# Distant Cousin:
# TWO WORLDS DAUGHTER

*A Novel*

Al Past

Distant Cousin: Two Worlds Daughter

A novel

Copyright © 2014 by Al Past

All rights reserved. No part of this book may be used or reproduced by any means, graphic, electronic, or mechanical, including photocopying, recording, taping or by any information storage retrieval system without the written permission of the copyright owner except in the case of brief quotations embodied in critical articles and reviews.

## Also by Al Past

*Distant Cousin*

*Distant Cousin: Repatriation*

*Distant Cousin: Reincarnation*

*Distant Cousin: Regeneration*

*Distant Cousin: Recirculation*

*Baroque Duets from Themes of Famous Composers*
(Charles Colin Pub. Co.)

*On Wings of Gentle Power*
Photographs to accompany the poetry of Barry Yelton
(Strider Nolan Media, Inc.)

*"I think that having fun is a social function, and it corresponds to my morals; I think about the reader who has to put up with these pages. He needs to have fun, he needs gratification; this is my moral. Someone bought the book, paid money, invests time: he has to have fun."*

–Italo Calvino

# Distant Cousin:
# TWO WORLDS DAUGHTER

# Chapter 1

It was a late winter day in the spring semester when, as he did every year, Dr. Ernest Cheever, senior professor at The University of New Mexico Medical School, led a small group of top medical students on a diagnostic tour for UNM-Med's Rural Medical program. In room 216 of the Doña Ana County Regional Medical Center, four medical students were wrapping up their examination of an elderly Hispanic woman with diabetes.

Cheever was scribbling notes on a clipboard as they talked. This particular case was not difficult, and the words the students were using, like *polydipsia* and *ketoacidosis,* were expected. The students were nodding at each others' comments, pleased with their diagnostic acumen. Only one bothersome obligation remained before they could move on to the next case.

"Ms. Mendez," Cheever said, coming down a little harder on the Mizz than absolutely necessary, "would you like a turn?"

On the far edge of the group, a small woman, a seventeen year old high school senior wearing the same white lab coat as the real students, barely nodded.

"Yes, sir," she said softly.

The med students watched with stony faces as the diminutive brunette held out a hand to the patient and began speaking to her in Spanish, as she had done with another patient earlier in the morning.

"Buenos dias, Señora Flores. Me llamo Clio Méndez," she said quietly. "Vivo en Mesilla. ¿Puedo examinarle, por favor?"

"Si, claro, señorita," the woman said, her voice encouraging, as if speaking to a granddaughter.

"Gracias," the girl replied. She clasped the hand between both of hers and held it for a minute. "A ver," she whispered, "con su permiso."

It took four or five minutes. Cheever impatiently scribbled a few more notes while the girl, unlike the real medical students, moved her hands around the woman's body, pressing lightly here, palpating there, but also listening on her stethoscope, and occasionally asking the woman a question. At one point she lowered her head close enough to the woman's face to smell her breath, though it wasn't obvious that she actually did so. She could have been merely examining her eyes. Her hands returned several times to the woman's throat and neck, fingertips moving gently, fractions of an inch at a time. Behind her the medical students smirked at each other. Finally she stepped back.

"Gracias, Señora," she said with a smile. "Es todo."

The woman held on to her hand a second.

"Gracias, mija," she said.

"Well?" said Dr. Cheever.

She collected her thoughts, glancing quickly at the most outspoken student.

"I agree with the overall diagnosis. Macrovascular complications are clearly present," she said, "but I found no sign of serious hypoglycemia. If surgery is planned I think the cardiovascular situation must be reevaluated first." She paused and looked at Dr. Cheever. "There is a significant aneurism in the external carotid artery, about an inch above where it branches from the carotid artery. It is large and could be a serious problem when surgery is performed on a hypertensive patient. It should be checked and probably corrected before any other surgical procedure."

Cheever squinted perceptibly. He jotted a note. One male student rolled his eyes.

"All right, then, let's head to room 224, if you please, folks."

The group filed past the main desk under the eyes of the floor nurse, RN Kimberly Martin, and Abel Lucero, the hospital human resources administrator, who had been going over personnel changes with her.

"Who's that girl, Abel?" she asked him.

"Huh? What girl?"

"With those medical students from Albuquerque." She nodded in the direction of the group wandering down the hall. "With that bearded professor?" she added.

"Oh, right, Dr. Cheever, with the Rural Medicine program. They were down in the ER yesterday. Now they're looking at cases up here."

"I know," she said, "but you see the kid following after them? Who is she?"

"She's not exactly a kid. She's a high school senior, but I agree, she looks younger. She's a project of Dr. Peebles'."

"The legend at the medical school? That Dr. Peebles? I thought he retired. I met him once, did you know?"

"I think he's semi-retired, whatever that means. I hear stories every so often. He seems to dabble in whatever strikes his fancy. The school gives him room to run, I guess. He's made them a lot of money over the years."

"And this girl is one of his projects?"

"Apparently. Cheever told me she's studied informally with Peebles for a couple of years. She's from down here somewhere, near Mesilla, I think."

"Huh. That's odd. What's the deal with her?"

"He said she's worked with curanderas for years. Peebles was so impressed with her medical skills that he got her permission to tag along with Cheever's fourth year students to see how she did. Cheever's supposed to keep notes on her as well as his own students. He's a little ticked off about that."

"With curanderas? You mean folk healers? Old women who burn incense and cast spells?"

"Now, now, Kim. I know you're from Baltimore, but it's a lot more than that. Curanderas have been a Hispanic tradition for centuries. They fill a niche in the local public health structure. They're basically harmless. Some are even helpful. Ask any old time doctor around here. They refer patients back and forth all the time."

"What's her name? Do you know her?"

"The HR guy at UNM-Med sent me her paperwork last week. I met her a couple days ago for an orientation. Her name's Méndez. Her first name, uh, let's see—Carol or Carla…Clio. That's it. Clio Méndez. Why so interested?"

"I dunno. She sort of caught my eye. She's dressed like the others but she's obviously not part of their group. She looks young and out of place. She tags along in back and they ignore her."

"Well, medical students are highly competitive. They probably resent her getting special treatment. Cheever wasn't keen on her either."

"Poor thing," Martin replied, sliding the clipboard under a stack of others. "She looked uncomfortable."

"Did you know, when I was little my parents took me to a curandera once?"

"Really? Why?"

"Well, I was having bad stomach aches. Our family doctor was stumped, and…oops."

The phone under Nurse Martin's elbow was beeping. She listened briefly.

"Yes, sir. He's right here. I'll tell him. Thank you, sir." She looked at Lucero. "That was Dr. Mitchell. He'd like to see you in his office."

"Uh-oh. It's too late for lunch, too early for supper. Must be trouble. See you later, Kim."

"I want to hear the rest of that story. Don't forget, Abel!"

Fifteen minutes later she was almost through making the changes to the duty list when the phone beeped again. Dr. Mitchell's secretary wanted to talk to Ms. Méndez, the girl with Cheever's group. She walked to room 224, knocked softly, and stuck her head into the room.

"Excuse me, doctor. There's a phone call for Ms. Méndez at the desk."

"Aha," he said. "Perhaps your bus is here." A student snorted. He checked his list. "If not, we'll be in room 227."

Nurse Martin led the girl to the phone as the group filed down the hall. She held the phone to her ear briefly and then hung up but remained in place, looking down at the counter.

"Miss? Is everything all right?"

"Huh? Oh, uh, yes, ma'am. I'm supposed to see Dr. Mitchell on the first floor."

"Ah. That's room 106, second door to the left past the reception desk."

"OK. Thanks"

Nurse Martin almost added "Good luck." She watched the girl walk by the elevator and disappear down the stairwell. Dr. Mitchell was the chief hospital administrator. She hoped Abel's prediction of trouble was incorrect.

The girl in question pushed open the door to a first floor restroom. She washed her hands and patted her face lightly with the wet paper towel, checking her reflection in the mirror.

She had to be in trouble. Nothing about being here felt right. Well, no, that wasn't accurate: being with the patients felt right. Even though she was no way close to being a doctor she felt she was helping at least a few of them.

It wasn't the hospital building that made her uneasy, or the staff. It was all of it together, the culture of the place. Healing was what she was interested in, but healing seemed to come after the business of medicine or the status of those who practiced it, with both of those second to considerations of money, which governed all. She couldn't look forward to spending years in an environment like this. Was she missing something?

She tried a smile in the mirror. It wouldn't fool anyone. Phooey. Tucking an escaped lock of hair into place, she pushed open the door to the passageway and headed to the main lobby.

In 106, Dr. Stanley Mitchell was conferring with Abel Lucero. Mitchell was wearing a white lab coat with the hospital ID card on a bead chain lying over his tie. Lucero, a file folder in his lap, was seated in front of Mitchell's chrome and steel desk. The only items on the desk were a computer monitor and keyboard and a telephone. On the left wall were a number of photos and plaques. Opposite stood a bookshelf with several dozen books and three garish trophies, one sporting a gold golf ball on a tee with the head of a garish gold 3 wood stuck to it.

"I know Peebles," Mitchell was saying. "Don't misunderstand me, Abel. I like the man. We owe him a lot. He's probably one of the fifteen or twenty most important figures in the establishment of modern medicine in this state. But he's been around a long time, a *long* time. He gets some odd ideas, and this thing with the Méndez woman is only the latest example. I wish I knew what he thinks he's doing with her."

Lucero shook his head and turned his eyes away from the glare through the plate glass behind Mitchell's desk. Mitchell could have closed the blinds had he wanted. Maybe it was his way of putting visitors off kilter.

"I wouldn't know about Peebles," he replied. "The politics of this is above my pay grade. But medically speaking, I guess you would say, he may be on to something with this young woman. Dr. Cheever's group has looked at a dozen or so patients so far, and she's had some surprising perceptions about four or five. Three that I know of have been checked out, and she was right in each case—detected things the others missed, that normally you'd need one of our scanners to find."

"Yeah, I read that in your file there. It does make you wonder."

"One gentleman swore she stopped his back spasms with a light massage."

"Oh, baloney. I've seen the placebo effect do that. Physical therapists can too. There can't be any way she can sense abnormalities by touch that careful palpation by an experienced doctor can't discover. The main problem as I see it is that she's upsetting Dr. Cheever's routine with his students. They need to concentrate, work together, and learn from each other, and she's distracting them. Cheever'll bitch to UNM-Med, and rightfully so, and it'll come back on me and I'll have to put out the fire, if I can." He grimaced. "I'm going to have to put a stop to it."

"Too bad," Lucero ventured, "Have you met her?"

"No," he said. "Have you?"

"I have. Gave her an orientation earlier in the week. Came on time, didn't have to be told anything twice, asked good questions. Seemed sharp."

The phone on the desk beeped discretely. Mitchell listened briefly, growling, "Send her in." He hung up while looking at Lucero.

Lucero thought she looked cool, self-possessed, and professional in her white lab coat, that is, if she were playing a doctor in a movie where high school students staffed a hospital. She barely smiled when Mitchell introduced himself. Oddly, when Mitchell shook her hand she held it a bit longer than seemed quite right. Cheever finally waved her to one of the other seats in front of his desk. She sat, back straight, hands clasped in her lap, holding her eyes on the edge of Mitchell's desk perhaps to avoid the glare…or maybe sensing what was to come.

Mitchell laid it out for her plainly. It didn't take long. She was creating a problem in his hospital. He was going to have to call an end to her presence on Dr. Cheever's team. He regretted it, but he hoped she would understand.

Still looking at the front of his desk, she waited a few seconds before raising her head. Her voice was lower and more deliberate than he expected.

"I understand, Dr. Mitchell. I know I was a distraction. Dr. Peebles wanted to provide me an opportunity to see if I might want to become a doctor. I do have some healing abilities, you see, but I don't understand them very well. Neither does he. He thought working with a professor and medical students might provide some insight. I apologize for disrupting the routine here. Please don't feel badly about letting me go. I was coming to the same conclusion myself."

"Healing abilities?" Dr. Mitchell prompted.

"Yes, sir."

"What healing abilities?"

"Uh, well, for example, when we shook hands just now I detected you have a problem with your upper right arm or shoulder. I think it is causing you pain. Isn't that so?"

Lucero saw the surprise in Mitchell's eyes.

"It is," he said, softly.

"I thought so. That's the kind of thing I mean. I don't know how I knew, sir. It's a problem with the tendons in your shoulder, is it not?"

"No. There's a problem with the cartilage in the joint itself. I'm having surgery on it next week."

She shook her head.

"I don't think it's the cartilage, sir," she said. "I don't believe it requires surgery yet, though it could become more serious if not treated properly. It could become a rotator cuff issue."

"That's not what our orthopedist determined."

"No, sir," she said. Several seconds passed. "Dr. Mitchell, if you would allow me, I could examine it right now. If I'm right I may be able to stop the pain for some time, perhaps for good. If I'm wrong, then no harm will be done."

He looked hard at her for two beats, shot Lucero a glance, then back to the girl.

"All right," he said, suddenly. "Abel, you can be a witness."

He stood, took off his lab coat, untied his tie, and began unbuttoning his shirt.

"Shall I leave my undershirt on?"

"Yes, sir."

Lucero couldn't believe what was happening. Whatever did Mitchell think he was doing? Lucero had read Cheever's notes but those gave only the vaguest idea of what the girl might do. Now they were going to get an actual demonstration. He watched in fascination.

Mitchell was a little soft through the middle, but was otherwise a fairly trim, middle-aged man. The girl took his right hand in both of hers and held it fifteen or twenty seconds. Then she began working her hands up the forearm, feeling the muscles, probing carefully around his elbow, moving on to the biceps and triceps of the upper arm.

In some places she squeezed or massaged the skin. In others her fingers were still or pressed down. She had him hold his arm away from his body so she could feel the underarm area. Her fingers slid under the t-shirt to the top of his shoulder, roaming over the bones and tendons. It looked gentle but several times she asked, "Does this hurt?" According to Mitchell's responses sometimes it did and sometimes it didn't.

The minutes passed. Something had changed--she was no longer exploring. Her head was turned to one side and her eyes were closed. She was humming softly in time with her breathing, like a person barely snoring: "Mmm...mmm...mmm."

Freaky! What the hell was she doing?

Oddly, Mitchell's eyes were also closed. His head wavered as if he were attempting to locate some faint sound. Both looked to be in weird, bizarre trances.

Her fingers kneaded the flesh of the shoulder firmly, pinching, rubbing up and down, side to side. A half dozen times or more they moved to different spots while she pinched an inch or two of skin and muscle between her fingers, long enough for her to make that peculiar hum several times. With her eyes closed, she had to be working by touch. It looked like her manipulations would be painful. Lucero prayed Mitchell's secretary would not poke her head in. This would be difficult to explain.

After some number of minutes, the girl stopped massaging, opened her eyes, and breathed deeply.

"There," she said. "I think I got it. How does it feel now?"

Mitchell opened his eyes as well, blinking several times. He moved his arm tentatively.

"Better. It doesn't hurt."

Gently, she lifted his arm out horizontally. He raised it the rest of the way over his head. She nodded.

"Good. Use the arm carefully for three or four days, please. If it bothers you any more, you may call me. Mr. Lucero has my number. Again, Dr. Mitchell, I'm so sorry to have caused you trouble. It was an honor to work with you, sir."

And with a polite nod to Lucero, she was gone. Mitchell moved his arm through a complete range of motion.

"I'm a son of a bitch, Abel. It feels normal. I'll be able to play golf again!"

"To quote the sage," Lucero cracked, "'Baloney. The placebo effect could account for that. Or a physical therapist.'"

Mitchell buttoned his shirt, raising his elbows several times.

"Yeah, OK, but no shit, Abel. She really did something to me, only I'm damned if I can explain what. It was weird. It felt electric, but also cold, and *not* just on the skin. It was deep in my shoulder. I can still feel it, sort of shivery and soothing. Did you notice anything unusual?"

"You mean besides a skinny little high school girl totally messing up the mind of a veteran hospital administrator? No, except for that everything seemed completely normal."

"Godammit, Abel. What the hell did she do? And how did she do it?"

"No idea, chief. Maybe you should ask Dr. Peebles."

Mitchell froze, his tie half knotted.

"Won't happen. Never forget the basic rules of administration. Number one: 'Act in haste. Repent at leisure.' And number two: 'If it ain't broke, don't fix it.' Forget Peebles. I'm gonna postpone that surgery. You get the hell back to your office and make us a tee time for Saturday at 9:00 am. If this shoulder hangs together that long I'm going to whip your ass. If it doesn't, well, don't throw that kid's phone number away. I don't know what she did, but if it doesn't last, I want another dose. Can you remember all that?"

## Chapter 2

None of Ana Darcy Méndez's neighbors would have ever guessed, had they observed her stepping out her front door and sweeping invisible dust over the edge of the narrow front porch of her house, that this small, lively woman had been born on a planet twenty five light years away, or that she was the world-renowned but reclusive celebrity who had been the first of her people to find their way back to Earth after some 3000 years of removal.

She had no close neighbors in any case, living as she did in one of the assortment of homes scattered along the 50 mile length of old Highway 28 along the course of the Rio Grande River in southern New Mexico's fertile Mesilla Valley.

One neighbor did in fact observe her: a retired welder from the tiny nearby town of Santo Tomás, who was enjoying a leisurely after-lunch bicycle ride in the interest of his problematic heart. He knew her as the wife of a prominent farming and ranching family, friendly and active in community affairs. He waved. She waved back.

Leaning her broom against the house, she eased into one of the four plastic chairs on the porch as the man slowly pedaled off to the south.

It was a warm winter afternoon. Abuelita Reyes' field on the other side of the highway, fallow for the moment, fell away to the barely flowing river, out of sight in the middle distance. On the horizon, under the deep blue dome of the sky, lay the low, wavy white border of the stark Chihuahuan desert. A faint quarter moon floated to the west, pale in the brilliant light.

She studied it, mentally filling in the disk suggested by the crescent to approximately locate Crater Albatagenius. The little Thoman base tucked into a debris field near one edge had been her home for many years. She and her faithful counselor, Hleo Ap Darshiell, had studied Earth until they decided it was

– 10 –

the original home planet of the Thoman people. The base was still there, as was Hleo, or rather his electronically preserved self. He had lived long past the death of his body in the circuits of the moon base computers, and with a little luck should live digitally well after her own life was over.

Her mind carried her far beyond the moon, across the trillions of miles to the distant solar system and the planet where her people lived. Some of them would still hold her in memory, even though there would have been no word of her since she departed on her voyage of exploration so long ago. What had become of her family? After eighteen years in her second life on Earth, with a husband, two children, and a large extended Earthly family, her home life was just what she had dreamed of as a young girl, comfortable, loving, and rewarding. Her turbulent first life seemed inconceivably distant. But it wasn't, really. That would soon be obvious to everyone.

Two polite squeaks jolted her out of her reverie. Diana, one of the family's two Siamese cats, wished to join her outside. She opened the door, was paid with a chirp of acknowledgment, and resumed her seat. The sleek gray-tipped cat paused wide-eyed at the steps to take in the panorama on all sides, ears swiveling, first together, then separately.

There were weighty decisions to be made about her family in the days ahead. For the first time since the twins had been born some seventeen years ago, everyone in her immediate family would be gone from their home for an extended period at the same time. The arrangements that situation required were daunting, and a little worrisome.

Her husband Matt and son Julio would be in Texas for nearly two weeks. That was no problem. They would be fine. Matt would see to that.

Daughter Clio's situation was less certain. Clio had always had a strong independent streak. Only two years ago she had sneaked off by herself into the mountainous back country of Mexico and gotten into very serious trouble with no one around to help. She was lucky not to have been killed. Now she wanted to accompany a public health team visiting underserved citizens in small towns and pueblos throughout New Mexico. She could drive and she had a car. But the idea of her attractive, petite, inexperienced daughter junketing around by herself, staying in who knew what kind of motels and dealing with the public was unacceptable. The fact that Clio had participated in many martial arts classes with her mother and thought she was capable of taking care of herself made no difference. This time some arrangement for her security would be absolutely necessary. That would be a problem. And Clio certainly wouldn't like it, which made two problems.

The cat had ventured off the porch to the lawn where she was delicately plucking and chewing grass with apparent relish, the tip of her tail curled into a graceful question mark which reversed itself periodically.

Her own travels would take her to New York City, where she had been many times. Then she and her uncle, one of three Thomans who followed her to Earth years ago, would fly to Switzerland, where she had never been. Traveling and appearing in public were always stressful but at least the Thoman delegation would have plenty of security and she should not be mobbed, one of her greatest fears. Given the likelihood of media interest in her uncle's news, there would almost certainly be additional problems, but there was nothing to be done about those now.

Their home, although vacant, would not be neglected. The modest house shared the shady two acre Méndez plot with the original main house where Matt's grandmother Abuelita Reyes and his parents Bert and Julia lived. Matt's father Bert would be the linchpin for the scattered family, acting as communication central and feeding the two dogs and three cats. Barring unforeseen emergencies, there should be few problems within the adobe walls of the Méndez family compound.

Diana suddenly hissed and streaked to the porch, tail puffed to three times the normal size. A scary diesel truck was blatting down the highway pulling a trailer full of heifers. Ana got up to let the alarmed kitty into the house, setting the broom inside. Son Julio, absorbed at the living room computer, didn't look up. She stepped off the porch to see how Matt was coming with his repair job.

The barn was at the opposite corner of the compound, with its big doors facing the back gate in the adobe wall. In the old days, a tractor could drive in through the gate and load with hay or feed, but no hay or vehicles were kept in it these days. The main room of the barn was a workshop.

Rajah and Rani, the two Rhodesian ridgebacks, lazed in a patch of sun by the back gate, following her with their eyes as she rounded the corner into the barn. Matt was tightening clamps on the corners of a window frame. He smiled when he saw her.

"Hola, wife," he said.

"What's that smell?" she asked. There was a spicy, foresty tang in the air.

"Cedar," was the reply. He checked the angle of each corner joint with a try square. "I just cut these half-lap joints. Now I'm gluing the sides together. Then I'll pop in a couple screws at each corner for reinforcement and mount the screens. Like this one. Check out the claw-proof screen."

"Very nice! Did you notice Raisin?"

Raisin was Clio's caracal, an African cat half the size of a mountain lion, with spectacularly tufted ears to make a bobcat jealous. Her name was a translation of a common pet name from Hindi, or so an Indian friend had told them. She was calmly looking down on them from her special hangout at the top of the stairs to the hayloft. The attention from below caused her to yawn impressively.

"Yup. She's my shop cat."

"I thought she hated the sound of your saw."

"She hates the table saw. The band saw I cut these joints with doesn't shriek like the table saw. She doesn't mind that. She loves carpentry."

Ana smiled at the notion of a cat appreciating woodwork. Matt carefully set the clamped screen on top of two others on the work bench. He wiped the blobs of glue off his hands and screwed the cap on the glue bottle.

"What have you got going on this afternoon?" he asked.

"I'm still working on our travel plans. Are you sure it will take you and Julio ten days just to go to a car race?"

"It's not really a car race."

"Well, what did you call it? The 'Texas Mile?' It sounded like a car race."

"It does sound like a car race. What it is is an old airport runway where people can sign up their vehicles to see how fast they can go for a mile. Each vehicle goes one at a time. There's no racing. They have a website. I'll show you later."

"Julio said it was one weekend, or Friday plus a weekend."

"Right. Add two days to drive there and two days back and you've got a week already. Then we're going fishing on the Gulf a day or two. We'll spend a few days at our Plan C Ranch, checking out the exotic game. Ten days, maybe twelve. It's a male bonding thing."

"I see," she said, looking dubious. "I'd like to visit that ranch sometime myself."

"Sure. We can do that. You're not missing a lot, though. It's a pretty plain Jane place."

The Méndez family had several refuges tucked away in case Ana's interplanetary identity was ever revealed and resulted in a tidal wave of media people outside their Mesilla home. Plan B was a ranch in Montana. Plan C was a ranch in an isolated area of south Texas. They already had a modified Plan A for their present home, involving security gates and a secret way to and from their property via the barn 200 yards to the south.

Matt glanced at the doorway to the twins' workshops.

"Where's Julio?" he asked.

"In the living room at the computer."

"Good." He spoke quietly. "I thought we ought to check out Plan C just in case, because of the news you and Rothan will announce."

"I agree, but it'll be another year or two before they arrive. Changes aren't likely until then. There'll be greetings, formal visits, clan ceremonies, a lot of socializing and politics. Julio and Clio will have to be a big part of it. They're the first children of two planets, after all. It'll be a huge deal to the Thomans, and it'll unavoidably change the twins' lives. Ours too, for sure.

"But for now," she continued, "there's Clio. You know she'll be traveling all over New Mexico by herself the next several weeks. She'll probably be fine but I'd feel better if she had someone with her."

"Yeah. I would too. Clio has the damnedest ability to get into scrapes. I imagine you and I have the same idea about what to do about that, don't we?"

"You mean Rob?"

Matt nodded. Ana had found Rob Coombs years earlier when she needed expert help getting her people out of an embarrassing situation. Coombs, a former Navy SEAL, had been a lifesaver, quite literally, then and on several more recent occasions. For the last two or three years, he had been running a branch of New York's World Security Services in Miami. Security services were just what they needed for Clio.

"We can't ask Rob," Ana pointed out. "Michelle's baby is due in four weeks and her doctor has her on bed rest. Rob should be with her."

"That's right! I'd forgotten it was that soon. How's she doing?"

"She and the baby are fine. She just has to be careful. I'll see them on my way to New York next week. For now, why don't I call Rob and see what he suggests?"

"Yeah, good idea. Rob's the best there is, though. Strange to think we might have to settle for second best."

Why was this blasted traffic moving so slowly? Clio's speedometer explained the problem: she was in a 35 miles per hour zone driving 50 miles per hour.

She needed to calm down. She slowed and looked for a place to pull off and gather her wits. The opportunity soon presented itself in the form of a strip mall parking lot clinging precariously to one of the ridges of the Organ Mountains overlooking Las Cruces.

The Corolla's engine settled into a purr as she shifted into park and set the emergency brake. Had she not done so, the car might have rolled to the bottom of the parking lot, thumped over the curb, and tumbled at least 500 feet to the bottom of the arroyo. People in the apartments awkwardly strung along the crest of the opposite ridge could have looked down at the wreckage. Similar accidents made the TV news several times a year.

She adjusted the air conditioner vents to blow directly on her face and stared in the general direction of the yuccas and greasewood bushes on the slope opposite. None of it registered on her brain. She sat back and breathed in the cool air. Even in the winter, a car under the sun in southern New Mexico could be uncomfortable.

She hoped Dr. Mitchell had not sensed how unhappy she had been to have him end her experiment among the medical students. They had all resented her presence but there was no point blaming him or the students. She could have endured even more than that if it had helped her better understand her upsetting ability to diagnose and heal.

She hardly knew what to call it. She was like one of those silly cartoon characters with bizarre super powers, except the cartoon characters at least knew what their powers were. She not only did not know, hers rather frightened her. What was it really? Could she control it? What were the possibilities? What were the limits? Where did it come from? *What was wrong with her?*

And what about the way she could sense the healing possibilities of plants? Was that the same thing or something different? Was she losing her mind? Was she a freak? Should she simply quit trying and give up on the whole business? The bottom line question: *Who was she?*

She couldn't give up. There had to be an explanation. She had improved Dr. Mitchell's shoulder. If that diabetic patient with the undiagnosed aneurism had been operated on it could have burst and easily killed her. She had found other overlooked conditions in several other patients. To not have acted might well have changed their lives for the worse or even ended them. She could not, she would not, give up on others, or herself either. Not yet.

Still, her poor parents were no help, though they wanted to be, and her brother, normally so closely attuned to his twin sister, was clueless. She felt isolated, cut off, doomed to a state so weird, so inexplicable, that it seemed it would drive her crazy.

If only there were someone she could talk to. Actually, there was one person whose opinion she valued that she might talk to. Aside from him, she had no other ideas.

The shrill voices of excited children snapped her out of her pensiveness. A mother laden with purchases was unlocking her car and loading a little boy and girl into car seats. The boy sported the knee socks and shiny shorts and shoes of a soccer uniform. That triggered her memory: she had a volleyball game this afternoon, one of her last as a member of Juarez Academy's "Lady Rattlers." That was good. The physical activity should be a welcome diversion, however temporary, from her troubles.

One of those troubles, minor as it was, was having missed lunch thanks to being kicked off Dr. Cheever's team. Food would help her play good volleyball later this afternoon and she could get that at home. She pressed down the brake pedal and released the parking brake. Shifting into drive, she headed back to the street.

## Chapter 3

Now that each member of Clio's family had a car, the parking space behind their house had had to be made so large there was only room for one row of Ana's garden squeezed along the back wall. (There were two more gardens in other spots.) She pulled in between Julio's RAV-4 and her dad's old pickup. The dogs well knew the sound of her engine and were not alarmed. Curled together in a patch of sun by the open barn doors, they watched her walk to the house with only moderate interest. She entered through the patio gate, tossed her shoulder bag on her bed, and headed for the kitchen. Julio was at the computer.

"Bubba," she said, opening the refrigerator.

"Hey," he muttered, staring at the screen. She poured herself some orange juice and eased into a chair at the dining table. From thirty feet away, Julio seemed to be manipulating a column of figures. She had drunk half the glass before he looked up.

"Tister," he said, finally. His brow wrinkled. "Hey." He checked his watch. "You're early. What's wrong?"

She knew it didn't show on her face. It was their twin meta-communication system, unremarkable to either of them.

"I got fired," she said.

"You what?"

Ninety minutes later she had explained her discouraging morning to Julio, eaten some leftovers from the refrigerator, explained it all again to her parents, and changed into her volleyball uniform. She was pulling her warm-up clothes off the hanger when Julio stuck his head in her room.

"You need a ride?" he asked.

"No," she said. "Friends are coming by. Thanks."

"So what did Mom and Dad say about your New Mexico trip?"

"They weren't gonna let me go at first. They had conditions."

"Conditions?"

"I had to agree to have a, an escort."

"An escort?"

"Someone to go with me. To make sure I stayed out of trouble."

"You're kidding! Like who?"

"Well, like Mr. Coombs."

"A Seal? They'd get a Seal to go with you? Are you serious?"

"It can't be Mr. Coombs. Michelle is expecting and he should be with her. Someone else."

"Like, who?"

"They didn't know. They haven't talked to Mr. Coombs yet."

"Oh, my God. And you agreed to that?"

"What else could I do, J-Man? They wouldn't let me go, otherwise."

"That sucks, Tister! So you're going to go help a public health team, but with a bodyguard, and he's a Seal?"

She was sitting on her bed, her sweatpants wadded in her lap, looking stricken.

"She said you and Dad would be gone and she would be gone too. I would be on my own. She's gonna pay whatever it costs."

"Oh, jeez," he said, shaking his head. "You think it's because you ran away to Mexico that time?"

"J-Man! I did not!" She sniffled. She sniffled again. "Yeah. Probably."

He sat on the bed.

"Hmm." They sat in silence a moment. "Well, how about this? What if I went with you? Would that do?"

"You can't. You and Dad are going to that car thing in Texas."

"They do it every year. We could go another time."

"You'd do that? For me?"

"Well, yeah? You'd do it for me, right? If I'd sneaked off to Mexico and nearly got whacked?"

She jabbed him with an elbow. Then she hugged him.

"Oh, Bubba. That's so sweet. I don't want you to miss your car race. I can go with a bodyguard, I guess. It won't kill me."

Her brother shook his head.

"I sure hope not, Tister."

Five minutes later she was sitting in one of the plastic chairs on the front porch waiting for her ride. The afternoon was taking on a chill. The warm-up suit felt good. She had told Julio "friends" were picking her up, but that was just to avoid snide questions from her brother. It was only one friend. She was having second thoughts too late about letting Shack pick her up—Shackley Tattersall. The third, no less.

He seemed to think more of her than she did of him, a minor source of annoyance, but it wasn't fair to hold it against him. He was OK, really. They were both graduating from Juarez Academy High School this spring. He had big plans he'd no doubt want to talk about. She had no big plans. The less said about them the better.

A flashy low-rider burbled down the highway with the windows down, banda music throbbing, the driver slapping the outside of the door to the beat of the tubas. What would Shack be driving? He had wrecked his Mustang in the fall, injuring himself badly enough to require the rest of the semester for convalescence and rehabilitation at his parents' vacation home in Aspen, or so she had heard.

The Tattersalls had moved to Las Cruces from Atlanta only three years ago. His father ran some sort of international trade company. They were country club types. She had only ever seen them at school functions.

There he came, in a spanking red, metal flake Mustang, scattering gravel as he braked to a stop with the passenger door even with the end of the walk. She got in, they hugged briefly and awkwardly over the center console, and the car took off in another spurt of gravel.

As expected he did most of the talking. He'd had fun recuperating in Aspen, easily kept up with his school work, and was looking forward to graduation, and most especially to heading off to Yale next fall, where he would study business. His father had gone to Yale, and why didn't she also go to Yale, which was a top-flight school? She just had to go to Yale. They were practically made for each other, would make a smashing couple, and would have a famously good time.

She managed briefly to admire his car, to say he looked good (in creased D&G jeans, silk polo shirt, and shiny loafers worn without socks), and that she hadn't yet decided where she would continue her education.

He was insistent that she simply had to attend Yale with him. It was her destiny. It was *their* destiny! Sure, it was expensive, but his father could undoubtedly get her a generous scholarship and also help give her a head start in life with his network of important contacts.

She could only say she'd think about it.

It was a relief when they arrived at the school.

Juarez Academy was in an old neighborhood of mostly one story adobe houses and small businesses with very limited space for parking. Shack had to park on the street three blocks from the school. It took him several minutes to lock the faceplate of the stereo system in the glove box and spread a sun shield over the dashboard to partially hide the interior. By the time he had set the car's alarm system, Clio had spotted several friends walking to the game.

One was an old friend and former schoolmate, Harry Saenz, now a community college graduate and trainer for Stallmann's Stables. Two young women were with him. One was a cousin of Harry's, a tall, solid girl Clio knew well: Carly Rivas, a classmate and fellow member of the volleyball team, wearing the team windbreaker that matched her own. Clio hugged Harry quickly as he introduced his date, Silvia Delgado, a dental hygiene student from Anthony.

As they neared the gym, a school bus lumbered past and eased to a stop. Members of the visiting team began disembarking. The sidewalk was getting crowded.

"We need to go in here," Clio said. "Why don't we meet you guys out front after the game?"

Before anyone could answer, a tall brunette girl stepped off the bus, bumping into Carly. The two girls spoke at the same time.

"Excuse me!" Carly said.

"Whoa!" the girl said, adding, "Well, looks like we drew the heavyweight team tonight!"

"Hey!" snapped Clio, "Watch your mouth!"

The girl looked down at Clio, smiling sarcastically.

"Ooo, I'm so scared!" she smirked. "We'll take care of you too...you little no-tits shrimp."

Eyes flashing, Clio pushed Carly toward the gym, leaving Shack and Harry and his date behind. Shack spied two girls he knew and told Harry he'd see him later. Harry and Silvia walked around the building toward the front entrance.

"That girl was nasty," she said to Harry.

"She was," he agreed. He was smiling.

"What? What's so funny?"

"She made two mistakes. She didn't recognize the two best setters on the team, for one, and for two, she made Clio mad. You don't ever want to do that."

"No? Why not?" They walked a few more steps.

"When she loses her temper there's hell to pay."

"Clio? Are you serious?"

"Oh, yeah." Harry was still smiling.

"Like, how do you mean?"

"A couple years ago, for example. It was a race day and I was showing Stallman's stables to her and a cousin. Two guys turned up who hated the cousin for some reason and they cornered him and started to beat him up."

"No!"

"Yeah. You should have seen Clio light into them."

"What? Clio? Two men?"

"Yeah. Tough guys, real ugly customers. Clio stomped 'em in fifteen seconds."

"You can't mean it!"

"Es verídico, I swear." He chuckled. "They were down for the count before they knew what hit them. I saw it and I can't tell you how she did it. Whappity whap, and they were on the ground. So that's two guys who know not to make her mad. Three, if you count me. Like I said, that girl could become a fourth."

The gym at Juarez Academy was a small, multi-use affair with a 300 seat collapsible grandstand on one side of the court. It was barely half full as Harry and Silvia chose their seats. Harry had watched a number of games at school and seen a few on television during the Olympics the previous summer, but he was hazy on the rules. Silvia had played in high school. She reviewed Harry: a game involved the best of five sets, each to 25 points, team members could only touch the ball three times in hitting it back to the other team, and so forth.

Clio's Rattlers lost the first set badly. The Panthers, from a private school in El Paso, were good. There was much shrieking from both teams and shouting from the crowd.

The second set was closer and took longer. The Rattlers made fewer nervous mistakes. The bumpers did better at stopping the ball and hitting it to the setters who consequently did better placing it high at the net for the attackers to spike to the other team. The Rattlers narrowly won the second set.

The coaches called a time out. The players stepped off court to drink and towel off.

"So what do you think?" Harry said.

"Carly's good," she said, "but I see what you mean about Clio. She's super quick. There was no way she should have saved some of those bumps. She's short, but she can spike, too, when she's up front. She needs to poach a little more. She could really light them up."

Harry wanted to ask for clarification but a whistle called the players back on the court for the third set. The Panthers clustered in a little circle, chanting and ending with a group hand slap. The Rattlers huddled briefly as well and moved into the receiving positions, with Clio on the front row left. The girl with the attitude was across from her in the center. Judging from the curl of her lip she must have said something snippy to Clio.

The serve, a high, looping ball, was bumped easily by Carly and set by the girl behind Clio. Clio leaped and faked toward the back of the opponent's court, but somehow hit the ball sharply at an oblique angle with her left hand, where it blasted off the side of Smart-mouth's face into the net.

"My God!" said Silvia.

The serve moved to the Rattlers who ran off four straight points. By the time they had won the third set, 25 to 14, Clio had made four impossible bumps (one only inches off the floor), one set, and three spikes, two of which had hit Smart-mouth, even though she was in the back row for the second.

The Rattlers easily won the fourth set (their third, and thus the game) by the score of 25 to 8. Clio made a number of cat-quick bumps and two spikes, the first of which smashed Smart-mouth on the left cheek. For the second, with Smart-mouth directly opposite Clio, Carly set her a perfect floater, high above the net. Clio soared upward as Smart-mouth shrieked in fear and turned her head away. Clio barely tapped the ball, which dropped at the girl's feet. Several people in the crowd actually laughed.

Silvia shot a telling glance at Harry.

"Now I see what you mean about Clio," she said to Harry. "That poor, silly girl. How embarrassing."

At the end of the game the teams formed the traditional moving lines where they traded hand slaps. Smart-mouth didn't seem quite as cocky with both sides of her face cherry red. Some of her hair had escaped from its scrunchie, giving her a dazed, disheveled look.

Clio slapped their opponents' hands along with her team. She wasn't proud of herself.

But she did feel a little better about getting fired.


Back at the Méndez house, Ana was on the phone.

"OK, Rob. That sounds good. Clio will meet him at the Albuquerque airport at 3:15 pm. It's a Southwest flight, and she'll be wearing, oh, I think a yellow hat. She'll have the number you gave me in case anything changes. Will that work?

"I can't tell you how much I appreciate your help, Rob. We were so fortunate to have you make this arrangement for us. I hope I get to meet him in the near future.

"Please give Michelle my best. My love to you both. I'll see you in two days!"

# Chapter 4

Dr. Thornton Peebles' office was tucked away on the third floor of a small building in the northeast corner of The University of New Mexico campus in Albuquerque. A stranger would have needed a map and a compass to find it, but Clio had been there many times over the previous two summers. She even knew where to park: far away. The walk was welcome after the three hour drive from home. She took the stairs instead of the elevator to further loosen her limbs.

It was an old building with a musty smell, full of mismatched offices mostly medical in nature but with a few science professors and the random sociologist or journalist. It contained a several small labs but no classrooms. It was a comfortable, human-scaled building. She liked it.

Peebles' office was one of the larger ones, on a corner of the third floor. He welcomed her with a gentle hug and then held her at arms' length with a beaming smile, eyes twinkling. A tall, elderly man with thin, barely visible hair and a ruddy complexion, he had old world manners, something that Clio understood and appreciated, thanks to her Thoman mother and Earthly great-grandmother. He ushered her to one of the two chairs not piled with papers, folders, medical journals, and books.

Clio asked about his family and shared the happy news of Dr. Peebles' fourth great grandchild. She admired the framed photo of the babe on his desk.

In return, he asked about her parents, whom he had never met, and her brother, whom he had. "I wonder what in the world that brilliant young man is up to these days," were his words.

Clio told him of the upcoming test of Julio's batteries, or rather the batteries whose design he had improved and patented. The test involved sending a battery-powered Toyota Corolla over a timed one mile course to possibly set a world speed record for its class (admittedly a very small class).

Peebles feared for Julio's safety but Clio reassured him that Julio would not be driving. The car was sponsored by Rocky Mountain Technical Labs of Albuquerque, she explained, which had hired a racing garage to insure the car was properly modified for high speed. They would also provide a team to transport and drive the car.

"Splendid, splendid!" he said, sitting back in his chair. "Such an innovative brother and sister. Would you like something to drink, my dear?"

"Oh, no sir, thank you. I'm fine."

"Well then, to the matter I am sure has brought you here. I so regretted to hear that the hospital director in Las Cruces saw fit to terminate your experience with Ernie Cheever's medical team. I read his report. It appeared to me that you were having some gratifying successes—did it not appear so to you, my dear?"

"I'm not sure, sir." She looked down at her hands. "I know I've caused you a lot of trouble. I'm very sorry for that, Dr. Peebles."

"Oh, my dear young lady, not so! By no means! You are the very opposite of a problem for me. I assure you that is the truth!"

He paused and studied her dejection. He finally spoke again, more softly.

"You do not seem convinced. Well, then, perhaps it will help if I explain why I have such hopes for you.

"You see, my dear, I began my career as a simple country pharmacist. It was a long time ago, and I worked on quite a primitive level by today's standards. I had no choice but to do the best I could with what I had. That is where I began my understanding of pharmacognosy, which has more recently been of interest to you as well.

"I felt I could do better, so I went to medical school and became a physician, after which I did in fact do better for decades. It was a satisfying career.

"Still, any doctor will tell you that he or she generally practices the art of the possible. We have many successes and help many people, but sadly, there inevitably remain those who are beyond our best efforts. I remember many of those cases to this day, and regret them deeply.

"Any physician will also have stories of inexplicable successes: spontaneous remissions, successful pleas to the almighty, of miraculous intercession by friends and relatives, or of incredible healings at the hands of this folk healer, or that shaman, or a quack 'medicine' or some even less likely agent of salvation. Few of these bear scientific examination. They are almost never replicable. Do you know that word? I mean they cannot be verified or repeated under study.

"But you, my child, you are different. Your diagnostic abilities, and your ability to heal, while not infallible, are recurrent. They have happened again and again, over time. The fact that neither you nor I can explain them is a problem, but that is not to say that they cannot be examined or that they can never be explained. Indeed, the possibility that there may be something of immense value to be learned from you is a marvelous incentive to pursue our examination however we can. Even if we learn nothing widely applicable to the practice of medicine, we may still learn something from you that was heretofore undocumented in human existence.

"I know you are discouraged, dear friend. I know it upsets you that you can effect healing in ways you do not understand and at other times you cannot heal when you would wish to. But I pray you will not give up. Instead, I would have you be joyful. You are actually able to create wellness in new and tantalizing ways! We will never have all the answers we wish—but we must seek those answers. I believe that quest is what makes us fully human. We owe the world no less."

Clio appeared to be studying the floor. When she raised her head he saw hope and doubt mixed in her eyes. Perhaps she was encouraged, a little.

"Come," he said. "Here's an idea. In all our work together over the last two years, I have heard about and documented dozens of your efforts to heal. Yet I have never asked you to examine me. What kind of scientist would I be if failed to learn first hand what we are investigating?"

She looked even more doubtful.

"I would be honored if you would examine me," he continued. "I am 83 years old, my dear. I assure you there are many things about me that could stand a little healing."

It was risky for him to become an object of study in his own experiment but he was tantalized by the notion that he might personally experience this extraordinary talent.

He regarded her cloudy face, adding, "I will sign a release if you wish."

Despite her reluctance she felt a smile flicker over her face. Of all the people she knew, this sweet man was as dear to her as her own family. To refuse would be impolite. Even if she failed she had to try. She sighed, stood, and held out her hand.

Her young girl's cool, smooth skin made his own seem coarse and dry. She laid her other hand on top, clasping his between hers for fifteen seconds or so, moving on to his wrist for a comparable length of time. She repeated the procedure with his other hand and wrist.

He waited for any sensation but felt nothing. She stood back.

"You have arthritis," she said. "Just a little. It pains you."

He nodded. That was true. That would have been a logical guess, in fact.

"May I examine your elbows and shoulders?"

He always wore a coat and tie. It took several minutes to remove those and his shirt. She held his elbows much as she had his hands and wrists. Then, begging his pardon, she slipped her hands under the neck of his undershirt and gently massaged his shoulders.

After several minutes she stepped back. Her voice was more confident.

"You have light to moderate arthritis in the joints I have examined. I think it is the same with your other major joints."

"How did you know I was feeling pain?" he asked.

"I don't know. I sensed it. I think the pain is worst in your feet and ankles."

Had she seen his cane behind his desk?

"You did not examine those. Is that a guess?"

"No. Well, kind of," she added, as if the lack of certainty irritated her. "It's what I think, that's all. Am I right?"

"Yes, my dear. You are right."

"I didn't check your vascular system. I'm best with that. I'm not as good with the nervous system, and still worse with organs. I could examine those but it would take much longer, and we'd need a table. If you like, though, I might be able to lessen your joint pain. For a little while at least, maybe longer. As long as we're experimenting."

That was what he was hoping for. It wouldn't be possible to take notes but he'd observe carefully and write it up later.

"Certainly," he said. "Please do!"

She had him resume his seat and began gently feeling his right hand. At first he thought she was massaging but a careful look showed she was using almost no pressure. Yet he felt the sensation of pressure. She felt the length of each finger and then several fingers at once, wrapping them with her own.

Gradually, he noticed his hand begin to tingle as if in an electric field. No effort was apparent on her face. In fact, with her eyes closed she almost looked asleep. She had moved to the wrist. The tingling sensation was now present there too. He could even feel it beginning in his elbow, ahead of her fingers.

Now she was at his shoulder, but using more pressure. That seemed logical. The faces of the joint were deeper there. Did that mean she was projecting some force that weakened over distance? Perhaps later they could test that.

She moved to his other hand and arm and repeated the procedure. The tingling sensation now encompassed both arms and shoulders. It was as though he had put on a jacket fresh from a freezer. His scalp contracted as if his ears were being pulled backward. He would have to…have to…. He was getting sleepy. Why should that be? He needed to remember this.

Her eyes blinked open. She knelt by his chair and pulled his right foot onto her knee. She pulled off the shoe.

He was going to call a halt, but his powers of speech failed him. There was his foot, white as a filet of tilapia. Before he knew it the bones of his foot and ankle were tingling. She pushed up the pant leg and worked over the knee joint. He fought for wakefulness, biting down on his tongue to try to stay awake. Her eyes were closed. She was breathing deeply and regularly, but not as if from vigorous exertion. She made occasional soft vocalizations, like someone asleep.

Suddenly he realized she was pulling on his shoes and socks. He'd slept despite his best efforts. It was as if he was coming out of anesthesia. The room felt cold. His joints felt cold.

Clio returned to her chair and waited for him to regain full consciousness. He was aware of her watching him doing so. It was so odd. He tried to speak. After several minutes he pushed himself slowly to his feet with the aid of the arms of the chair. He put on his shirt and flexed his hands and arms and turned his head from side to side.

"Whatever did you do?" he was at last able to ask, his voice thick.

"I fixed your joints. Or tried to."

"How sure are you that you did so?"

"I know I improved them. I could feel that. I don't know how long it will last."

"You could feel that? Extraordinary. I could feel it too. Were you aware of turning something on, or of concentrating on doing something?"

"'Concentrating,' yes."

"Were you thinking of anything else, or just that?"

"Just that. Focusing."

Steadying himself against his desk he took a few tentative steps, breathed deeply, flexed his shoulders and neck, and felt the world returning. Two pigeons on the window ledge bobbed their heads in the sun. A shuttle bus rolled up the street toward his building.

He eased the tie over his head, turned up the collar, and snugged the knot under his chin. He put on his coat, wondering what had been the action here? There were medicines that could possibly have done it, but he'd swallowed no medicine, had no shot, been slathered with no ointment. The placebo effect could not be ruled out, but he doubted it strongly. His skin still felt crawly. He walked to the door and back flexing his wrists and fingers. The joints worked smoothly and without pain. How long would that continue?

There was much to investigate here. She regarded him evenly.

"Your circulation is good," she said, "as if you exercise regularly. Your blood pressure is normal, or slightly higher than normal. You are taking a statin. I can usually detect those. I think I detected another strong drug but I can't identify it."

He sat. The tingling she seemed to have caused was only a part of it. Before that, how had she known he felt pain at all?

"You actually sensed my joint pain?"

"Yes, sir."

"In the areas you touched, but were you guessing about my feet?"

"Sort of. That was a little confusing. I wasn't sure."

"I apologize for the fuzziness of this question, but I do not know how else to put it: what do you sense when you sense pain? What are the signals like?"

"I don't know! It's so confusing. It's like, like static, or tree leaves in the wind. Sometimes one voice is obvious, sometimes two. I can't sort them out if there are lots of them. I can usually find the ones for pain and the vascular system the easiest."

He sat and studied her face. She wasn't embarrassed. Dr. Peebles would never embarrass her. She let him think. Still, after a while she looked down at her lap.

After a full minute he asked, "Dear Clio, do you ever listen to classical music?"

"Sir? Uh, yes, I do."

"So you know what a symphony orchestra sounds like?"

"Yes, sir."

"You can hear the difference between the brasses and the strings and the woodwinds? Yes?"

"Yes."

"And you can hear the different instruments in each of those sections? The trumpets as distinguished from the baritones and tubas? The violins from the cellos? The oboe from the bassoon?"

"Uh, I guess so. Yes, sir."

"And maybe even the first violins from the second violins?"

"I don't know. I don't remember trying that."

"All right. Now, just imagine someone hearing a symphony orchestra for the first time. Don't you think it would sound like noise to them? Perhaps like trees in the wind?"

She nodded slowly.

"Consider: you can differentiate over thirty different symphonic sounds at the same time. How do you do that?"

Her eyes told him that was a new idea.

"You practiced, didn't you?" he said, a twinkle in his eye. "You listened. If you could see the orchestra, you associated the sound with what you were seeing, so that now you don't have to see it to know what you're hearing.

"Maybe you can do that with your diagnoses. Maybe practicing will help. Aren't you going to tour with a public health team? That could be the perfect opportunity for you. You won't be responsible for diagnosing. Others on the team will do that. But you might be able to compare what you sense with what is known about the patients. That may help you match your sensations to particular conditions. No one else on the team needs to know what you're doing. There would be no pressure on you, unlike your experience with Dr. Cheever's students. What do you think? Is that worth a try?"

"Yes, sir, it is. I never would have thought of that. I was confused. I didn't know how to start. Now, maybe I do."

"Excellent, my dear. I hope you will be patient. It might take a little time. Ah! Speaking of time, would you join me for lunch?"

"I'm sorry, sir. I'm picking up a friend at the airport soon. I should be going. Thank you so much for seeing me this morning. I am so grateful for your help."

She got to her feet. He followed.

"Oh, no! I must thank *you*, my dear, not only for what you have done for my tired old bones, but for allowing me to personally experience your uncanny abilities. It is one of the highlights of my medical career, and something I would have thought impossible. We simply must pursue this at the earliest opportunity. When you finish your tour why don't I call several eminent medical researchers I know and set up an exploratory study, hm? We would start with the basics: your abilities, family medical history, and of course your DNA genetic code. And then...."

"Oh! Uh, uh, no, Dr. Peebles. I couldn't do that. Please, sir!"

"I know you are shy, my dear, and of course you are very young, but you need not dread participating in a medical study. I promise you being the subject of a study like this one will not be in the least onerous."

She sat down again. Her agitation was obvious.

"I...uh...it's not that, sir. It's...it's...."

"Or are you perhaps leery of becoming an object of popular curiosity? I can assure you your identity will be kept strictly confidential. You should know that this state's medical school is beginning to take alternative medicinal practices more seriously these days. There is nothing there that should worry you."

Her mind was racing. She had been taught at an early age that the secret of her mother's origins must be kept within the immediate family only. Doing so was second nature to her and her brother, and reinforced by observations at school, where the exchange of secrets between friends was a currency far dearer than money. Abuelita, her father's grandmother, had often expressed contempt for women (it was usually women) who gossiped, but Clio noted that Abuelita herself enjoyed nothing better than a juicy tidbit of news about someone she knew. Secrets seemed to cry out to be shared.

Yet her parents had of necessity trusted Ana's secret to Dr. Dave, Julio's professor friend and business partner, who had kept it faithfully for several years. Matt's father and even Abuelita had also had to be informed, though Matt's mother Julia had not. Julia had had several strokes which seemed to have rattled her judgment, causing her to occasionally say embarrassing things. She loved Ana like a daughter in any case, so it hadn't been deemed essential to explain to her that her son's wife was the famous girl who had come from another planet.

Clio's closeness to Dr. Peebles went beyond professional communality or a teacher/pupil relationship. There was genuine affection, a personal concern between them that was more than science or medicine. She thought she could trust him. Besides, given that he was the most likely person to help her come to understand her perplexing abilities, it might actually be important that he know who her mother really was.

Even if she was wrong, it seemed all but certain that her mother's secret would have to come out in the next few years. So what did it matter?

Peebles watched her sit and think, lost to the world for a few seconds. He had no notion of what was upsetting her, but he could wait. If she needed time to decide something she could have it.

Finally she looked up.

"You'd better sit down, sir," she said, "please."

He did, slowly.

"Please keep this to yourself, Dr. Peebles. It's a family secret."

He waited.

"It's not me, sir. It's my mother."

He had just begun to wonder why her mother might object to having a famous daughter when she spoke again.

"My mother is Ana Darcy."

She could count the seconds it took for that to sink in: about three. His mouth actually dropped open.

## Chapter 5

Goddam jetway. Hate jetways. Trapped like a mouse in a bucket if things go to hell. Shit!

Shit! Shit! Shit! Shit!

Steady man. Control yourself.

He shot a glance behind—people jammed up around the bend. Three military haircuts in camouflage uniforms, lugging big, camouflaged packs. Good sign. In front a college girl with purple streaks in her hair, backpack over one shoulder, right hand hanging down with a book, index finger keeping the place. Probably OK. Up ahead a family: man and woman loaded down, two kids, a boy, chest high, bored, and a whiny cotton-topped girl, smaller, both with backpacks. The girl's is pink plastic. Teddy bear under her arm. Should be alright.

Shuffle, shuffle, shuffle. Damn jetways.

The plane'll be worse, packed like cigars in a box. Reach the hatch, check the info plate on the jamb. Seven years old. Gotta be millions of miles on it. Should fly, though. Damn well better. Seated in business class. Could be worse.

He worked his way toward his seat assignment. On the aisle. Can't watch the engines for oil leaks, but if something goes south with the passengers can move fast if necessary. Toss the carry-on bag in the overhead bin, ease into the seat. Sneak a check of those already seated down the aisle. They seem OK except for one curly haired guy who looks jittery and a young guy not dressed well enough to be a businessman who looks too calm. Have to watch those two. Pisser that the Beretta had to be checked in the suitcase.

He sat and dragged the seat belt out from under his butt. Scope out the little emergency lights running down the port side of the deck. Trace 'em to the emergency exits one, two, three, four rows ahead, left and right. Remember that: four rows. The soldiers bumping past on their way to tourist class. They were smiling. They should be. They were alive, and of sound body.

The file of passengers stopped moving past. Son of a bitch! A fat guy with a ticket for the window seat. He got up and moved into the aisle to let the jerk in. He must weigh 280 pounds, 290 with cologne. Sit back down. Where'd that goddam belt go? Sitting on it. Crap.

Three hours and change from Miami to Dallas-Fort Worth. Double crap.

Things were slightly better forty-five minutes later. The plane was at altitude, the flight was smooth, and he was beginning to feel the pricey bourbon the stewardess had brought him. No emergencies yet.

He pushed his seat back a couple notches and wadded up the empty packet that had contained a dozen tasteless pretzels. For sure, the days of excitement and adventure were over. Had to happen. He just hadn't expected it would be when he was only 35, for Christ's sake. Nor had he expected there'd be so few good jobs for ex-warriors. Law enforcement had no appeal—too dull and too poorly paid. Stupid cheap bastard taxpayers. They'll get what they pay for and deserve it. In the meantime, there was RobboMan.

He had to admit he was thankful for Rob Coombs. Once a Seal always a Seal. Seals stick together. A lieutenant working for a chief? No problem, as long as the checks cleared. The security job Coombs had for him was anything but exciting but the pay was decent, worth a try for a little while at least. Coombs was his Seal poster boy for becoming at least part way domesticated: had a wife with a kid on the way, regular hours and mostly desk work to keep him off the streets. The assignments Coombs had given to him so far had been no sweat.

And then there was the occasional perk, like this gig Coombs put him onto. It would probably be dull too, but as RobboMan pointed out, where else could you work for a woman from another planet?

Freakin' airlines never gave enough leg room. He shifted position, crossing his legs uncomfortably. His damn stump was killing him.

Jabba the Hutt to his right was dozing over the Sky Mall catalog, radiating aromatic heat. He reached up and fine-tuned the air nozzle in an attempt to send the stench somewhere else.

No stewardess, wandering passenger, or curious child was looking. He reached into his jacket pocket and pulled out a Ziploc bag containing a toothbrush, a pissant tube of toothpaste, and a three ounce plastic bottle of mouthwash. He poured half of it over the remaining ice in the plastic cup and replaced bottle in his jacket. He took a sip. His "mouthwash" was a helluva lot better bourbon than the stuff the airline had sold him. Time for a little toast. "Here's to you, Homeland Security. Bite me, sumbitches."

When Michelle Stratemeyer first saw Ana Darcy it was as a troubled middle school student sent home from school. Now, eighteen years later, Michelle was a lawyer and fluent speaker of Luvit, Ana's native language, and one of Ana's oldest and best friends on Earth. Several inches taller than Ana and married to another friend of Ana's, Rob Coombs, she was seemingly in glowing good health, and extremely pregnant.

Twenty agreeable minutes chatting in Michelle's kitchen began the pleasant process of catching up on their lives. During a short break while Ana poured more tea, Michelle called a Philippine restaurant to order lunch. When she returned to the table Ana was staring at a note pad with a puzzled expression, pencil in hand.

"Something wrong?" she asked.

"Oh, no, it helps me to remember a word if I write it down. I want to remember the name of this lovely red tea."

Michelle found the box on the counter.

"Here it is. 'Rooibos,'" she said, spelling it slowly.

"Thanks. Now this word too, please. You said it, but I didn't get it."

Michelle studied the paper.

"Oh. That's 'preeclampsia.' Sometimes it has a hyphen: 'pre-eclampsia.'"

Ana shook her head.

"I never heard of that."

"You should be glad. It's not that rare, really. My doctor said it's more a combination of things rather than a single condition. Mainly, I have to watch out for high blood pressure. That's why I've spent so much time at home in bed these last few weeks, and why I'm drinking herbal tea. But I'm fine, really. I've been able to do a surprising amount of office work by computer. I've even packed up some of my mom's bric-a-brac."

Ana frowned and picked up the pencil again. Michelle spelled it, hyphens and all.

"Is your mom happy in her condominium?"

"She loves it. She says it's perfect for a retired lawyer, even though she won't actually retire for another year or so. That way we can overlap until the baby is a year old and I can take over her duties."

She was giving Ana a quick tour of the baby's room and explaining how she and Rob planned to remodel the house now that it was theirs when the doorbell rang. Lunch had arrived.

Ana had had lumpia and chicken adobo before, but pancit bijon and ginataang seafood were new and delicious. Michelle searched out the seafood dish on her laptop and was able to tell her it was shrimp and scallops sautéed with red curry, coconut milk, eggplant, and garlic. Ana jotted that down too.

While they finished the meal, Michelle asked Ana about the rest of her travels.

"Hleo wouldn't tell me a thing," she complained. "He said Ambassador Darshiell would be making an announcement tomorrow."

Ana smiled.

"Hleo always was a…a sticker? For regulations?"

"Stickler?" Michelle ventured.

"Yes, thanks. …a stickler for regulations. The Tribal Council ordered the Ambassador to keep it secret. I had to beg Hleo to tell me just a little, so I could make plans for the family. But I can tell you. You're family." She put down her fork and leaned forward. "They're sending another vessel. With six to ten people. Hleo couldn't say exactly when they will arrive. It'll be another couple years or a little more."

"Oh my gosh! Six to ten?"

"Yes. Hleo wouldn't say anything about them. I don't think they'd been selected yet. I assume they'll be high ranking, each probably expert in two or three fields. They wouldn't have heard about my disobeying orders and coming to Earth, so I have to think they're coming because of the technical data and historical observations Hleo and I sent long ago. They're in for a big surprise."

"Are they ever!" Michelle's cup clanked in the saucer. "And you might be too, you know…."

"I know. And Matt and the twins also. This will change everything. I worry about that." She looked down at her plate. "I worry a lot about that."

The captain's tinny voice garbled something about a "final" approach to Albuquerque. Every flight was final, dumbass. Once you're up, you're coming down. That's a given. Would they walk away from the landing? *That* was the question.

He drained the last of his "mouthwash."

So what the hell was this job gonna be like? He was working "for" a woman from another planet but not "with" a woman from another planet. Didn't look like he'd get to meet her on this gig. Pisser, man. He'd never, ever forget what Ana Darcy looked like in that skimpy tank top and black pajama bottoms. Foxy! He'd remember that forever, even though it had been the middle of the goddam night. Suddenly there she was: a SEAL's dream calendar photo, stepping out of her sexy sports car from outer space, along with a boy and girl and a man. The girl had been holding on to a concussed RobboMan so tight the corpsman had to pry him loose to haul him to sickbay. He hadn't paid much attention to either kid after that. Why should he, after Ana Darcy passed him the tactical tip of his life? She earned him and his team a big fat Silver Star, but for all the good that had done he ought to pass it on to her. She'd accomplished the hard part the free world had failed at for ten years. He and his squad had only done what they always had done. She was the one who located the mope right down to the last square yard of his life.

It wasn't until two days ago when Coombs briefed him that he learned the man was her husband and the two kids were her children, for Christ's sake. They had been on a family outing: the wife from another planet, her husband, and their two kids, your basic little home-style armed raid on a Pashtun compound.

RobboMan said she was as good as a SEAL in a jam and maybe she really was. But would he recognize her daughter now? He remembered a little kid, more or less, big enough to hang onto Coombs' head, but not as big as her brother. Coombs said they were twins, about seventeen now. Not that it mattered. Hell, for the per diem he was getting he'd change diapers if it came to that. She'd supposedly be wearing a yellow hat, but things never went as planned. At least Coombs had given him her cell phone number.

The pilot didn't have to be embarrassed by the landing. It took twice as long as it should have for the passengers to shuffle out of the plane, of course. Once again, he was ambling along in a crowd of schmucks. At least they'd all been through security. No one would be packing heavy weapons.

Stay invisible, man. Walk close behind this big guy and his even bigger wife. Goddammit, his goddam leg hurt. Straighten up, you fuckin' gimp. Look normal. Follow 'em past a bored security guard across the line into insecure territory. Stick close until they get through the chumps awaiting the arrivals, until…wait, wait…now!

He stepped behind a column and pretended to search his pockets for something. Turned a little and sneaked a casual glance around the column at the crowd he'd just walked through. Too damn many unsifted people on the loose here.

Off to the right, a girl in an ugly yellow cowboy hat. Well, more chartreuse than yellow. Seemed to have a boyfriend with her. Tall girl. Taller than the boyfriend. Nah, forget her.

No yellow hats. Crap! Where in the hell is that kid? Nonchalantly, he pivoted to see around the other side of the column. Still no yellow hat. Shit.

He was reaching for his cell phone when damned if he didn't notice a young girl in a yellow baseball cap not ten feet away. She was staring straight at him, bold as brass, positioned much like he was, behind the next column in the row, in full view. How had he missed her? Where in Christ had she come from?

Fuck. If she were the enemy he'd have been a dead man.

Nothing to do but walk over to her. He stopped three feet away. Her face was expressionless. He kept his the same way. They regarded each other.

"Lieutenant?" she said, finally.

"Call me Fergus."

"Yessir," she replied. "Have you checked any baggage?"

"Yup."

"Baggage claim is this way."

She didn't say squat until they were in her car leaving the airport. Maybe she resented his presence. Or maybe not—he wouldn't have said anything in this crowd either. Low profile. Always best.

She really was a kid, a full head shorter than his five feet eleven. Skinny, too: small hands, thin arms, little sneakers. Might weigh a hundred pounds. Looked fourteen except for the watchful eyes and controlled movements. She was pretty much keeping track of the people around them like he was.

In the sun the shoulder-length pony tail pulled through the hole in her hat showed dark gold rather than the brown it had appeared inside. Making allowance for her age and size she was trim, not a bad looking kid. Kind of like her mother, come to that. Anyone watching would figure the two of them for a father and daughter. So this was who he was going to bodyguard, or be an escort for, or whatever? How hard could that be?

She led him to a silver Corolla in the short term lot. Oh, shit. Of course she was going to drive. Why hadn't he anticipated that? She'd better be a hell of a good driver.

He was not going to be a good passenger.

## Chapter 6

It only took a few minutes for Clio to exit the airport and merge onto Interstate 25 north. Traffic was mercifully light.

Her "body guard" was a rangy brunet man of thirty-some years, and not movie star handsome—more like supporting actor handsome, unremarkable. His eyes were keen, though, and the lines of his face and jaw suggested a residual hardness beneath the surface. He seemed uneasy. He was sitting with his feet braced against the firewall, one hand gripping the door ledge and the other pressed into the seat, as if he expected a collision. She was a careful driver but decided it would be more polite to overlook his nervousness.

As to manners, they had not yet properly greeted each other. Her mother, always scrupulously polite, would have expected better of her. In fact, he had said nothing to her yet, and she had said nothing to him. The longer it went on the more awkward she felt. Someone had to begin.

"Thank you for coming, Lieutenant Fergus. Did my mom explain the situation to you?"

He was leaning slightly forward, apparently sneaking a glance in the right side rear view mirror but replied as readily as if he expected her question.

"'Fergus' is all you need. That's what everyone calls me. I'm not a Lieutenant any more. She said you'd be part of a public health team traveling around the state and that she didn't feel right that you should do it alone. That was about it."

"Yes, sir, that's what I'll be doing. Mom wouldn't let me go by myself. I tried to argue with her but I lost. I don't resent having you with me, but I didn't want it. I'm sorry. I have to be honest."

"Sure. I understand. I'll be honest too. If you were my kid, I'd want what she wants. From what little I know of your mother, she has reason to worry about security."

"Yes, sir, she does. That's why we needed your help before. I'm grateful for that, by the way. I never thanked you."

"No problem. Glad to do it. She repaid us in spades, you know."

"I know. I've wondered about that. Was it terrible?"

"Terrible? Depends on your point of view. From yours, yeah, you probably would have called it terrible. From Al Khalifa's point of view, it was worse than terrible. It was the worst. From ours, it was business as usual—except that in this one case, it was terrific too. Couldn't have been better. And for innocent people everywhere, it was exactly right."

"Was anyone with you hurt?"

"A couple. Minor stuff. No one died. It was a clean op."

"Gee. After all that, now here you are with me. I'm not my mom, you know. Probably only ten people know who I am. No one cares about me."

"Your family?"

"Of course, my family. I mean no one else knows who my mother is. I'm just this weird little person nobody knows."

"If you say so. So tell me: what are you doing on this deal? You seem a little young to be going around with doctors and nurses. That might help me figure out what I'm supposed to be doing."

"Well, do you know what a curandera is?"

"Mmm, has to do with curing, I guess. Some sort of witch doctor, right?"

"Not exactly. It's a person, usually a woman, who uses traditional plants and stuff as medicines and who helps people who are ailing. I'm sort of a curandera, except—this is going to sound crazy—I can actually heal with my hands, some of the time. Not all the time. I don't know how I do it. I kept Rob Coombs alive until we reached you, back then. But I don't know how to control it. I don't know what else I might be able to do. It's really bugging me. A doctor friend suggested I tour with this rural health team. I'll be a gofer mostly, but I'll also see lots and lots of people who need help, and I'll probably get to practice with some of them. Maybe it will help me understand what I can do. Maybe I'll be able to control it better."

In the rear view mirror, an eighteen wheeler was looming behind them. She eased the car's right wheels onto the shoulder to leave extra room as it thundered by in the passing lane, its chrome hub nuts flashing silver spirals at eye level. Fergus went as rigid as if he had been tased.

It was not a close call. Watching the truck pulling ahead, Clio finally lost patience with her body guard.

"It's OK," she said, a little shortly. "I'm a careful driver."

Fergus settled slowly into his seat, his eyes tense.

"I know you are," he said. "Don't mind me. It's those overseas deployments. Over there if you drive slow, they'll kill you. You never stop, not at stop signs, not at red lights. Keep moving. If you stop, you're dead. Anything unusual in the road is potentially dangerous. React fast and live. It's a really hard habit to break."

She had nothing to say to that. Fergus gradually collected himself.

"I remember you holding onto Coombs," he said, finally. "I didn't know what the reason was."

"I'm good with the vascular system, and the lymph system," she said. "I kept the swelling down as best I could. I was so frightened."

"Hmm," he said, pushing himself into a more normal seating position and flexing his shoulders. "Coombs said you'd done something to him, but he couldn't say what. He said his only memory was his head felt like it was cold and shrunk to the size of a walnut."

"I don't even know what I'm doing. That's what I want to work on."

"Weird."

They were coming up behind a lumbering RV with Minnesota plates. She eased off on the gas, checked the mirror, pulled out and went around it. Fergus managed to control himself. She reset the cruise control.

"I have a copy of our approximate schedule I'll give you when we get to the hotel," she said. "Mom said Seals have medical training. Is that right?"

"You betcha. Mostly emergency stuff, battlefield medicine, the basics. We're not doctors."

"OK. So you could be a medical volunteer on these visits, all right?"

"I guess so. Where are we headed?"

"Oh, sorry. I should have mentioned. The medical team doesn't start for two days. We're going to Santa Fe now. A cousin of mine is an artist. He's having his first exhibition ever at a gallery there tomorrow. It's a really big deal. I'm so excited for him. I can't wait to see it! You might like it too."

"Oh, yeah. That reminds me."

He reclined his seat and twisted around. He began wrestling with his suitcase on the back seat. She heard a zipper unzipped. He pulled out an object wrapped in a t-shirt which he unrolled to reveal an automatic pistol, a clip of ammunition, and a nylon holster.

He glanced at her. She was cool, not even surprised.

He crossed his left leg over his right, pulled his cuff above his ankle, and strapped on the holster.

"Mr. Coombs also had a knife," she said.

He slid the clip into the handle of the pistol.

"I got one of those in the bag too," he said, "but this is handier. One size fits all. Better to have it and not need it than the other way around."

She was watching the road again. He pulled his pant leg over the pistol and holster and raised the seat back.

"What sort of painting does your cousin do?"

"I don't really know. I only met him once. He lives on a ranch in Mexico. It's probably western art. He's really talented."

"If you only met him once, how do you know he's talented?"

"Oh. Well, he wanted to sketch me. He did an amazing job. That's not easy."

"That's right. It's not."

"Are you an artist?"

"No. I took a drawing class in college. It's hard."

"Where did you go? What was your major?"

"University of Washington. International studies." He snorted. "Then I joined the Navy. The Nav gave me a doctorate in international studies, you might say. The sort of major where you learn or die."

Over the remainder of the short drive to Santa Fe, Clio learned more about what a conventional international studies major entailed, and Fergus learned that Clio had no idea what to major in. More surprising, she didn't even seem eager for a college degree as much as exploring medicine, healing, and pharmacology.

Their hotel turned out to be moderately upscale and with the obligatory Spanish colonial theme. She had ID cards for each of them that pronounced them members of the medical visitation team and exempt from the state hotel tax.

Their rooms were on the fifth floor. His was nearest the elevator. He inserted the card in the lock, received a green light, and opened the door, setting down his suitcase to hold the door open. He was going to ask her what time to meet in the morning, but she beat him to it.

"The gallery reception is at 1:00 pm. I'd like to sightsee a little in the morning, if you don't mind. Could we meet for breakfast at 8:00 am?"

"Sure," he said. "Wait for me to knock on your door, please. We'll go down together."

"Also," she continued, "I apologize for not meeting you properly this afternoon. I know you already know, but I'm Clio Méndez, sir."

She held out her hand. He took it automatically.

"Right. OK. And I'm Fergus."

He unfolded his fingers from her hand but she held on. He pulled lightly to no avail. She was looking blankly at his shirt.

"Uh…." he said.

Still grasping his hand she looked up at him.

"You're in pain," she said in a matter-of-fact voice. "Your right leg is hurting you. I can relieve some of that. Maybe all of it."

He jerked his hand free, frowning.

"I don't think so."

"It won't hurt. I promise."

"Never mind," he said, anger in his voice. "A whole hospital full of VA combat rehab specialists did their best and this is what I've got. I can live with it."

"Please, Lieutenant Fergus. I can help."

"Forget it, kid." He kicked the suitcase into the room with his good leg. "I'll see you in the morning," and he shut the door in her face.

## Chapter 7

Matt was enjoying his first-ever extended trip with his almost-grown son, but it was hard to tell if Julio was enjoying it as much as he was. Despite his active, brilliant technical mind the young man had an undemonstrative nature. He didn't miss much, but he generally kept his thoughts to himself.

They had just turned south off Interstate 10 at Kent, towards the Davis Mountains. Julio knew the area well. The Méndez family had a history there. Indeed, the family history had begun there, and Julio knew most of it. Still, from time to time he learned things he hadn't known. His sister, for example, once asked a question he never would have thought of asking on his own. They were having a simple supper of leftovers while Ana was in town at a dinner meeting. Out of the blue, Clio asked, "Dad, when did you know you were really in love with Mom?"

His father had swallowed whatever he was eating, took a sip of tea, and explained that he had first searched her out because he was a newspaper reporter and she had been a mysterious fugitive from several branches of law enforcement. It figured to be a good story. He found her, met her, and had been astonished by her claim of having come from another planet. Partly because of that claim (and partly in spite of it), he found himself enjoying her presence more and more over several more interviews. It wasn't until she left the Williams ranch to try out for the Olympics that he realized he might never see her again and would miss her desperately: she had taken permanent residence in his heart. When she not only returned to the area after the Olympics but actually asked to see him again, *that* was the moment. He was head over heels in love.

Julio reflected on that as the truck climbed into the mountains. So many of his friends' families were troubled one way or another, yet he and his sister never doubted their parents' love for each other or for them, and the security that came with it.

His parents had their disagreements. His mother got nervous whenever he and his sister were out on their own. She kept careful track, usually by phone. She didn't like it when the three of them had target practice behind the barn. His dad wasn't thrilled when their mother jaunted off on some international mission. Most of the serious trouble the family had experienced had been as a result of such trips. Yet they compromised. Their problems never overwhelmed the family. Was that normal?

Well, duh, how normal was it to have a mother from another planet? Maybe the family closeness came from the unique situation of having a wife and mother born twenty-five light years away. Whatever the cause, could he and Clio ever hope for such happiness in their own relationships? Clio was interested in boys, to some degree. He was interested in girls to some degree also, like Dhwani, the math-crazy girl from India….

The truck slowed slightly. Up ahead a police car was on the shoulder of the road, light bar flashing brilliant blue and red. As they passed, he saw the Mustang in front of it. A highway patrol officer was standing to one side writing a ticket. Gotcha, Julio thought. The Mustang reminded him of the car one of Clio's would-be boyfriends drove, one of the annoying ones, that Shack fellow. Clio seemed annoyed by him too, fortunately.

Clio just hadn't run across any boys that she clicked with. She definitely had a wild streak, though, like when she ran off to Mexico to search for that Indian healer guy. That was more than wild—it was dangerous. She nearly got killed. She should have been smarter than that. She was probably smarter than he was, but she sometimes did unpredictable things without thinking them through. His sister was hard to understand.

His father had just said something.

"Sorry, Dad. What was that?"

"I said you're awful quiet, son. Whatcha thinking about?"

"Oh. Uh, the batteries, Dad. And, uh, also the Zimmer's place, on the other side."

Another time, they might have stopped at the Williams' ranch, on the far side of the Davis Mountains between Fort Davis and Alpine, to visit Ana's sister Ianthe and her husband Scott Zimmer, where the Zimmers had a vacation home in the low mountains above the vast Williams Ranch. The home had been a wedding present from Dwayne and Rhoda Williams and Jack Benning, head of the law firm that scouted Ana for the Olympics. The Méndez family had also used the cozy little home several times as well. At the moment, though, the Zimmers would be in New York City with Ana and her uncle Rothan, to attend Rothan's press conference.

Instead, they called a halt for gas and lunch in Alpine where in unspoken male solidarity they chose the kind of food they never had at home: chicken fried steaks smothered in savory cream gravy and fries.

Julio drove from Alpine to Del Rio while his father relaxed, and Matt took the wheel for the last leg into San Antonio.

They checked in to the historic Menger hotel just after sunset. Dating from 1859 and furnished in frontier Victorian style, the Menger had accommodated Theodore Roosevelt and Babe Ruth, among others. It was even rumored to host a ghost, perhaps of Sam Houston. It was close to the Alamo and San Antonio's famous River Walk, in effect a below-street-level riverside tourist mall along the San Antonio River, with restaurants, shops, galleries, souvenir stores, and even boat tours on the river. But Julio's hunger came before tourism.

Matt led him to Rosario's Restaurant, a short walk away in the King William historical district, where he treated his son to a gourmet TexMex meal, quite different from their accustomed New Mexican cuisine.

To walk off the meal they checked out the famous Alamo. It was closed though lit spectacularly by floodlights, so they strolled the River Walk until Matt, tiring of the throngs of tourists and conventioneers, ducked into a quiet bar for a beer. Julio had a licuada, made from blended fresh strawberries.

Matt was answering his son's question about why there should be a "Governor's Palace" several blocks away when Julio unexpectedly shot his dad a look and Matt paused his narrative. A Dixieland band on the opposite side of the river (a hundred feet away) was performing one of Louis Armstrong's Hot Five classic tunes at a night club but Julio shook his head slightly and nodded a fraction of an inch at the table behind him.

Two nicely dressed couples in their thirties were chatting over beer and tostadas and salsa. One of the men was speaking.

"…blows my mind," he was saying, "It's just amazing. They're traveling trillions of miles, *trillions*, at 97% the speed of light, and they have no idea what they're headed to!"

One of the women spoke up.

"How can that be? The first Thomans arrived almost twenty years ago."

"I know. It's hard to savvy. I'm gonna make a neat unit out of this for my science classes. See, the folks on Thomo don't even know yet that Ana Darcy and their ambassador and the others are safely on Earth and doing well. They won't know for another five years!"

The woman was confused.

"But they're sending more people who'll be here in a year or two? They had to know, didn't they?"

"No! Their 'current' information is 25 years old!"

"Well, but…."

"They're coming based on the reports that she sent them about Earth 25 years ago. They have no idea what's happened to Ana Darcy and her uncle yet. In fact, if you think about it, the most up-to-date Thomans are the ones headed this way, who have to be intercepting the news being sent back to Thomo!"

"I don't get it," the woman said.

The other woman laughed and spoke up.

"OK, Gerald. Let an English teacher have a turn. Imagine a river, Debbie. Someone upstream is putting notes in bottles and dropping them in a river, OK? Let's say the bottles take 25 days to float downstream to headquarters. So they drop one in the river every day, maybe a couple times a day. Downstream, they get the notes when they are 25 days old. One day they read something that makes them want to send visitors to the people upstream, so they put people in a boat and start speeding upstream. On their way, they can read all the notes that are still floating down to the starting point, where those there have yet to read them. See?"

"I guess so," Debbie said.

Matt looked at his watch, drained his beer, and glanced at Julio. Julio nodded and pushed back his chair. Outside, on the River Walk, they set as brisk a pace as they could through the throngs of tourists.

"Obviously, we missed something important in the news today," Matt muttered. "But we can make the 10:00 pm wrap up."

It was the lead story on the international news: Julio's great uncle, the Ambassador Plenipotentiary of the People of Thomo, Rothan Darshiell, was speaking from a podium at the embassy flanked by the other three Thomans on Earth, his nieces Ana Darcy and Ianthe Darshiell Zimmer, and Herecyn Cymred. Beaming with pride, he announced the anticipated arrival in a year or two of the third voyage to Earth from Thomo.

"Oh, jeez," said Julio, "Did you know about this?"

"More or less," said Matt. "Mom gave me some idea."

"Double jeez."

The Ambassador was taking questions from media people. Over the next few minutes it became clear that all the information he had came from pre-launch plans and that it was anticipated that six to twelve Thomans, chosen for their expertise in multiple areas and their ability to represent the entire Thoman population, would make up the crew. Most surprising was that the plans included a return voyage to Thomo, bearing an exchange crew from Earth.

Julio was thunderstruck. The family had guessed that something like this might eventually be in the offing, and now it was evidently going to happen. Julio well knew that his parents had gone to great lengths to keep their mother's identity secret, as much for the benefit of their children as themselves. Over the years since her arrival amid a stupendous burst of publicity, things had settled down a bit. He was even able to forget, some of the time, that he and Clio were the first humans ever to be born of two worlds. Given the Thomans' love of ceremony, status, and order, not to mention the inevitable publicity storm of Earthly media, the two of them were sure to be celebrated to a ridiculous extent. They would never be able to avoid the resulting glare of fame. His life, and Clio's, would surely become some kind of living hell.

He did not feel Thoman in the least.

Almost invariably soft-spoken, he looked at his father in amazement.

"Holy shit," he said.

His father's face was dead serious as he replied.

"Uh-huh."

## Chapter 8

Ana decided to travel from Zurich to Davos by train rather than automobile. Rail was a mode of transportation she had rarely experienced on Earth, though her own planet, Thomo, had several kinds of rail transport. She loved being able to move around freely while in motion, even though this particular ride was only two hours long and she had little need to move around. More happily, the train allowed stupendous views of snow-covered mountains and peaceful, snug valleys, similar to vistas she had seen in Colorado, but much more domestic: settled, neat, and comfortable.

Uncle Rothan would arrive the following day. He had been delayed by a meeting with several officials of the United Nations dealing with his announcement of the third Thoman expedition. Sister Ianthe should have arrived in Davos hours before Ana, flying with her husband Scott on a plane chartered by media representatives.

Ana was traveling alone, which she much preferred. Had she been with her uncle or sister she would have had to travel as herself, and that would have created problems she preferred to avoid. Traveling anonymously with a backpack, sunglasses, and a Zagat guide to Switzerland under her arm, she was spared the annoyance of being a celebrity. People around her behaved normally.

She was not looking forward to the "World Economic Forum" conference at Davos. As a youngster on Thomo, she had always dreaded the ceremonial functions that had been part of her notable family's life. At the time, when it had occurred to her at all she thought she was a bad daughter, uncooperative and rebellious. Now, many years later, she understood that she had actually been shy. She still was. Although she could hide her feelings and function well enough, she simply did not like crowds of strange people. But this was another command performance. She would have to work a crowd again. She *had* to. The reputation of the people of Thomo would suffer if she did not.

She was way too famous already, what with the long public memory of her peculiar status as the first of her people to return to Earth after thousands of years' absence, and especially after the publicity stunt of being in the Olympic games, followed closely by the news of the colliding meteoroids. It had seemed such a good idea at the time, but now that it was over, the aftereffects continued to loom ominously over her life.

Her personal renown was by no means the only problem ahead. When the newest Thomans arrived, ceremonial and public functions would be frequent and unavoidable. Thomans too were sure to celebrate her achievement. As if that weren't enough, the epic poem Hleo had composed exalting her supposed heroic deeds would make it even worse.

The unbearably worst part was that their little family could be torn apart. Their many friends and relatives in New Mexico would never think of them in the same way again. How could they continue to live in the peaceful place where they now lived? Her children would become icons, unwilling symbols of the historic reunion of the people of Thomo with the people of Earth. Julio and Clio were children, innocent children! They were *not* symbols!

The train was slowing. She had to get control of her emotions. There was nothing to be done now.

She took a cab to the Belvedere Hotel, tipped the driver, and strolled through the entry colonnade into the lobby. Ten minutes' effort in a stall in the women's room changed her from an unremarkable tourist to an informally dressed but recognizable Ana Darcy, judging by the reaction of the desk clerk, who slid her sign-in card and room key to her beaming broadly, not even asking for her name.

Despite dozens of people chatting here and there in the lobby she made it into an elevator without attracting notice. Yesterday in New York, Uncle Rothan's aide, Pavel Sugarek, had told her the Thomans had four rooms at the end of a hall, two on each side, but she was surprised to find a desk in the hall before the rooms. The man behind the desk stood as she approached.

"Good afternoon, Ms. Darcy," he said. "I'm John Morrison, with World Security. Welcome to Davos. Your room is 480, right here. Your sister is waiting for you."

And so she was, a welcome sight indeed.

Different as they were, Ana got along well with her sister. Tall even without heels, beautiful, self-assured, and with calm common sense, Ianthe radiated elegance. She had terrific fashion instincts, which Ana did not, and she wore her clothes well. Ana, caring little for fashion, generally opted for simplicity, which sometimes made her feel a little self-conscious.

Ianthe didn't love crowds, but neither did she mind them. Like Ana, Ianthe was reserved in company, but her smiles were warm and gracious if not quite as radiant as those of her nervously overcompensating sister. Strangers seemed to find Ianthe simultaneously appealing and intimidating.

Ana was happiest in small groups, in the person of "Ana Méndez," where she could converse and relate comfortably. As "Ana Darcy, the Girl from Outer Space," or "Ana Darcy, Olympic medalist," she felt herself regarded as the kind of vacuous celebrity people merely wanted a signature from, or to touch or be photographed with, so they could brag about it to their friends. Encountering such people was what she most dreaded about this conference—that and Herecyn Cymred.

Ana had a history with Herecyn. Before leaving Thomo on her mission to Earth, she had refused Herecyn's offer of marriage. It had been made for political reasons, but she didn't love him and couldn't stand the idea of being married to him. He was one of several reasons she didn't mind leaving Thomo forever.

The arrival of the Thomans' second expedition, with Ianthe as Herecyn's wife, was a considerable shock. To make it worse, it didn't take Herecyn long to become intoxicated by the very earthly idea of making lots and lots of money, getting himself and his fellow Thomans in serious trouble. Ana nearly lost her life righting Herecyn's wrong. Ianthe divorced him, later marrying the journalist Scott Zimmer.

Over the years since, Herecyn had at least partially rehabilitated his reputation and apparently would be attending the Davos convocation, according to Uncle Rothan. Thomans were nothing if not meticulously formal in public. Ana prayed her early training in etiquette would enable her to conceal her dislike of the man.

Ana's fears turned out to be the subtext of Ianthe's conversation. Ianthe knew Ana would be tense among all the strangers at Davos, and that Ana might not be able to avoid encountering Herecyn, so she steered her subtle pep talk partly to prepare her sister should there be a chance meeting. She concluded just as there was a knock on their door.

It was Pavel Sugarek, the Ambassador's longtime aide.

"Good afternoon, Mrs. Zimmer," he said, "and Ms. Darshiell. I'm a little late. Sorry. I had to stop to chat with too many people. That happens at Davos."

"Your timing is perfect," Ianthe said, turning to her sister. "I asked Pavel to give you a quick introduction to the conference," she said. "It can be confusing. This is my third time, and I still don't understand it all."

Sugarek, a young man from California with a talent for languages and the workings of diplomacy, had been Rothan's aide for years. He was efficient, naturally diplomatic, and had a wry sense of humor. Ana liked him.

"I know you prefer structure in affairs like this, ma'am," he said to Ana, "but I'm sorry to tell you that whatever structure there might be here exists mainly in theory. Most participants, in fact, will tell you that randomness is one of its main attractions.

"There is a program, to be sure, but most participants cheerfully ignore it and improvise. At any time and any place, you should expect to encounter the world's foremost innovators, scientists, engineers, bankers, theologians, politicians, philosophers, and business people…to name just a few."

"Oh, my," Ana said. "If only the people of the Third Expedition could be here…."

"I have no doubt they'll be invited to later conferences. It's heaven for networkers and deep thinkers." He gathered his thoughts a moment. "Let me lay out the general organization for you. Then you can follow your bliss, as it were.

"First, the daytime hub of the conference is the Congress Center, a short walk from here. You'll find lecture halls, lounges, cafés, and many, many espresso bars, drink stations, fruit stands, and the like. There is a schedule of presentations, but everyone feels free to wander about and improvise.

"This hotel, the Belvedere, is the night time hub. All present will have gone through a security check and there'll be parties, music, and endless conversation.

"The late-night hangout is the Europa Hotel, with piano bars and parties until dawn. It can get pretty wild and security is not strong there. You may wish to avoid that.

"The overall theme of the conference this time is something like 'Planetary Risks: What Is To Be Done?' The panel discussion you will be a part of is one of the prime events. It's at the Congress Center, the day after tomorrow."

"Prime events?" Ana asked.

"Right. Most Davos conferences have a central celebrity. One year it was a former American President. Two years ago it was a movie star/philanthropist. Last year, it was the Chancellor of Germany."

"What about this year?" she asked.

He looked at her, no expression on his face. He said nothing.

"Oh, no," she gasped, "Oh, dear."

## Chapter 9

Clio had been to Santa Fe many times with her family. By her high school years its many attractions had begun to grow on her. She had come to understand and love the historical buildings, the variety of cultures, the architecture, museums, theater, music, dance, and on one transcendent night, the opera, Handel's *Giulio Cesare*. This visit, however, was supposed to be different, or so she hoped. She had developed her own interests, she had her own car, and she could decide for herself where to go and what to see.

But it wasn't turning out that way.

She wasn't alone.

She had a body guard.

None of her friends had body guards. How should one act when one had a body guard? As if the body guard were a welcome presence, maybe a friend? Or as if that person were merely a lackey, beneath notice until needed? Or something in between, as someone with only an ancillary but non-trivial reason for his presence? The dilemma followed her everywhere.

There were additional considerations: she knew her body guard from his previous assistance to her family, and she appreciated his expertise. She wanted to like him. But it was not clear that he wanted to like her or was even terribly interested in being a body guard. The area around the Governor's Palace, for instance, was full of interesting things: art galleries, people selling jewelry and handicrafts from blankets, tourists from all over the world, and more. She loved immersing herself in the scene and interacting with those who caught her interest. But Lieutenant Fergus, the former Lieutenant Fergus, hung back, watching everything with lazy eyes, apparently bored, seemingly indifferent to her attempts at conversation. He either didn't want to be distracted from his job or he was simply unfriendly. Whichever, he was always *there*, in the background and in her mind.

That bothered her. Did it matter? After all, it seemed highly unlikely that she actually needed a body guard. Fergus was mainly the corporeal proof that her mother worried about her. Suppose he stayed in his hotel room. It would make no difference, really. In fact, why not simply drive off and leave him?

No, she couldn't do that. He would contact Mr. Coombs, or worse, her mother, and she would be in serious trouble. The bottom line was that she had told her mother she would accept the presence of a body guard as a condition of her participation with the rural health team. To back out now would break her word. She would dishonor herself, and in so doing dishonor her mother. That was the Thoman way to think about it, and she couldn't help it. Evidently she really was part Thoman. Phooey.

They only had to get through this weekend. Once the rural medical program started, her body guard could take on selected additional duties of a medical assistant and maybe actually be useful. At the moment, well, he was a man. Men were usually hungry. She would take him to lunch.

The body guard in question was having not dissimilar thoughts. His morning had been utterly boring, but for a security man boring was good. No one who had been in combat needed to be reminded how quickly things could go sour. Boredom was, in fact, beautiful, even though it could never be taken for granted.

He was paying close attention to their surroundings without being obvious about it, but even so he felt he stuck out like a pig at a picnic. Anyone studying them from a distance might have thought he was stalking her; he, a 35 year-old man, lurking around this cute little girl with the tight jeans and the pony tail. No one seemed to be watching them, though, and vehicular traffic looked routine.

The lunch break was welcome. He could walk normally enough since the surgeons had left him his knee, but after all morning on his feet his stump ached like a bastard. Food would be welcome, provided they sat down to eat it.

A half hour later he realized the kid had picked a hell of a fine restaurant. She asked him if he'd ever had New Mexican food. As if the Navy had a strong presence in freakin' New Mexico. But it turned out the food was outstanding: filling, spicy, lots of cheese and great sauces, way better than the Cuban chow in Miami. He'd been leery of the chili strips on top of his steak, but she promised they were not that hot and she was right: they were tasty, lightly sautéed, crunchy, perfect. From an international studies standpoint it was pretty obvious that civilization in this place was as old as the Mayflower or even older. That's how the food tasted: ancient, worked out, settled, cultured. Good stuff.

The kid seemed to feel she should chat over the food, get acquainted, maybe become a pal, but he just wasn't up to it. Sorry, kid. Pain did that to a body. He'd do the job for two weeks and that would be that.

After lunch they walked to the East Meets West Gallery where her cousin's exhibit was opening. It was a couple blocks off the old town square (she called it a "plaza") in an old building, but fancied up—shiny wood floors, clean beams and plaster in the ceiling. Pretty decent crowd inside, maybe a hundred people in what looked to be three good-sized rooms. The kid found her cousin right off, young guy, handsome, lots of hair down the back of his neck and western clothes. She ran to hug him. He kissed her cheeks left and right, excused himself from the people he'd been talking to, and they ambled into the next room, talking Spanish a mile a minute.

He paused by the entrance and checked the place out. Good security system, cameras covering pretty much everything. Windows alarmed. No other obvious access points except a door at the back of the place, but it was a solid door with three locks.

The people were dressed better than typical tourists: no flip-flops, no bags of souvenirs, no cheesy t-shirts. About a third were artsy looking—parsley eaters, maybe parsley smokers. The rest were average citizens of all ages, decently dressed, and looking at the art. Didn't see any potential perps who looked likely to abduct or shoot the kid.

There was a counter inside the entrance with a visitors' book and a stack of cards advertising the show. He nodded to a nut-brown young woman with long, straight black hair behind the counter. To the left was another gallery where Asian art of some kind was on display. An easel to the woman's right held a poster with a picture of the cousin over the name "Doro" and a print of a sandy-haired girl with a dreamy expression on her face over a hazy gold background. Looked a lot like the kid. Could actually be the kid—she said Doro had drawn her.

He scanned the paintings on the walls of the main gallery. There were some fine renderings of horses, portraits of the type a proud owner might display in his trophy room, and others of horses at full speed carrying jockeys in colors. There were paintings of ranch life: a wrinkled old shepherd with a staff, dog, and sheep, an Indian-looking cowboy lounging in the shade with a cigarette, young children playing some kind of game in a dirt yard with chickens in the background, and a half-dozen others in a similar vein. A few paintings were of animals other than horses, both domestic and wild, including one particularly striking bobcat, but the ones that seemed to attract the most viewers were less representational, maybe personal to the artist, or maybe just puzzles.

The kid was still in the back gallery with Doro, so he decided to not worry that some schlub might grab her. He could wander around the main gallery and look more closely at the art.

Doro had talent, if Fergus was any judge. For sure, the guy could draw—there were pen and ink pieces, charcoal renderings, and water colors, many of which clearly had real character. The oil paintings (or gouache or who knew what the hell the medium was; he'd only had that one drawing class) seemed more substantial. Most were representational but a few were abstract and a couple were, what, symbolic? Metaphorical? They made him think of that famous Mexican artist Frances...Flora...*Frida*. Frida Kahlo, that was it. Lots of personal and Catholic-looking stuff tucked into those paintings.

So many people were clustered around one particular item that it was barely visible. He eased behind two shorter women to see what was so interesting. It was the painting which had evidently supplied the face of the girl on the poster at the entrance, another puzzle painting, packed with images whose meaning was not obvious, at least to him.

It was big, almost the size of a card table, and featured a young woman (who really did look like the kid) taking up most of the middle, sort of floating in a golden haze, looking oddly sleepy and alert at the same time, as if she were dreaming...or maybe she was protecting the guy somehow. Who knew? Her left hand lay on a chestnut horse and her right hand on a recumbent man. Her eyes, an odd pale hazel, were cut to the side and down, toward the man. She had a hint of a private smile, like the Mona Lisa. Around the margins, ensconced in rose bushes, cacti, and any number of probably identifiable native plants, were various animals: hummingbirds, doves, a lizard, snake, rabbit, and the like, with the faintest suggestion of some sort of nimbus, or maybe halos, around all of them, including the man and woman. The man was on his back, head toward the viewer, one knee drawn up, his face not visible. Somehow, the horse looked pleased. Despite the seemingly injured man, there was a peaceful feeling about the picture, as if all were well with all the living things around her.

The people in front of him were discussing the painting, making comments and posing questions he wouldn't mind knowing the answers to himself. Who was that woman supposed to be, and what was the story on the horse and the downed man? What was the idea behind all those other plants and animals?

Several more people had come up behind him. He stepped back to make room and noticed the gallery door being opened by yet another visitor.

It was a well dressed man, a cut above the casual visitor—quality suit, sharp tie, polished loafers. The man scanned the room while holding the door open. What the hell was he looking for? That could make a body guard suspicious.

The man looked out to the sidewalk and nodded. Ah, of course—a woman on the sidewalk was pushing in a wheelchair. The geezer in the chair had to be eighty at least, and skinny enough that his shirt collar looked two sizes too big. He wore an expensive looking tweed coat, a red bow tie, and a navy blue beret set at a rakish angle. His face was pale, contrasting weirdly with his bright eyes. Once fully inside, he said something over his shoulder and the woman swung the chair to the right. The trio began a slow counterclockwise circuit of the paintings in the "Doro" gallery.

Behind them, the receptionist made a beeline for the back gallery, maybe to alert Doro that there was a VIP out front. The wheelchair rolled slowly down one side wall, the geezer nodding as they went by sketches and portraits and then turned down the back wall where Fergus was standing with his group. They politely made way for the chair. As the chair reached the mystery painting the old man held up a hand. The three in his party studied it along with those already there.

"Ahh," he said after a long pause, and "Hmmm," laying one finger alongside his nose, and finally, "Marvelous. Exquisite!"

Fergus could see no reason to be quite that excited, but movement from the back gallery caught his attention. The receptionist was returning to the front counter. The truly striking woman with her headed straight for the man in the chair.

She was smiling warmly, reaching out to clasp the hands extended to her by the old man.

"How wonderful to see you again, Jerry," she said. "You are looking terrific today!"

"Thank you, my dear," he responded in a raspy voice. "You, on the other hand, are as beautiful as always. I don't think you have met my assistant. This is Axel Baldwin, Cynthia. Axel, please meet our host, gallery owner, and consummate curator of art, Cynthia Blatherwick."

While they shook hands and exchanged pleasantries, Fergus watched discreetly. The woman was a real drink of water: tall and elegant in a long, swirly black dress and top, wearing no makeup and needing none. She could have been 30 or she could have been in her early 40s. Her long, dark hair swung gracefully and her face was lively and intelligent. She radiated confidence and innate class. Under different circumstances, he would have been interested in her, more than interested.

"You must have heard about the double vajras just added to the Tibetan gallery," she said. "They're extraordinary. We were lucky to get them."

"Yes, indeed, I'd love to see them. I can only hope your price will not be out of my league."

They both chuckled. Evidently, the old man was well fixed.

"At the moment I'm interested in your new discovery: Doro," he continued. "I had heard something about this particular work already. I find it completely striking. What can you tell me about it?"

"It's an intensely personal piece," she replied. They regarded the painting together. "It was inspired by a young woman he met on a large ranch in the mountains of northern Mexico, a girl, really, with extraordinary healing abilities who could cure horses as well as people, by touch. He himself was once injured and treated by her. He had not believed such a thing possible. It was unearthly. He said she changed his life."

Fergus could see the old man's profile. He was hanging on her words, his face almost a pantomime of astonishment. He stared at the painting but spoke to her.

"Is the artist here today?"

"He is."

"I'd like to meet him."

"Certainly. I'm sure he'd like to meet you too!"

She headed to the back gallery. The old man, who didn't seem like a "Jerry" at all, continued his rapt gaze on the painting. In less than a minute she was back with Doro, and the kid in tow. She kept the introduction simple.

"This is Doro Mendoza, Jerry. Doro, this is Mr. Girolamo Bianchi," she said.

OK, then, thought Fergus: Girolamo shortened became Jerry. He didn't look much like a "Girolamo" either. The old man held out a spidery hand and Doro shook it lightly.

"It's an honor to meet you, sir. And this is my cousin, Clara Montez."

The kid stepped forward and shook Jerry's hand. Clara Montez? That wasn't her name. Why the hell did he say that? And why didn't the kid react? Something hinky was going on here.

He'd no sooner had that thought than he realized the kid looked like she'd smelled a skunk—a frown flashed across her face. She released his hand and stepped back.

"Please excuse me," she said. "My dad is waiting for me outside. It was nice to meet you, sir...."

And she was out the door. What the damn hell? As unobtrusively as possible he eased back from the group as the old man was saying something to Doro about "your extraordinary picture." He nodded at the receptionist and walked out of the gallery as if he had not a care in the world.

Where the hell was the kid? There was no sign of her on the street, blast it. Apparently she could not only appear at will (if their airport meet was any indication) but also disappear at will too. He had to think a moment to remember where she had parked her car. He headed in that direction and there she was, behind the wheel, just sitting there. He sat in the passenger seat. A minute crawled by.

"Clara Montez?" he said, after a bit.

"It's an alias. Julio and I had aliases when we were little."

He wondered why, but never mind.

"And Doro was good with it?"

"When the gallery owner asked Doro to come meet someone, I was afraid I'd be recognized. That stupid painting! It looks just like me! It's so embarrassing! I told Doro to use my alias. And also if anyone asked if that was me in the painting, to just say I was the artist's model, nothing more. I had to get out of there."

He thought about that.

"So...that *is* you in that picture, huh? You healed a horse and that man?"

"Oh, not really. The horse had pulled a muscle, a couple of muscles. I showed the trainer which ones, and how to ease the sprain and retrain the horse correctly, that's all. The man was Doro. Some guy slugged him. But nothing was broken. There really wasn't anything to heal. But I guess Doro thought otherwise. It wasn't that big a deal."

Well, alright then, that explained it. Doro must have got a little carried away. He painted a bunch of touchy-feely Catholic hocus-pocus and now the kid, instead of having a great advertisement for a career as a witchy-woman healer, is in danger of being outed as the daughter of a woman from another planet.

If he ever got another security job like this one he'd be very surprised.

Clio picked at her fingernails. He shifted his weight on the seat and pain shot up his right leg. Fucking right foot. Son of a bitch was gone and it was still killing him. Fucking stump was killing him too, piercing pain at the end of the bone. Goddam docs had done their best. It'll go away, they said. Or it won't and you'll have to live with it. Damn it, he could use a drink. Shit, he could use *two* drinks.

The kid's breathing had settled down. That encounter shook her up more than he would have figured. He had another question.

"Something bothered you when you met that old fellow, didn't it?"

Her face fell. Her voice shrank.

"Oh, Fergus. That was so terrible."

He waited. She had closed her eyes.

"What was?" he said finally.

"That man, that sad old man. He's sick, Fergus. He's very, very sick. I don't think he's going to live very long. That poor old man. He's dying. And he knows it."

# Chapter 10

Father and son were heading south from San Antonio on Interstate 37. Julio was mentally composing a text message to his girl friend, but it was a halfhearted effort, since Dhwani was now back home in India and he had not seen her in over a year. She was gregarious and fun-loving and beautiful and unforgettable, and one of the smartest girls he'd ever known. She loved mathematics and physics and computers and didn't need anything to be dumbed down. She didn't even mind when he practiced his Hindi with her. It was great fun to be with a person like that. But she was on the other side of the world, and she didn't seem that thrilled with a long distance relationship. He couldn't blame her for that. Even so, he enjoyed just having her for a friend.

If only his poor sister knew a boy that appealing, it might take her mind off her problems. As far as his twin sense told him, she just wasn't that interested in boys. There weren't that many to choose from, it was true. He saw that Shack character take her to her soccer game in his flashy red Mustang, but from the way Clio acted afterwards it was apparent he annoyed her more than anything else. Fair enough: he didn't like Shack himself. Something about Shack was....

"What do you think, son?"

"Sir? About what?"

"About this country we're driving through."

The countryside had not made much of an impression. Compared to the mountainous desert they'd crossed the day before, the barely rolling, feature-starved land looked fairly lush, but that was all.

"Oh. Well, it's green, I guess."

"Yeah, it is, sort of. Semi-parched, is probably how the locals would see it. Tough to make a living on this, I imagine."

– 61 –

Civilization had dropped off quickly as they left San Antonio behind, but the fields and pastures along the interstate showed few signs of production: occasional herds of cattle, a few goats and sheep, one large plot of olive trees, and not much else besides oil field equipment and commercial vehicles of various kinds. His father's comment got him thinking about the place they were headed.

"So, about our 'Plan C' ranch? How big is it?" he asked.

"Pretty large," his father said, "about twelve sections, roughly. A section is a square mile. It comes to 8000 acres, give or take."

"Dang," he replied. "Does it make money, or what?"

"It does, actually, even though it's in even drier country than this. It's mostly what they call brush country, full of cactus and sticker bushes higher than your head and so thick you can't walk through it. Ours is profitable, believe it or not."

"Really? From oil?"

"No, not yet. Eventually, maybe. They're always exploring for it around here, and finding it, increasingly. It could happen. No, our income is from deer."

"Deer?"

"Yup. Deer and birds. The brush country is great for hunting, and folks are happy to pay a lot to come hunt here. Hunting leases in south Texas are either on open land, where the native deer can traipse through at will, or spreads like ours, with fences to separate the area deer from the managed deer. Our place has a wildlife manager who sees to it that the deer are healthy and large and that the bucks are trophy bucks. I feel two ways about that, but from the point of making income from the land, that's the way to go. Game management makes this land good for something. It covers the expenses, so it doesn't cost us anything to own."

"How did we come by it?"

"That was Hleo," Matt chuckled. "The whole thing was arranged by a long-dead counselor from another planet. Hleo has great business sense. You'll remember that he still has a lot of that money from the crooked corporation that kidnapped Mom. He worried about what would happen if our family could no longer be safe on our New Mexico ranchito. Years ago he recommended we purchase a ranch in Wyoming, which we did. It has a caretaker too, and a modest house we should be comfortable in, if we had to move there.

"He's always thinking. You know that. You've worked with him on technical stuff often enough. He thought we should have a second fallback place, and this is it. For all I know he has another that we don't even know about. It wouldn't surprise me."

"So there's a house here too?"

"Right. There's sort of a lodge, for the hunters, and a house for the caretaker and his family. The game manager lives in a nearby town. Off a little way in the brush is a home for the owner of the place, who's almost never there. That's us, of course. We're going to change that for a few days, kind of. We're going to be 'friends' of the owner, who invited us to stay at his place. Would you believe, Hleo even has an answering service in Las Cruces that'll cover for us?"

"Yessir, I believe it. Hleo thinks of everything."

An hour south of San Antonio Matt exited the interstate, looped over to the east side, and headed eight or nine miles down a farm-to-market road, turning onto a narrow county road. Ten minutes later he pointed out the sturdy, eight foot chain-link fence marching down one side of the farm to market road.

"There," he said, "this is the place."

"Quite a fence," his son observed, watching the tall posts whip by.

"Expensive," he replied. "Note how the manager plowed a fence row on the other side. Otherwise the brush would take over the fence."

It was neither forest nor pasture, but rather a solid wall of dense, scrubby bushes, smallish trees, and undergrowth. It didn't look like something a deer could get through, though a cat might. The fence seemed endless, but three miles down the road his dad turned in through an open double gate.

The parking area was about an acre of hard-packed white dirt. One car and three fancy pickups were parked there, plus a camping trailer, its tongue resting on a stand, and, of intense interest to Julio, a large truck with an awning unfolded along one side bearing the legend "Rocky Mountain Racing" in large, red letters.

At the back of the parking area sat a wide, two-story wood frame house with a peaked metal roof and a gallery across the front. They drove slowly past it, a barn, several corrals, two compact houses, and down a narrow lane through the brush to a gate. Matt rolled down the window and punched numbers into a pad. The gate clicked and swung open and they eased through to a small parking area before a modest home with a gallery much like the main building.

"Plan C. Here we are," he said. "Give me a hand carrying stuff inside and then I bet you'd like to go visit your race team."

It only took two quick trips, barely enough time for Julio to register that the cottage was a pleasant little place with one main room for living, dining, and cooking, three tiny bedrooms, and a bath and a half. Never mind exploring: he had a racing team to check in with.

Beth Melson was one very hot girl, if she could judge herself—but who better to judge, really? She was overdressed for this dusty all-male macho hunting hideaway, but that was the males' problem, not hers. Which was not to say that she had no problems: she had several, and they were intensely irritating.

One problem was the horribly boring SAT study guide lying open on the table before her. Her father expected her to be working through it while he was off having fun shooting things. But he would pay her way into Baylor University no matter what her scores were, so what did studying vocabulary and math matter? So annoying!

Even more irritating was her boyfriend Taylor, who had just texted her (he didn't dare call in person) that he wouldn't be arriving today after all. He was probably afraid of what she would say about his not showing up, and he darn well should be afraid, the dweeb. His excuse was that his father was working on some big petroleum deal in Houston and couldn't get away. He had promised her they'd spend all day seeing the sights and checking out the cars and motorcycles at the Texas Mile, but nooo, he had to wait for his daddy to make a little more money. The dummy.

Despite her boredom, she actually was making a little progress with her studies: the breeze across the gallery had just turned four pages of her study guide. She needed another Coke, dammit. Where was that dumpy Mexican waitress when you needed her? She pushed her chair back and stretched out her shapely legs and admired her Tony Lama ostrich leather boots.

A door opened behind her and a young Mexican-American man emerged carrying something like a tool box. He stopped in his tracks when he noticed her. She loved it when that happened.

"Do you work here?" she asked him.

His mouth dropped open. He said nothing. He must be either stupid or, more likely, stunned by her beauty.

"Could I have another Coke, please?"

His mouth slid into a smile.

"Sure. Be right back."

He set the toolbox on a chair and disappeared inside.

Julio chuckled as he reentered the lobby. Something about that girl triggered his sense of the ridiculous. The main room of the Plan C Ranch was without pretense, clean, neat, and comfortable, nice but not extravagant. It was a hunting lodge, after all. The gorgeous creature on the front gallery looked like a model for an expensive fashion label in a glossy magazine advertisement. She was out of place but she acted as if that was the fault of the place, not her.

"The girl out front needs a Coke, please," he said to the harried woman in the kitchen, who was stirring a simmering pot of carne guisada. It smelled great. "I'll take it to her," he added.

"OK, I'll get you one," the woman said. "Thank you, sir."

While she went to the refrigerator he scanned the walls of the room, which sported a dozen or so taxidermized animals: trophy deer, a coyote, a javelina, and one extraordinarily out-of-place animal: the giant head of a not particularly handsome moose.

The woman handed him the Coke. He had to ask.

"What's a moose doing up there?"

"Oh, that's not from here," she said. "One of our hunters keeps it there. He used to have it in his house, but when he got divorced his wife got the house and she wouldn't give him his moose head. He hired two men to sneak in and steal it for him."

Julio looked at her in surprise. She waved dismissively.

"So then his ex-wife hired her own guys to go to his new house and steal it back." She paused for dramatic effect. "So he got his men to break in and steal it back again. But that time he brought it here, so she couldn't steal it anymore."

"¡Qué cosa!" he said, shaking his head.

"De veras," she cackled.

He carried the can out to the gallery and set it in front of the princess. She surprised him by thanking him.

"Don't mention it," he said, picking up the toolbox.

"You don't really work here, do you?" she asked.

"Not exactly. I'm bringing those guys something they need, that's all," he said, nodding toward the Rocky Mountain Racing truck.

She frowned.

"I went over there to see what they were doing, but they couldn't be bothered," she said.

"Well, the Texas Mile is sort of a competition. Maybe they were just being careful."

"More like rude," she pouted.

"If you promise you're not a spy, I'll talk to them. Maybe they'll give you a look."

"Oh! Why, thank you very much!"

She watched him walk across the parking area. She knew he was flirting with her and if he didn't work here he probably worked somewhere else. She didn't mind. He had fine, square shoulders and a terrific, tight butt. That made up for a lot.

Julio recognized Deke and Carlos working at a fold-out table under the awning that rolled out from one side of the truck. Both were absorbed with instruments. He got along well with the four-man team, which included a mechanical engineer, an electrical engineer, and two experienced racing mechanics, all of them "car guys." On this job, with a car powered by batteries and two electric motors, and the platform already tuned, reinforced, and tested front to back, top to bottom, the team's bright red shirts were remarkably clean.

Deke looked up as Julio neared.

"Hey, Julio, you made it!" he said.

"Yeah. Just got in. Hi, Carlos. What're you guys up to?"

"Running some diagnostics on the power output. I'm still not happy about the thermal curve."

"I've been thinking about that too. I did a little work in my shop at home. I brought a couple things you might check out. They should help with that."

"God, I hope so," Deke said. "We're running right up to the ragged edge now, probably beyond."

"Where are Pete and Repeat?" he asked. Pete and Paul, brothers, were the rest of the Rocky Mountain Racing team.

"They're checking out the track and finishing up the registration and inspection. They should be back mid-afternoon. Or else they'll call," Deke replied.

"Good. Have you guys been out there?"

"Yeah, we dropped by yesterday afternoon, when we got here," Carlos said. "It's one hell of a scene—cars and motorcycles everywhere, trucks, trailers, people all over the place. Some great cars. And noise? Just wait till you see it. And hear it and smell it!"

"Some year maybe we can enter a fossil fuel vehicle," Deke mused. "I'd like to try to set a speed record with a diesel motorcycle."

"First, find a millionaire," Carlos laughed. "A crazy millionaire."

Julio set the toolbox on one end of the table, unsnapped the latches, and pulled out a small box with wires protruding, wire nuts protecting the bare leads. With both hands he lifted out a heavier object, a solid plastic case containing rows and rows of his yttrium-lithium batteries.

"Aha!" said Deke.

"Right," Julio replied. "The box contains a controller with chips for a modified power regimen that takes this battery into account along with the main ones. This battery is bulked up, modified to give max power all through its curve, but only lasts a minute or so. I programmed it to kick in at about 400 yards from the speed trap, but it's adjustable. You can play with it."

Carlos squinted at the battery.

"Well, that's fine," he said, "but what does it weigh? We gotta remember our power-to-weight ratio. That and the finish-line temperature of the batteries are what Deke means by the ragged edge."

"For its weight, the power in this outdoes the present batteries by 40%. You'll see. Surely you can find some weight to cut somewhere on the car."

"Forty percent? That's worth doing. If we goose the car at the right point just before the trap we oughta get another five or ten MPH out of it."

"That's what I'm hoping," Julio said. "You can put the instruments on it and run some load tests. They should tell the tale. It looked good in my shop."

"Hell, to save weight we can cut off the sun visors and the floor mats and the glove box lid and…for five MPH we'll find stuff."

"I know you will." He glanced at the lodge. "Hey, has that girl on the porch been over here?"

"Yeah. A groupie wannabe. We were busy. We ran her off."

"Well," Julio responded, "she might wannabe a fan of Rocky Mountain Racing. You got any of those bumper stickers with you?"

"Oh hell yeah, in the cab. Help yourself."

"I'll give her a couple. Public relations, right? What are you all gonna do about lunch?"

"The lodge provides that. Food's good, here. Feeding time's 12:00 to 1:30."

He looked at his watch. It was nearly 11:30.

"Good deal. Maybe Dad and I will see you there."

Deke and Carlos watched him walk back to the lodge, bumper stickers waving from one hand. Carlos winked at Deke.

"It'll take more than that for true romance with that chick, don't you know."

Deke blew a puff of air through his mustache.

"Way more," he said. "Nothin' but trouble there, pal."

# Chapter 11

"Where the hell is that bleeding sod?" Nigel Dunston grumbled. He snagged a pastry off a table while he wandered around Davos' Congress Center. The place was buzzing with people chatting earnestly in small groups. No one paid him more than a glance, probably because his white badge proclaimed him a member of the media, one of the lowest of the low in this exalted crowd. Conference rules said that only the main sessions could be reported. Everything else was strictly off the record, and that made reporters useless, lower than whale poop.

Dunston, a technical producer for SANECOR, or Satellite News Corporation (commonly known as INSANECOR by employees), figured he was more expert in his field than a lot of these supposed luminaries were in theirs. For example, that damn fool Buddhist monk to his left. Shit, the guy had blond eyebrows and blue eyes—who the hell did he think he was fooling with that stupid orange robe, anyway? Ommm to you, you flaming chav asshole.

He sucked the sugar off his fingers and grabbed an apple off a pyramid of apples on a table of vegetables and fruit, dislodging two other apples which rolled off the pyramid onto the floor. He kept walking. It was a big, rambling place, with hundreds, probably thousands, of people, all juicy potential targets for his unique skills. He had already seen over two dozen big shots he recognized, any one of whom would have attracted a crowd in London. This was going to be a fun group to work on.

At the end of a hall he came to a wide room with a long wall of windows overlooking ranks of neat apartment buildings with snow-covered mountains in the near distance behind. Mixed groups of people were scattered along the windows standing or seated around tables, all gabbing away. He stood to one side, munched the apple, and scanned the lot.

Ah. There was his man. He was not far away but on the near side of the room rather than by the windows, and talking to an attractive, middle-aged woman. Dunston headed that way but stopped short and waited to be noticed. Ben was touchy about his women and touchy about being interrupted and generally touchy about most things. What could you expect when his father was the CEO of SANECOR, and a sodding billionaire? But no matter: you had to coddle people like that if you wanted to get ahead.

He watched Ben play up to the woman. The bloke was good. Her face was animated with interest—she touched her hair at least three times in one minute. There was no denying the man had people skills when he wanted. There was also no denying that those skills hadn't done much to help him reach the upper strata of SANECOR. He was pushing forty and his old man still hadn't worked him into the high-paid management position he expected, something he invariably griped about whenever he was in his cups. Well, cream and bastards rise to the top. So why not you, eh? Tough chips, Benedetto. (Couldn't call him that to his face—he hated his real name.)

Finally Ben noticed him standing there eating his apple. He talked another minute with the woman, shook her hand while patting it and smiling, and headed his way.

"Nigel the Digel," he said. "You made it."

What a hoary, stupid play on his name. Typical.

"I did."

"What'd you bring?"

"The usual. Plus two new James Bond items. I'll try them out and let you know if they work."

They would never discuss the particulars in public. The only reason Nigel was at Davos was because he had figured out how to hack celebrities' voice mail (and the voice mail of lesser beings as well) even after those celebrities thought they had been careful to protect them with passwords. He had other tricks up his sleeve, too. The revelations his discoveries had provided had enabled SANECOR's printed tabloids to make millions of pounds and kill countless trees for over five years.

Ben had tasked him before they left London: he needed at least one tremendous scoop to fuel some huge, exploding story that would cause headlines to ripple around the world. Ben hadn't added, though Dunston knew he had thought it, that such a coup would be a big lever in his attempt to be made CEO of the satellite operations once his father had taken over the entire, giant corporation.

Nigel didn't give a tinker's damn about Ben's next job, but he loved creating trouble. If there were some way he could stir up enough of that, then his own future might be a bit more rosy. If not, well, it would still be fun to screw the nobs.

Ben looked at his watch.

"Late afternoon," he said. "Not much will happen here now. Let's find us a bar and plan us a little night crawling, eh what?"

From experience, Nigel was generally skeptical of Ben's ideas. This one was one of the exceptions.

"Lead the way," he said.

As it turned out, they barely missed a possibly newsworthy event. Five minutes after the two media men had headed to what Ben claimed was an Old World bar with a New Age mixologist, the featured celebrity of this year's Davos conference, Ana Darcy, walked out of the building, passing within feet of where they had been standing.

She was in the company of her sister and her sister's husband, and it was only because her brother-in-law, a tall, solid man, positioned himself to shield her from view of the people by the windows that she attracted so little notice.

They emerged from the building into a numbingly cold wind and failing light. Ana pulled a knit cap over her head as they began the walk back to the hotel.

"Thanks for rescuing me, Scott," she said.

"Glad to do it, sis," he said. "How was your afternoon? Were people crowded around you the whole time like they were just now?"

"Oh, not really. Maybe. Most were polite. I shook so many hands I could hardly sign autographs. I didn't expect so many would ask. This doesn't seem the right place for that. It's all right," she said, her voice soft. "I got through it."

They walked a few yards in silence, their breaths visible before them.

Scott thought back to his days as a divorced, starving journalist, fixated on doing a story about the woman from outer space. She had been an obsession, his personal crusade of salvation. He had given up drugs in pursuit of her—even tobacco—and he lucked into an interview that led to several more stories that made his name and his career, and also introduced him, providentially, to her sister, his present wife. He very well understood the fascination people had with Ana. He also understood the reasons for her shyness in public. Misadventures with the wrong people had nearly cost her her life more than once.

"Well, that's good," he replied after a few moments. "Maybe your panel discussion in the morning won't seem such a big deal now."

"Oh, no, that's a formal situation. It's predictable, and orderly. We sit up front. The audience sits before us. I'm used to that. That's not a problem. There are eight people on the panel, including Uncle Rothan, and he'll talk more than anyone else. My part, about the Second Planet Foundation, will be easy. I'm not worried about that.

"This afternoon," she continued, "people were telling other people where I was and they kept coming over to meet and talk until I was in the middle of fifteen strangers, talking about nothing to many people at once. That makes me nervous. I hope it didn't show."

"It didn't," her sister chuckled. "You were smiling, they were smiling, and if I hadn't known you better I'd have thought you were thrilled to meet them all."

"Well, they did seem like nice people, but I can't say I got to know anyone much. Rothan's secretary, Mr. Sugarek, told me that was normal at Davos. My goodness, it's beautiful here," she added.

They looked up at the sky, rapidly fading to a deep blue behind dark striations of high clouds. On the snowy slopes of the mountains, lights were coming on in houses and streets. It could have been a Christmas card.

"Watch your step," Scott warned as they approached a puddle of slush on the sidewalk. "You see why some of the women carry their high heels in a bag and walk around in boots."

They were getting close to their hotel.

"I agree that most folks at the conference are nice people," he went on. "They're some of the most creative, innovative people on the planet…but a few may not exactly qualify as 'nice people,'" Scott continued.

"No doubt," Ana replied. "Matt once said that high achievers tended to be trouble makers."

"He's right," he said, "some more than others. For example I met one fellow this afternoon who is most definitely a trouble maker. What's more, he wants to meet you. He said he has some sort of business proposition for you."

"Oh! Who? What business proposition?"

"He wouldn't say, but I need to warn you about him. His name is Silvio Bianchi, and he's the CEO of Satellite News Corporation. You might have heard of him."

"Yes! I think I read something about him. He's very, very rich, and, and he's being sued for something, isn't he?"

"Yes indeed, several things. Some have to do with corporate skullduggery…."

"With what?"

"Skull…oh, sorry. 'Skullduggery' means underhanded or unscrupulous behavior. But that's the least of it. Lots of CEOs do that. No, I mean being sued for personal things, like extramarital affairs with minors, for example, young women sixteen or seventeen years old."

"Good heavens! That's Clio's age!"

"Right. He's over seventy years old. But they say he's very dashing…attractive, that is. If you meet him it might be a good idea to watch yourself."

"Oh, dear. And he's here? And wants to see me?"

"He's here. He's one of the superrich and an international big shot. And yes, he wants to meet you. At least, that's what he said."

"Oh, my goodness. If I see him I'll be very, very careful. Thank you, Scott!"

"Please don't worry, sister," Ianthe said, patting her arm. "I'm sure you have handled more difficult people. Husband," she added, glancing at Scott, "why don't you introduce Ana to that lovely bartender at our hotel? I think he's the nicest person I have met here so far."

"Excellent idea! He's a real gentleman—you'll love him, Ana!"

Scott could see she was intrigued. Despite the slightest frown there was a twinkle in her eyes.

"I barely drink at all, Scott. But I confess, something soothing would be welcome right now…especially from a true gentleman."

And so it was that an hour later, Ana had made the acquaintance of Signor Domenico Magro, the bartender from the Palace Hotel in Varese, Italy, just over the border from Switzerland, making a guest appearance as celebrity mixologist for the Davos Conference attendees. In his fifties, with a solemn face and kind eyes, wearing a red bow tie and crisp white shirt, he invented a cocktail just for the famous extraterrestrial philanthropist and her sister and husband while chatting politely in accented, gracious English. Ana loved the theatricality of its production: shaken with ice in a shiny martini shaker and poured with expert flourishes into crystal martini glasses, the drink was an extraordinarily delightful revelation: deliciously cold yet comfortably warm.

The cocktail made the most enjoyable hour of Ana's day. Scott, who had watched it being mixed, thought it was a mixture of brandy and amaretto with a dash of banana syrup and possibly something else he couldn't identify. Whatever it was, Ana carried a glow of contentment with her the rest of the evening. She resolved to invite Scott and Ianthe to return with her tomorrow evening after the panel discussion she was secretly dreading. It would be easier to endure if she knew another one of Signor Magro's wonderful cocktails would be the reward.

## Chapter 12

The kid seemed to have settled down after her encounter with the geezer. She drove back to the hotel steadily enough. Hadn't said a word so far, though.

So the old goat was dying, was he? He was plenty old, for sure. Looked fairly weird all togged out with that beret and pasty complexion, but dying? Except for being in that wheelchair he seemed pretty lively. Hell, we're all dying. Maybe this was just more of the kid's Catholic bullshit.

He wanted to ask her how she knew he was supposedly dying but screw it. Not part of the job description.

Finally she said something.

"Doro's going to pick me up this evening. He's staying with a friend and we're going to have dinner and visit for a while at the friend's apartment. Mom knows Doro. If she were here it would be fine with her. We won't go anywhere else and they'll bring me back to the hotel. We won't be late and I'll let you know when I'm back."

He thought about that. What the hell? *In loco parentis*. An evening off....

"Hmm," he said. "Before midnight, OK?"

"Yes. Busy day tomorrow. Can we start at 8:00?"

"Sure."

As promised, cousin Doro and some equally smooth looking young guy picked her up several hours later in the hotel's porte cochere and purred away in a shiny white Lexus. Just a guess, but it looked like he didn't have to worry about the kid's virtue.

An evening off. Unexpected. He stepped to the curb and looked down the street at the row of small stores on one side and a strip mall on the other. Security guys missed nothing: there was a liquor store down there. He'd seen it. He headed that way.

His aching stump gave him a stab of pain as he pulled the door open.
"May I help you, sir?"
"Yeah. You got Johnny Walker Red?"
"Sure do."
"Gimme a pint. No, wait."

He thought a second. Better to pace yourself, lay in a supply. You never know.

"Gimme six."
"Six it is. Coming right up."


Clio and her cousin Doro were sitting on a sofa watching Doro's friend Mark tend to a charcoal grill on the little balcony. The sliding glass doors were closed to keep the smoke out.

"This is a such beautiful apartment," Clio said.
"It is," Doro agreed.
"But it's so small!"

He looked at her significantly.

"It's big enough for two bedrooms," he said, quietly.

Doro had come out to Clio but she didn't know if he was out to everyone. He lived in Mexico and she knew Mexicans had their own take on sexual orientation.

"I didn't mean that. I don't care about that. It's just that I expected him to have a house, or at least a big apartment."

"He mainly lives in New York City. He's only here during the opera season."

"Tell me again what he does."
"He's a lighting designer, for operas."
"I didn't know you could make a living 'designing' lights."

"Prima querida, lighting is important! He's famous for setting the mood of whole operas with his lights. Light is important everywhere. Look how beautiful the light is here in Santa Fe. It's important in painting too."

"Painting." Clio made a face.
"What?" he asked.

Their host was turning ears of corn, still in their shucks, on one end of the grill, and adjusting skewers of vegetables and meat on the other.

"That old man at the gallery today," she said, still frowning. "What did he have to say to you?"

"He was, uh, encantado…?"

"Fascinated?"

"Yes, thank you. He was fascinated by your painting. Digo, 'your' painting. You know the one. He wants to buy it."

"Really? Would you sell it?"

"I don't want to. I'd like to keep it."

"I'd like you to keep it too, so no one else ever sees it."

"Ay, no, prima! It's a wonderful painting, the best thing I've ever done! Besides, he offered me $25,000."

"You're kidding!"

"¡De veras! I told him I'd think about it."

"He must be rich!"

"Si es, un verdadero rico. Cynthia Blatt…Bla…I can't say it. You know, the gallery owner. Cynthia told me he's a billionaire. And she didn't mean in pesos."

"So who is he, anyway?"

"Se llama Girolamo Bianchi. He's originally from Italy. He's a big media chingón. Pardon my word. I mean a big shoot? Big shot! With newspapers and tv and stuff like that all over the world."

The sliding glass door rolled back. Mark stuck his head in.

"Hey, can one of you see the rice cooker?"

"I can," Clio answered. "There's a green light on it."

"OK, great. Dinner in three!"

He slid the door shut. The smoke that drifted in smelled heavenly of onions and marinated shrimp and bacon. They could see Mark laying kabobs on a platter.

"Doro, that old man is sick. He's terribly sick."

"I know. Cynthia said he moved here from the east coast because there's a cancer center he likes here, but also because of the opera season and concerts. And art, I guess. And the light!"

"If he bought your painting I'm afraid he wouldn't enjoy it very long."

The door slid open again.

"Let's eat!" Mark said. "Doro, can you open the wine?"

"¡Qué sí!"

Clio hated alcohol but she wasn't worried this time. She'd seen water glasses on the table at each place. A polite sip or two of wine was all she needed to get by.

They dropped her off at the hotel at 11:45.

"That's a very interesting young woman," Mark said, a block later.

He held the car to a sedate 30 mph to stay in synch with the traffic lights. A taxi and a food service truck passed in the opposite direction.

"Really," Doro said.

"She actually did those things in that painting?"

"That all happened, yes. I told you what she did to those two guys who tried to beat me up."

"Hard to believe."

"Well, yes. Unless…how do you say? You had to be there?"

"That's how you say it."

"I didn't tell you one thing, the most important thing."

"What?"

"She was, I don't know, working on my jaw, where they hit me. I don't know what she did but it stopped hurting under her hands. I felt like I was floating. Her face was very close. I could feel her breath. Then she moved even closer, to kiss me. That's when I told her I was gay."

He paused.

"And?"

"She said 'yes.' And then she kissed me."

"She did?"

"Yeah. But it wasn't sex. It was…it was…like she was saying it was OK, like it didn't matter, like nothing mattered except she loved me, like, like, oh caray, like *I* mattered, you know? Just as a person. It was like, she, me bendició…she blessed me." He paused a beat. "That sounds stupid. But I'll always remember that. It changed the way I think, about her, about people, about everything. That's why I had to do that painting."

Mark shook his head in the darkness.

"My friend, that's not stupid, not stupid at all. It sounds like a miracle."


He woke up at 7:45 the next morning and looked at his travel alarm. It had gone off but he hadn't heard it.

"Shit," he muttered, dragging himself out of bed. He pulled on his jeans and his prosthesis and a sock and the other shoe and headed for the bathroom. There was a slip of paper under his door. He picked it up. "I'm back," it said in girlish handwriting. "See you at 8."

"Shit," he said again, and resumed his trip to the bathroom. He hadn't been there long when he heard a knock on the door.

"Ahh, shit."

He still had shaving cream on his face. He wiped it off and went to the door. There she was, all perky in blue sweat pants and top.

"I knocked last night but you didn't answer so I left you a note," she said.

"Sorry," he said. "I'm a sound sleeper. Long day."

What a bunch of crap. He was a SEAL. OK, a former SEAL. He could stay up for days, carry boats out of the surf, swim for miles, jump out of helicopters, climb mountains, goddammit. Here he was making excuses to Tinkerbelle.

"I've had breakfast," she said. "Now I'm going to spend some time in the hotel's gym. You can join me after you have breakfast, if you want."

Her face bore no expression, but he knew a challenge when he heard one. Shit.

"OK, great. See you there."

He took his time at breakfast. No reason to hurry to a damn gym. He'd visited one a couple times in Miami but the results didn't sizzle his endorphins.

The gym, in the basement, had about a dozen Nautilus machines, a pull up bar, a small trampoline, and a rack of weights on a stand. Better than expected. The kid was working on her pecs, what there was of them.

He took off his long-sleeved shirt. The t-shirt would do for an upper body routine. He'd avoid the leg machines. He adjusted the seat of the biceps machine, set the weight light to start, and eased onto the seat and did two quick sets of 10 to warm up.

He watched the kid out of the corner of his eye. She didn't have much weight on her machine but she was moving as if in slow motion, taking at least thirty seconds to complete each sweep. Her face was flushed with effort, glistening under a light sheen of sweat. Reminded him of Conoly, old Racker Conoly. He used to lift like that. Said it built more muscle. Where the fuck was Racker now? Probably counting the days till they sent him home, the puke.

He got up and adjusted the weights to 100 pounds. Two more reps and on to the triceps machine. The kid was doing deltoids now, the seat down low and pushed forward. Still working it slowly. Might be worth trying himself but definitely not now. Couldn't let her see him copying her.

It took him a half hour to go through the machines. He was rubbing his hands with hand sanitizer the hotel had thoughtfully provided while the kid did some bouncing on the trampoline. She was having a ball. Finally she stopped and joined him for some hand sanitizer.

"Now I'd like to run, if you don't mind. There's a high school not far from here. They have a track. You can run too, if you'd like."

Another challenge, but he had to decline. They'd tried a blade prosthesis on him, but it hurt worse than the one he stayed with. Give the muscles another year to adapt, they said. The dopes.

"I think this time your security detail will just maintain the perimeter."

"OK, sure," she said.

Ten minutes later he had scoped out the deserted stadium and track and taken a seat in the stands fifteen rows up. The day was clear and crisp and the light soft. No wonder Georgia O'Keefe decided to stay in New Mexico.

The kid was on her second lap on the 440 yard track, stripped down to a tank top and shiny little running shorts. Her waist looked to be his hat size. She picked up the pace on the third lap. She ran three miles, faster and faster until she eased off on the last one.

Then she did some stretches in one end zone and began running 100 yard wind sprints, one after another. She did four. She walked a half lap, did more stretches, and ran three more miles.

It finally dawned on him that he should have been hearing cinders crunching underfoot, but she whizzed by almost silently. After studying her stride for several laps he realized she was not coming down on her heels; there was no pounding of the track. Each stride touched down on the toes first. Her heels never seemed to touch the ground.

Was she showing off? Training for some high school thing? This was a serious workout for anybody, much less a little kid.

She pulled on her track suit and they headed back to the hotel to clean up. The parking garage was two blocks ahead when she spoke up.

"It's close to time for lunch. I need a shower and then we can go eat, if that's OK."

"Sure. You don't have to ask. I'll follow you anywhere."

"I know that. I'm sorry. I never had 'security' before. It just seems polite to ask. What kind of food would you like?"

"Really, I don't care."

"C'mon, Fergus!" she said, frustration in her voice. "I had some of what you ate over there, those MRE things. They weren't that good. Here you can choose almost anything. So why not choose?"

"It's not that big a deal. It's your party. I'm just along for the ride."

"Oh, bother!"

She turned into the entrance, rolled down the window, and slid her room card into the parking garage kiosk. The wooden arm went up and she drove up the ramp.

In the elevator she tried again.

"Did you honestly like the New Mexican food you had yesterday?"

"I did, yes."

"Would that be all right again today?"

"Sure."

"All right then. I need carbs so it's fine with me too."

The elevator doors opened. He motioned her back with a "wait" gesture.

"Security first, ma'am," he said, checking the hallway and standing aside. She saw the twinkle in his eyes. She glared at him.

"You are such an annoying man," she clipped, striding past.

He watched her march down the hall half pissed off. Not bad. Maybe the kid was feisty after all.

An hour later she drove to a nice-looking neighborhood restaurant. As she cut off the engine she reflected that although many of her friends might think it was cool having a body guard, in practice it was a terrible drag, and especially so with this body guard.

"Have you been here before?" he asked.

"No."

"How'd you pick it?"

"I used an app on my phone. It's supposed to be a nice place. They have a big menu. Why do you ask?"

"Just wondered."

Oh, right, he "just wondered." He probably had some security reason for asking and it was probably a stupid reason. Only the third day and she was already so tired of this. Now she had to get through another meal with him.

The waiter departed with their orders, leaving them with iced tea, tortilla chips, a nice salsa, and a bowl of excellent, hot pico de gallo with diced onions, tomatoes, and jalapeños in lime juice—red, white, and green, like the Mexican flag. Clio was digging chips into the latter as if it were a salad. Fergus preferred the former.

"So why do you lift weights?" he asked.

What business of that is yours? she thought, but she thought again. Some minimal level of conversation was necessary, or the meal, and the day, would be ruined. Her mother would expect her to make the effort.

"I'm not very strong," she replied. "I guess that's obvious. I get that from my mom. I have good reflexes, which I also get from her, but we both have to work to develop more strength."

"You run like a greyhound. Do you get that from her too?"

"I must. We both have high metabolisms. That's why I'm starving right now. She would be too."

"Hmm."

He dipped some salsa onto a tortilla chip and scanned the room quickly. No one was near. He lowered his voice.

"Coombs said your mother was an ace at hand to hand combat. Is that true?"

"I guess. She's had plenty of lessons. I used to go with her."

"Hmm," he said again.

"Do you do any martial arts?" she asked.

"Just the basics, like our medical training is basic. My kind prefers hardware, the lethal kind. If a conflict comes down to martial arts something's gone bad wrong. We try to avoid that."

She nodded and changed the subject.

"Why did you want to know how I chose this place?"

He sipped his tea.

"Suppose, when you walked in here a few minutes ago someone on the other side of the room began watching you. Does that mean Hey, check out the cute chick? Or does that mean he's seen you before and is trying to place you from an earlier visit? Or does it mean he has some nefarious purpose in mind? In the one case the guy might be a threat. In the other, I might embarrass all of us if I were to treat him as a threat. Big difference. See?"

"Yes…maybe." She twiddled an empty sugar packet in her fingers. "It seems unlikely, though."

"It is," he admitted. "You probably don't need a security guy. But you're stuck with one. Sorry about that. Aha. Here we go."

The waiter was approaching with a tray. Further conversation was curtailed by two beef enchiladas, in her case, and a large, thin steak sizzling on a puddle of mild white cheese and tomato sauce topped with chili rajas in his.

"Did you order soup?" he asked, looking at the shallow bowl before her. It looked like cheese soup.

"They're in here, under this sauce," she said, pushing some sauce aside and cutting off a bite of an enchilada hidden underneath.

"Oh, yeah," he said. "Looks good."

"It really is. Want a bite?"

"No thanks. Another time. What's with these blue tortilla chips?"

"They're made from blue corn."

"Of course they are."

The food seemed to put him in a good mood which lasted through their return to the hotel, the checkout, and the drive to their next destination, the small village of Tasajillo, sixty miles north. It sat at the junction of two state highways, nestled between two national forests. Fergus wasn't impressed.

"Looks like the truck stop time forgot," he said, "with trees."

"The Rural Medical team selects underserved places," she replied. "There's no interstate highway near, mainly little towns with lots of poor people nearby. There's where we'll be staying: El Faro."

"El what?"

"'The Lighthouse.'"

"Ah. That explains the sign."

The motel, built in a long, square U shape facing the highway, sported a neon sign over the office at one tip of the U, which did indeed feature a stylized lighthouse. It was not on, since it was still daylight. The painted image of the lighthouse behind the neon tubes had faded to chalky pastels. A fenced area enclosing an empty swimming pool filled in the U.

He sat in the car while she checked them in. It had been a good day—not much time on his feet…correction: foot. No pain to speak of, a modest workout, good food, not a bad gig so far.

They had adjoining rooms near the far back corner of the U, with two inner doors separating them. A person in either room could lock the other room out. They were basic and clean, if a little used. He'd lived for months in far worse. It didn't take long to move in.

The kid stuck her head in as he was hanging his few clothes on hangers.

"My cell phone battery is dead. I need to tell Mom we're here. Can I borrow yours to send her a text message?"

"Yeah, sure."

An hour later he parted his curtains to see a small caravan of cars, a van with a logo on the door, and a U-Haul truck pulling in. The kid knocked on the door that joined their two rooms.

"Looks like most of the team has arrived," she said. They'll be needing to set things up at the school. I'll go help. Do you want to come too?"

The kid just didn't get their professional relationship. If she was going then he was going, end of story. "Want to" was not a part of it.

"Sure," was all he said. But not all he thought: "Standing. Toting crap for hours. Gonna hurt like a bastard. Shit."

## Chapter 13

Beth Melson was sitting in the gallery of the hunting lodge once more, only slightly happier than she had been the previous morning. There was still no word from her stupid boyfriend, her father was off hunting again, and she hadn't got to see what that racing team was doing up close. In fact, today the team had packed up and headed to the track after lunch. The SAT study guide never crossed her mind.

On the positive side, the Mexican boy was friendly. He said he and his dad would be happy to give her a ride to the race track to see the action, and she could probably get a look at the car after the race. She'd seen his dad in the dining room, talking Spanish a mile a minute with the cook. He seemed a friendly, easy going man. They weren't hunters. Maybe they were relatives of someone on the staff.

The truck they picked her up in was almost a vintage model, clearly a veteran of hard service, and no way a state of the art machine like her father's. All she needed was for it to get there and back, though, and it seemed capable of that.

Julio had explained his slender relationship with Miss Melson to his father, and was grateful to receive only a minimum of joshing in return about his new "girl friend." Matt had, in fact, quickly concluded that the exquisite Miss Melson was nowhere close to his son's type. He was surprised and impressed, though, by his son's conversation with the girl on the half hour ride. Julio wasn't shy, but neither was he a people person or a party animal, and was generally reticent around strangers and in crowds. Today, however, he had just the right questions for Ms. Melson to keep her happily talking about herself, her travels, her friends, high school accomplishments, shopping acumen, and random other triumphs.

The result, as far as he could tell, was that the girl learned next to nothing about Julio.

Matt paid the admission fee at the entrance to the former Naval Air Station and followed the flag wavers' directions to a parking area alongside a runway, where the cars and motorcycles would try to set speed records. He parked among hundreds of cars, motorcycles, and trucks—mostly trucks. The sound of revving engines became obvious as soon as he opened the door.

"Hey, Dad!" Julio said from his side. "Look at this!"

He was pointing at the interior of the pickup parked next to them, a large, flashy four-door diesel, idling with no one in it.

Curled up asleep on the passenger seat was a tiny white poodle, evidently enjoying the air conditioner.

"Humph," Matt shrugged, "I thought Texas was hell on dogs. Evidently not any more. Let's go find the team."

"Cute little dog," the girl said. "I have one like that."

It didn't take long to locate the Rocky Mountain Racing team thanks to the New Mexico state flag someone had attached to the dish antenna on top of the team van. Matt thought it was a good sign that the flag was barely flapping in a modest breeze. It shouldn't affect the race results much if at all.

The van and race car were in a long line of vehicles being prepped by their crews, behind a rope line.

Julio excused himself, showed a card to the man tending the line, and was allowed to pass under.

"Is Julio on the team?" she asked.

"Yes," Matt replied.

"Is he a mechanic?"

"Not really. He helped in the early stages."

"He did? What did he do?"

"Well, this whole thing is sort of his idea."

She was peering at the car, forty yards away.

"That car," she said, "it's a Corolla?"

"Right."

It took her a minute to process that.

"Did they put a big engine in it?"

"No. They put two little engines in it. Motors, really. About the size of a small wastebasket. Each."

"And it's supposed to go fast?"

"They sure hope so."

"I don't get it."

"They're electric motors. The car is battery powered."

"What? How fast will it go?"

"We'll find out. The record for an electric car at the Texas Mile is 175 mph. They hope it'll beat that."

"A *Corolla*?"

"Actually, the type of vehicle doesn't much matter, as long as it's small and streamlined. It's the batteries that are being tested as much as the vehicle."

"You're kidding!"

He looked at his watch.

"We'll find out in about an hour. You want to check out the starting line?"

That was definitely where the action was. About two hundred yards away a sleek, incredibly expensive looking knee-high yellow sports car was spinning its tires to heat them up for better traction, the engine screaming impressively amid clouds of horrible smelling smoke. The driver goosed it to the starting line, a man waved a flag, and it roared away, engine and tires screeching. Behind it, another crew maneuvered a muscular motorcycle into position, its cowling dotted with stickers of sponsors. Its rider also spun the back tire. The whole area was permeated with the smell of exhaust, fuel, burning rubber, and hot oil.

By the time they'd watched the motorcycle and the two next vehicles scorch down the track, Beth had begun talking to several rangy boys and excited girls. Matt saw the writing on the wall.

"Let me have your cell number," he said. "I'll call you when the Corolla's ready to go."

Barely acknowledging the favor, she readily headed off with her new friends. Matt watched four more vehicles tear down the track, one every five minutes. Shortly after each ran through the timing trap at the far end the speed was announced over the loudspeaker to varying applause and cheers.

Matt understood why a driver might want to heat his tires up for better traction. But there seemed no sense in a vehicle blasting off the starting line as if in a drag race. They had most of a mile to build up speed for the end, where it counted. A mile was surely plenty of distance for acceleration. He guessed it was done out of nervousness or, more charitably, showmanship. Would the Corolla driver do that? Wouldn't that heat up the batteries too soon? Well, what did he know? He wandered back toward the staging area to look for his son.

Julio, a few minutes earlier, had been surprised to find the racing team calm, basically waiting for the signal to advance to the starting pad.

Pete and Repeat were sitting on the tailgate of the truck. Carlos and Deke, chewing on an unlit cigar, were fooling with the car, one taking a final look at the connections under the hood, the other testing the telemetry.

"How's it looking, guys?" he said.

"Ready to go," Pete said. "Tested six ways from Sunday. Nothing else to be done."

"Did that controller and booster battery work out?"

"Yeah, they did, in a bench test anyway. We couldn't take it out for a run to be 100% sure, but this electric stuff is so simple—it's got to work. It could be the edge we were looking for. You do that in your shop?"

"Yeah. I just got this particular unit from the fabricator. It's a modification in the yttrium deposition. Should allow a higher power throughput with little or no cost in thermal falloff."

Repeat nodded.

"That's what our dummy run indicated. We might find out in a few minutes. Carlos adjusted the timing sequence and figured out where to get it to cycle in at the right point on the track no matter what speed the car's going at the time. This is strictly a one race performance."

"I hope it works."

"Me too. That bonus Rocky Mountain promised if we set a record will come in mighty handy."

The loudspeaker blared "Contestant #184 on deck, please."

"OK," Repeat said. "Four to go. Let's get you belted in, Pete."

Matt decided to watch the Corolla head down the track from where he was, near the van. He'd miss no fireworks when it left, and the crew had mounted a monitor high on the side of the van that would indicate the car's speed every second. That was what was important. He dialed Julio's temporary girlfriend. She was at the starting line and would join him when it was over.

The little Corolla looked decidedly humble amidst the customized hot rods, sleek motorcycles, and quarter million dollar sports cars. Its factory paint job (white) was salvaged a little by the huge yellow lightning bolts down both sides, along with logos of Rocky Mountain Racing, a tire company, and several other automotive suppliers. The main clues that it was not an ordinary Corolla were the airfoils on the front, back, and sides. They would have been laughable on a street car but somehow suggested seriousness of purpose at this time and place.

Julio had told him the airfoils were computer controlled, to keep the front end down and both ends steady at all speeds. The driver had only a manual override in case of emergency.

When its turn came, it rolled to the start silently except for a couple short bursts of the throttle to heat the tires—the front tires. Most of the other contestants were rear-wheel drive. It looked to Matt almost as if invisible hands were pushing it into position.

The flag went down and the car took off smartly, with only a pronounced whine from the electric motors and gearing and the sound of tires on pavement. It soon receded to a dot.

Matt eyed the monitor on the van: 60...85...98. The numbers were increasing very rapidly, and the whooshing sound the car made was still audible...110...130...150 mph. The rate of increase slowed but the numbers continued to rise: 165...173...180.

Was it close to the timing trap? He had forgotten to ask Julio how long the "race" would take...190...194...Matt held his breath...and then all of a sudden 199 became 208. At 216 mph the number started decreasing. What did that mean?

The public address system clicked on.

"Folks, we have a new speed record at the Texas Mile! Rocky Mountain Racing has shattered the record for a battery powered car: 211 mph! Congratulations, you guys! Next up, we have entry #189."

The Rocky Mountain team and friends were going crazy backslapping each other, high fiving, hugging, shaking hands. The Corolla returned on its own power via the taxiway next to the runway, apparently none the worse for wear, and stopped in front of a huge Texas Mile banner. The driver got out, removed his helmet, and stood for photographs with the rest of the team. The still photographer and video crew finished quickly and began packing up their gear.

Back at the van, Pete and Repeat checked the car over while Julio talked to the film crew and two men with them. Deke and Carlos had let down the ramps and were waiting to load the car into the van.

Beth Melson, who had materialized out of the crowd, noticed the two crew members standing around, plucked up her nerve, and asked if they would show her the car. Deke, in an exceptionally good mood, volunteered, raising the hood and talking about batteries, motors, and miscellaneous electronic components that made no sense to her. She asked about the box Julio had delivered to them yesterday. Deke pointed it out: a supplementary battery bolted to the firewall.

"Did Julio do anything else, or was that all?" she asked.

Aha, thought Deke. Well, hell. Julio's batteries were really responsible for the team's extra month's salary this year. He decided to help Julio with his girlfriend.

"He designed these batteries. They're high-output, energy-dense, low-temperature batteries. You just saw 'em push this crate over 200 mpg."

"He did?"

"Oh, yeah. He's quite an inventor."

"Seriously?"

"Seriously. He also invented a power control circuit that's in about every Toyota made now. Hondas too, I think."

She looked taken aback. She had evidently underestimated Julio. Deke was enjoying her befuddlement.

"Made him a lot of money, that circuit," he went on. "A ton of money. These batteries will, too. See those guys he's talking to? They're from Toyota. They sent that film crew. Their tech guys will be going over all the data on the car's performance today. Some day they'll put his batteries in their electric cars and he'll make even more tons of money."

"He will?"

"Damn straight," Deke winked. "And not just millions. Hell, he's already made millions from that power control circuit. Electric Toyotas? Are you kidding me? Hundreds of millions!"

She was uncharacteristically quiet as they started the drive back to the lodge, commenting only that the little poodle was still asleep in the truck with the air conditioner on, after three hours. Julio and his dad were talking anyway.

"How come that monitor showed 216 mph but the official time was only 211?" his dad wanted to know, adding, "I say 'only' as if 211 mph isn't plenty fast enough."

"We blew it," Julio replied. "The extra battery provided more power than the test instruments indicated it would. The car was still accelerating beyond the speed trap. If we had known the supplemental battery had that much reserve power, we'd have had it cycle in a few seconds earlier. The batteries were not even too hot to touch afterwards!" he chuckled. "Toyota's going to love that."

Beth was thinking. She'd wondered if Deke, with his twinkly eyes and nasty cigar and sly smile, had been kidding about Julio, but maybe not.

"That guy with the cigar said you designed those batteries," she blurted. "Is that right?"

"Oh. Not exactly. We started with lithium ion batteries. They're excellent as they are, except for a tendency to get hot under load. They're used in a few expensive cars now. All I did was add an yttrium substrate during the ion deposition process. That gives more power and reduces the heat significantly. It's a modification rather than a new process."

"Yeah, but you and Dr. Dave patented it," his dad pointed out. "If Toyota wants it, they gotta come to you two."

"I guess so."

"The guy said you invented a power circuit too, that's in Toyotas and Hondas."

"Well, yeah," Julio admitted, "That was long time ago. I was in first grade. That was practically an accident."

His dad started describing a toy bulldozer that young Julio had nearly destroyed this very truck with, but Beth barely paid attention.

She was musing about dollars…millions of dollars. Hundreds of millions of dollars.

# Chapter 14

After three days at Davos Ana was experiencing serious conference fatigue. Thousands of the most creative people on Earth were in attendance, but there was simply no opportunity to settle in for an extended, thoughtful conversation with just one or two individuals.

The two sessions she had been a part of had gone well enough. She had few problems in formal settings, which she had grown up with on Thomo. Her father, basically the "Secretary of State" for the combined tribes of the planet, was forever dealing with formal situations. She was a teenager at the time, but after she was selected for the mission to Earth it was often necessary that she appear before groups. Even though she had not enjoyed the experience, the ceremonial structure served to get her through them.

The first panel discussions on Sunday, about the many risks to Earth, environmental and otherwise, and the Monday morning session, on the results of the Mars expedition with the Thoman shuttle, were mainly carried out by the other panelists. Uncle Rothan, an experienced speaker and professional diplomat, was eloquent as usual. Her contributions were minimal.

It was the rest of her waking hours at Davos, famous for free-form discussions and spontaneous encounters, that were the problem.

Back home in New Mexico, as Mrs. Ana Méndez, her conversational strategy was to get other people talking, and contribute as necessary. It was easy to do and occasionally interesting. Here, however, despite the superabundance of talkers, almost no one she met wanted to talk about themselves: she was the one who was invariably the center of attention (and often the center of a crowd), and who was asked the same questions over and over. Her answers had become rehearsed. She found she was echoing herself.

"What was it like traveling twenty-five light years to our solar system, Ms. Darcy?"

"Didn't you get tired of living all those years in that tiny base on the moon? Whatever did you do there?"

"How did it feel to win all those medals in the Olympic Games, Ms. Darcy? Do you still have them?"

"How did you feel when you had been kidnapped by the Mafia, Ms. Darcy?"

"How did you ever survive that terrible experience in Peru, Ms. Darcy?"

"Do you feel lonely living at that isolated ranch in Montana? Do you have companions or visitors?"

"Would you consider a visit to our home/charity/board of directors/foundation/city/province/country, Ms. Darcy?"

"Would the Second Planet Foundation be interested in joining ours in a combined philanthropic project to (fill in the blank)?"

"What can you tell us about the Thomans who are on their way to Earth?"

There were exceptions. Probably a higher proportion of attendees than among the general population were able to regard Ana as a real person. Her encounters with these people were generally brief, because often interrupted, but even so, she found some quite engaging.

There was a prominent Muslim sociologist, for example, who had studied Thoman social structure using resources provided by the Ambassador's office and the website the embassy maintained, and who wished to refine some of the information those contained by asking an actual Thoman. He was intrigued with the comparatively smooth functioning of the Thoman tribal government as contrasted with the often intractable and tumultuous tribal relations in the Middle East.

There was a classicist from Oxford, an expert in the works of Homer, Vergil, and Gilgamesh, who wanted to know more about the role of Thoman epic poems in modern Thoman society. (Ana did not see fit to tell him that the most recent one of those epics was about her.)

There was an elderly astronaut who had actually walked on the moon and who had been, in a literal sense, a neighbor of Ana's for several days. That gentleman had some trenchant observations about living on the surface of the moon in a small, totally self-contained environment. He admitted being jealous of Thoman space vehicles which made their own gravity, thereby avoiding the problem of bone loss suffered by astronauts in the weightless International Space Station.

He wished Ana to convey his admiration and thanks to the Ambassador for suggesting the Mars Shuttle Expedition, which among other things produced that magnificent photo of the Earth and the entire orb of the moon, taken from 100,000 miles away. It was as miraculous, in his opinion, as the famous "Blue Marble" photograph taken by the Apollo 17 astronauts from only 28,000 miles.

One of the world's great organists, a young Korean woman, was delighted to confirm what she had heard about Ana, that she particularly loved the music of Bach. Their discussion wandered into abstract concepts of patterns in music, and of the multidimensionality of Bach's music in particular, though Ana struggled to understand the finer points.

Ana was, in fact, somewhat intimidated by the braininess of the typical Davos attendee, and more than a little self-conscious of her own lack of knowledge about their many fields. Added to her inborn reluctance to mix with so many strangers, she felt uncomfortably ill at ease most of the time.

Help was at hand, fortunately, in the person of Pavel Sugarek, the Ambassador's aide. Ana had liked him when she'd first met him years ago as a recent college graduate with a major in Slavic languages. Now, after years of diplomatic work, he had proven himself creative, quick minded, and adaptable, in addition to being an affable young man.

He was a member of the Ambassador's entourage but not an official invitee to Davos, and as such he was free to accompany Ana for hours on end, which he seemed happy to do. He knew of Ana's dislike of crowds so he suggested a simple solution: whenever her situation became too tedious, frustrating, or nerve wracking, she had only to pass him a secret signal whose meaning he would understand to be: "Get me out of here!"

So it was that late Monday afternoon Ana was having a decent chat with several doctors associated with Surgeons to the World, which her own Second Planet Foundation had worked with in the past. The name of the director, Dr. David Schwartz, inevitably came up, prompting one doctor to recall how distraught Dr. Schwartz had been when it was thought that Ana had died during the mishap in Peru. That led to more questions about the incident, drawing in a number of nearby listeners and leaving Ana once again trapped, for at least the fourth time, on a topic she'd rather forget.

She gave her standard answer, that she couldn't remember much about it (which happened to be true), and that she had never been so cold and hungry in her life. While speaking, she glanced toward Pavel, her savior. He was thirty feet away, not facing her, with his cell phone to his ear. Darn!

"What hospital were you taken to?" someone asked.

"Oh," she stammered. Pavel had snapped the phone shut. He saw her, and she gave him the signal: a fleeting, significant look. "Oh," she said, "I really can't remember right now. But…."

Pavel stepped through the group and touched her arm.

"Excuse me," he said to the group, and turning to Ana said, "The Ambassador tells me you have a meeting in ten minutes."

"Oh, dear! I forgot!" she said, and to the group, "I must go. Please pardon me," adding with a smile, "I was going to say that to this day I cannot stand cold weather."

She tucked her hand around Sugarek's arm, to indicate, she hoped, that they could not stop to talk. In less than a minute they were fifty yards down the hall, headed toward the Congress Center exit. Thank the stars for Pavel. He was—how did Matt say it?—quick on the uptake? Or was it quick on the upkeep?

They claimed their coats at the door. The evening air was decidedly chilly. She truly did not like cold weather.

"Thank you so much, Pavel. I don't know what I would do without you."

"It was my pleasure," he said, keeping his voice as low as hers, though few people were out walking. "May I assume you are already looking forward to the next Davos conference?"

"Goodness, no! But if I have to come for some reason, I'll insist that you come with me."

"If the Ambassador wishes, I might return, but it won't be as much fun without you," he chuckled.

"It was clever of you to think of a meeting."

"Actually, you do have a meeting, but not immediately. That was the Ambassador on the phone. A certain VIP insists on meeting with you."

"Insists? Who?"

"You might have heard of him: Silvio Bianchi."

"Oh! Oh, yes. Scott Zimmer warned me about him yesterday. He's not a very nice man, is he?"

"He has that reputation. Hopefully, he'll be on his best behavior at Davos. TheAmbassador said Bianchi wanted to invite you to a late night party at the Hotel Europa, but he told Bianchi he absolutely forbids you to go outside the conference secure area. So Bianchi said he'd arrange to see you at the Belvedere, tomorrow evening. There'll be other people there too, so it should be all right. But I'll be with you in any case."

"Did he say what Bianchi wants to talk about?"

"No, just that he has a deal for you of some kind, a business deal."

"I never make business deals. The Ambassador and the foundation do all of that for me."

"Well, good, then. You should have no problem tomorrow."

Stupid goddam conference. His steps echoing down the stairwell sounded like the emptiness of his future. There were throngs of people taking the elevators up. Only way to get down to the cheap rooms without waiting until midnight was to take the stairs. Bleeding sods. Bloody conference was running over with optimists. What he needed was pessimists, people with grudges, complaints, preferably in bars nursing their complaints with alcohol. Plenty alcohol was disappearing in the bars and clubs of Davos late at night, but none of the booze-soaked optimists had any usable dirt. The Davos conference was looking like a complete waste of time.

Five B, six B, seven B, there it was: eight B. He knocked. He waited. Finally a latch clicked and the door opened a crack against the chain. Dunston's gimlet eye scanned him from within.

"It's you," he said.

Who the hell else would it be looking for the likes of you?

The door shut, the chain was freed, and Dunston opened the door and let him in. He looked almost happy, which was rare.

"What's up? You find something good?"

"Maybe," he replied, locking and latching the door again. "Come see."

He led him to a round table and two chairs against the tiny window, curtains drawn tight. On the table sat a laptop and a mare's nest of cables and black boxes. Dunston typed in a password and begin arranging things on the screen. It took several minutes. Video of a panel discussion appeared: eight men and women behind a long table.

"All right then," Dunston said. "Dull stuff, this. I'll mute it. Irrelevant. But note, third from the left the Ambassador from Thomo, and next to him his niece, Ana Darcy. See?" He consulted a slip of paper. "Now, let me move the timeline along…there. Now watch."

The Ambassador was talking. One woman on the right took a drink of water. A man on the left end was jotting notes. Another covered his mouth and sneezed. A minute passed.

"Well?" Dunston asked. "Did you see that?"

"I didn't see any reason to bring me down here, no."

"I'm not surprised. Now look at this."

He opened another window, sized it to a wide, narrow rectangle, and positioned it under the video of the panelists. A fuzzy line began crawling across the green field.

"This is the output of the cell phone scanner. I'll run the video back to where it started…and now I'll run the phone graph from the same point…there. Now together. Watch."

The fuzzy line started moving. After about twenty seconds it expanded into a burst of fuzzy spikes. Numbers appeared beneath it.

"That's a call to a cell phone somewhere within fifty meters," he said. "Ignore it. Keep watching."

The panelists were talking back and forth soundlessly. Another thirty seconds passed and then the fuzzy line popped up with more fuzzy spikes and numbers. Dunston waited a bit.

"Did you see that?"

"See what?"

"Ah, you still didn't see it. That's why I'm the best there is at this. Let's run that by again, but this time keep your eye on Ana Darcy."

He watched. Ms. Darcy was sitting straight in her chair, listening to the Ambassador saying something. She looked down at the table briefly and her arm briefly moved out of sight as if to scratch someplace and then returned to the table. She still appeared to be listening to her uncle. It was a small movement, not unlike the others on the panel were continually making. But thanks to Dunston's cell phone track, there was obviously a fuzzy burst from the cell phone recorder at the exact same time.

"Ah," he said.

"Right!" Dunston chortled.

"What does that mean?"

"It means, old chap, that she got a cell phone call just then. And she reached into her pocket and turned it off."

"So?"

"'So?' So how many people do you suppose have Ana Darcy's private cell phone number, eh? I went online to try to find a number for her. There ain't any, my friend."

"Hmm."

"So I put my man in London on it—you remember, the fellow whose name I won't tell you because what he does is right dodgy, OK? He could run it down if anyone could."

"And what did he find?"

"I sent it to him yesterday, actually. He spent hours, and what he found was surprising. First, it was a text message. But it was encrypted and he hasn't cracked it. Said he might never; he'd never seen one like that. Couldn't even get a toe hold on a crack."

"Yeah? Well?"

"There's one thing about it that couldn't be encrypted: where it came from. That's what some of those numbers mean. With the right access and a bit of grease to the right office drones, he can get phone records from just about anywhere, just like the cops can. So do you want to know where it came from?"

"Where, dammit?"

"Now, let me have my fun, Ben. Don't rush me. I get bloody little fun as it is. See, if the call had come from London, say, or New York City, or Jalalibad, we'd be shat upon, now, wouldn't we? Never sort out all those ruddy buggers. But no, we're in luck. It came from a place so small there's only one cell phone tower within range. Are you ready for this? It came from Tasajillo, New Mexico!"

"What?"

"Population about 600, dear boy. How hard could it be to find someone who knows Ana Darcy among 600 people, hey?"

Ben tried to let his normal cynicism hide the unfamiliar sensation of hope he felt blooming in his breast.

"Well, that could be someone telling her her dry cleaning is ready."

"Oh yeah? You think the dry cleaner was an encryption expert? What if it's her boyfriend? Or hell, her girlfriend! She can't be a hermit, me lad. You know that. She's no different from you nor me. She's got to be up to something with someone. She has to be! And wouldn't it just be peachy if you and I could break the news to the world?"

## Chapter 15

"Thank you, Alice."

"You're welcome sir."

She stood back and straightened his smoking jacket.

"Would you like a tie, sir?"

"No. I'll be informal this afternoon."

He glanced at the drip stand against the wall.

"They tried to poison me again, but I beat them. I survived."

"That you did, sir. You had a good nap. You look rested."

She helped him into his wheelchair and pushed him out to the sun room.

"It's a glorious afternoon, sir."

"Just beautiful. Help me into the recliner and adjust the blinds for reading, please."

"Yes, sir."

The spacious condominium occupied a corner of the building. Two walls with floor to ceiling glass gave onto a spectacular panorama of suburban Santa Fe. He loved the view. He was so glad he hadn't bought that estate on the north side. It had been horribly expensive and he didn't need the room. He didn't entertain any more, and had never cared to have extensive grounds to maintain. That was expensive too.

"Will you have supper at the regular time, sir?"

"No, I'm not hungry. Ask the cook to serve at 8:00 pm, please. She knows what I want."

"Yes, sir. Will there be anything else?"

"Some tea, please."

"Yes, sir."

He felt down the side of the chair to the buttons and pressed one, raising the foot rest. He considered the stack of magazines and books on the end table next to him but didn't feel alert enough to read. His attention was drawn to a framed photograph to one side. He picked it up and studied it.

Ms. Blatherwick had kindly taken the photograph at his request and had it printed and framed for him. He had studied it for hours.

The painter, Doro, clearly knew and understood the plants and animals that crowded the margins. The accuracy and visual interest of each lent authenticity to the larger figures in the painting: the horse, the injured man, and the girl floating over them, as it were. The girl's expression was difficult to characterize but somehow he found it comforting. The longer he contemplated the painting, the more it radiated a peace that eased his mind.

He felt sure that Doro's young cousin was the girl in the painting. Ms. Blatherwick said Doro had told her she was just the artist's model, but he didn't believe it. He'd seen her himself, briefly, at the gallery opening. There was something unusual about her—the keen eyes, perhaps, or her quick, precise movements. She had certainly read him correctly when he shook her hand. She had known instantly he was a basket case.

He set the photo down and picked up the stereo remote control. A little Verdi would help the afternoon go better.

He must have dozed. There was Alice. She had said something.

"What was that, Alice?"

"Mr. Baldwin is downstairs, sir."

"Oh. Good. Ask him to come up, and you may take this cold tea away. In ten minutes, bring hot tea for the two of us, please."

He turned off the music. Axel Baldwin walked in a few minutes later.

"Good afternoon, Axel."

"Good afternoon, sir. You're looking well today."

"I can function. For a while. Have a seat, please."

"Thank you."

"What's the report on the board meeting?"

"They're not happy, sir."

"No, I expect not. *I'm* not happy."

They sat in silence a moment.

"I still haven't made a decision. Family! It's hard to give up on one's family."

A longer moment passed.

"How long have we known each other, Axel?"

"Umm, twenty three years, sir."

Twenty three years. Axel could be his grandson. If only. Alice brought the tea tray and left while his thoughts took him over for a minute. Axel sipped his tea. They were comfortable with each other.

"I need a favor, my friend."

"Certainly. Just name it."

"It's about this painting," he said, looking at the frame on the end table. He paused.

"Shall I raise your offer?" Axel prompted gently.

"No. Not yet, anyway."

He pointed at the picture with a bony finger.

"This young woman," he said. "What do you know about her?"

"The subject of the painting? Ms. Blatherwick said it's just what it looks like. She's a healer; she heals with her hands. Supposedly the artist was healed by her. And the horse too."

"Yes. Well. And what do you know about the young woman who was with Doro at the gallery opening?"

"She looks a lot like the woman in the painting. Ms. Blatherwick said she was the model."

"And do you believe that?"

"I have no reason not to. It seems obvious."

"Yes. But do you think she is the actual healer?"

"I couldn't say, sir. It seems unlikely…that a girl, or anyone, could heal simply by touch."

"It does seem unlikely, doesn't it? Yet Doro seems to believe it. His painting shows intense conviction—even love, and a surpassing spiritual peace. You will recall I met that girl. I shook her hand, anyway." His eyes moved to the framed photo. "I think she is the healer in the painting. I would like to meet her in person, Axel, here. Could you bring that about?"

"I think so. Yes, sir."

"I knew you could. Thank you Axel. Pour me a little more tea, will you, please?"

---

Pavel met Ana at her hotel room. They headed down the hall, nodding at the guard at the desk.

"Are you sure I'm dressed appropriately?" she asked. "You said 'Davos casual.' Is this 'Davos casual?'"

"Absolutely," he replied. "Perfect. You look lovely."

Only that morning she had purchased tweed pants and a collarless tweed jacket to wear over a high-collared burgundy blouse. She had little confidence in her fashion taste in her present rarefied context but she liked the look, and most important, the new clothes were warm. She wore no necklace, but had tiny gold studs in her ears.

"You are an excellent diplomat," she said with a smile.

"I saw your sister and brother in law coming out of the elevator. They were dressed up too. Where are they going?"

"To the Hotel Europa."

"Ah!"

"Scott said there would be, uh, some kind of crowd…a 'raffish' crowd? Is that it?"

"'Raffish.' Right. That's the Europa."

"I don't know that word."

"Oh, uh…unconventional, boisterous, maybe."

"Hmm."

The lights on the elevator buttons indicated the elevators were elsewhere.

"Let's take the stairs," Ana said. "I'm in no hurry."

Sugarek pushed open the door for her and they started down. The stairwell was deserted.

"I wonder if the group we're meeting will be raffish," she said.

"It's possible, but don't let that fool you. Lots of the world's richest one tenth of one percent are here. You've met some already. They are their own society, their own club. There are some big egos among them and some are certainly raffish, but they never stop working even when they have fun.

"They make a regular circuit every year: Davos, Sun Valley, the California TED conference, the Aspen Ideas Festival, Monaco, and so forth, all over the globe. They're more citizens of the world than of individual nations. Their outlook is global, not national."

"Rothan ought to love that. He's global too."

"That's exactly right. He does love it. He's a member of their club, even though he can't match their money."

"Because he's global?"

"Yes, because of that, but also because he represents a whole planet himself, which makes him unique, and because he's a philanthropist at heart."

"I thought these were businessmen and scientists and professors."

"There are some, but many are industrialists and politicians and technocrats. They often have their own pet philanthropies: health, education, technology, and so forth. Here at Davos they talk philanthropy and politics. At other meetings around the world it might be technology or education. No matter what or where, it's usually from a business perspective."

"I'm not going to talk about business. I know little about it."

They had reached their floor. Sugarek paused with his hand on the door.

"This should be all right. Maybe Bianchi has a pet philanthropic cause to talk about. Remember, if things get awkward, you have me. Just shoot me one of your looks!"

Ana felt a little better once she saw the meeting area. It seemed people were assembling for several meetings. Four meeting rooms opened onto the same common area where a bar and tables of fruit and hors d'oeuvres were available to all. The food looked delicious. She knew it was silly, but the presence of free food never failed to attract. Apart from saving money, the buffet looked convenient and hassle-free.

Unfortunately, by the time she had loaded a small plate with assorted delicacies, sampled a few, and received a cup of punch from Pavel, she had been recognized. She managed to eat half the items on her little plate while dealing with two, then three, then four people asking the expected questions when she recognized Silvio Bianchi entering at the far side of the common area. His face would have been familiar from news coverage of his several scandals but he was hard to miss in any case. Accompanied by an entourage of five, wearing a stylish probably Italian sport coat, and with an animated face and confident swagger, he was clearly used to being the center of attention.

He got off to a bad start with Ana.

Over her years on Earth, Ana had learned to relax her Thoman standards of etiquette. There were times when she reverted, though, as during formal appearances at the United Nations, in very rare television appearances, or most recently in panel presentations with Ambassador Darshiell at select, prestigious conferences like the G-8 World Economic Forum in Milan and at Davos. On Earth as on Thomo, the formal framework helped people function smoothly and events run manageably.

Silvio Bianchi, on the other hand, seemed to assume that ignoring formal rules in favor of informality conveyed in-group status, as if he and Ana were such renowned celebrities they could behave as if they were the best of friends even if they weren't. In fact, he carried it to such an extreme that he gave Ana a real kiss on the cheek instead of the properly formal, more polite air kiss. This was a much bigger faux pas to a Thoman than an Earthling. To Ana, such unwarranted familiarity went beyond buffoonery to outright rudeness.

Being Thoman and well schooled since childhood at controlling herself in public, she allowed no inkling of annoyance to show. Had her sister been present, Ianthe would have gasped at Bianchi's crude brazenness. Pavel Sugarek, for all he could speak Luvit, was male and not Thoman and the significance of the kiss escaped him completely.

Ana endured ten minutes of clumsy, suggestive jousting with Bianchi and his publicity people and business and legal aides before he invited her and Pavel into the conference room for their presentation. She still had no clue what it might be about.

It didn't take long to find out. They arrayed themselves around an oval table with a projector and screen at one end, Bianchi at the other. His face lighted up as he began recounting the many shortcomings of the two movies made years earlier about Ana's life: the unauthorized Hollywood version and the unauthorized cable TV version. The inferiority of these efforts, he said, was an insult to history and failed to achieve the level of quality which would be worthy of the reunion of the peoples of two planets.

But now, with the help of the vast Bianchi media empire, Ana had in her hands the power to right the record and leave humanity a true and accurate, *authorized* account of her stunning adventure. To that end SANECOR had optioned and was fully ready to finance the world's most brilliant film makers to produce the film, no matter how many hundreds of millions of dollars it might take.

Ana realized what kind of project Bianchi had in mind as soon as he mentioned movies, and instantly decided to have nothing to do with it. She did not need to be more famous (quite the contrary) and the historical record could be satisfied—was being satisfied—by historians, social scientists, and physical scientists, in print.

Bianchi assumed she would view his proposal as a stroke of genius compounded by generosity. That was not a problem. She would assure him it was indeed an idea of immense boldness, and she would eagerly take it before her Second Planet Foundation for consideration (and then forget about it). All that remained was to endure the rest of this presentation, again not a problem. She was Thoman. Thomans were inured to long discussions.

Bianchi passed to one of his assistants who began an elaborate PowerPoint show detailing the film studio and running down a list of the proposed film luminaries who were supposedly eager to begin making what they were certain would be an Oscar-winning landmark film. It ended with slides from a possible story board outline of the movie.

Sensing it was now her turn, Ana professed herself flattered and delighted with the concept and promised to recommend it to the board of directors of the Second Planet Foundation at the earliest opportunity.

Bianchi, ruddy cheeks glowing, stood and demanded a group photo to commemorate the beginning of the glorious project. A publicist and an aide produced cameras and associated hardware, and the principals lined up behind the table, Ana and Bianchi in the center. While the camera person focused, Bianchi laid his arm behind Ana's back and surreptitiously pulled her closer, squeezing her breast from the side. She instantly moved his hand away. No one seemed to notice her flash of anger. The camera clicked several times.

Bianchi, smiling and undeterred, announced, "And now a kiss, to seal the deal!"

With the same hand, he pulled her neck to him and planted a kiss square on her lips. Or rather, he began to plant a kiss: at the same time Ana brought a hand up and gave his right ear a hard twist.

"Oww!" he bellowed, "Shit!"

The room went deathly still, except for Bianchi, grimacing in pain.

She stepped back, her eyes like daggers.

"God damn!" he said, hand to his ear.

"You, sir, have no honor," she said through clenched teeth, and stormed out of the room.

Pavel couldn't exactly follow her unobtrusively, but he did the best he could.

Most of the SANECOR employees at Davos heard what had happened to their boss within half an hour of the event. They knew from long experience that it was yet another not-to-be-mentioned exploit by their lusty boss, and a firing offense to be caught repeating. Consequently the news spread rapidly.

One of the last to hear, oddly enough, was Bianchi's son Ben, who was at the Europa hotel enjoying a world class martini in the company of a nubile, sweet-smelling marathon-running brunette museum curator from Atlanta. Of course it would be Nigel Dunston who would call and tell him the news. Nigel loved spectacular disasters like that, and Ben did too, even though his future success probably depended on his father's success.

Most of his father's embarrassments, like this one, were of his own making, but this time there was a huge difference. This foul-up might represent an opportunity for him to rescue his own father, and *that* surely had to nail down his own chance for promotion in SANECOR…and maybe even to replace his father when he took over the entire company. The chance was important enough for him to jot the curator's cell number on his palm and promise with a wink and a kiss to return as soon as he could.

When he arrived at his father's hotel suite it was to discover that gentleman sitting amid the wreckage of half the furniture in the room, a water glass half full (or maybe half empty) of whisky in his hand, his face like a thundercloud.

"I heard, Pop," he said.

"That bitch!" his father said. "That goddam bitch!"

The other chair still standing in the room had only three legs remaining. Ben sat cautiously on an end table and looked around. His father had destroyed the other end table too. The last person to make his dad this mad was the judge who wouldn't lower the million dollar bail on that "sex with a minor" thing. The case was still pending.

"Yeah," he agreed. "Say, Pop, I might have something on her."

His father's gaze migrated slowly from the broken vase and scattered flowers on the floor at his feet to his son's face. He stared at least fifteen seconds. Ben rolled out a little more information.

"Dunston and I have snaffled out a close friend of hers no one knows about. Might even be a girl friend. Won't know until we investigate. It's in the American west. Could check it out if you like."

He kept staring at his father, waiting patiently. Pop was famously hardheaded. At times like this information took a while to soak all the way through. Finally, screwing his eyes halfway closed, he mumbled something.

"Get her."

"It'll take some boodle."

Another ten seconds passed.

"Don't care. Just get her."

"'At's the spirit, Dad. We'll get right on it, Dunston and me. We're good. Don't worry. Start tomorrow, we will."

Ana's little hotel room had a mirror over the low dresser. She studied her image. Her temper had gotten the better of her once again. She had been stupid. It would not have killed her to have been kissed by that buffoon. Now she had probably created a scandal that would soon reverberate throughout Davos and maybe beyond. What had she been thinking? That was the problem: she hadn't been thinking. She just reacted.

The terrible evening had been made worse when she and Pavel ran into Herecyn Cymred in the lobby. Up to that point she had been fortunate in avoiding him at Davos.

No one who watched their encounter would have known of their dislike for each other. After all, they were both Thomans. Each warmly greeted the other. They exchanged pleasantries. Herecyn asked about her meeting with his very good friend Silvio Bianchi. She said it had gone well, and that she would consider his kind offer of assistance. She asked him about his activities at the conference. He said they had been delightful. They wished each other well.

In the elevator she had been so angry she was trembling. Pavel barely dared to hold her hand in his, patting it with the other.

Poor Pavel. She looked down at the dresser. She was leaning on her fists. Slowly she straightened up and forced herself to breathe and relax. She pulled a tissue out of the dispenser and blotted her eyes. She'd stay one more day, just to show she was Thoman, proud, and had not disgraced herself.

But she had.

## Chapter 16

Fergus had never given much thought to how the daughter of a woman from another planet might behave, but he had to admit that this one had a lot of energy. After two days her purpose in being here as well as the work of the rural medical team was becoming clear. He felt fortunate he didn't have to follow her around every minute. He would have been a pathetic, limping, bitching wreck.

He had seen the team schedule. It listed twenty to twenty five people all told: two family doctors, two physician assistants, and a number of specialists—an endocrinologist, an orthopedist, two pediatricians, a cardiologist, even a dentist, each with assistants—plus several nurses, nurse aides, and several lab techs. The roster varied slightly from day to day.

They were set up in the gym of the Tasajillo elementary/middle school. (The older kids in the area were bused to high school in another town.) From a security standpoint it was a pretty good situation. The school was two blocks off the state highway where there was some traffic, but not much. Parents, buses, kids, and most teachers used the front of the building. The gym entrance was at the rear of the building. Medical team members, a few teachers, and most of the patients parked in back in a small parking area meant for the athletic field.

During the team's visit the gym was off limits to everyone but the medical types and their patients, but he had managed a quick look inside. Plumbers had rigged a temporary scrub area behind sheet plastic walls. The medical staff shared the teachers' rest room and lounge. Other examination areas had been created with more plastic sheeting. Several medical machines had been set up, including an autoclave, a dentist's chair and stand, even a small X-ray machine.

The patients had appointment times but there were walk-ins as well. There was much traffic in and out of the gym. The business of filling out forms, transcription of diagnoses and prescriptions, and so forth was considerable, and conducted in the lobby of the gym. That's where the kid came in. Several aides handled that but they were usually overloaded. The kid made herself useful in helping them and explaining diagnoses, prescriptions, and doctors' advice to patients, often in Spanish.

With no obvious kidnappers or rapists lurking in the corners, the need for his security services was not urgent. He could work from his cover story, as the kid's ex-Navy corpsman uncle.

For one thing, the team had no fixed time for lunch, each member eating whenever he or she could steal a few moments. He got them to pass around a clipboard with an envelope clipped to it so they could jot down their food preferences and drop the approximate amount of cash into the envelope. He then drove to the three restaurants in town (Mexican, a hamburger joint, and a fried chicken and meat loaf place), picking up bags of food to deliver to the teachers' lunch room.

He couldn't blame the kid for looking hard at him when he asked for her car keys, but driving in this small town was not a problem. There was almost no traffic and only two stop signs between the restaurants and the school. What with keeping the car in first gear so the engine screamed if he forgot to drive slowly, and gripping the steering wheel with white knuckles, he was able to drive without incident.

That good deed helped the staff look on him favorably, and once the kid let it be known that her uncle had been a corpsman in the Navy the staff was willing to trust him to fetch the correct medical supplies and instruments from the truck as needed. His prosthesis hurt him but he could easily sneak breaks to let it rest.

Considering what World Security was paying him, this was by no means a bad gig.

For her part, Clio too was pleased with the team procedures, but after two days she needed some quiet time to sort things out in her mind.

"Are you starving?" she asked Fergus as they got out of the car at their motel.

"No, not really," he replied. "Are you?"

He could always eat, but her schedule was his schedule. She still didn't understand that.

"I kind of have a headache. I'd like to take an ibuprofen and lie down for an hour. Would you mind knocking on my door in an hour or an hour and a half, and then we could eat?"

"Sure, no problem."

She skipped the ibuprofen but she did lie down after kicking off her shoes and pulling the second pillow over her head. It wasn't really a headache but she had a slight swimming of images in her vision. These could signal the onset of a migraine headache, but for some reason she didn't think that's what this was. In any case she needed to think over the experiences of the past two days and she didn't need her eyes to do that.

The setup of the rural medical team was almost ideal. To all appearances she was a community volunteer who made herself useful wherever needed. At least that's how the nurses and aides acted. The doctors barely noticed her at all, which was perfect.

She *was* being useful, and not just by helping with paperwork. Many of the people who showed up for medical care were not used to dealing with modern medicine and its providers. For that matter, many of the providers were not used to explaining things to people who needed even more explanation than typical patients in the city of Albuquerque. True, the doctors were trying to deal with as many patients as they could. Long explanations required time that could be devoted to other patients in need. Nor did all the medical people speak good Spanish.

She was helping with that.

Darn it! Even with her eyes shut her vision was still swimming. She remembered that odd episode by herself in the high mountains of northern Mexico when she had had similar crazy visions. These were not as severe…not yet, anyway.

What had she been thinking about? Oh: the people she had met.

In her brief experience at the hospital in Las Cruces all the patients she had dealt with had been seriously ill. She had little experience with normal people of all ages from the general population. But in the past two days, she must have met over fifty individuals, from infants to the elderly, most of whom were comparatively healthy. There could hardly be a better sample to work with.

The benches in the lobby of the gym were perfect for sitting and talking to people who had just seen a doctor. A few questions about their families or general wellbeing were all it took to get started.

Best of all, it was natural to hold the hands of the elderly, or shake hands with the men. Caressing children was not only natural but expected, even if the children were only accompanying a parent who was seeing a doctor. In the traditional culture touching children was almost a rule. In the old days not to touch a child one admired was thought to invite the *mal de ojo*, or evil eye, on that child. Nowadays that stricture had receded to mere custom, but it was a custom parents noticed. Observing it in modern times amounted to good manners.

Generally, she would ask the persons she was sitting with if they had any questions about what they had been told by the doctor, if the doctor had overlooked anything important, or if they had any other concerns. Twice, she had gone back inside to ask doctors for clarification, mildly annoying them, but she didn't care.

It was wonderful to have a professional's diagnosis before her while she formed her own impressions through physical contact. It was a little like taking a test to which one had the answer key. Having the diagnosis before her enabled her to refine, or attempt to refine, the impressions she was receiving. She'd met half a dozen patients with diabetes, for example, but there are different kinds of diabetes. Problems with major organs had always been difficult for her to sense.

Still, in two patients she thought she detected conditions not caught by the doctors. Fortunately they were not urgent or life-threatening, so she kept them to herself. Were she to send someone back inside for a second look she would be remarked upon. She couldn't have that.

She had told Dr. Peebles that the sensations were like tree leaves in the wind, but that wasn't really accurate. His analogy to symphonic music wasn't quite right either. What about flowing water? That had many subtle qualities: dripping, rushing, bubbling, flowing, etc.. But no, water wasn't right either. What she was experiencing was unlike anything else she knew.

The diagnoses she read from the reports varied widely: osteopoenia, gastric reflux, arthritis, rheumatism, sinusitis, low grade infections, colds, rosacea, lupus, cancer, migraines, drug addiction, nutritional problems, on and on. It was difficult to impossible to consistently correlate what was on the papers with the onslaught of impressions she sensed. Still, she was getting better at recognizing some of what she sensed even if she couldn't explain why.

For the first time, she realized that the auras of everyone had much in common. In fact, when she thought about it, human auras were not that different from the animals she had examined: cats, dogs, horses. All living things (animals, at least) seemed to have an aura of some kind that she could detect. Accurately dissecting that aura, however, was beyond her.

Her great grandmother, Abuelita, had a distinctive pattern that was familiar: thin, strong, lean. The children she had met on this tour had loud, wide patterns in general. Some adults' patterns were loud and wide as well, yet with "dents," or "holes," or depressions. One very elderly woman, frail and skinny and with serious arthritis, had the loudest pattern she'd ever felt. One toddler, oddly, had a thready, seemingly weak aura, despite being chubby and lively.

She sensed herself getting better at recognizing some of the subtle differences in auras, however impossible these were to describe. Apparently one set of differences had to do with the blood, another with the lymph system, and yet another with muscles. Nerves, bones, joints…too many, too complex…each body produced a symphony of signals…no, "symphony" was the wrong word… darn! The swirling in her closed eyes was taking over her brain…. In desperation she clutched the bedspread with both hands.

"Um. What? Who's.…"

She pulled the pillow off her face and pushed herself up slowly, blinking her eyes hard as the visions faded. Someone was knocking on her door. The room was stuffy, uncomfortably warm.

"Just a minute, please," she said, getting up carefully. She steadied herself against the wall.

"You OK?" Fergus said when she opened the door.

"Yeah. I was sleeping. Sorry. I.… Oh!"

Her knees almost folded. Fergus grabbed her. He guided her to a chair.

"Are you sure you're all right?"

"Uh-huh. I got up too fast. My headache's going away. Let me wash my face and we can go eat. I'll be fine."

The cold water helped restore her equilibrium. She stared at her reflection over the towel in her hands. Fergus had held her forearm, his other hand on her opposite shoulder. Four days ago she had shaken his hand, but now his aura was different. It was the second time she had been inside his personal space: besides pain in one leg there was also a peculiar change in his upper body. Was it his aura, or merely his odor? Or both?

If she had to guess, she would guess that he had been drinking alcohol.

## Chapter 17

Julio, in shorts, running shoes, and sweat-dampened sweatshirt, was having iced tea on the gallery of the lodge after a four mile run down the county road that ran along the southern edge of the Plan C hunting ranch. His dad had run with him but had gone straight back to the "owner's" cottage—their cottage—for a shower.

Sunday afternoon he'd helped the Rocky Mountain Racing team load up the world record-holding Corolla and stow their tools. Then he and his dad and the team had driven into Beeville for steak and potatoes at a fancy, if oddly out of place, English pub in the center of town. It had been bustling with tourists and speed enthusiasts, and service was slow but the food was good. Several knowledgeable people noticed the jackets of the team members and congratulated them on their unlikely speed record.

The next morning the racing team had headed back to Albuquerque. On their own again, Matt asked the wildlife manager to give them a tour of the ranch in one of the ranch's four-wheelers. The ranch was easily large enough to get lost in but it wasn't unattractive country, not all brush by any means. There were rolling pastures, dry creek beds, and large stands of stately, gnarled live oak trees, all good land for deer, wild pigs, turkeys, and migratory birds. Dove and quail season, the manager told them, were wildly successful, nearly as profitable as deer season.

Since his visitors were from out of state, the manager gave the two of them a lesson in the meaning of "brush country." This included pointing out some of the more common sticker-bearing plants in the area: huisache, blackbrush, prickly pear, granjeño, guajillo, and the like. By far the most formidable was catclaw, with hundreds of recurved thorns, smaller and sharper than rose thorns, that grabbed clothes and skin and drew blood as one struggled to get free.

The brush was largely worthless, the manager said, the heritage of cattle driven north by Spaniards in earlier centuries. The seeds they dropped from the desert plants they had eaten took root and eventually conquered the vast grasslands which had originally covered the area.

One type of plant caused Julio a double take: the mesquite trees, many as tall and twisted as the live oaks, but covered in fine, fern-like leaves and bearing large, formidable thorns. Julio knew the mesquite as a bush, not a tree. The desert country where he lived was covered with millions of hummocks of windblown sand with thorny mesquite branches sticking out on all sides. These were the same plant, the manager told him. These trees are what you'd have if you watered those bushes a little more and kept the sand away from them.

They saw only a few does and fawns. The big bucks hid out during the day, coming out at night to eat from the automated feeders which scattered corn and nutritional pellets to ensure the healthy growth of these profitable animals. And there were windmills, of course, in this land of little running water. Julio had loved windmills from childhood.

Following the tour, late Monday afternoon he and his father cooled down after their run by walking the last quarter mile back to the lodge.

"Winter's different down here, eh?" his dad cracked.

Julio nodded, flapping his sweatshirt to get some cooling air under it.

"So, now that you've seen it, what do you think of Plan C?" Matt asked, still puffing a bit.

"I like it," Julio replied. "I noticed the garage behind the cottage. I guess that's where we could keep the pod?"

"Right. The fence around it and the house is secure. It's far enough from the lodge that no one would hear the pod, at night, of course."

"I don't know that we'd want to hole up there for any length of time."

"No, probably not."

"Is this anything like Plan B, in Montana?"

"Not really, no. We can check that out in the summer, maybe. It's too damn cold there now. It was a ranch owned by a movie star for a while, so it has a much fancier house and an airstrip. There's a foreman and some staff there, but they live a couple miles away."

Julio mopped his neck with the bandanna.

"What about tomorrow?"

"Tomorrow we'll drive down to Rockport, on the coast. We can go to the beach, check out the sights and have some great sea food, and the next day we'll take a charter out into the Gulf and try some fishing."

"Not too sure about that," Julio shook his head. "Waves and my head might not go well together."

"Way ahead of you, son. I checked with your sister. She said meclazine was good for that. It's sold over the counter. I have enough for both of us."

"It better work. If not, she'll hear about it."

A half hour later he had finished his iced tea on the gallery. His dad should be out of the shower and he was about to go for a shower himself when—whoa!—here came Beth Melson, in skintight pre-worn-out blue jeans and a colorful western snap shirt. The shirt was snug on her. He wondered what those snaps might do if she sneezed.

"Hi, Julio!" she said. "Whatcha been doing?"

"Hey. Not much. Went for a run."

"You're out of tea. Need some more?"

"Huh? Yeah. I do."

He started to rise.

"No, I'll get it. You rest."

She smiled brightly and disappeared inside. She was easily the best looking animal he'd seen on the whole 8000 acres. She seemed a good deal friendlier than she had been Sunday. Maybe she was slow to warm up to new people. If so, he understood. He was the same way.

In several minutes she was back with a glass of tea in each hand.

"Can I join you?"

"Sure. Thanks."

The bench was a three-person affair, but she sat in the middle and watched as he squeezed the lemon slice into the tea and stirred it with the straw. He really was a handsome boy, even all sweaty and stubble-cheeked. Especially all sweaty and stubble-cheeked. You'd never dream he was a millionaire.

"Mmm. Thanks," he said, after a long sip. He leaned back and stretched his legs. "So, is your dad still hunting?"

"Not today. He's at the country club with his buddies. He said he'll hunt two more days and then we go back to Houston."

"Ah."

They passed another fifteen minutes making small talk. He was struck more and more by how very friendly she was, even rubbing his forearm and patting his back for emphasis several times. She was a party person, she said, and that was what she had missed most over the last week. That gave her an idea! It was so beautiful out here in this wide-open, vacant country they should have their own party, their own private party!

Julio received this news as he did most news, with outward equanimity. Inwardly, it was another matter. First, as a rule he didn't like parties. He liked talking with interesting people of all ages, but at the parties people his age tended to favor, thoughtful conversation was rarely a priority. While a party of just two people had potential for thoughtful conversation, thoughtful conversation with this particular person seemed unlikely.

There was another factor: Julio's little voice. He didn't think of it by that name, but if he had been asked he might instead have called it a scientific procedure, or perhaps a rational attitude. He generally pondered problems at length, whether technical or interpersonal, trying to be receptive to thoughts floating just outside his awareness. Often enough, his thoughts gelled and the proper course became clear.

At the moment, he was feeling increasingly uneasy over the drift of this conversation. When he understood that Beth's party plans included sneaking beers from her father's stash and a couple of blankets against the cold night and even a pillow, he suspected that she had in mind something a good deal more intimate than the typical party. There was more: her perfume and the careless way she allowed her thigh to rub his were adding disturbing variables to the equation.

This, he realized, must be the golden opportunity most of his male classmates had dreamed of. His first sexual experience had yet to be, and he had thought about it probably as much as any other healthy young male would have. Why not now? Beth was eminently desirable, clearly willing, and, best of all, without any claims on his future that he could see. He would return home, she would return home, and that was that. No one else had to know. Yet his unnamed little voice haunted his conscience. Something wasn't right here. Occam's Razor had always guided him before: the simplest solution was the best. In this case: decline. That was simplest.

At the same time, he knew he couldn't refuse without hurting her feelings terribly. She clearly thought she was irresistible. She would be crushed, personally insulted, if he refused her. He couldn't bear to do that. The Thoman part of him rebelled at delivering such a brutal message. What in blazes could he do?

He realized she had just asked him a question.

"Oh. Uh, tonight? Um...I can't. My dad and I are visiting relatives in Beeville. We haven't seen them in years and I have to go with him. How about tomorrow night? The moon will be nearly full. Will that work?"

He watched her react. She was a bit disappointed but yes, tomorrow night would work. He smiled as best he could and took a drink of tea, looking over the rim of the glass at the parking area.

He and his dad would leave in the morning at dawn. It was horribly rude to cut and run and she'd be furious, but that was better than an outright refusal. He'd leave her a note of apology, maybe begging a family emergency. It was a chicken-hearted trick to play on someone and it made him feel terrible. Most of his friends would say he'd been a buttheaded idiot, and maybe he was. For sure, he wasn't proud of himself. But he wasn't going to change his mind.

Who in hell was calling him at this damn time? He pulled out his cell phone and glanced at the screen: Nigel Dunston, the damn fool. He'd call him back later, after this little bit of sucking up was over. Nigel better have good news. He shoved it back in his pocket as a maid opened the door and let him in. He announced himself.

"Let me see if he's ready, Mr. Bianchi. I'll be just a minute."

It was less than a minute. She led him to a small dining room. The old man was in a wheelchair at the far end, a cup of tea in front of him and a newspaper folded to one side. He looked terrible, all shrunken down and frail. Might not last another week. Excellent! That could mean a giant step up. The old relic watched his entry keenly enough, though.

"Afternoon, Grandpop," he said. "You're looking good."

"Nonsense. How are you, young man?"

Young man. Right. Hell, he was forty.

"I'm good, sir, just fine. I was in the neighborhood and thought I'd stop by. Nice place you have here."

"You're in a neighborhood halfway around the world. What brings you to New Mexico, grandson?"

"Paper's doing a story on the modern American West. Probably because of a couple recent movies. You might've seen some. The West is huge right now, everywhere."

"Is that so?"

"That's true. And so naturally I volunteered to come over and do my part. Just between us, it was mainly so I could come to Santa Fe and visit my dear Grandpop."

"I see. Well, thank you for that. And how's your father?"

"Oh, he's pretty good, mostly. With one exception. Maybe you heard about that."

"Are you referring to this?"

He opened the newspaper—not one of theirs, of course—to a front page photo of their son/father in mid-grimace, eyes starting out of his head, his face inches from the face of an obviously angry Ana Darcy. His hand was on the back of her neck and she was twisting his ear nearly off his head.

"Uh, yeah…that's it. He shouldn't have done that. Tried to kiss her, that is."

"The damn fool. He has no class."

"That's what she said. Reportedly."

"I'm not sure even ten million dollars worth of lawyers can keep that jackass out of prison."

"Well, they have so far."

"That's one thing I can say for you, grandson. You keep your peccadilloes out of the headlines. Usually."

"I've been lucky."

The old man looked stern.

"That's a joke, just a joke, sir!"

"This family," he shook his head. "What happened to this family? I swear I don't know. But I'll tell you, young man…."

His grandfather launched into an impressive ten minute tirade about how the hand of destiny had not yet written the complete story of the Bianchi family, no indeed! Fate was fickle but people often got what they deserved, yada yada yada. He tuned out as best he could. He'd heard much the same thing many times before. The old stick was probably shortening his life even more with all the energy he was putting into his doomsday diatribe. OK, fine, Grandpop. Have at it.

Forty minutes later he had found a quiet bar to return Dunston's call.

"What news, Nigel?"

"I finally pulled the right string with the telecommucations blokes. Took a lawyer and twenty thou, but we have access to their phone records in New Mexico now."

"So why aren't you here, dammit?"

"One last little technical problem. You don't appreciate the innovations your humble servant has to call into being, pal o' mine! We need a scanner with a range over 50 meters, more like 200 meters, and directional. There wasn't one... until now, that is. Thanks to me, there's a tech team finishing one up at this very moment. It should be ready tomorrow, and I'll be on my way to join you for the grand fox hunt."

"Shite, I hope so. Can't wait to find a better place to be. Call me each step of the way, blast it. I have a birthday in six months."

He put the phone in his pocket, drained his scotch, and signaled the bartender for another. He'd spent a discouraging morning checking out the nowhere town of Tasajillo. So Ana Darcy got an encrypted call from there, huh? Dunston had wisecracked it wasn't likely her dry cleaner or the person she'd left her pets with. It'd be his luck if it was a wrong number, or maybe someone just passing through.

The town was composed mainly of rundown, tired little houses and a few businesses on the highway: a couple gas stations, a truck stop, two motels, four small eateries, a garage, a pawnshop/loan office, a couple churches, a second-rate grocery store, an elementary school, and a couple state offices, including one for the forest service.

The city hall was an aged building the size of a house. Hell, it even incorporated the local cop shop. All of four pickup trucks were parked in front. What was it about Americans and pickup trucks, anyway?

It was hard to imagine a place less likely to contain someone of interest to the famous girl from outer space. He and Dunston would try the space-age gizmo for a couple days and then go home to Blighty and think of something else to try. Crap. What else was there to do?

## Chapter 18

The working day was almost over when Fergus returned from a late restaurant run with lunches for four of the medical staff. He delivered the plastic bags to a nurse aide and scanned the lobby. The kid was at her accustomed bench at the far end. But hold on—the man sitting with her didn't look like a patient. The guy was wearing a suit. As he watched, the man turned his head. Aha. It was the snappy dresser who was with the old man at the art show.

They were talking easily enough. There seemed no need for security, but just in case he sidled to the mid-point of the lobby where she could see him. They had evidently finished their chat. The kid glanced his way as the two of them stood. He handed her a card, they shook hands, and he left. She came to meet him.

"You met that gent before, right?" he said.

"Yes. His name is Axel Baldwin. He works for Mr. Bianchi."

"Hmm. What'd he want?"

"Mr. Bianchi would like to see me again."

Fergus thought a second.

"Uh-oh," he said.

"That's what I thought, too. But he promised Mr. Bianchi wasn't looking for a healer. He loves that painting. He wants to talk about it and about Doro. And me, I guess. I didn't want to, but he said Mr. Bianchi is very sad these days and it would make him feel better."

"So...are you going to do it?"

"I said I would. I'm not doing anything important in the evenings. He's really sick, Fergus. If a visit would cheer him up, then I'll go."

"When?"

"As soon as we finish here and change. He goes to bed early, so we'll be back by our bedtime. He lives on the north side of Santa Fe. It won't take an hour to get there. I hope you don't mind."

"Not at all."

He almost added another wisecrack about how it was his job to follow her wherever she went, but he held back. She knew that as well as he did. Asking if he minded was probably politeness on her part, but it was a courtesy wasted on him. Over the last ten years he'd gotten a little rusty in the manners department. Still, it was obvious she genuinely felt sorry for that old guy. The way her brow wrinkled when she mentioned his sickness was kind of touching, even to a hardened war cripple.

There was no rush hour traffic on the state highway and only slightly more heading north to the outskirts of Santa Fe. The sky was overcast enough to reduce the sunset to a handful of wide, dark orange bands on the western horizon. It was quiet in the Corolla.

"So, have you been satisfied with the first three days?" he asked.

"Yes, I think so," she said. After several seconds she continued. "It probably wasn't clear what I was doing. At least I hope it wasn't. I haven't told anyone on the medical team. I haven't told you, either.

"You see, I'm pretty good at sensing some conditions, especially if they're close to the surface, like the blood and lymph systems, parts of the nervous system, and most bones and joints. I was able to partially control Mr. Coombs' concussion, for example. That involved both blood and lymph vessels. I first learned I could do this by checking my great grandmother's high blood pressure. Muscles and joints came later.

"The interior organs and smaller glands are much harder to interpret. It's very confusing. In the gym I can meet lots of people and compare what I sense with the doctors' diagnoses they've just received. It's a wonderful opportunity. I think I'm getting a little better at it."

She paused. She was talking too much.

"I'm pretty sure I could help reduce the pain from your prosthesis," she added.

"We've been through that," he said, "but thanks anyway."

"I hope that didn't happen because of what Mom told you, about that man."

"It didn't. It was a different evolution, about six months later."

"Was that why you left the Navy?"

"No. I left because I could no longer serve with the SEALs."

"Oh." A second later, "Are you married? I'm sorry; you know a lot about me but I barely know anything about you."

"Divorced."

"Oh."

"No children."

"I'm sorry, Fergus. It's really none of my business."

He exhaled softly.

"That's all right. I'm kind of an edgy guy. You probably noticed. My wife ran off while I was in rehab. It wasn't her fault. I was hard to get along with, I know. Not like now. I'm a pussycat now."

"That's good. Well, if you change your mind about your leg...."

"Don't worry. You'll be the first to know."

The address turned out to be one of a circle of luxury condos accessed through a lighted guard post. They were met at the door by a young woman who introduced herself as Alice, Mr. Bianchi's housekeeper. She wore a pale blue blouse with an embroidered dove and the words "La Paloma" over the pocket. She led them into a small dining room.

"Mr. Bianchi will be with you in a few minutes. He asked me to tell you that he would be pleased if you would accept a modest supper."

Clio had resigned herself to eating late, on the return trip. She glanced at Fergus, who nodded ever so slightly, and they sat down to be served a wonderful Italian meatball soup, fresh bread with a buttery brie, and a salad of lettuce, toasted walnuts, scallions, and pears. She glanced at Fergus during the meal. He nodded again, more emphatically this time.

The woman returned as they were finishing.

"Mr. Bianchi will see you now, miss," she said. "Sir, there's a dessert, if you would care for one."

She escorted Clio to a wide room with drapes drawn over two walls and a number of chairs, a sofa, bookshelf, and media cabinet. Bianchi was seated at the far end in one of two wing chairs angled toward each other, with a small table and lamp in between. He wore a dress shirt and green bow tie. A lap robe covered his legs.

"Miss Montez is here, sir," she said.

"Thank you, Alice."

Clio heard the woman back away.

"Miss Montez, please, have a seat."

Clio took the other wing chair. Bianchi studied her keenly.

"Thank you so much for coming. I didn't think you would."

She returned his gaze, her face neutral.

"You will pardon me for not offering to shake your hand," he said. "That got us off on the wrong foot last time."

"I'm very sorry about that, sir. I didn't mean to be rude. I was surprised, that was all."

"You are too diplomatic, miss. It was because you knew instantly that I am barely clinging to life by my fingertips, that I am in fact beyond curing."

She looked at her hands, clasped in her lap.

"I know it, you see, despite what my doctors tell me. Please be at ease about that. I do not expect anyone to save me from my fate. Not even a courageous young woman."

He studied her another minute. She studied him back. She didn't know what else to do. Finally he spoke again.

"I should explain why I wished to meet you. I owe you that much for your trouble."

He smoothed a wrinkle in the lap robe.

"In my long life, Miss Montez, I have made a lot of money, money beyond understanding, far more than anyone needs, more than any family needs, more even than a corporation needs. For decades that was all I cared about.

"I replaced the religion of my ancestors with the religion of money. I neglected my family. I taught them by my example to love wealth."

He was pausing for breath between phrases.

"My illness was identified nine years ago. The odds of surviving were small, they said. But I had the best doctors, the best hospitals, the best of everything. I thought my wealth would save me.

"After three years I grew impatient, and after five, angry. After seven years of inexorable, increasing illness I finally accepted that I am facing the end and that I have wasted my life on unimportant things. Everyone around me except Mr. Baldwin regards me as an obstacle standing between them and more money than they already have.

"I began to despair, but not about death. Whatever happens after death will take care of itself. Rather, what bothered me was the ancient question: what is a good life, and how does one live it?

"I will spare you the steps I took in cogitating the matter. At the end, I have come to the realization that the only answer that satisfies me is that we all matter. All living things, including the earth, matter a great deal, because that is all we have, ultimately. We must nurture it, share and preserve it for those who follow us. We must love…well, but we don't. That is enough for now."

He paused, his eyes on her.

"Your cousin's painting has affected me deeply. It is based in reality, isn't it?" She nodded slowly.

"I thought so. It's obvious. What is he to you, if I may ask? A boy friend, perhaps? That does happen, between cousins."

"No, sir," she said quietly. "He's a distant cousin. I met him only once before, two years ago, when we discovered his family."

"Ah. And the events suggested by the painting? They really happened?"

"Yes, sir. The horse had sprained some muscles. Doro was attacked by two bullies."

"And what did you do?"

"I showed the horse trainer how to treat and strengthen the horse's muscles. I eased Doro's pain."

"Can you explain how you did that?"

"No, sir. I have some abilities to heal, but I don't understand them very well. That's why I'm working with the rural health team."

"I see," he said. "I sensed that mystery in the painting. But there's love there, too, an extraordinary, pure love, glowing with compassion. The reverence for life is immensely affecting. The picture is never far from my thoughts. To know it was born in actual events, involving a very real, self-possessed young woman is a great comfort to me."

He covered his mouth and yawned.

"You must pardon me. I tire easily these days. I am so very grateful to you, Miss Montez, for agreeing to meet me again. You are a breath of fresh air."

His endurance was clearly reaching its end. She stood.

"It was an honor, sir. Thank you for your hospitality. I am not afraid to shake your hand this time."

"Thank *you*, my child," he whispered.

She took his hand, prepared to hide her reaction to the sensations she knew would overwhelm her, but the effort was unnecessary. He was falling asleep. His head tilted down slightly.

She laid her left hand over their clasped ones and stood quietly while a minute passed. His breathing was soft and slow.

She slipped her left hand inside the placket of his sleeve to hold his scrawny wrist. She looked to one side and concentrated.

He was completely asleep. She stepped carefully behind the chair and reached over the back to place her hands along either side of his neck. It was awkward but she stood there, his neck and jaw cradled between her palms. She closed her eyes and lost track of time.

Fergus rubbed a finger across a smear of dessert left on the plate, licked it off, and regarded his nearly empty coffee cup. The kid had been gone over a half hour.

He pushed his chair back and got up to search out more coffee when the hall door opened and there she was, looking wrung out, small and tired, her eyes shiny.

"You OK?" he asked.

"We can go now," she said.

"I'll tell Alice," he said, nodding toward the kitchen door.

"I'll be outside," she said.

And so she was, leaning against the driver side door.

"Are you good to drive?" he asked.

"Yes. The fresh air helps a lot."

"You sure you can drive?"

"Better than you."

"That ain't sayin' much."

Once they'd left the suburbs behind, Fergus had to ask.

"So how was the old guy?"

"He's really a sweet man, Fergus. It's so sad."

"Is he that sick? Could you tell?"

"Oh, yes, it's terrible. I think he has some form of cancer of the blood. There are many types. It's all through him. And he's having chemotherapy. There's some kind of strong poison in him. I felt something similar in a woman this morning. She was being treated for breast cancer. But Mr. Bianchi was worse, much worse."

"Did you work on him?"

"Yes, a little. The poor man went to sleep while I watched. I don't think I helped him. I'm afraid he's right. His disease is incurable."

"Well, he's had a long life. Made plenty of money."

"He's not afraid of dying. He told me he's wasted his life. That's what's sad."

Fergus thought about wasted lives as the darkness streamed past. Tell me about it, he thought. Finally he replied.

"Well, I guess that can't be cured."

"Maybe it can, sort of," she said. "He said he finally realized that all we have is each other. We have to look out for each other. He knows that now."

"Hmm."

You still need money, he thought. The rich forget: even poor people need money to live. They need it worse, in fact.

"What's in the bag?" she asked, nodding at the white paper bag he'd set on the console.

"Huh? Oh. Alice didn't want you to miss dessert. It's cheesecake. It's great. You've got a treat to look forward to when we get back."

"How thoughtful! I should have thanked her. What nice people...."

# Chapter 19

What a cursed, nowhere, no-account little village, thought Ben Bianchi, eating his surviving French fries one at a time. Impossible to conceive that someone might have texted Ana Darcy, the world-famous extraterrestrial multi-Olympic medal holder, from this miserable burg.

Granted, the town was in scenic country: low, forested mountains, long red bluffs, lots of scenic pastures of sheep, cattle, and goats. There were probably ranches and estate getaways for big shots up in those mountains. Maybe an owner of one of those called her. The county tax office ought to show where they were and what they were worth, and maybe the owners too. All he'd have to do was go visit them one at a time and ask if Ana Darcy hung around there. Sodding job that would be.

According to a loafer at the gas station, the restaurant where he was eating, Silvia's, was the best place in town. At first it seemed prophetic: that was his father's name. Now that he'd experienced the plebeian quality of the food, it might still be prophetic. His father wasn't all he was cracked up to be either.

The waitress, a solid, dusky young woman fond of chewing gum, brought him the check. At least the food was cheap. In London or New York it would have been two or three times as much. Not that he cared.

"What does 'Tasajillo' mean?" he asked her.

"That's this town. That's where you are."

"No…I, oh, never mind. Tell me, do any celebrities ever come here?"

"Celebrities? Like, movie stars?"

"Anyone famous."

"The owner said that John Madden used to come here."

"John Madden?"

"He was a football announcer, on TV. He was afraid to fly. He took a bus everywhere. But that was before I was born."

"Well, any since then?"

"Umm…Eric Joeffry?"

"Who's he?"

"He's on C.S.I. Las Vegas. He's handsome! He sat right over there. I served him! I got his autograph!"

"Well, lucky you."

He left a small tip on the table and went to the cash register behind a rangy man paying for takeout, three clamshells in a plastic bag. After the guy pocketed his change and headed out the door, he handed over his own check. While the cashier was waiting for his credit card number to clear, he asked her the same question he'd asked the waitress, slightly modified to avoid a repeat of the airheaded answer.

"You ever get any big shots through here?"

"Big shots? Here? Not many since the Interstate, not that I know of."

"What about in the last week? Any important people here since then?"

"Not really. 'Less you count the doctors. They think they're big shots."

"What doctors?"

"'At's a buncha doctors and nurses from Albuquerque, set up a medical clinic at the elementary school. They're the only visitors recently, until deer season at least."

"At the elementary school, huh?"

"Yeah. That guy that just left? He's a runner for them, takes them food. He's headed there right now."

He managed to get out of the restaurant in time to see the taillights of the chap's car disappear around a corner three blocks away. By the time he reached that intersection himself, the car was gone, but he made the same turn and only had to search another five minutes to find the school to the right. He parked in front and walked past the flagpole to the front door.

The entry was a small vestibule of chicken wire-lined safety glass. A guard was waiting for him at the end.

He had a story ready. Playing up his British accent always helped in America.

"Good afternoon. I'm looking for a Dr. Ken Stevenson, please."

"Would he be an educator or a medical doctor, sir?"

"Medical. He told me I could find him here."

"There's a medical team in the gymnasium. The entrance is at the back of this building."

"Aha. Right. He's probably busy. I was to meet him for lunch but I was unfortunately delayed. Are there a number of doctors there, do you know?"

"There's a bunch, yes."

"Including specialists?"

"I expect you could staff a small hospital with all a' them."

"How long have they been here?"

"They began Monday. They'll be here through next week."

He excused himself, went back to his rental car, and drove it around the back of the school. Indeed, there was a lot of activity there, people going in and out and quite a few cars in the parking lot. Right, then. He drove back to the highway and turned toward Santa Fe.

It wasn't hard to imagine Ana Darcy seeing a doctor, for reasons medical or personal. Personal would be better, of course, the more personal the better, like a randy, rich surgeon. But there was no way to tell which doctor it might be until bleeding Dunston brought the new scanner.

It'd be a total pisser if the delay meant they missed finding Ana's man (or woman) friend. He looked at his watch. An hour back to Santa Fe. Well, what was a body to do? He'd get there just in time for happy hour.

Matt had agreed to meet his son at one of the outdoor tables of a Vietnamese restaurant two hundred feet from the beach. The breeze off the Gulf was rather too chilly for dining and there were no other open air customers. That was just as well. He slipped his cell phone back into the watch pocket of his jeans. He had a cup of hot coffee to sip and he didn't mind waiting. He had some important things to think about.

The Rockport-Fulton part of the Texas Gulf Coast was flat and almost featureless as far as he had seen, but they had found much of interest along the shore, which despite development retained an engaging local character.

They'd seen nothing to equal the excitement of the Texas Mile, but simply roaming around stumbling onto things of interest in casual male fashion was very pleasant. Julio had been particularly impressed by the Fulton Mansion, a solid, stately home from the 1870s on the National Register of Historic Places. He liked its innovative indoor plumbing, central gas lighting and heating well enough, but he was astounded at the way the walls had been constructed: they were twelve inches thick! The three and a half story house had walls made of one by twelve inch boards stacked flat and nailed together, a stupendous volume of lumber. That probably explained why the house had survived a number of hurricanes.

The Fulton Mansion was a well-known tourist attraction, but they also found interesting non-touristic things by simple luck. Today, for example, father and son had strolled through a beachfront neighborhood so upscale that some of the residences had boats moored behind their houses. In a circle where four condos faced each other, they found five men polishing three immaculate vintage cars.

Matt and Julio, aided by street cred from the Texas Mile speed record patch on his jacket, began chatting with them. Two were lawyers and three were businessmen. After fifteen minutes showing off their cars, Julio happily accepted an invitation to go for a ride. Matt talked ten more minutes with the one man who stayed behind, before heading back to the restaurant near their bed and breakfast to await the return of his son.

An elated Julio was dropped off a half hour later in a resplendent red 1934 Chrysler CB sedan with chromed bug-eye headlights *and* chromed fog lights, and an hour after that the two of them were contemplating the remains of a world-class multi-course meal whose exotic dishes they could never hope to pronounce.

Matt cracked open his fortune cookie (Weren't those supposed to go with Chinese food?) and looked at his fortune: "You will have an unexpected adventure soon," it said. He flattened it out face down on the table and set the salt cellar on it. Julio was looking out over the tables on the patio outside. Two Asian men, one young, one old, were on the fantail of a shrimp boat, working on a winch engine. He could hear the clanks of their tools on the exhaust manifold.

"Tomorrow we tour the wildlife refuge?" he asked his father.

"Maybe not," Matt replied. "Our plans might have changed."

"Yeah? How come?"

Matt glanced around. No one was within two tables. He pulled out his phone and manipulated the screen a bit. He slid it to Julio.

"Check it out," he said.

It was a Yahoo news page: there was his mother, twisting the ear of an extremely unhappy-looking man who was obviously trying to kiss her. Julio's mouth dropped open.

"Dang!" he said, and then, in a lower voice, "Holy crap!"

Matt let him absorb that a minute.

"Have you talked to Mom about this?"

"Sort of. More like she talked to me about it."

"Jeez, who is this dope?"

"Only about the biggest, richest media guy in the whole world. You can read the article with the photo later. He's quite a lech, it seems. There's a sex with a minor case pending against him in England, it says."

Julio shook his head in amazement.

"Mom looks furious! Man! He's lucky she didn't knee him in the slats!"

He tapped the "Back" button to get rid of the image and returned the phone to his father. He studied the table a few seconds before speaking again.

"How'd she sound?"

"You know your mother. I think she was madder at herself than at Mr. Billionaire. She lost her cool and created a scandal, two of her least favorite things."

"Poor Mom!"

"She can't stand being in that place anymore; she's too embarrassed. She's coming back early."

"Yeah?"

"Yeah. So I suggested maybe she might need to get away for a little while—say, like a nice peaceful cruise along the Intercoastal Canal. She thought that sounded good.

"Son," he continued, "I know you didn't care much for fishing on the Gulf. As you rightly pointed out, there was nothing to see out there but water. But on the Intercoastal Canal, we'd have a couple days of good sightseeing, on peaceful, smooth water, away from crowds and stuff. Could you do that?"

"You bet! Did you rent a boat or something?"

"No. You remember that fellow I was talking to when you drove off in that Buick, the sunburned guy in shorts? Turns out he's a ship broker. That's an agent, like a middleman, between people who buy yachts and companies that build yachts. He told me he's picking up a yacht in New Orleans and delivering it to someone in Corpus Christi. I just called him and asked if we could ride along if we picked up the tab for the fuel.

"He agreed. He said the yacht has a crew of four and it would be a good chance for them to learn the ropes with a few passengers--test out the galley and practice their duties and so forth. Would you like that?"

"Are you kidding? That sounds fantastic!"

"One more thing. Mom wants to drive back home over the roads we used to drive when she…uh, when she first arrived. For old time's sake, I guess."

He paused.

"Yeah? So? That's fine. Is there a problem?"

"A small one. We'd either have to sit three in the front, which is not comfortable, or put one person on that hard bench in the back."

"Well, I don't m...."

"And besides, that truck is older than you are. However, we meet Mom in New Orleans the day after tomorrow. Whaddya say tomorrow we drive to Corpus Christi and do a little truck shopping before we fly to New Orleans?"

Julio's eyes gleamed.

"Excellent! I know the perfect person to ask for advice—me!"

Fergus always welcomed the end of the kid's work day. It meant the end of his work day too. He could get off his feet, sip a libation from his stash (which he'd been able to augment on the lunch runs), and watch TV in his room. It was dull, but not only was dullness good for a security man, dullness was welcome in his life generally. The more the better, in fact.

The El Faro motel was only three-quarters of a mile from the school. He was sure the kid would rather walk. He suspected that she didn't because she knew he would be in pain and felt sorry for him. Piss on that. He'd almost rather she walked anyway. He had experience with pain. He could take it.

She was an active little critter for sure, with lots of energy. A couple times he'd heard her jumping rope in her room.

"Looking forward to Friday?" he asked, as they belted in for the short trip back.

"Yes," she said, the pitch of the word falling off slightly as if she wasn't really. "I'm feeling, I don't know what, overloaded, maybe, with all the input I've been getting. I need some time to think about it all, sort it out, I guess. I'm looking forward to a weekend at home."

"Your parents aren't back yet, are they?"

"No, but my grandparents and great grandmother are there. You'll like them. You'll like the place, too. It's real peaceful. I hope you like the animals. I miss them too."

"Hmm," he said. Peace. The warrior's goal. What bullshit.

Out of habit he always scanned the cars in the motel when they returned in the evenings. The place had about thirty rooms. Tonight there were only ten cars and trucks there. He recognized five as belonging to medical people, concentrated in the half of the "U" nearest the office. Their two rooms were at the bottom of the "U" on the opposite side. The clerk told him that was because they only had two pair of adjoining rooms and that was where they were. There hadn't been any other lodgers at that end since Monday, but tonight a tired white van was parked at the next to last room of the far leg of the "U." In the gathering darkness the drapes indicated the room lights were on inside.

He waited on the sidewalk while she unlocked her door.

"You wanna go eat in a bit?" he asked.

"Sure. In about an hour?"

"Fine."

He watched her go inside and close her door. The TV was on loud in the room where the van was. He waited to enter his own room until her drapes lit up. Can't be too careful when you're guarding a kid half from another planet.

He kept thinking about that as he visited the bathroom, turned on the window heat pump, and poured himself a little snort. He sat in one of the two chairs and propped his feet in the other.

The first time he'd seen the kid was in a forward deployment camp in Afghanistan two years ago. It was completely bizarre. She had floated down to a soft landing in the middle of the night in a tiny spaceship built on her mother's planet. Her parents, her brother, and a half-dead Robboman Coombs were with her. God almighty that was a weird night. Her mother was good-looking but all business. From another planet…Christ.

He was on the point of turning on the TV when he heard a commotion outside…a woman screaming? He jumped to his feet and parted the drapes. A mini-van was parked this side of the white van. Several people were struggling. One of them was the kid. Shit!

He flung open the door, took stock of the scene. The screaming woman was standing by the open middle door of the mini-van. A man in dark clothing was down on the pavement while a second was flailing away at the kid. Somehow the kid was ducking and juking and then the second man went down.

He yanked his pistol out of the ankle holster and was halfway there when a third man came boiling out of the room and crashed into the kid's back, smashing her against the front fender of the mini-van. He got there just in time to slam his pistol into the back of that man's neck, the son of a bitch. The God damned sorry bastard. He could kill the lousy piece of…the kid was hollering something. Stop? Stop what? The man before him slumped to the ground. He took a step back and looked around.

The kid had evidently had the breath knocked out of her. She'd sagged back against the van and slid to the pavement. The woman had both hands to her mouth, an expression of horror on her face. There was a toddler in a car seat in the van.

Fergus forced himself to calm down. The kid was ok for the moment. He looked at the woman.

"Do you know these guys?" he asked her.

She stared at him several seconds, finally shaking her head.

He pulled out his wallet and handed her a sheaf of twenties.

"I suggest you try another motel, ma'am," he said. "The cops'll be here soon, and you don't need this."

It took her several seconds to register what he said. She accepted the money, closed the middle door of the van, got in and left in a hurry. Two of the three men were still down. The third was rolling around in pain. He picked up the kid and carried her to her room as she protested in a strained voice that she was OK.

"Yeah, sure," he said, laying her on the bed. "I'll be right back."

After unlocking the door that connected to his room, he went out her room door and closed it, entered his room, locking the door, unlocked his adjoining door and went into her room and locked her outside door. He peeked out the drapes. One of the mugs had made it to his hands and knees. Let the healing begin.

The kid was curled up on her side, still struggling for breath, holding a tissue over her nose. The tissue had bloody smears on it.

He picked up the room phone, dialed the desk, and told the clerk there'd been a fight and to call the cops.

Now for this crazy kid. What in God's name did she think she was doing? In fact, why the hell not ask her?

"What in God's name did you think you were doing?"

He started mopping blood off her nose and upper lip. She pulled back.

"What do you mean what was I doing? That man was roughing up that woman. He was probably going to rape her! She had a *child* in her car! What do you think I was doing? I stopped him!"

"Are you out of your mind? There were three of them! Each one outweighed you twice over!"

"I *did* stop two of them. I didn't see the third. That was my mistake. And I paid for it."

She had her hands wrapped around her middle. She'd hit that fender hard, right about belly button level, and her face had bounced off the hood but he didn't detect any ribs broken.

"You were lucky. *We* were lucky, God damn it! If you'd been killed I would have paid for it too, you little hellcat!"

"Me? You call me a hellcat? What about you? You were trying to kill that man! If I hadn't stopped you I think you'd have kept hitting him until you did kill him!"

"Yeah, well…. Tell you what. See if you can heal yourself, kid. I've done about all I can for now."

## Chapter 20

Clio had taken two ibuprofens a half hour earlier but she still hurt from head to hips. The room was dark. Fergus had turned out the lights when he returned to his own room. He said to leave them off until the cops had gone.

Sure enough, five minutes later the drapes started showing soft flashes of red and blue. She could hear men talking on the sidewalk outside. Fergus must have left her out of his narrative: no one knocked on her door, for which she was grateful. The police left and quiet returned.

She didn't regret stopping those two men. It wasn't all that dangerous since they didn't have guns or knives and she was able to face them one at a time. They were big and slow, and not familiar with the martial arts moves she used. Fergus was right about her being foolish, though. She should have been more aware of her surroundings, should not have been surprised by the third man.

That and the physical pain were only two of many things that bothered her.

Another was the unpleasant feeling of coming down from an adrenaline rush. She had seen it happen to her mother several times but hadn't appreciated how weak and shivery she would feel. Deep breaths helped clear her head, but they also hurt her abdomen.

Fergus himself was another worry. The savagery in his face as he continued to punch that third man was frightening. It was as if something had snapped in him. He had called himself "edgy," but what she had seen went way beyond that.

As watchful as she was normally, he was more so. He reacted to unexpected stimuli like a cat, as if permanently tense and ready to jump. Maybe he had some degree of post-traumatic stress disorder—after as much combat as he would have been involved in, it seemed possible. Then there was his crack about the ineffectiveness of rehabilitation therapists. Either he had given up on them, or they had given up on him; which of the two wasn't clear. But it was worrisome. What kind of life could he lead in that state?

One worry, at least, was finally beginning to fade an hour after the event: Fergus's harsh words. Being shouted at was a new and unpleasant experience. Her initial hurt feelings caused her to snap back, which didn't help matters. Now, mostly calmed down, she regretted her words.

She sat up carefully, using her arms to take weight off her abdomen, and sipped some water. She had reduced pain in other people—could she do so for herself? She might have tried except for one thing. Healing required her to concentrate, to focus from a calm center and a positive mental state.

She didn't have that tonight, not even close.

In the adjoining room, Fergus sat in one of the chairs between the bed and the window. The gloom provided by the light leaking from the bathroom was all that was necessary for mulling over the events of the previous hour.

The two cops seemed basically competent. They accepted his story of rescuing a just-arrived young mother from a bunch of drunken louts. They'd check her out with the desk clerk, which was good, and they'd verify that he was associated with the U.N.M. med team working at the high school. It helped that he was in his t-shirt. They'd connected the tattoo on his forearm with him being a former Navy SEAL with medical training. That made running three miscreants off by himself more plausible.

He described the van. They searched the room and came up with beer and booze bottles, a smear of coke dust on a table, some shreds of weed, and a collection of fingerprints. When they left they said they'd keep an eye on the motel and the middle school for a few days. They probably wouldn't, but he could handle that job himself.

He took a generous sip of Johnny Walker and poured in another two fingers from the pint bottle.

OK, so he hadn't taken out three ragmops himself. The kid had accounted for two. How the hell had she done that? She was fast and in great shape, yes, and maybe she had gone to martial arts classes with her mother like she said, and maybe she had learned some great moves, but this had not been a gym fight. A sparring session in a class and a real fight were two completely different things. People with no combat experience usually fell apart when a fight was for real. Even decently trained cops screwed up more often than not in combat situations. Hell, half his arduous SEAL training had been about thinking fast, acting with discipline, and adapting to changing situations on the fly.

The truth was probably that the kid had been extraordinarily lucky. She sure folded up like a cheap card table once the wind had been knocked out of her.

He took another snort of whisky. His left hand was stiffening up. He held it up to the faint light coming through the drapes. Two skinned knuckles; all four hurt. He remembered slamming the side of his pistol into bozo number three with his right hand. He must have continued with his left, but he couldn't recall it. The kid implied that he'd hit the guy time after time. That wasn't like him. Had he blacked out? What did the therapists call that…combat rage? Something like that.

God damn it, what was the matter with him? He'd worked his ass off and gone through hell to become one of the elite few, one of the best soldiers in the world, and he'd made it. He'd been part of an amazing team, a team with esprit, with guys he could rely on and who could rely on him. They'd taken difficult, dangerous assignments one after another and made them routine. He was proud of that, even though he had to keep it to himself.

And now…what was there? Not a hell of a lot. He could be some kind of ancillary SEAL, maybe, behind a desk. He could write a book. (Not.) He could be a security consultant. But where would he ever find another team like that? Where was the challenge and the excitement? What was there to look forward to?

His glass was empty. He picked up the bottle. There was a bare splash in the bottom. He tilted it gently and watched the golden liquid flow back and forth. Then he removed the cap and drained it.

On the other side of the double doors, Clio had finally calmed down. She got up, went into the bathroom, and looked at herself in the mirror. Her face was mostly clean, the nose and left cheek a slight reddish purple. There'd likely be more bruising later. Her abdomen was still sore, but she'd get over it. She took a hot shower and felt better.

She lay on the bed, pulled out her Kindle, and tried to read with little success when car headlights flashed on the drapes. She stood against the wall and pulled the drapes back an inch to look out. A woman was getting out of a car. She carried a large plastic bag and knocked on Fergus's door. Words were exchanged and the woman got back in the car and drove off. A minute later Fergus knocked softly on the adjoining door, opening it a few inches.

"Need some pizza?" he asked.

Did she ever. He had ordered drinks too. The pizza was still hot. It was wonderful. She was in a much better mood by the time she had finished.

"That was great. Thank you," she said.

"You bet," he replied.

"Did you learn anything about those men from the police?"

"No. They found some dope in the room. They might be dealers. They were certainly users."

"I wonder if they'll come back."

"I doubt it. But we'll take no chances. Never underestimate the power of a stupid person. Or three."

She winced as she shifted position in the chair.

"Are you hurting?"

"Some. I took two ibuprofens."

He nodded but said nothing.

"You're wondering why I don't heal myself."

"I am?"

"Well, aren't you? It's logical that you would be."

"It is?"

"You're being annoying again, Fergus. I've never tried working on myself and I don't feel like starting now."

"Right."

"Anyway, I think I don't want to wait till Saturday to go home. I'm tired. I need a break. Let's head back in the morning, OK?"

"I promised the nurses an early lunch. They set up things by 7:30, you know. We could leave about 10."

"Perfect."

He put the empty pizza box in the bag, picked up his soda, and headed for the door.

"Oh, and Fergus?" she said.

"Yeah?"

"Thanks."

"You're welcome."

"Not for the food this time. I meant thanks for taking care of that third man."

"Ah," he said. "You're welcome for that too." He started through the door but paused. "You did good, kid," he added. His face was unreadable. "See you in the morning." And he passed into his room, closing the adjoining door with a soft click.

## Chapter 21

At the unlikely hour of 8:00 am Ben Bianchi found himself parked across the street from the Tasajillo Middle School, yawning constantly but with hope hot in his breast. The rising sun streaming in the open window made his eyes water, but it had to be that way: in his hands at last was the gadget Dunston had had his boffins create and which he had delivered to Ben in person at the Albuquerque airport the previous afternoon. It looked to be a wonderful invention, potentially worth millions to SANECOR's less scrupulous journalists in the future, provided it worked as demonstrated.

Dunston had instructed him in its operation before running to catch a return flight—something juicy was developing with the royals, he said. The device wasn't complicated. Dunston had programmed his own cell phone ID code into it as well as the code of the phone which had called Ana Darcy's cell phone. When Dunston stood on the other side of the airport parking lot and made a call on his phone, the ID on the thing in Bianchi's hand had blinked furiously. Excellent!

The unit was not large—about as big as a baby's forearm—but the antenna was a small umbrella the size of a dessert plate. It was necessary to point it out the open window when in use but for now he held it inside the car lest passersby notice. There were two extra sets of batteries on the seat beside him, along with a $1500 digital camera, billed to SANECOR, of course.

If anyone in the school used that same phone, he would know about it. Sooner or later, though, he'd have to pee. That could be a problem.

Tucker Crawley's life was becoming a living hell. Every damned thing that could go wrong had gone wrong, and today wasn't likely to be better. He threw his cigarette stub out the window and lit another. His throat hurt like a son of a bitch, but not from the smokes. That fucking girl, a goddam scrawny teenager, had somehow popped him in the throat and left him wheezing so hard he damn near passed out. And he was the one trying to stop that stupid asshole Fdez from hassling that woman! Christ, it was hard to find good help nowadays. He needed Fdez as interpreter, but Bagger was good only for his brute strength. He could be replaced, easy.

How difficult was it to understand the business plan? Guns for dope. It should be simple, right? Sell it but don't smell it, right? Any jackass should know that. But Fdez and Bagger? Nooo, those dumb shits had to "test" it a little. And see where it got them: go a little crazy, do something stupid, and get the beating of their lives, the turds.

He had been content with a little booze, himself. Set the example, right? Well, anyone who wouldn't learn from the example would become the example. Bagger got whaled so hard he might be dead by the end of the day, and good riddance. There's your example.

The sale and the transfer hadn't gone perfectly: there'd been trouble. That was followed by trouble with his crew. And they'd had to run like muggers to avoid even more trouble with the cops. And now he had to face Schultz, the end of the line for trouble. He wasn't afraid of many people, but cross Schultz, screw up bad, and you could end up sleeping with the maggots. Schultz didn't put up with incompetence.

He slowed and took his exit, lighting another cigarette while he did so. Might should light two. Gotta get his broken ass pumped for this meeting. Had to be face to face. Schultz avoided phones when the subject matter was business. It was bound to be unpleasant.

Schultz's headquarters was on the western fringes of Albuquerque where civilization thinned out to junkyards, ramshackle bars, and rundown houses. He and his wife worked from a double-wide trailer at the back of a gravel parking area, the whole surrounded by an eight foot privacy fence. The sign on the fence said "Sportsmen's Guns & Pawn," over the words "Second Amendment Spoken Here" in foot-high red letters. Two pickups with oversize knobby tires were parked at the nostalgic hitching post out front. An American flag hung limply from an angled pole off the front gallery. You'd never guess that this was a multi-million dollar outfit.

He pulled open the iron-bound door under two surveillance cameras and entered to the sound of a tinkling bell.

Cassie, Schultz's solid, platinum blonde wife, was showing automatic pistols to a man and woman. Two lay on a green rubber mat along with laser scopes and empty magazines of various sizes. The woman hefted a small automatic and pointed it at the trophy deer on the wall. To the right, two bearded men in camouflage shirts and pants were poking around a display of black powder accessories. Cassie nodded minimally at him.

"Tucker," she said.

"Cassie," he replied. "He in back?"

"If he's not in the office, he's in the workshop."

"Right."

He walked to the end of the glass display case offering rows and rows of lethal-looking pistols. With a lump in his stomach to match the lump in his windpipe he pushed through the door to the inner sanctum. Schultz was at his desk.

Cassie ran the store, but Schultz made the serious money: guns for drugs, basically. The profit margin was incredible. Mexican drug lords loved American arms. Lately they had been going for fully automatic assault rifles, rocket-powered grenade launchers, even mines and machine guns. They generally paid in cocaine, crystal meth, weed, and whatever else was in demand in the states. Schultz sold it and washed the cash somehow. What he did with it then was a mystery.

Tucker was never comfortable around Schultz. He was a big man, muscular once but now running to fat. If you overlooked his shaved head, rakish chin whiskers, and intense eyes, his pudgy face looked like a canned ham. He wasn't smiling.

"What's the report?" he said, omitting the pleasantries.

"Coulda been better," he admitted. There was no point in pretending different.

Shultz's eyes were cold.

"Details," he said.

"The Meskins only brought two thirds of what they promised. Said one of their mules got caught. So we only gave them two thirds of the arms. We left the rest at the shack and passed the goods on to the Chicago man, but he was pissed."

"Fuck. I am too."

"That ain't all. Bagger and Fdez got drunk and hassled a woman at the motel. I ran out to stop them, but there was already a guy there from another room who put them down, and me too." There was no way in hell he was going to admit that a pint-size girl had accounted for him and Fdez. "We had to bail outta there pronto," he continued. "The cops came after that, but we got away clean."

"*Fuck!* Are you sure?"

"Yeah, I'm sure. Fdez repainted the truck this morning, just in case." He'd used brown latex house paint. The truck smelled like crap. "Bagger was peeing blood this morning but we ain't takin' him to no doctor. If he dies, he dies."

"Are you telling me one guy whipped you three tough guys?"

"Yeah. The bastard was a real fighter, efficient. Like a professional."

Schultz's eyes narrowed.

"What'd he look like?"

"I didn't see him good, but he was average size. Short hair. He had a tattoo on one arm."

"Short hair? What kind of tattoo?"

"The light wasn't good. Maybe like a bird? Holding a fork? I couldn't really tell."

"*Are you shitting me?* A bird holding a fork?"

"Yeah. Maybe."

"FUCK!"

Schultz nearly came out of his chair. He had puffed up to a third bigger than normal. Tucker couldn't see why.

"What's that mean?"

"That's a SEAL tattoo! That's why he's a fighter! The fucker's a government man! God DAMN it! Sumbitchin' government men are sneaking around everywhere down here. They've been trying for months to nail my ass to the wall, the shits! DEA. ATF. FBI. Customs. All of 'em. I have this place swept for bugs twice a day because of those fuckers. I can't go to the crapper without worrying about who might be sneakin' up the pipe. Bastards!"

He slammed his desk with both hands, shot to his feet and began pacing, massaging his right fist with his left hand.

"Those assholes are gettin' too fucking close, *too fucking close*! I've had enough, Tucker! Enough! It's time to do something."

He sat back down, still raging. Tucker froze in place, trying to remain calm while Schultz glared at the wall. Finally, he spoke again.

"All right, godammit. I've been careful for years. They can't pin nothing on me. They can't connect us. That's what I pay you for. I want you to do two things. First, long range: if Bagger lives, fire him and find someone else. I leave it up to you whether to fire Fdez or not. He speaks Meskin, so if you do fire him, find someone else who can.

"Second thing, soon, like days, a week at most: find that government man. Just don't kill him. The fucking government will turn inside out if you kill him. But I want to meet that piece of shit! Can you do that, Tucker?"

Tucker held Schultz's gaze until finally he had to blink.

"Yeah. I'll find a way. I can do that."

It was 8:25 when Fergus delivered his second load of breakfast taquitos to the medical staff. The kid had been sleeping soundly when he left the motel at 5:30. She'd probably be up and ready to go now, and since no one else professed a need of food, they could leave early. He had four extra taquitos for them to eat on the road.

He was about to leave the gym when he saw that Axel Baldwin fellow headed inside. In his suit and with his hair slicked down he looked like an insurance salesman, or maybe a pill pusher from a pharmaceutical company. He held up and waited for him in the lobby.

"Good morning, Mr. Fergus," Baldwin said, holding out his hand. Fergus shook it.

"Morning," he replied. "I bet I know why you're here."

"I won't take that bet," Baldwin said, smiling engagingly. "I wish you could have seen Mr. Bianchi's improvement over the last few days. Meeting your niece did him a world of good. You were so very generous with your time. The poor man has been terribly ill, but something about your niece revived him more than anything in the last year, for a few days, anyway.

"He had another dose of chemotherapy yesterday. That always makes him feel bad. I think his depression is returning as well. He would hardly talk to me this morning.

"So yes, as you guessed, I came to ask you and your niece if you could possibly consider another visit. I know it's a terrible inconvenience, but do you think there's a chance you might be able to see him once more?"

Fergus thought a second.

"Well, maybe. I can't speak for my niece, but I'll ask her. That's one thing. Another is that she's pretty well exhausted after all her activity this week. Right now, she's headed home for the weekend to recharge. If she agrees to come, could I call and tell you later this morning?"

"Absolutely. That would be wonderful. Just telling Mr. Bianchi that she'll be coming in a few days will improve his weekend. I appreciate it too, I assure you."

They said their farewells, shook hands again, and Baldwin headed to the parking lot. Fergus inserted Baldwin's business card in his wallet, told the reception aide that he'd see them on Monday, and headed out himself.

He was ten steps from the gym when his cell phone buzzed. Blast! It was one more nurse, wanting a taquito. He looked at the bag of four in his hand. If he gave the nurse one, he could save another trip to the cafe. The kid might be willing to go halves with the third one, and they could get on the road that much sooner.

Four minutes later he tossed the bag with the remaining three taquitos on the seat and started the Corolla. Rather than take his usual route—a road crew had been working on that side earlier—he drove around the other side of the school and back to the motel to get the kid.

He was looking forward to a little recharging too.

Ben Bianchi nearly wet his pants when he saw the scanner's little light was blinking. That meant the phone that had called Ana Darcy was in use. Unbelievable! It worked! And of all things, there was a man outside the gym talking on a cell phone! He wagged the antenna back and forth to make sure. Yes, that was the phone and that was the man.

He grabbed the digital camera snapped a couple of shots. The man walked back into the gym. Score one for Dunston! First contact had been made. Excellent!

Did he get a decent photo? He had to know. He switched on the camera's view mode and thumbed to the best shot, zooming it to see more detail. It looked like...huh? That runner chap? The worker bee who fetched the food? This was no surgeon, no big shot, just a fellow who delivered food to his betters. Why the hell would Ana Darcy have anything to do with such a man? Something didn't add up here.

He'd been fooling with his camera too long. When he looked up, the man was back outside, getting into that little car he had been driving. It began to move. He tossed the camera on the seat beside him and started his own car. The prey was already out of sight behind other cars, but he was surely headed to one of the town's several inferior eateries. He pulled out and zoomed down the street only to come to a road crew and flagman working in the intersection in front of him. Four men were laying down new school zone markers. One had a blowtorch, one was sticking down broad, white stripes on the smoking-hot macadam, and a third was standing by with a heavy roller. The fourth man, holding a paddle that said "STOP," stepped to his car.

"We'll be through in a minute sir. Please stand by."

"Up your arse!" he mumbled, shifting into reverse.

A horn sounded behind him. Sodding hell! Another car! He was trapped!

He raged and fidgeted while the men took the requested minute and several more besides to let him through. The runner's car was out of sight, but he knew it had to be headed to one of three places. Once past the road crew, he headed toward the most obvious choice, the Mexican café, considering how and when to confront his mystery man. He hadn't thought of a cover story yet, but one would surely occur to him.

Axel Baldwin didn't regret the hour's drive to have a five minute conversation. It was a simple courtesy, really. A favor was always best requested in person. It was a matter of respect (and, not coincidentally, harder to turn down than with a phone call). He expected the girl, Clara Montez, would accept the invitation her uncle was bringing her. Healer or not, she had seemed intelligent and compassionate, so much so that to have offered to pay her would have offended her. He was sure of that. She was no fool. Mr. Bianchi certainly couldn't stop talking about her, and he was famous for not suffering fools.

As for himself, he rather enjoyed dealing with Mr. Fergus. He was direct and decisive, quite unlike what might be expected from an uncle moonlighting as a chaperone.

The parking lot, half full of cars and trucks, was quiet except for a woman behind him unloading a chattering child. He pushed the remote unlock button in his pocket and started to open the car door when a sudden movement in the near distance made him pause and looked over the roof of his car. Someone in a car parked on the street was aiming something...not a gun, fortunately...some kind of microphone? That was weird.

The microphone disappeared inside the car. Shortly after came a bright reflection in the same window, a small circle. It seemed a camera or telescope of some kind was being pointed at the gym. He glanced to his left. Mr. Fergus was walking out. The man was evidently photographing Mr. Fergus. How bizarre.

He got in the car, fastened the seat belt, started the engine, and eased to the exit as the paparazzo or spy or whatever he was pulled out and drove by in front of him.

Hey! He *knew* that face! It was…could it be….? It looked an awful lot like Mr. Bianchi's grandson Ben! Ben had visited his grandfather last week. Whatever was he doing taking photos of Mr. Fergus? This was totally perplexing. At least his boss had chosen the darkest available window tint for his Avalon. Ben didn't seem to have recognized him or even noticed him.

There was another close call when he found himself hemming Ben in at the road work site, but Ben blasted through it as soon as the flagman stepped aside.

How extremely odd. Should he mention this to Mr. Bianchi? Mr. Bianchi regarded his grandson as the feckless spawn of an irresponsible parent, and was never surprised by the exploits of either son or grandson, but why bother a sick man with such an oddity? On the other hand, Mr. Bianchi was deeply concerned about his family.

Undecided, he reached the highway and turned toward Santa Fe. He had at least an hour to think about it.

## Chapter 22

Traffic was light, so the kid could drive with one hand and eat with the other. Fergus was pleased she ceded him the third taquito in its entirety. He was getting a serious Jones for New Mexican food. The flour tortillas were still warm and smelling heavenly of warm flour. The cook had added green chile rajas to the scrambled eggs and potatoes (in all three) and sausage (in his), plus a few sprinkles of cilantro. They were perfect, and not available in Florida.

She said it would take five or six hours to get home, and she would leave it to him to decide whether or not they should stop for a late lunch. The kid's eating habits were strange. She could chow down with the best of them—he'd seen her do it—but most of the time she just nibbled. That might explain how she stayed lean.

The drive was pleasant enough. South of Albuquerque the forests played out, but desert mountains were usually visible in the distance. It was attractive country without being spectacular. She didn't chatter constantly, but she said she needed to fill him in on her family and animals.

With her parents and brother elsewhere, there were three people at home: her grandparents and great grandmother. Each knew different things about her mother and he needed to keep them straight.

Her grandfather and great grandmother knew her mother was really Ana Darcy, from the planet Thomo. (He still had trouble believing that himself.) They did *not* know, however, that Ana had been kidnapped by Al Khalifa, the number one terrorist in the world at the time, and had been rescued by her husband, children, and Rob Coombs, in an armed raid on a compound in northern Pakistan. (He had trouble believing that too.)

The grandparents did not know of the existence of the pod, Ana Darcy's little gravity-powered runabout, which had carried the rescuers halfway around the world to her and then located her in that isolated compound. Oddly enough, the great grandmother did know about the pod. The kid said she'd been taken up in it for a thrill. The old lady could keep her mouth shut, apparently.

The grandmother had a history of strokes. Sometimes her mind didn't track quite right and she said things she shouldn't. The family was afraid she might let out Ana's secret to her friends, or even blurt it out accidentally. Thus she did not know her daughter-in-law was Ana Darcy. She still believed the initial cover story about her son marrying a foreign student from Argentina. She loved her son's wife at any rate, and that was what mattered. It was safest, the kid suggested, that he not mention Ana at all, unless one of the others brought her up.

That would be no problem for him. His professional life had depended on remembering the details of briefings. He had given a lot of them himself.

He saw no reason to be briefed on her animals, but she did it anyway. They had a couple of dogs. He'd never had a problem with dogs. And she had three cats. Fine. He liked cats too. But she wanted to "introduce" him personally to the animals early on. That was OK if she insisted…but were introductions to animals really necessary? Whatever….

"I think I got that," he said. "Now, here's something for you. That Baldwin fellow came to see me this morning. He said his boss perked up considerably after your visit. But he's had more chemo and is down again. He'd like to see you again, if you can manage it."

"Oh," she said. She frowned. "Well…that's hard for me, Fergus. I really can't do much to help him. I don't think he can last very long, the poor man."

"I'm not sure you need to do anything for him. From what Baldwin told me, Bianchi livened up when he told him he was coming to ask you to visit. Maybe he just likes you, you think?"

"It's probably because he's so fascinated by Doro's painting. I guess I could see him again. But Monday and Tuesday will be long, busy days at the clinic. That's when the specialists are scheduled. Wednesday should be better."

"OK. Baldwin asked me to let him know. I'll call him now."

He pulled the business card out of his wallet and left Baldwin the message. Then he slid the phone back in his pocket, sighing quietly.

He wasn't looking forward to the weekend. The home of the first alien to come to Earth from another planet had to be practically an armed compound, probably like the one that old Bianchi fellow lived in, with controlled access, lights at night, and a gate guard. There might be a tiny, manicured lawn for the animals, with the adults cooped up inside. It would be one thing if Ana Darcy herself were there, but with only three old people and the kid it was bound to be tedious, and probably awkward.

Still, he could take it: he was being paid well. He could relax later, when he got back to Miami.

Tucker was a worried man. Responsibility did that to a person, and he hated responsibility. It was making him good money so far, but it could also get him killed if he wasn't careful. He spent the whole drive back to the shack thinking about how he might learn more about that goddam "government man," if that's what he was, who had busted up their party. The high school girl who had done most of the busting was not as much of a problem because ultimately, Schultz was the problem, and it was Schultz who wanted the government man. Tucker didn't need to run the extra risk of messing with a schoolgirl. He already had enough trouble.

The road took him through Tasajillo, and on a whim he stopped at the El Faro motel to talk to the clerk. There were only a few cars and trucks in the place and none at the far end where the thug in question had been. The clerk claimed not to have been on duty that night and couldn't give him a name even if he had. It was against the law, he said. Even the offer of twenty dollars couldn't loosen his conscience. But he did say that the medical people had gone home for the weekend, and would be back on Monday.

"What medical people?" Tucker asked. The clerk was willing to accept the twenty to explain that a bunch of doctors and nurses and volunteer gofers were holding a two-week clinic at the middle school. They'd done a week, and were coming back for one more.

He thought about that as he resumed his drive to the shack. The "government man" might be coming back. That would simplify things considerably.

He was headed up into the forest in the horrible-smelling van (fuckin' Fdez had painted the dashboard with that goddam acrylic latex too) when an idea dawned on him. Jesse! Jesse Connor. They had met as cellmates at the Springer Correctional Center. Tucker had done a year, but Jesse had been caught with only a few ounces and got out early for good behavior.

Jesse's experience at the Correctional Center actually had been corrective, unlike Tucker's: he had got his LVN certificate and was now working at a nursing home in Santa Fe. He had some medical training and just as important, a uniform! A further lucky stroke: LVN's weren't paid for shit. An extra couple of hundred would be a big deal to him.

Jesse lived behind the Harley-Davidson dealer in Bernalillo. Tucker would cycle down there Saturday and slip him a hundred or two to call in sick Monday and go to Tasajillo to volunteer as a gofer. Tucker chuckled to himself. Hell, Jesse had the gift of gab and was twice as smart as Fdez and Bagger put together. He could dig up info on the "government man" and no one there would be the wiser. And there was nothing illegal about it!

Maybe that would be enough to get Schultz off his back.


They were about two hours from their destination, according to the kid's estimate, when her cell phone tweetled. She put it to her ear and listened a minute. When she began speaking, it was in some language he caught not a word of. It wasn't Spanish or French or German, or Pashto or Dari, which he had heard enough to recognize. Best guess: it was her mother's native language. He couldn't remember the name of it, but it was soft sounding with a lot of back-of-the-mouth sounds, kind of like Russian, maybe. Interesting. The kid could speak Spanish, too. It was nearly fifteen minutes before she slid the phone back into her jeans.

"That was Mom," she said.

"Yeah? So how is she?"

"OK. Did she tell you where she was going?"

"A conference, she said."

"Right. At Davos."

"Davos? I didn't know that. That's a big deal."

"I guess. Mom hates that sort of thing. She said she left early. She's going to meet Dad and Julio and do some sightseeing for a week. She was calling from the Houston airport. That's why she spoke in Luvit."

"The Houston airport? Does she have security?"

"No. She uses disguises."

"You're kidding."

"I've watched her practice. She can change into a college girl on spring break in less than ten minutes. Mr. Coombs said she was a Russian boy once. Fooled him."

"What a hoot."

"She said they should be home next weekend. You might get to see her again."

"I wouldn't mind at all. Your mom is pretty cool, I hope you know."

She checked her mirror, flipped on the turn signal, and changed lanes to pass an elderly pickup piled high with scrap metal. She cancelled the signal and changed back to the right lane.

"If you say so," she said.

By mid-afternoon he figured they were an hour from their destination. He was confident they were not being followed. The kid asked if he was hungry.

"About like you, probably," he said.

She phoned her grandfather, told him their ETA, and listened a short while. She said they'd see him soon and pressed the off button.

"He's taking my grandmother and great-grandmother to a garden club meeting and then to the grocery store. They'll be home a little after we get there. We'll have supper with them in a couple hours, probably. Will that be OK?"

"Sure."

He concentrated on the scenery. Las Cruces was on the slopes of some truly formidable desert mountains. The kid said they were named the Organ Mountains because early explorers thought they looked like the ranks of pipes in a pipe organ. He couldn't see it, but agreed they were majestic.

She left the Interstate and began negotiating city traffic. Like Santa Fe, Las Cruces had a different look from other American cities he had seen. Most homes and smaller buildings had flat roofs, often with beams sticking out of the walls near the top, sort of pueblo style. Many seemed to be built of stone, masonry, or adobe, and none that he saw of framed wood. There were lots of arched doors. If not for the cars, businesses, and billboards he could have been in another country. He was musing about other cities with unique looks—San Francisco, New Orleans, Portland—when the kid spoke up.

"This is the town of Mesilla, on the right," she said.

It didn't look much different from what he'd already seen except there were more houses jammed together and fewer splashy stores with metal siding.

"It's very old," she went on. "Las Cruces has almost grown around it, but it's the nearest town to us. If we drive somewhere tomorrow, I'll show you the plaza and the church at one end. There's a great restaurant and even a bookstore on the plaza."

No comment seemed required but he managed a polite "Hmm."

After another mile or two the area became more rural: fewer buildings, with farmland appearing between and behind them.

"This is our street, I guess you'd say, Highway 28. It follows the Rio Grande, more or less, off to the right, all the way to El Paso. There are huge pecan orchards further on. Dad said they produced twenty six million pounds last year."

"No kidding!"

That really did surprise him. On the right the horizon was solid desert. On the left was a craggy desert mountain rage. Pecan trees? The glimpses he'd seen of the Rio Grande didn't suggest it had enough water for acres of pecan orchards. He was still mulling that over when they rounded a bend. Not far ahead was a tall adobe wall on the left. The kid slowed the car, checked her mirrors, and turned in through an entrance. So this was it, the home of Earth's first extraterrestrial.

Technically it was a gated compound: there was a gate, but it was wide open, and there was no guard. She eased past a substantial, two story adobe house, past a smaller house off to the right, to park next to a RAV-4 and another Corolla. The kid jumped out and began hugging two large, excited yellow dogs. They looked alertly at him when he opened his door, but she said something to them in a foreign language and they sat. They looked like Rhodesian ridgebacks, a male and female. The male had to weigh as much as the kid.

"This is Rani," the kid said, indicating the female, "and that's Rajah."

She came around the car, rubbed one of his hands between hers, and presented them to the dog to sniff. She said something unintelligible and both dogs ran off.

"C'mon," she said, popping the trunk. "Let's take our stuff inside."

He looked over the place as they went in. There was a barn in the far left corner. At least a dozen huge trees—he had no idea what kind—provided shade for most of the enclosure. He could see plowed fields through a wrought iron gate in the back wall, apparently intended for vehicle access to the barn. In the distance were the kid's "Organ Mountains."

To his surprise the extraterrestrial celebrity Ana Darcy lived in the more humble, smaller house with her family. It was clearly an elderly structure with additions built on later, not quite random but certainly not out of a builder's book of house plans.

Inside the front door was a single family area that included a kitchen, dining room, and living room. It was neat and attractive but neither opulently furnished nor terribly large. The kid led him to a newer section in back, two rows of smaller rooms separated by a narrow patio open to the sky. Her room was first on the right, then a bathroom, and then the guest room, where he was to bunk. Her brother's room was across the patio, tucked in with a gym and laundry room.

She greeted her two slinky Siamese cats, curled up on her bed, and then dragged him back outside.

"You need to meet my other cat," she said. "Have a seat over there and give me a couple minutes, please."

She indicated some lawn furniture behind the main house, arranged around a table and a barbecue grill.

It was a pleasant evening. He took a seat and watched her go inside the barn. The barn was two stories high, of modest size, board and batten construction, with a cupola on top, and in decent repair.

The two dogs lay down under the table.

Why was she being coy about this cat? It must be special. A bobcat? It would be great if it were a bobcat.

He stretched his legs and contemplated the garden areas along the walls in several locations. It looked like Ana Darcy might be a gardener too. So how would he feel if he were on a totally strange planet, with different plants, different animals, different everything? Damned uncomfortable, he thought. But that's what happened to Ana Darcy. From the looks of this place, she seemed to have figured it out pretty well. No wonder she prizes her privacy. If people knew she lived here it would completely screw this up for her.

He breathed in the rich smell of a river and plowed fields. Not bad, for being in a damn desert, not bad at all. After dinner, maybe the kid would have things to do or friends to visit and he could find a way to enjoy some serious nips.

The side door of the barn opened and the kid headed his way. She sat in a chair next to him.

He looked at her.

"Wait," she said. "She's cautious."

He waited.

He waited some more.

The kid clucked her tongue. A cat head appeared in the doorway. It stepped halfway out the door, looked their way, and hissed. It was startlingly loud.

"It's all right," she whispered. "She doesn't meow. She hisses. She has lots of different ones. That one means 'I see you. I'm watching you.'"

She clucked her tongue again. The cat came to her ten feet at a time, pausing to check on all sides, staying to the side of the yard away from him.

It was no bobcat, but it was stunningly beautiful, whatever it was. It had the shape and approximate tawny color of a mountain lion, but it was smaller, a little over knee high and maybe forty pounds. The face was sharply featured, with fierce pale blue eyes rimmed in black with white margins. The ears were its best feature—tall in proportion to the head, and black on the backs, with additional long tufts of black hairs that flopped this way and that as she swiveled her ears.

It approached the kid close enough for her to scratch its jaw. It hissed again, showing some very serious fangs.

"I'm watching you too, kitty, believe me," he whispered.

In civilian life he'd seen his family's angry housecat make two veterinarians and an aide back off. The vet told his father that if a cat had a stinger in its tail, it would have six ways to hurt you instead of just five. This animal could have emptied a football stadium. But the kid didn't seem worried, so he decided not to be worried.

"That's a gorgeous cat," he said, in a low voice. "What the hell is it?"

"She's a caracal. That means 'black ears.' They're from Africa."

"Super," he said. "Maybe tomorrow she'll let me touch her."

"Probably," she said. "She gets used to new people pretty quick. I'll exercise her tomorrow and you can watch. She can jump eight feet."

"If she were after me, I could jump ten."

The kid actually cracked a smile.

"You wish."

## Chapter 23

Ana expected to be exhausted after fast-forwarding through eight time zones, changing from a college girl on vacation to a businesswoman in the Houston airport, and finally meeting her husband and son, but she hadn't anticipated a two hour taxi ride through heavy traffic to a marina in Galveston. They couldn't converse much with a cab driver present, but that didn't matter: she dozed leaning against Matt for most of the way. The ride cost $200!

Fortunately, the marina had a yacht club with a restaurant. The smell of food perked Ana up remarkably. Husband, wife, and son eagerly sampled the area's fresh seafood: fried crawfish tails, shrimp ceviche, and grilled Gulf red snapper.

To his parents' surprise Julio declined dessert. He couldn't wait to see the yacht, and volunteered to find the slip where it was supposed to be moored and report back. Matt shared cheesecake with Ana, and once that had disappeared he ordered crème de menthe over ice for them both.

Finally, they could talk. Ana was subdued.

"I'm tired Matt, more tired than usual after a trip." She sighed. "I've done many things I regret in my life, but this time…."

"I can't agree, wife. You have a kind heart. Everyone knows that."

She looked down at the deep green liqueur and ice.

"One person's rudeness doesn't justify another's."

"On Thomo, maybe," Matt said gently. "Not here, not always. Once again, sugar, you've united the entire planet. Believe me, everyone wants to give you a medal for finally putting that jerk in his place."

He picked up his glass.

"Here," he said, holding it before her, "To your health, babe."

She barely smiled, but she raised her own glass.

"*Nazd rawii.*"

They sipped. The liqueur was smooth and sinus-expanding. Ana sipped again.

This wasn't the time to review his wife's harrowing scrapes. Matt changed subjects.

"Did you talk to Clio?"

"I called her from the airport. She's at home for the weekend."

"Ah, good. Did she say anything about her medical experiences?"

"A little. She said the clinic was perfect for seeing a wide variety of health problems, but she's still trying to understand what she finds and how she responds."

"How's she doing with Fergus?"

"She said they get along well enough, but he's no Rob Coombs."

"Well, it's kind of awkward for a seventeen year old girl to have an ex-Navy SEAL for a bodyguard. Did she mention any problems?"

"No, just that she wants to rest a few days. She's going back for the second week Monday. She saw Doro Mendoza at his art gallery exhibit in Santa Fe, though."

"Great! If the exhibit is still there the week after next, maybe we can...."

He stopped in mid-sentence. Julio was back. He pulled out a chair and sat down.

"I found the yacht! You gotta see it! The captain said we'll sail the middle of the morning tomorrow, after they install a part for their radar. But we can sleep on it tonight! It's fancy! Wait till you see the cabins!"

Matt looked at his wife. A tiny smile played at the corners of her mouth. She held up her glass of barely sipped crème de menthe.

"Get me a plastic cup to pour this into and I'm ready."


Fergus had predicted Ana Darcy's family would be high society, but he was pleasantly surprised to find they were pretty much regular people. More to the moment, the women were terrific cooks.

The table had been cleared of all but dessert, small dishes of pale green pistachio ice cream. He was really going to miss New Mexican cuisine and he told them so.

"Thank you, Mr. Fergus," Julia said, obviously pleased.

"Everyone likes it, including us," said the kid's great-grandmother. "That's why we fix it."

"How come it isn't more widely known?" he asked.

"I think it's the chilies," Bert Méndez said. "They don't travel well. You have to be here to really enjoy them at their best."

The matriarch was studying Clio.

"Clio, dear, you look droopy, child," she said. "Why don't you head off to bed?"

"I will, Abuelita. Let's clean up first, though."

"¡Ay, qué tontería! Don't worry about that. We'll just load the dishwasher and push the button. We do that every day of the week. It's easy. You run along, dear. You need to sleep."

The kid suppressed a yawn.

"Maybe I will. I'll help more tomorrow." She gave each family member a quick kiss on the cheek, adding, before she left, "I'll leave the front door open, Fergus, but please lock it when you come in."

"Leave it open? Is that safe?" he asked.

"It's fine. The dogs are watching. Good night, Fergus."

"Buenas noches, chica."

His accent was terrible and he knew it. The great-grandmother's eyes twinkled.

"Well," she said, "I think I'll go push that dishwasher button. Julia?"

"I'm tired too. I believe I'll go up and get ready for bed. Please excuse me, Mr. Fergus."

Fergus watched as the little elevator chair on the staircase smoothly carried her upstairs.

Bert leaned toward him and whispered, "It's safer that way. She's had some strokes. She's not always steady on her feet." He pushed back from the table. "Many evenings I like a beer after supper. Would you join me?"

"You bet."

The great-grandmother came out of the kitchen as Bert went in.

"Clio has always had excellent manners, Mr. Fergus. Her brother does too. Why does she call you simply Fergus?"

"I asked her to, ma'am. That's what everyone has called me since I joined the Navy."

"I see. Well. Everyone except me, then. I'm sorry. I'm too old to change. Good night, Mr. Fergus."

"Good night, ma'am. Thanks for the terrific meal."

The little chair had returned to the bottom of the stairs. He watched the older lady rise out of sight as Bert returned carrying two bottles. He handed him one.

"Here we go. Why don't we move to the parlor?"

Fergus looked at his bottle. There was an Aztec warrior on the label.

"Indio beer? Never heard of it."

"It's made in Monterrey. They don't export much. I guess they drink most of it themselves. Don't blame them. Pick a chair while I close the drapes."

He tried it.

"It's good." He took another sip. "I was wrong. It's excellent."

"Yeah, I think so too. It looks dark but it's mellow rather than hoppy."

Fergus was happy. He hadn't expected to find good company or booze at Ana Darcy's house, and here were both. Fortune had smiled on him for once. Bert waved him to a chair and sat down himself.

"Have you followed the news in the last week, Fergus?"

"Not much. Why?"

"My daughter-in-law has been featured. Some rich bozo tried to kiss her in public. She, uh, she refused. Spectacularly."

"Your granddaughter talked to her on our way down here. She said her mother wasn't having a good time. She was heading back to meet her husband in Houston."

"Right. She created quite a stir at the time. We decided not to tell Clio about it if she hadn't already heard. Julia watches all those tabloid TV shows and they all played it up big. I was afraid Julia would mention it at dinner, but she didn't. Might've been because my mother told her to keep it quiet. She listens to my mother."

"I do too. She's impressive."

"I need to thank you for keeping an eye on Clio. That's got to have its awkward moments."

"Oh, not really."

"I'd almost have let her go by herself, but her mother wouldn't hear of it."

"You can't really blame her."

"No, you can't, that's true. Anyway, I hope you're not bored out of your mind. Do you know what she's doing with that medical bunch?"

"She said she's trying to learn more about healing."

"Right. She can heal. I mean really. I've seen her do it. Julia had a major stroke at our dining table two years ago—all of a sudden stopped talking and nearly fell out of her chair. Clio jumped up and put her hands on Julia's head, and in a few minutes she was all right. The hospital ER found no sign of a stroke. I have no idea how she did it. Neither does Clio. That bothers her. She's trying everything she can think of to figure it out. Her mother's never seen the like either, not even on her home planet."

Fergus sipped his beer and thought back to the first time he'd seen Clio: in the back of that crazy little space ship of her mother's, with Coombs' head clasped tightly to her breast. The SEAL medic said Coombs had been hit so hard he had a hairline skull fracture and a concussion and should have died in minutes.

Maybe the kid really did save his ass.

But whatever, she was never going to get her girly little hands on his goddam leg.

Ninety minutes later he headed back to Ana's house with the beginnings of a welcome buzz clouding his brain, thanks to three better-than-average beers. Two or three more nips from his stash and he'd be there. One of the ridgebacks huffed at him in the darkness but let him enter without a mauling.

He locked the front door, soft-walked through the living area to the patio, visited the guest john on the left side, and crossed to the right to head back to his room.

The kid had left her door open. One of her silver Siamese cats was nestled against the door jamb, paws folded underneath, eyes closed. He glanced inside as he passed and saw only a lump under the covers and the tip of a large cat tail slowly waving back and forth on the other side of the lump.

The kid was better guarded than her mother could ever hope for.

## Chapter 24

"Your eggs are cold, sir. Can I get you some more?"

"No, thanks, Alice. I've had enough breakfast. I'd like to move to the sun room, please."

"Certainly, sir."

He was depressed this morning and he knew it. Axel had just departed, after reporting what little he had been able to learn regarding grandson Ben's real purpose in New Mexico. That had killed his appetite more than the medicine had. Axel had told him the managing editor of SANECOR's news division said young Ben was on assignment from his father, with an unlimited, non-reporting expense account. He knew no particulars of that assignment but he did know the division currently had no stories in progress dealing with the American west.

Alice steadied him as he gingerly moved to the recliner by the window.

"Thank you, Alice."

"Would you like some coffee, sir?"

"No. The chemo has ruined my taste for it. I'll have tea."

"Yes, sir."

He sat lost in thought. Sun room? Today was overcast. Wind and rain were predicted. It suited his mood perfectly.

On assignment from his father, eh? So now the young scoundrel was sneaking around a medical team that was providing basic health services in Tasajillo, New Mexico? For his *father*?

That father, his own son, was not a complicated person to those who knew him well. Indeed, he was a base, primal, barely civilized human being. What the devil could he possibly care about a rural medical team?

He found himself staring at the opposite wall where an original Picasso hung, a colored pencil sketch in six lines of a clown's head. Too damned cheerful. Far more appropriate to have Bellini's Head of St. John the Baptist. He refocused on the steaming tea cup perched on the newspapers at his elbow.

Silvio, Silvio, what are you up to?

Fergus awoke at dawn as usual, relatively clear-headed, not always usual. He allowed himself a minute in bed for orientation. The bedroom was small, neat, and simple. He had slept in Ana Darcy's house. How bizarre.

He sat up, put on his prosthesis, and stood. The window looked west. Dawn had reached the sky but not the trees around the house. He stretched, pulled on his jeans, and tucked in the t-shirt. This was the best he generally felt each day.

He eased into the bathroom between his room and the kid's, noting that her bedroom door was closed. She was probably sleeping late.

Fifteen minutes later he was shaved, dressed, and ready to see what might be edible in the kitchen, but then he heard a dog barking outside. From the patio it sounded like it was on the east side. He unlatched the gate at the south end of the patio and stepped out into the yard.

The kid was there, facing away from him, in a blue sweat suit, evidently doing some kind of tai chi routine, going slowly from pose to pose. It looked serious, the movements smooth and balanced.

One of the dogs was trying to provoke the kid's big cat. The cat was ignoring it from a comfortable crouched position where it could stare out the back gate.

The dog noticed him and stopped barking at the cat, which prompted the kid to notice him as well.

"Good morning, Fergus," she said.

"Morning."

"Did you sleep well?"

"I did, yes. Is this part of your wakeup routine?"

"Huh? Oh. No. The dogs and I went for a run. I'm loosening up now, that's all."

"A run? In the dark?"

"It wasn't that dark. We only went four miles." He must have frowned. She added, "Not on the road. Through the fields." She nodded toward the back gate. "It's safe." He kept staring. "I wasn't able to work out enough during the week," she explained.

"Right," he said.

She picked up a towel and water bottle.

"Are you ready for breakfast?"

"I think so."

"Good. Me too."

It wasn't hard to feed Fergus. He was agreeable to everything. That bothered Clio.

He acted like an employee. He *was* an employee, in a sense, but he was also more than that: he was a certified hero and former Navy SEAL whose team had caught the world's most wanted terrorist. It was embarrassing for her, a high school girl (which is how she thought of herself), to be his "boss." If he were only more outgoing and friendlier, it would be easier to have him as her shadow. She looked up to him, but he wasn't easy to be with.

He wasn't old. He had exceptional abilities and accomplishments. He was in good physical shape and not bad looking. But he wasn't companionable.

At least this weekend they didn't have to be together. She made sure of that. She was home for lunch and dinner but otherwise visiting friends, working out in her mother's gym, or looking in on Stallman's stables.

Fortunately, Grandpa Bert and Fergus got along well. They made something of a production of grilling hamburgers in the evening, perhaps, she observed, as a way to get out of the house, tell stories, and drink beer. For her part she spent that same hour reviewing commands with the dogs and exercising Raisin with the bird lure.

This would be her last evening at home for a week. She helped Grandma and Abuelita clean up and then chatted with them awhile in the kitchen before heading off to bed, early again. Grandpa and Fergus were watching a basketball game in the parlor.

When she got to her bedroom she realized she wasn't at all sleepy. She was tired, but not from the tremendous amount of physical activity she had exerted today. On the contrary, that had energized her. No, it was her head that was tired. She had accumulated hundreds and hundreds of impressions of people over the week, including multiple impressions of several, but it was raw data. How would she ever sort it out?

She shut her bedroom door and headed to the barn with a quilt and pillow under her arm, Raisin following. Instead of going into her shop she took the steps to the loft above and climbed the ladder to the cupola at the very top.

The cupola was a tiny room roughly six feet square with screen instead of windows. It allowed heat to escape in the summer. In the old days the hay in the loft just below could breathe without danger of catching fire spontaneously. A padded bench ran along one side.

Clio clicked her tongue and Raisin jumped up from below. The cupola was one of the cat's favorite hangouts, but now it was a little chilly. She brushed the cat hair off the bench and sat down, pulling the quilt over her legs. Raisin sat next to her and began her settling-down routine, licking the fur on her flanks into shape.

There was enough moonlight to see the upper branches of the cottonwood tree in the back corner of the compound, the few remaining leaves waving in the breeze. She leaned her head back against the boards and closed her eyes. Two coyotes wailed back and forth in the distance.

In the silence, Raisin's tongue sounded like a liquid metronome. She laid her palm on the cat's shoulder, gently rubbing the muscles over the shoulder bones. Her coat was warm.

Her eyes still closed, she turned her mind inward. What was she sensing?

Raisin's aura. It was…strong. "Round," somehow. No: Julio would say "spherical." Alive, vibrant.

She moved her palm to the cat's neck. It felt the same; no change.

She opened her eyes. Barely visible on the ledge of the screen window was the dried husk of a beetle. She picked it up with her left hand and tossed it against the opposite wall where it made a faint click and a second when it hit the floor.

Raisin's aura compressed instantly, though her ears only barely twitched, the long hairs at the tips waving slightly. She paused her licking a bare second, and then resumed.

Clio was neither a philosopher nor a psychiatrist. "Compressing" was an inadequate notion for a totally indescribable concept. The conceptualization of a "round aura" was ridiculous on its face, but nothing she had any experience with was comparable. The cat had registered a minor change in her immediate vicinity, which she had detected. Or had she?

Softly, she clucked her tongue. Again the aura flickered.

She slid her hand to the cat's ribs and made a kissing sound. The aura wavered once more, though it might be thinner, less dense, somehow. Other than that, it didn't change.

She scratched Raisin's jaw. The cat stopped licking and sat erect, the better to be scratched. Cupping the ear between her thumb and index finger, Clio scratched the top of her head affectionately.

Could she affect Raisin's aura by somehow focusing her mind on the cat's mind? She shut her eyes and held her hand steady on Raisin's head. Her own breath lightly riffled through her vocal cords, emerging through her nose as a soft "mmm." She tried to suppress the sound in case it disturbed Raisin.

Raisin didn't seem disturbed. Clio kept concentrating…but was it working?

Fifteen seconds later Raisin closed her eyelids to slits and began purring.

Aha…but did she cause that to happen or was it a coincidence?

It was impossible to tell. OK, then stop trying. She redirected her thoughts from Raisin to her own sensations: the way her fingertips parted the hairs on Raisin's head and her nails moved lightly over the skin underneath. Let Raisin have her "mind" back.

The purring abated. She still couldn't be sure it wasn't coincidence. She focused once again on Raisin's aura.

The purring began again. The "roundness" expanded, impossible as that seemed. Or perhaps it had become denser or stronger. Words failed her. Was she actually affecting another being's mind?

If Raisin's aura had changed at the unexpected sound of a beetle bouncing off the wall, could she make it change with her mind alone? Could the concentration be a sign of alertness?

With her hand still on the cat's head, she tried to make Raisin's aura contract. It was a purely mental activity and very hard to control. She tried harder… and harder. Darn! *Harder!*

Raisin opened her jaws a little and hissed softly. It was not a hiss of alarm— more like unease.

"It's OK," Clio whispered, sliding her hand down the cat's body and rubbing her side. "It's OK." She was almost sure her mind had just contacted the mind of another living creature, at some fundamental level of which she had barely been aware before. That was encouraging, and more than a little weird: *very* weird.

She reflected. When she had so desperately tried to save Mr. Coombs and Grandma, she had had no idea what she was doing. Now she realized she had been sensing *and* acting at the same time, out of fear and panic and confusion. At least she had acted, because she had to, but she had done so without thinking, as if by instinct. But what if she could concentrate on one effort at a time—sensing and then acting? She hated those terms. What about "receiving and sending?"

It was so frustrating. Dr. Peebles' comparison with music wasn't bad either, but nothing described it accurately. Phooey. If she could make it work, did it even matter?

Now she really was tired.

Slowly, she swiveled in place and lifted her legs over the cat and down onto the pad. She draped the quilt into place over her body and turned on her side. A minute later, Raisin lay along the very edge of the bench with her weight against Clio's legs. She began purring again.

Thus cuddled cozily together in their private place, Clio pondered over and over what she had learned, until she drifted off to sleep.

## Chapter 25

Tucker decided not to park the van on the streets that ran alongside the parking lot to the gym. It would be too visible, even though it was no longer white, but a dirty (and stinky) brown. That damn government guy (or whoever he was) might recognize it. Instead, he parked on the street at the far end of the gym parking lot, under a tree with low-hanging branches. He had adequate sight lines and there was no possibility of being seen against the light thanks to the thick shrubbery along the curb.

He lit a cigarette and checked his watch. It was 8:30 am, later than he wanted to be, but scattered showers slowed him down on those curvy mountain roads. He was a late night person, anyway. Early mornings were a freaking hardship.

There were lots of cars and trucks in the gym lot, and a constant drift of people in and out. One good sign was a Harley-Davidson motorcycle parked to the left of the entrance. Jesse Connor was on the job. Jesse had better find out something useful, or he could forget the second hundred bucks.

It happened earlier than he expected. His cell phone went off at 9:45. Jesse wanted to know where he was. Smart guy, Jesse. Fdez or Bagger would have passed information over the phone, but Jesse remembered: assume they're always listening. Schultz had drilled that into him, and he'd drilled it into Jesse. Ten minutes later Jesse came out of the gym and Tucker met him on the side street. He drove a couple blocks and pulled over.

"What'd you find out?" he asked him.

"I got the reception nurse to let me look at the roster," he said. "I got his address. He lives in Miami. I wrote it down for you."

"Is that all?"

"I talked to him, but he wasn't saying much. I didn't want to push it. He's no dope."

Smart guy, Jesse!

"Yeah, that's probably best. Gimme the address."

"You need anything else?"

"Nah, but don't take off for a while. Don't wanna make that guy suspicious. Hang around till the afternoon." He handed him five twenties. "That's still good pay for a day's work."

"Yeah, not bad. You need anything else like this you know where to find me."

Tucker thought about that as Jesse got out and hoofed it back to the gym. People always liked Jesse—friendly face, easy smile. What's not to like? If he just had a larcenous heart he could be a great con man.

He looked at the address. It meant nothing to him. He was many things, but he was no detective. Schultz would know how to run it down. But he couldn't phone it in. It meant another goddam three hour round trip to Schultz's store. He'd better get started.


After two days on the water, Ana realized she'd been wrong to expect much time to herself in a boat, even if it was a luxurious yacht. But now she finally had several hours to sit and think.

It was hard to imagine a more different environment that the one she had just left in Switzerland…unless it might be the southern New Mexico desert where she lived. The coastline of Texas offered few visual attractions, being low and unrelieved by hills or large buildings, with the exception of the occasional resort or industrial complex. Marine traffic on the waterway was varied and moderately interesting, but not as interesting to her as it was to her son.

Matt and Julio had gone ashore in the launch with several crew members, who were taking a part from one of the yacht's diesel engines to be fixed in Port Lavaca. Matt and Julio mainly wanted to sightsee, but Matt also volunteered to shop for several items Ana wanted from a grocery store. The yacht's cook, a student in a restaurant program in Houston, wanted to try Ana's Thai shrimp recipe. That required green curry paste and coconut milk among other things, which the on-board galley did not have in stock.

Under other circumstances she would have loved to tour the wildlife preserves and parks and islands which stretched along the coast. For now, however, it was just as well the schedule belonged to the captain and to the eventual owner of the yacht. She was content to be merely a passenger. She had added the term "shakedown cruise" to her ever-growing lexicon of odd English words.

The yacht was rocking gently at anchor in Matagorda Bay, close to a fishing pier at Port Lavaca, a town of perhaps 15,000. The two remaining crew members were below decks, with the engines. She had the foredeck to herself, under high scattered clouds with moments of welcome sunshine. A raucous assortment of sea birds swooped low over the boat in a vain hope that the yacht was really a shrimp boat. The salt water smell was pleasant.

It was a good opportunity to reflect on her life and her family.

Despite having had many wonderful years with her husband and children, she saw little prospect of ever living a normal life on Earth.

It had been crazy from the beginning: being hunted down and captured by soldiers, leading to her fame in the Olympic games and the ensuing business of the meteoroids. She had never dreamed that following Dr. Sledd's advice to become famous would have had such lasting effects. Then there was her "leaving" Earth after being kidnapped, followed by her "return" years later, resulting in even more publicity...and then that terrible incident in Peru which was most unfortunately videotaped.

And now she had committed this foolishness at Davos, creating a lurid public scandal with a wealthy, influential media magnate. That photo would no doubt haunt her forever. Could she have been any more stupid?

She found herself staring at distant figures running around at the shoreline. Some were tiny: young children. It was a family outing, perhaps. Her eyes began to sting. During that Peruvian disaster she had been pregnant but had lost the baby.

And now her children were seventeen. It was a difficult age. It had been a terrible age for her too—she had run away from home when she was not much older, twenty-five light years away from home. The twins were not likely to do that.

Julio would do fine. He had his father's low-key personality, and his talents seemed likely to lead him to secluded laboratories or the like where he could work and innovate with the world little noticing.

Clio's case was more worrisome. She had her mother's temperament, and though she was not particularly at odds with her parents and her world as her mother had been, her stubbornness and impulsiveness had already gotten her into more danger than her mother had at a similar age.

Then there was the strange business of her healing abilities. Since childhood Clio had been fascinated by curanderas, herbs, medicine, and healing. In recent years she had performed three astonishing, undeniable, and inexplicable acts of healing, with Matt's great-grandmother, Grandma Julia, and their SEAL friend Rob Coombs. At this very moment Clio was trying to understand that ability, and control and even develop it. It was hard to see how she could do so without attracting unwelcome notice sooner or later.

A sudden cat's paw breeze added an extra chill to Ana's thoughts. She zipped her jacket closed. It was surprising how a warm day on land became a cold day on the water.

Some of their family's problems came from outside the family. There was the matter of the approaching emissaries from Thomo. Whether in two years or three, their arrival seemed certain to turn their world upside down. Hleo wouldn't know how many newcomers there would be, or anything about their tribal affiliations, until perhaps a year before they actually landed. That was because the mission would have launched not long after the final choices of passengers had been made. Thus, traveling nearly at the speed of light, they would be chasing the news of their own arrival, which Hleo would receive barely ahead of them.

It was comforting that her Uncle Rothan was already the official representative for the four Thomans presently on Earth. As the "Ambassador Plenipotentiary," he would be more responsible than Ana for assisting the new arrivals in acculturating and settling in, as well as helping to organize their efforts for best effectiveness.

But the newcomers brought other problems. On Thomo, she had been the second highest-ranking person of the Darshiell clan, next to her father. Since her father had almost certainly passed away by now, her sister Onela would have taken his place. But that did not change the fact that Heoren Darshiell's eldest daughter outranked her no matter how separated they were. Now she was on a different planet, the Thomans' planet of origin, and married outside the Thoman clan structure. Yet her former rank would matter, somehow, even though there was no Thoman office for her on Earth. What that might mean could not be foretold. There was no precedent for it.

It would also matter that Counselor Hleo, who maintained the lunar station, had written a great Thoman epic about her. Ana had to admit that Hleo's poem was an impressive effort, though it seemed to her little more than an exercise in public relations. But even so, Thomans had enormous reverence for their historical epics, and the approaching Thomans were certain to accord Hleo's epic, and its subject—her—high status as a result. She was, in fact, the only Thoman to become the subject of an epic while still alive. Hleo insisted that the reunion of Thomans with their distant cousins on Earth after thousands of years' separation justified that innovation. The new arrivals might agree or they might disagree. Again, there was no precedent.

She sighed. It was impossible to know what unpleasantries might lie ahead for her and her husband and children. At a minimum she needed to explain the situation to Matt so he would know better how to prepare, as far as possible. Beyond that, it was ridiculous to worry about what might happen in the future.

But she worried about it anyway.

The hour and a half trip to Schultz's firearms emporium took Tucker two and a half hours, and he arrived dirty.

"Cassie," he said to Frau Schultz on his way in.

"Tucker," she replied, glancing up from stacking a display of boxes of shotgun shells. "He's in the shop."

The shop was a concrete block building the size of a double garage behind the store, which was a double wide trailer up on blocks. The shop was a formidable windowless building with security lights and cameras at each corner. Tucker rang the bell and was admitted.

"What happened to you?" Schultz growled, taking note of his grimy hands and sleeves.

"The piece of shit van broke down. Had to replace the master cylinder and then bleed the brakes."

"Come in," he said, holding the steel door open.

Shultz had his reloading bench in operation: rotating turrets of brass casings passed under dies, things happened, and the result was a large pile of automatic pistol ammo. Looked like 10 mm. to Tucker.

Shultz was not one for small talk.

"Whatcha got?" he asked.

"I got a man inside," he said. "Got the home address of that guy with the tattoo. This is it."

He handed Schultz the slip of paper. Schultz squinted at it.

"Miami," he said.

"Right. My spy's a friendly sort. Tried to chat with Mr. Tattoo, but he wasn't saying much. Decided not to push it. Didn't want to alert the guy. I figured you'd know how to run this down."

"I might," he replied. "Cassie has a sister there. I'll get her to check it out. In the meantime," he added, turning to a safe the size of a movie star's refrigerator, "I got something for you to do."

He twirled a combination into it, levered the heavy handle, and pulled it open. Two thirds of the contents were rifles. Down one side was a stack of big drawers. He pulled one open and grabbed something out of it.

"Here," he said, "This is $20,000. Go to Delgado's Auto Center a half mile down the highway on the left. See Jerry Delgado and tell him you work for me and you want a reliable used truck or van. Buy it in your name—got that? In your name. Bring me the receipt and the change. I can't afford you breaking down on a run—too goddam much money at stake to risk it on a freakin' leaky master cylinder. I'll see if I can get an answer out of Cassie's sister by the time you get back. Now beat it."

Tucker wasn't all that fond of small talk himself, so he left in good spirits. Happy birthday to me, he thought.

He was back in an hour, in a clean seven-year-old Suburban, with the panel truck configuration—perfect! No windows in the back for anyone to see what was being hauled around. Excellent. It didn't stink, and the truck was black, just right for not standing out.

He pushed the doorbell button. Schultz yanked the door open five seconds later, looking hotter than a turkey fryer.

"That son of a bitch!" he rasped. "That bastard!"

"What?" Tucker asked.

"That address. It's not a residence. It's a goddam office! 'World Security Services,' out of New York City. Cassie's sister knows about them. Everybody who works there is former military—SEALs, Delta Force, Rangers, the whole lot." His bullet head looked about to explode. "I'll tell you what it is. It's a CIA cover for people who do stuff off the books, black ops, the bastards! I knew it! I knew it! Shit!"

Goddam, thought Tucker. No wonder that guy wasted him and Fdez and Bagger. He totally forgot about the high school girl. Schultz was near to losing his mind, storming around cussing and slamming things onto his workbench. Finally he slowed down a little and glared at Tucker.

"All right, goddammit. This is the last fucking straw. One way or the other...."

The safe was still open. He opened another drawer and grabbed something.

"Here," he said, handing him a black plastic case the size of a slightly flattened hot dog bun. It must have weighed four pounds. "It's a bomb. Don't drop it, jackass!"

Tucker nearly did drop it, in surprise.

"It's C-4 and a cell phone. And some magnets. Stick that on the firewall of the fucker's car and leave it. I still wanna talk to him. I want you to grab him and hold him for me to talk to. But if he gets away, all we gotta do is dial this cell phone and that's one less government man we got to worry about."

Tucker held the thing as if it were a bomb. Well, it *was* a bomb.

"Now," Schultz went on, "gimme the receipt and my change. It better show the trade-in value of that piece of shit you left there, too."

## Chapter 26

It had been a long Monday for the kid—she was too tired to decide which of the town's four restaurants she wanted to have dinner in. Fergus pointed out that pizza in her motel room had worked well before, and she went for that gladly. She ate every bit of her half of the pizza.

The order included a free dessert, an insult to dieticians everywhere: six bread sticks made from pizza dough and dabbed with white icing, which she nibbled while they talked.

"Does your gut still hurt?" he asked.

"No. I'm over that."

"Got a headache?"

"No."

She'd spent most of the day sitting and talking with sick people. How hard could that be? But he said nothing.

"Why do you ask?"

"You seemed pooped."

"Well, yes. I was. I am. It's…I don't know. I told you what I was trying to do. It's hard. It's frustrating."

"Healing?"

"There's more to it than that. I'm still trying to figure it out. First, I…I try to feel what's happening with people, what the problem is. I don't know…maybe it's like they say the blind develop super hearing. It's not sight, though. It's a sense I can't describe. It's weird."

"So that's first…."

"Yeah. And then it's, like, after I find something, doing something about it. I don't know how I do that…I guess I do it with my mind. I don't know what else it would be."

"Hmm. That's pretty out there."

"It is. It used to scare me."

"Can your mother do that?"

"No. She's never heard of anything like that, even on Thomo."

"And doing it makes you tired?"

"It did today. I've never worked with so many people in a short time."

"Did you actually heal anyone?"

"No. Well, yes, I guess. Sort of."

He waited.

"I don't dare do too much. Like today, a woman came with a migraine headache. Doctors can't do much about those, but I was pretty sure I could help. But if I had, she would have told other people, maybe even a doctor, and then they'd notice me and I'd be in trouble. So I can't. But I did anyway, a couple times. Did you hear that crying baby this morning?"

"I sure did. Everyone there did."

"She had colic, poor little thing. She was really in pain. I held her while I talked to her mother. I was able to make it go away. The mother thought the baby just liked the way I held her.

"And then earlier this morning I talked to an old man who'd had a blood test. He had tape over the puncture but it was still bleeding. He was going to go back to the nurse, but I pulled the tape off and wiped it with a cotton ball and touched it with my fingers. I made it stop bleeding."

"How?"

"I can't put it in words. I just made it stop. I guess I closed the capillaries or the vein, I don't know."

"Jeez, we could have used you as a medic in country."

"I can't do surgery."

"You'd have been a big hit if you could stop bleeding. Lotta bleeding over there."

"I can also help with pain."

She looked at him reproachfully.

What she meant was obvious. He said nothing. She spoke again.

"I think you like your pain."

"What?"

"Some people do. They really do. It hurts but they welcome it."

"You think that or you know that?"

"It happens. I've seen it. I saw it today."

"That's crazy."

"Yes, it is. I agree."

She let that sink in. He looked at the pizza mess on the table.

"I think I'm about done," he said, standing and picking up his drink. "I'll leave you the breadsticks."

It took forty minutes in the hotel hot tub before his stiffened limbs loosened up, and two scotches to make his innards warm to life. Flaming hell, what a day. Ben Bianchi began taking stock of his situation.

He'd spent seven hours sitting in a freezing automobile, afraid to run the engine to provide heat for the attention the warm plume of exhaust might call to him. The result was that the windows of the car fogged up to where he could see nothing. He had to leave the driver's side window halfway down to aim the scanner's antenna at the gym and keep an eye on the building, making the inside of the car even colder. Since there had been a chilly rain off and on all day his entire left side and the car seat under him had soon gotten wet and cold. Damnably cold.

The worst part came soon after his arrival at 9:00 am. A gorgeous yellow Corvette parked near the gym entrance. The man who got out carried a coat hanger with a plastic drycleaner bag over white garments inside: obviously a doctor, and a doctor with style.

Not five minutes later the scanner blinked that the phone was in use. The doctor was barely visible, standing inside the entry doors with another man. Was he on the phone or were they talking to each other? It was impossible to tell. The damn plate glass was covered with posters and notices that got in the way. They either shook hands or exchanged something...a cell phone, perhaps? The other man walked outside. It was the food runner. Blast!

It had bothered him all weekend that some errand boy for a medical team would have telephoned Ana Darcy at Davos. That simply made no sense. But the doctor's presence put a new light on the matter. He was clearly wealthy, with a good opinion of himself. He looked a cut above, perhaps a specialist, maybe a surgeon. That made a certain amount of sense. He could have been the one who had called Ana Darcy, and the food runner could have borrowed his cell phone to place orders for the food.

He squirmed sideways to let a hot water jet pulse on the small of his back.

Damn it, but this whole operation was a shot in the dark. There were other fish that could be fried. Dunston had called Sunday positively chuckling over a possible rift in a royal marriage. A big fat scandal like that was looking like a much more promising target for his efforts. He'd give this one more day to see who owned the cell phone. Then, that afternoon, whether successful or not, he would barge in there and ask some embarrassing questions. If that didn't produce results, then the hell with it.

Aha. The waiter from the dining room was coming with a third scotch, right to the hot tub. Thank you, my good man. And thank you, expense account.

# Chapter 27

Tucker and Fdez sat in their comfortable almost-like-new truck and watched it rain. Tucker cracked open the windows on the downwind side a little to reduce the buildup of cigarette smoke.

"Can't grab him like this," he grumbled.

Fdez said nothing.

"Good time to stick on that bomb of Schultz's, though. Visibility is down."

Fdez lit another cigarette. Tucker stubbed his out in the ash tray.

"I'm gonna do it," he said. "Be right back."

He popped open the center console and dug the thing out from under the wad of maps and phone books he'd transferred from the old van. Jamming on his hat, he opened the door and stepped out, sliding the bomb into his back pocket. Fdez watched him amble off into the murk.

Clio picked up the requisite paperwork from the admittance nurse in the gym lobby and guided an elderly woman into the gym proper. The woman was a little tottery; she had a cane in her right hand. Clio held her left hand for gentle support.

"High blood pressure and arthritis," Clio thought. That was the easy part. "And something else—maybe an endocrine problem." There was a good chance she would later help the woman go over the diagnosis and learn what the doctor had found. That was the beauty of working with this medical team.

"Uh, miss?"

One of the doctors called her over. He was middle aged with a halo of pale blond hair around a large bald spot and laugh lines around his mouth.

"Yes, sir?"

"That man with you, your uncle?"

"Yes?"

"Is he ex-military?"

"He is, yes, sir."

"I thought so."

"How could you tell?"

"He was in here a little earlier when an aide pushing the EKG cart knocked over a metal chair. I thought your uncle was going to jump out of his skin. He was ready to rumble."

"Oh."

"Has he seen combat?"

"Yes, sir. He lost a foot."

"Ah. Probably a bomb, maybe an IED. Most likely a concussion too. He has the symptoms. That's not an official diagnosis, mind you, but he should be checked for that."

"He's had some therapy, I know."

"Yeah, that would be for the foot. The military's way late recognizing how common and how serious brain injuries are. They tend to treat brain injuries as if they're somehow the soldier's fault. There are new scanners around that can identify and even localize concussion trauma. I can get him a name and address for the nearest one if you think he'd go for it."

"He might. Would it help him?"

The doctor pressed his lips together.

"Unfortunately, no. Even with a precise diagnosis, we can't fix concussed brains. Some day, maybe, but not today."

"Yes, sir. Well, I'd appreciate the address. I plan to be in medicine for some time. They may figure out a treatment some day. There's no hurry, sir. I'll be here the rest of the week."


The "uncle" in question was standing at the dark end of the gym lobby staring idly at the rain visible between posters exhorting students to "Come to the Tasajillo Carnaval!" and "Let's All Kill the SBA Test!" He was bored but he didn't mind. Boredom was his preferred lifestyle.

The rain was fluky, alternating between torrential showers and hard, wind-blown sprinkles. The time of day couldn't be guessed from the darkened sky. Thunder rumbled in the distance.

There was only one person in the parking lot, walking toward the gym. Why hadn't he parked closer, the damn fool? The rain picked up again, making it hard to see, but it was a man, with a hat and a beard. Oddly, he wasn't hurrying. Small side-to-side movements of his hat indicated he was glancing at the cars around him.

The man was passing between a pickup with a camper shell and the kid's Corolla as a curtain of heavy rain obscured him. When it let up, the man had disappeared. Fergus started, instantly alert. Now the guy was walking away, toward the back of the parking lot. He must have knelt down between the kid's car and the pickup truck next to it. In fifteen seconds he was again obscured by a shower.

Could he have slashed a tire on one of those vehicles? The habits acquired from years working in places where random people were trying sneaky ways to kill him returned in a flash. He slipped out the nearest door and stood under the awning, reconnoitering. At the moment, the rain blotted out everything over fifty feet away. He pulled up the hood of his windbreaker and headed toward the Corolla, parked in the second row of vehicles.

Both it and the pickup looked OK, no flat tires, no scratches, no broken windows. He squatted down to look underneath. Nothing there.

Once again the rain let up. Staying low, he raised up enough to see over the other vehicles to the back of the parking lot. Where did that guy go? A light blinked in the distance, then went out. It was a door on a truck or van, parked sideways to the gym, opening and then closing.

He waited another two minutes. The vehicle was still there.

This had to be checked out. He sat on the wet pavement and leaned over. Cold water immediately chilled his butt. First, the Corolla. It was dark under the wheel well. The disk brake seemed ok…shock absorber ok…rack and pinion… too dark to see. He wormed the little Maglite out of his jeans and twisted it on. Lying on his side on the pavement, cold water soaking him the length of his body, he extended both arms under the car, one holding the light and the other feeling around. Radiator hose…a/c return hose…fuel line, probably…all felt sound. He fumbled all the way up to the exhaust manifold but found nothing obviously out of place.

The flashlight was reflecting off some part of the steering rack. It was either shiny or wet. Since it was under the hood; it shouldn't be wet. He rubbed a finger over it, but his hand was wet too. There were faint lines spaced regularly around it. He dug in a fingernail. It felt like plastic, soft plastic. The steering rack under it was cast metal, rock hard. He pushed the shiny thing and it moved a fraction of an inch. When he grabbed it and pulled, it came loose in his hand: a long, narrow box. The lines he'd seen were strips of black electrical tape. It was heavy.

Fuck. It was a bomb! Had to be! His mind flashed into its military mind-set in less than a second.

He sat up and leaned against the car, unaware of his freezing skin, breathing hard. He contemplated the damned thing. A bomb. Why? Why that guy? Something bothered him—the beard. He hadn't paid much attention at the time, but one of the chumps the kid had put down had had a beard. The guy had been rolling around trying to breathe at the time but he was sure the asshole had had a beard. Maybe the sneaky son of a bitch was trying to get even! Shit!

What the hell should he do now? Call the cops? They'd damn sure go after those bastards. They might even get lucky and catch them.

Then what? Arrests. Lawyers. Witnesses. Participants. Giving evidence. *Checking identities.* Oh, shit. The two reasons for this operation were to protect the kid from harm and not to spill the fact that her mother was from another planet. That would come out in any investigation—it had to—and he'd be in a world of shit with World Security, and the kid and her mother and family would be exposed and super-pissed at him. Shit!

So what about this bomb? Was it set to go off if the engine were started? Not likely—that would make it pretty delicate for what that schlub had done with it. No, the guy would want to watch the kid (or him, come to that, or both of them) get in the car and blow the whole thing up while he laughed. There were no wires sticking out of it, so it was not connected to the starter motor. It was tightly sealed with tape. Had to have a cell phone inside wired to the detonator. The guy could call it in when the time was right, the son of a bitch.

He sat there, getting wetter by the minute, thinking. Then he decided. All right, you goddam jackass. We'll see about you, hot shot.

Fdez was sitting in the driver's seat, the dumbass, focusing binoculars through the windshield. Tucker yanked open the door and startled him.

"Move your ass over, man."

Fdez hoisted himself over the console and squirmed into the passenger seat.

"You should have been watching me. What was you doing?"

"I did watch you. I saw you stick it on and head back. You were doing all right. But then I noticed something else. I needed to use the wipers to see it better, man. That's why I was in your seat."

"So what'd you see, a nurse with her blouse stuck to her tits?"

"No, man. Look over there. See that blue car on the curb?"

He pointed at the half dozen cars parked in front of the houses which faced the side of the parking lot. One, maybe a eighty yards from them, was dark blue.

"Yeah, I see it. So what?"

"There's someone in it."

"OK…so?"

"Two times, now, he's opened his window and stuck something out. Can't tell what it is. Might be a camera or a gun or something like that. Pointed at the gym. Then he runs the window back up."

"You shittin' me?"

"I ain't! Here's the binoculars. Check it out. Maybe he'll do it again."

Well, crap. Fdez didn't have the imagination to make that up. So who the hell could it be, and doing what? There would seem to be no reason to be stalking a patient coming here—they all lived in this area anyway. What about someone with the medical bunch? Hmm. There was only one nominee he could think of: the "government man." Was he bent, and was this another government man after him? Did they sneak around on each other? Were they all after the same guy?

If Fdez was right, whoever that was represented a potential threat to the two of them and by extension to Schultz. They better be damn careful to check this jerk out good. Wouldn't do to have a witness.

The best choice for now was to wait and watch and see what they could learn.

The thunder was getting louder. Rain was coming down in torrents. Time to move. He rose up enough to see over the hood of the Corolla. No one was within twenty feet—couldn't see much farther. Good enough. He stuck the bomb in his back pocket and ran around the back of the Corolla on the side away from the gym, in a low crouch, and crossed the parking lot. Stumbling over the curb, he looked both ways, praying that anyone out driving in a car would have the headlights on, and crossed to the opposite curb.

He was thoroughly soaked. The rain and wind were furious: couldn't be better. He snugged the hood around his face and began trotting away from the school, following the curb. At the intersection he slowed and looked toward the truck. There was too much rain to see it. Perfect!

As best he could remember, there were only a couple houses along the street at the back of the gym parking lot, and some, but not much, shrubbery. He crossed the intersection diagonally. Still no one within view, no one on the sidewalk or a porch. OK, team: time to boogie.

He dropped to the ground, more dirt and rocks than lawn, and began crawling forward on his elbows. It was reminiscent of SEAL boot camp except there was no razor wire overhead and no nearby explosions. In three or four minutes the back end of the truck came into view. He stopped and studied it while the rain washed freezing mud down his sleeves. The truck had prominent rear view mirrors on both sides. They should be running with droplets of water. Even if the guy was looking he'd not see him down low…probably. More slowly now, he crawled closer, using a row of shrubs as a shield.

Closer…closer…check the one mirror he could see from here, on the passenger side. Water was indeed dripping off it, and pouring off the sides of the truck. His face was the only light colored part of him by now. He eased off the curb into the river of water rushing down the curb and kept crawling with his head down. Look up…crawl a little more…look up…a little more. Freezing water flowed straight into his shirt. His balls were surely shivering. A guy could drown doing this. At last he could touch the bumper.

There was no way he could reach the front and stick the bomb on the engine, but a truck had a steel frame like a ladder that ran the full length, so there'd be an I-beam at each rear axle that would do in a pinch. Carefully feeling for it, he stuck his head under the bumper. Yeah, there's the place, next to the right rear tire over the leaf spring. The bomb wouldn't rub the body above it, wouldn't scrape off against anything on the road, wouldn't be jarred off. Holding it firmly with both hands, he set one edge against the beam and felt the magnets bite. Rotating it as slowly as possible so as not to make a click, he laid it full against the beam. Nudge it: yes, it was solid. It would stay. All right. There you go, fucker: a little present from Ana Darcy's SEAL Team One.

Twelve minutes later he was back at the Corolla, unlocking the trunk. He'd never looked in the trunk. Box of first aid stuff, twelve volt air pump, and twelve volt trouble light…someone set the kid up right. Couple of empty nylon shopping bags…and a black nylon zipper case. What's in that? Sterno stove, Sterno cubes, two bottles of water, and aha! a Mylar and polyester emergency blanket! Excellent.

He draped the flimsy "blanket" over the front seat and sat on it, shedding water onto the floor. Now he could drive back to the room and shower and put on dry clothes. He took inventory and realized he was soaking wet, filthy with mud, way colder than shit, his teeth were chattering and he was shivering like a bastard.

A crack of lightning a block away startled him and no doubt everybody in the gym. He laughed out loud and pounded the steering wheel. Yes, by damn! An honest-to-God SEAL evolution! Outstanding!

# Chapter 28

"Hello?"

"Hey. This is Fergus."

"Are you all right?"

Uh-oh. Had she seen any of what he'd been up to?

"Of course. Why do you ask?"

"The rain is terrible. Someone said you went outside, but you didn't come back!"

"Right. I was caught out and got drenched. I'm at the motel now, getting dry clothes."

"Oh, good. I was worried. It looks awful out there."

"It's not that bad. Listen, why I called: your appointment with Bianchi is mid-afternoon, so don't you think we ought to leave a little early to allow for the weather?"

"Good idea. Why don't you pick me up in forty-five minutes?"

"Roger. If it's still raining I'll call when I'm out front."


What with the heavy rain and a pickup truck between him and the Corolla, Ben Bianchi hadn't seen the Corolla leave. He barely noticed its return, an hour later. What he really noticed was when his scanner started blinking wildly. He pressed the window's down button and held the antenna in the opening to try to localize the call. There, visible through the steady rain, was that Corolla with its lights on, at the entrance to the gym. The best signal came from that precise direction. The food runner looked to be on another run.

The call ended. The car didn't move. A minute passed, and a woman ran from the gym and jumped into the passenger seat. The car eased toward the far side of the gym and turned toward town, the brake lights making red dots on the droplets on the window. Another restaurant errand, most likely. They'd be back in half an hour or less.

It's now or never, he decided. When that damned food runner comes back I'll confront him. He'll tell me what I want to know or I'll threaten him with making up something about him and Ana Darcy and splashing the headlines around the world. With photos!

"Damn! You were right, Fdez! Look at that window!"
"See? I told you, man! What the hell is that?"
"Dunno. Maybe an antenna?"
"What's it mean?"
"It means let's think about this a tad bit. Plan it out. I'm tired of sittin' here. You wanna make something happen?"
"Fuckin' A, man."

Ben was absorbed in working through the fourth iteration of a completely outrageous yarn he would headline "Mr. X's Love Affair With the Extraterrestrial Ana Darcy" when a large truck pulled to a stop right next to him, the driver-side door five feet away. Before he could make out any details about the driver, the door opened and a man stepped out and knocked on the window. He pressed the down button, stopping when the glass neared the bottom.

"Yes?" he said.

A fist crashed into his jaw and knocked him silly. The next thing he was conscious of was lying on a metal floor, trussed hand and foot, his clothes uncomfortably wadded in the wrong places about his body, his mouth taped shut.

What in Christ's name was happening?

His whole head hurt. The phrase "ring like a bell" floated oddly to the surface of his scrambled thoughts. Now he knew how apt that was. He was in that truck! Centrifugal motion pushed him to one side. They were moving. It was a mistake! It couldn't be anything else. It was all a mistake!

Fdez leaned against a fender and watched Tucker going through the collection of items from their catch's pockets. He was supposed to be the lookout but there was nothing to look out for. He brushed the droplets of water off his leather jacket and smiled.

Tucker had never asked him about his name. His real name was Yzaguirre, hard for gringos to pronounce but it was better they didn't know it anyway. His first name was Eladio and no one knew that either. The jefe of the second gang he had worked for as a youth was also a gringo. When he asked him what his name was they were driving down a street in Nogales, passing a sign that said "Fdez Juncos," denoting a particular intersection on Avenida Fernández. "Call me Fdez," he said, and it stuck. The gringo had no clue. Tucker was a gringo too, no big deal, but the guy in the truck was a bolillo, puro anglo-sajón, with a ruddy face like a slice of baloney. No balls, either. Fucker had pissed himself.

"What'd you find?" he asked Tucker.

"He works for something called Sanecor. He's got him a press pass. Might be a reporter of some kind. And see this? It's a passport. A *British* passport. With his picture in it."

"No shit?"

"No shit."

"So what now?"

"That's the question. I'm gonna ask him what the fuck he's doing here, rough him up a little if I have to, without damaging him. Schultz would shit if we busted him up and he turned out to be some big shot. You know Schultz. Got a mean streak and a quick temper to go with it. We gotta be careful. We'll take him to the shack and put him in storage. Tomorrow maybe we'll wrap this up and bring in Schultz, let him handle it."

"That's a plan."

"Fuckin' A."


Fergus had been right about the weather. Clio took over the driving when they bought drinks at the café in town, and was pleased to find that the rain had lessened. She drove ten mph slower than normal and they had no problem.

Alice met them at the door and led them to the dining room, where she set Fergus up with coffee and pastry, magazines, and a small TV.

"He's ready for you," she said to Clio.

"How is he doing?" she asked.

"Much better. He's been looking forward to your visit all day. Thank you for coming again. It makes him so happy."

"Ms. Móntez is here, sir," she said, moving to one side to allow Clio through.

Bianchi was in the same recliner. The drapes were closed. A lamp was on at the table by his side, with several books, magazines, and a newspaper alongside. He did look better, still gaunt and pale but bright-eyed and alert.

"So good to see you again, Ms. Móntez. Please, have a seat. Would you care for some tea?"

"Yes, sir, thank you."

He raised his eyebrows to Alice, who nodded and disappeared.

"How are you, young lady?"

"I'm fine, sir. And how are you? You look better today."

"Today is a good day. I am grateful for every good day, and especially for your willingness to come again."

"Don't mention it, sir. I'm honored you would have me."

His eyes sparkled.

"Very prettily spoken, Ms. Móntez. Your manners are admirable. On your previous visit you mentioned that you were working to better understand your healing abilities. Have you made progress in that?"

"I think so. I'm not sure. It's hard to tell. I have nothing to compare it to, and there's nothing in the medical libraries that's any help. That I've found, anyway."

"That's a shame. I know the responsibility is worrying to you. But I urge you to persevere. Even such a lost cause as I can recognize the unparalleled benevolent potential of your talents. Ah, thank you Alice."

The housekeeper delivered the tea and retired, closing the door gently. Bianchi watched Clio add a cube of sugar and stir it in. He leaned forward in his recliner.

"And now, my dear, I must ask you a question. Do you happen to be related to Ana Darcy?"

The spoon stopped its motion. Clio tried to keep her face neutral but realized she probably failed. She swallowed as imperceptibly as she could. Allowing a little surprise to show, she looked up from her cup.

"Why do you ask?"

"For two reasons, my dear. First, it strikes me that you have a remarkable resemblance to Ms. Darcy."

Several seconds passed. Clio spoke again.

"And the second?"

"Yes, the second. Have you been following the news?"

She said nothing.

"For example, have you seen this item?"

He picked up the newspaper, unfolded it, and handed it to her. There was her mother, face sharp in anger, twisting the ear of an obviously shocked and pained elderly gentleman.

"This happened at the World Economic Forum meeting in Davos, Switzerland, last week. The man in the photograph is an ass, and Ms. Darcy gave him what he richly deserved.

"Unfortunately, he is also the head of a media empire, and I have reason to believe he is trying to use his media powers to do damage to Ms. Darcy any way he can to get revenge." His face darkened. "It embarrasses me to have to tell you that this man is my son."

She stared at him.

"I have learned that one of his reporters is hanging around your medical team. My guess is that he is looking for you."

Clio was trying with all her might to channel her mother's Thoman social armor. She forced her breathing rate not to increase while her mind raced ahead. The thugs she and Fergus had met could not be reporters. Bianchi was talking about someone else entirely, someone whose presence neither she nor Fergus had suspected. Had anyone been lurking around the medical team? She realized she looked paralyzed. Bianchi was speaking again.

"I feel sure this person means you no personal harm. But I must admit, no one in the world would dream that Ana Darcy had an almost grown daughter. It would be the story of the year—of the decade! Were that to be published, it would set off a tidal wave of unstoppable curiosity. I'm sure this would be terrible news to Ms. Darcy…and to you. *If* you are her daughter."

Clio's skin had gone cold. This was what her family had been dreading when the next group of Thomans arrived.

But that was years away. This was now. She swallowed again, still thinking. If their identities were to come out now or later, there was nothing she could do about it.

And there was no point being afraid: she was half Thoman. She should be proud! She took a slow breath and composed her face. She looked evenly at Bianchi.

"Ana Darcy is my mother," she said quietly, adding, "And I am her daughter."

Bianchi sat back.

"Spoken with spirit." he said. "It is an honor to meet you, young lady. Now I can tell you that I am the chief executive officer of the corporation of which my son is the president. As such I am not without considerable influence in its affairs."

He paused a beat.

"I vow to you, Ms. Móntez, that I will do everything in my power to prevent the publication of any mention of your parentage in any of the corporation's various media. Indeed, I have already begun. I wish I could guarantee success, but I cannot quite do that." A quick smile crossed his face. "I will, however, fight to the death to accomplish that goal. That, I do promise."

She barely registered his words. Whatever was going to happen to her family would happen. She could worry about all that later. Right now, she thought she could feel this decent man's aura shrinking—basically defenseless. Even if she failed to help him, how could she not try?

She stood and held out her right hand, palm up. He waited several seconds before placing his on top of hers. His fingers were cold. She laid her left hand over his, holding it between both her hands. After another few seconds, he added his on top. His eyes were bright.

She closed her eyes and began focusing her mind.

***

Fergus heard a noise in the hall and checked his watch. The kid had been in there a long time. The doorknob turned and there she was, looking somber and tired. Alice came from the kitchen and persuaded them to have a small supper. The kid took a chair next to him.

"So how'd it go?" he asked, his voice low.

"OK," she replied. "He went to sleep."

"Ah," he replied as the cook came out of the kitchen bearing a tray.

"I'll tell you the rest later," she added.

The meal, anchored by a wonderful ricotta cheese and pasta frittata and salad, was gone in a half hour. They were finishing off their dessert—savory cannolis with a silk-smooth filling and crunchy pastry shell—when Alice returned.

"Excuse me. I see you're nearly finished. Mr. Fergus, Mr. Bianchi would like a word with you if you don't mind, sir."

"Oh. Sure, you bet," he said, setting down his napkin and shooting a glance at the kid. He got up and followed Alice into the hall.

The old guy sure had a fine room to be sick in, he thought, glancing over the minimal but high-quality furnishings. The man himself was in a recliner with a blanket over his legs.

"Pardon me for not standing to meet you, Mr. Fergus," he said, holding out his hand. "I'm no longer as spry as I once was."

Fergus shook the bony hand, barely daring a squeeze.

"Please have a seat."

"Outstanding dinner, sir. Your cook is to be complimented. Thank you for taking such good care of us."

"You're very welcome, Mr. Fergus, but it is you two who are taking the care. I can't tell you how the visits of your niece revive me."

"I'm glad to hear that, sir."

"I asked to see you to tell you a little of what I have already imparted to your niece. It's always best to get one's information first hand, I have found, and you, I think, need to know what I have learned.

"To begin, Ms. Móntez has told me the true identity of her mother. I see that surprises you. She did so because I asked her about it. I came to suspect as much from information Mr. Baldwin gathered at my request, you see. She merely confirmed it, most courageously, I might add. And so I now ask you, sir, if you are really her uncle."

"I...am not."

"Just so. You are, then....?"

"You could call me her security contingent."

"Exactly. You are ex-military, yes?"

"Yes."

"I thought so. Very good. Her mother is to be commended. The information I have is something you need to know, then. Ms. Móntez, regrettably, is not a close follower of the news of the world. Since you have been busy with her, perhaps you have not kept up yourself. For example, have you seen this?"

He handed Fergus the newspaper.

"Good God," he said.

"Yes. That man, with characteristic, monumental bad judgment, attempted to kiss Ms. Darcy, whom he had just met, in public. She, as you see, quite put him in his place."

"She sure did."

"That man is the president of Sanecor, Satellite News Corporation, a worldwide, multibillion dollar media empire."

"Right. I thought he looked familiar."

"Your expression tells me you are putting it together, sir. Very good. Yes, he and I share the same last name. He is my son, for better or worse. Usually the latter. Among his other characteristics, he is self-important and excessively proud. I am certain he deeply craves revenge upon Ms. Darcy for his public embarrassment.

"Through my contacts, I have learned that a Sanecor reporter is in this area working on a story. New Mexico is an improbable area for a story for a British tabloid, and it aroused my curiosity. Last weekend I happened to have this newspaper lying open on the table while I was looking at a photograph of Doro Mendoza's intriguing painting. I think you are familiar with it?"

He turned up a picture frame lying face down on the table. They regarded the two images side by side.

"Does it not strike you that Ms. Darcy and the young woman in this painting bear a strong resemblance? I have never met Ms. Darcy, but those who have tell me she has an extraordinary presence. I had thought the same of young Ms. Móntez when I met her briefly at Ms. Blatherwick's gallery, and much more so when she visited me here last week.

"Thus it finally dawned on me, Mr. Fergus, that if these two women were related, and if that reporter got wind of it, it would provide an excellent means for my son to create a very great deal of mischief for both of them. Do you see?"

Fergus waited a good ten seconds before speaking.

"I do, yes."

"I have discussed this with Ms. Móntez. I am certain the reporter does not represent any physical danger to her. Social danger, or psychological, is another matter. I have told her that in my capacity as CEO of Sanecor I may be able to suppress the story. I will work on that this evening.

"Still, I thought it wise that you should know the situation. It might have a bearing on your decision-making."

Fergus looked at the old man with new respect.

"Yes, sir," he said. "It just might."

It took ten minutes to work through city traffic and reach the highway to Tasajillo. It was cold and there was a light drizzle in the air. The wipers swept the windshield once every five seconds or so. The kid said nothing. Once she had engaged the cruise control she still said nothing.

"Bianchi told me what he told you," he said, waiting for her to reply. When she didn't he continued. "What do you want to do about it?"

"I don't know," she sighed. "What do you think I should do?"

"Well, even if we figure out who the reporter is, we can't stop him. We might just make it worse. You need to avoid the guy completely. The best course is for you to disappear as soon as possible, like tonight."

"I hate to miss the last three days, though."

"Aren't there other ways to do something like this? What about at a hospital?"

"I tried that. It didn't work. I got in the way. The state does these medical clinics every six months. The next one is a long way off, darn it. Tomorrow they vaccinate all the school kids and give them a quick physical. I'm needed for that. Can we leave tomorrow after work?"

"I don't advise it."

He didn't want to scare her with the little episode of the dopers and the bomb. Better by far just to leave town clean. He decided to resort to the nuclear question.

"What would your mother say?"

"We both know what she would say. But Mr. Bianchi said the reporter meant me no harm. I want to leave tomorrow."

"If you insist. But I'd like you to wrap it up as early as you can so we can grab our gear and go. OK?"

"OK."

Fergus was annoying her again but she couldn't bring herself to snip at him. In all honesty, she had to admit that this time, he was right.

## Chapter 29

"This was a lovely evening, husband. Thank you so much for arranging it. I can barely hold my eyes open. I'm going to call Rob and Michelle and then go to bed early. I hope you don't mind."

"Of course not, love. I'd like to hear their news too—Michelle must be about due by now, right? Please give them my best wishes."

He watched her pull out her phone and head outside. Julio was out there too, walking and talking on his phone. Was there something about cell phones that required walking?

The microwave dinged. He removed a cup of coffee, poured in a little milk, and sat in an easy chair under the mounted head of a trophy buck, propping his feet up on a stool. His boots were dusty.

She had called him "husband" rather than using his name. That little formality in her speech, most often used when others were present, was a clue she was slightly ill at ease. He expected her to be tense and embarrassed with herself after her exploit at Davos, but it was taking her more time than he would have predicted to settle down. A novel three-day cruise on a fancy yacht hadn't been enough, nor, apparently, had tonight's extra-cost luxury option for hunters at the Plan C lodge: a catered barbecue under the stars, with a honey-voiced guitarist performing tejano favorites in the moonlight. Even Julio, not normally attuned to social refinements, enjoyed that.

She seemed cool toward their Plan C arrangement, too. True, the cottage was small, not something for long-term occupation, but it was comfortable. Maybe she missed the mountains. So did he. They needed to visit their Plan B ranch house in Montana and compare. They might even consider a Plan D closer to home.

Come to think of it, Ana hadn't been that surprised about Julio's speed record at the Texas Mile, but that could have been because she was far from being a car enthusiast. She'd traveled to Earth for years at 178,000 miles per second, after all. Her son's 211 mph record was trivial next to that.

The front door opened to admit Julio.

"What news from your sister, son?"

"She's fine. Busy. They're vaccinating all the school kids tomorrow. She said she's getting a little better at diagnosing."

"Ah, good."

"She asked about our schedule, when we expect to get home."

"Well, we'll take our time. Might stay at Scott and Ianthe's place on the Williams' ranch a day or so. Best guess: home Friday, maybe Saturday. You think?"

"OK. I'll text Clio. She wanted to know."

"Did you tell her about our new truck?"

"No. I wanna surprise her. She'll love it, I bet. Mom wasn't that thrilled."

"No, but remember: she didn't grow up in a car culture like we did. You made a good choice, I think, son. It's comfortable, plenty of room for all four of us…drinks gas, though. All trucks do, really."

"Yessir, but the Honda Ridgeline has one big advantage."

"You love that trunk, don't you?"

"I do! It's the only truck with a lockable compartment under the bed. Perfect for batteries, Dad!"

"Yeah, well, we'll have to see about that. Messing with it will void the warranty. You'd have to do some major monkeying with the engine and brakes to turn it into a hybrid."

"I know, Dad, but I'll be careful. I promise."

"I want to break it in first. I'll let you fool with it next year or the year after. You don't want to have to buy me another truck to replace a boogered one, even if you can afford it. Did Clio say anything about Fergus?"

"Nossir, not a word."

"Good. Must be working out. I wasn't sure about that."

Julio was tapping in the text message to his sister when Ana appeared, face tired but radiant.

"It's a girl!" she beamed. "Seven pounds, three ounces! Mother and baby are fine!"

"Hallelujah!" Matt said. "I bet Rob is a nervous wreck."

"She just said Rob's very happy. Charlene is with her. And guess what the baby's name is?"

"Oh! Ah…hmm…would 'Ana' be a part of it?"

"Lily Ana! Isn't that sweet?"

"Very sweet, sugar."

He got to his feet and hugged his wife tenderly. That might be just the pick-me-up she needed.

"Why don't you plan to visit them soon?" He winked at her. "Lily Ana! Very, very sweet!"

## Chapter 30

Wednesday had been a long, busy day for the kid, but her energy level looked as high in the late afternoon as it had all morning. Youth and optimism. Pain in the ass. Dammit, it was a long day for him too. His stump was killing him. It was time to hit the road and end this gig...possibly with one of the bottles from his stash. Yes!

Elementary-age kids were everywhere, not quite running wild but with the same level of shrill excitement, and there were enough mothers and babies to make school officials confident of future employment.

One of the mothers was working through a set of rosary beads. Good luck, lady. You'd best just leave a message—God's been on an extended holiday. He clearly isn't that worried about your baby's health or the violence his people are wreaking upon the helpless of his world, and that's a fact. Got the scars to prove it.

Now the kid's handling two rug rats at the same time. She must have picked up germs from a hundred people today, half of them nose-wiping ankle biters. She means well, but she's doing what? Diagnosing health conditions? Curing people with her hands? Oh, sure, girl. More like charming them with your bright smile, like that poor old wreck Bianchi, so pathetically grateful for a cute young woman who'll massage him to sleep. Who couldn't use a little healing like that? But hey, pops: you're still gonna die. There are no free passes on life's highway, no matter how much money you got.

If there are any reporters around here they must be very good at being invisible. No bearded guys in Suburbans, either. No one at all lurking in cars in the parking lot—but securing the perimeter was a good opportunity to take a couple slugs from the pint stashed in the car, at least.

Dammit, it's going to be good to get out of here. The money is excellent, but it was disappointing not to work with the woman from that other planet. Working with her kid? The kid is different, quirky, running some kind of medical shtick. She might even believe it herself. Hard to tell.

Four p.m. Time for one last visit to the car? No, better not. We'll be driving together the rest of the evening. Better to wait a day and get good and anesthetized on the plane, once this gig is history. Can't happen soon enough.

Clio was so absorbed working with groups of children that she nearly forgot to pause for lunch. Never before had she had so many contacts with dozens of children in a row. She was experiencing a flood of potentially useful impressions even though she didn't have time to concentrate on each one.

The auras tended to be vibrant and complex, probably because of the children's youth, high growth rate, and relatively robust health. There were many siblings among them, and she was beginning to realize that those auras did indeed show some commonality. In eight or ten other cases she was also able to receive impressions from mother and child, and there, too, she thought she could discern familial patterns in their signatures, though describing their characteristics to someone else would have been impossible. A double blind test might help, but that was out of the question for now.

She ate lunch by herself, in a corner, doing more thinking than chewing, mulling over some of her past studies. Basically, the purpose of the approximately 30,000 genes humans carry is to create thousands, perhaps millions, of RNA chains. The RNA molecules flow throughout the body, causing the appropriate cells to manufacture the millions of proteins which make life possible. There were estimated to be hundreds of millions of different types of these proteins.

Making matters still more complex, every person's complement of proteins is unique, including some inevitably faulty ones. A few are malformed enough to result in illness. Bovine spongiform encephalopathy (mad cow disease) was one such, caused by a particular reversed protein. Humans could contract it. There was no cure.

She knew that since human DNA had been decoded, the next holy grail of analysis was to identify the human "proteome," the body's inventory of proteins, whose untold billions of combinations and interactions seemed nearly incalculable, an even bigger challenge to supercomputers than the weather system of the entire planet. Every human was an impossibly complex galaxy of tiny bits of life, literally a living stew, continually reproducing, changing, and interacting.

She must have dreamed of this stew before—the first time was in the Mexican desert several years ago: tiny dizzying bits of life, swirling whorls of molecules. Was that what she sensed? If it was, she despaired of ever adequately comprehending it. If it wasn't, then what was she sensing?

She used to think she might be going mad. Now she no longer thought that. She had no idea what to think. Her brother had a comparable predicament with his search for what he called the "unified field theory." She had seen him tantalized by almost, but not quite, understanding the force of gravity well enough to harness it as a means of propulsion, as Thomans had done. She thought her own problem was worse, though. Hers had to do with the process of life itself, and she seemed to have some poorly-understood ability to affect it. That was a terrible responsibility. Julio did not have to worry about that.

A tiny doll-faced little girl in a sequined pink t-shirt, ruffled pink pants, and tiny pink sandals was staring up at her, holding a googly-eyed purple velvet hippopotamus to her chest. Beyond, a troupe of little boys in jeans and blue shirts from a parochial school were filing into the gym.

Her half-eaten lunch went into the waste bin.

"Hi, mija!" she said to the little girl. "Let's go find your mother!"

---

The tide of school children ebbed by 4:00 pm, but it took Clio until 4:40 to pay her farewells to the head nurse and staff she had worked most closely with. They thanked her for her help and begged her to come back for the spring clinic. She met Fergus by the gym entrance and they headed back to the motel.

There were six or seven cars and trucks at the motel, including one sleek Infiniti two rooms away from theirs—some well-heeled businessman, Fergus thought idly. But he thought differently when he and Clio got out of the Corolla. Both front and back doors of the Infiniti opened at the same time.

"Hands on the car. Don't move," a voice said.

Two men, with a sawed-off shotgun and an automatic pistol. He glanced at Clio. A third man had come up behind her out of nowhere with another shotgun. The kid looked furious.

"No chance," he said to her, slapping the roof with his palms. "Do it."

In less than a minute they were bound hand and foot with nylon ties, hands behind backs. They quickly found his gun and knife.

"Guy has a wooden leg," one said.

"Don't matter. Let's go," said the other.

He recognized the man on Clio's side—the big guy he pounded hard last week.

They were pushed into the Infiniti and driven around the far wing of the motel. On the other side was a shuttered gas station and that damned black Suburban. Their captors transferred them to the cargo area of the thing and rifled their pockets, turning off their cell phones and putting everything in a green nylon bag. The bearded guy cautioned Clio's man to not be so rough with her. Why would they care?

The Suburban started moving. The bearded guy was driving. The other two, the big dumb one and a wiry Hispanic with a thin halo of beard encircling his chin, were on the bench seat behind the front seats, swiveled around to keep the shotguns pointed at him and the kid, their backs against the passenger side panel.

There were no windows in the back except two small ones in the rear doors, above their heads. He did his best to tell which direction they were traveling. They were on the main highway through Tasajillo, heading north. Several minutes later they turned west at the Mexican restaurant—light from the familiar tall, colorful sign shined through the windows. Start counting the minutes, in case it might matter. The kid looked plenty worried but hadn't panicked. Good going, kid. Stay cool. No other choice for now.

Clio was as surprised as Fergus. She considered attacking the man on her side, but Fergus's quick warning stopped her. She was treated roughly but not hurt beyond being pinched by the nylon ties and manhandled, literally, into the Infiniti and then the bigger truck. These were the drug dealers they had beaten up the week before, when they were hassling that young mother and child. It seemed stupid for them to take the chance they had taken just to get even, but something Fergus said came back to her: never underestimate the power of stupid people.

Once before she had been attacked and thrown into the back of a vehicle and she would never forget it. It was only because of her gravity tag and her family searching for her in the pod that she and Harry weren't killed. But now, her family would have no idea that she was in trouble. They weren't even home. The pod sat in its hangar. Her gravity tag was useless.

There was a Seal with her, though. OK, a former Seal, one whose conditioning was more than a little doubtful. She was thoroughly and desperately frightened.

Fergus estimated that the Suburban was traveling 50 mph or a little faster and heading mostly west, up a fairly steep, curving road. It was now dark. He saw no street lights or other lights of any kind from his angled view of the front and rear windows: it was a country road or highway, up into the mountains around Tasajillo. He'd not been on this highway before and he hadn't studied an area map to know where they might be, dammit to hell.

These sons of bitches. Who'd have guessed that an expensive Infiniti with tinted windows would have two jackasses hiding in it? These bums were not reporters, for sure. Bianchi must have had his head where the moon don't shine about that.

He and the kid were in the dumper big time. Shit, they'd been within ten minutes of blowing town and wrapping up the gig. Now he could be headed to the Seal hall of shame, goddammit, or maybe just an unmarked grave. Two unmarked graves. God *damn* it!

Fifteen to twenty minutes passed. The Suburban slowed and turned right, off the road onto an unpaved surface. They rolled slowly maybe a hundred yards and stopped. The big dumb one got out. He must have opened a gate—the Suburban eased another short distance, backed in a circle, and stopped.

The bearded driver got out, leaving the Hispanic man and his shotgun to watch them.

Lights came on outside. Metallic rattlings. The bearded guy gave the dumb guy muffled orders. One of the Suburban's back doors opened.

"You first," Beard said to the kid. "Scoot this way. Don't make me come get you."

She scooted, feet first. Beard grabbed her wrists with one hand and cut her ankle tie with the knife in his other hand. He marched her off. There was a metal on metal clang.

"Now you," Beard said to him. "No funny stuff," he said, cutting the ankle tie. The Hispanic guy on one side and Beard on the other guided him into a large chain link cage. They shut the chain link door and locked it with a padlock.

"More bird dogs. A full house." Beard said. "C'mon, Fdez. Let's get those crates loaded."

He backed the Suburban to a shed behind a dilapidated house trailer.

Fergus took in the situation. He and the kid were locked in two of three dog pens, it looked like, each about six by twelve feet, on a single concrete pad. The end cage was occupied by a disheveled, very unhappy-looking man, also with his hands secured behind his back. He was on the pudgy side, stubble-cheeked, with sandy hair and a florid complexion, and looking wide-eyed at him as if he had two heads.

The chain link sides were solidly anchored by corner posts set in the cement. Overhead were a series of hog panels, sixteen by four feet each, made of heavy welded wire on six inch centers and held in place with heavy wire twists, impossible to remove without a bolt cutter. Each cage contained a plywood dog house with shredded tar paper tacked over the top. They were about the right height for a human to sit on.

Lighting, what there was of it, came from a string of a half dozen bare bulbs strung from the tree over the cages to a house trailer. The trailer had seen better days. One window was boarded up and screens over the other windows bore ragged holes. Some of the blocks the trailer rested on had sunk into the ground, giving it a decided list. Patches of mold were growing up from the bottom edges of the aluminum siding.

The Suburban was backed to a small metal shed behind the trailer, the kind of shed normal homeowners would keep a wheelbarrow and lawnmower in. This shed, it seemed, contained heavy metal cases. Chinwhiskers and Beard were straining to hoist each one into the truck. The cases looked gray or olive green in the darkness. Fergus had seen plenty of cases like that in his previous employment: munitions, and weapons. This put the "drug dealers" into a different category, and not a better one.

Stupid helped lug the cases, but only barely. He must still be feeling the pounding he'd had the previous week. Once finished, Beard began lecturing Stupid. He was speaking emphatically enough that Fergus could make out the basics: keep watch, don't mess up the prisoners, don't get drunk, and stay awake until they got back, about midnight, or else someone would have his ass. The someone's name sounded like "Shits," but that couldn't be right.

Beard and Chinwhiskers got in the Suburban and drove away, turning right, up the highway away from town. Stupid shut the gate and went in the trailer. The lights went out.

It was a chilly night. There was most of a moon somewhere above the trees, enough to make out Clio seven feet from him, leaning back against her dog house. She looked stressed.

"You OK?" he asked.

After several seconds, she nodded minimally.

"Good," he said. "Hang in there."

There was nothing else to say. He looked at the man on the other side.

"Who are you?" the man asked. He had a British accent.

"I was going to ask you that," Fergus replied.

"I'm a reporter," he said. "I've been looking for you."

Holy crap, Fergus thought, there really was one. He needed to play this cool, and so did the kid.

"Me? Are you nuts? What the hell for?"

"You placed a call to Ana Darcy, the woman from the planet Thomo."

"I what? That's bullshit! You are definitely nuts."

"I'm not. You have made calls on that same phone while I've watched. There's no mistake."

"Don't tell me there's no mistake. Anyone with a cell phone can give all kinds of examples of weird mistakes from butt-dialing on up. Ana Darcy. Don't I wish."

"You called her. I can prove it. And I want to know why."

"So do I, jackass. I'd love to talk to Ana Darcy, but I promise you, Chuck, I've never called her on this phone or any other phone. Now I have a question for you. Why did these scuzzy goons grab your Limey ass and stick it in a cage, huh? Answer me that, Chumley."

Even in the dark he could see the man's face fall.

"I don't know why." He took a shuddering breath. "Why did they grab you?"

"That one I can answer. I displeased them. They were hassling a woman at the motel and I beat the shit out of them."

"By yourself?"

"Well, no, to be honest, not by myself. My niece helped. They don't care for her either."

"Now you're the bullshitter."

"OK, have it your way. Here's another question. You've been here a while, evidently. So what do you do when you need a john, hey?"

"I've been here a day. I piss through the wire in back. For the other they took me to that outhouse this morning," he said, nodding to his right.

He squinted into the gloom. Damned if there wasn't a dilapidated old-fashioned wooden outhouse sixty feet from them. It was probably full of spiders. The kid would freak big time. He wasn't too thrilled himself. He was going to ask the guy how he slept, but he didn't bother. The answer was quite obvious: not at all.

# Chapter 31

"Why you driving so slow, man? This is gonna take all night."

"I'm driving so slow because we're hauling a thousand pounds of stuff that'll send us to prison for twenty years if we get caught with it. If you'd done a better job of arranging that last sale we wouldn't have this problem. Schultz don't want this stuff neither, but he can keep it safer than we can. Besides, it won't take all night. What do you care, anyway? You got chicks waiting for you or something?"

"That Schultz is crazy, man. Whatsamatter with him, anyway?"

"Crazy like a fox, Fdez. You and me, we done time, right? Not Schultz. Schultz don't fuck up and he don't stand no one else fuckin' up either. That's why he's a rich sumbitch. That's why we make good money working for him. But you gotta be careful and follow his rules. If you don't, he gets mad. And you don't wanna make him mad, Fdez. Trust me on that. That's when he really gets crazy. I heard he killed a guy for not following his rules."

"Yeah, OK, I can dig it. Since you put it that way, everybody I work for is crazy. Especially you pinches gringos."

"You got that exactly backwards, you crazy Mex. Gimme a cigarette. I'm plumb out."


It was freakin' awkward having his hands tied behind his back. He ended up half sitting, half leaning against the dog house, taking a little of the weight off his upper body with his hands on the plywood behind him. After a half hour or more, the cold was settling in. It looked to be a long night.

The reporter was sitting slumped in a stupor on the cold concrete, sighing from time to time. The kid was keeping herself together, pacing back and forth and doing leg stretches.

This was nothing for a Seal. He'd lived through Seal POW camp, been kept awake and beat half to death over a damn week. Compared to that, this was a picnic. For the kid it might count as the midterm exam of a character test. So far, so good.

The lights came on. He glanced at the kid. She looked back, face neutral. The reporter was zoned out, not registering the sudden illumination.

With a screech of aluminum against cement, the back door of the trailer scraped open. Stupid stepped out, a beer dangling between the fingers of one hand. He belched loudly, rubbed his forearm over his nose, and headed their way.

In the dim light his eyes were puffy, hair uncombed, and there was a residue of white dust on his upper lip. He seemed to be trying to inventory his prisoners, but counting to three seemed too much for him.

The reporter wouldn't meet his eyes but he snarled at Fergus, who glared back. Then he moved to the kid's cage and studied her. He tipped up the bottle and drained it, letting it fall from his fingers. He pulled out a ring of keys.

"I better take a look at you," he mumbled, sneering through the wire. He stepped to the lock.

Bad move, Fergus thought. No way I can let you do that.

"Hey, dick brain," Fergus said, "You remember me, don't you, shithead? The guy that pounded your ass into the pavement? You scared to try again? Even though my hands are tied? How about it, blubber butt? Or are you only man enough to take it to a kid?"

Stupid looked sidelong at Fergus. His jaws clenched, but he took hold of the lock to the kid's cage.

"Hey, pussy," Fergus snarled. "I'm talkin' to you, chickenshit. Big man, huh? Fuckin' coward. Bench-warmer on the jerk-off team, aren't you? C'mon, dog turd. You scared you'll get your clock cleaned by a no-handed man? A second time? What a sorry fuck."

Stupid stalked to Fergus's cage, growling like a bear. Fergus continued heaping abuse on him while the guy fumbled the lock open.

Here we go, he thought. The only option was to seize the advantage if he possibly could, and keep it. If he couldn't, he was going to get a beating.

As soon as Stupid stepped inside he charged into him with a roar of his own, trying to ram a shoulder into the guy's midsection and knock him down or wind him. If that succeeded, he'd improvise from there.

Stupid managed to get a meaty arm up before Fergus reached him, reducing the force of the collision. He followed that up by slamming his other arm hard across Fergus's neck and back, nearly knocking him to his knees.

Fergus pushed into him as if the guy was a tackling sled, but Stupid already had his back against the inside of the cage and didn't give way. Instead he fought back, clumsily but effectively. He had arms.

Fergus tried to knee him but he was expecting that and turned to the side or raised one of his own legs. Unable to use his own arms to retaliate or block punches, Fergus was forced to give ground until his back was against the long side of the reporter's cage. Stupid leaned in against him, indiscriminately punching at ribs and kidneys. Fergus was seeing stars. The pain was incredible.

He was on the point of losing consciousness when he realized the guy had stopped punching. It dawned on him, like it must have on Stupid, that they were hearing a high, shrill sound so loud it was almost painful. It took Fergus several seconds to realize it was the kid, screaming at Stupid. Then she began shouting. And Stupid was listening.

Fergus sagged to the cement, faint with pain. He forced himself to concentrate on her words. She was berating Stupid, mocking his masculinity as he had. Somehow it sounded much worse coming from a young girl. Fergus was too dazed to follow it all, but the phrase "limp dick" got through. So did "shriveled."

Her words seemed to hit close to home. Stupid remained standing over him, curling and uncurling his fat fingers, inches from Fergus's face. Suddenly he bellowed, kicked Fergus in the stomach, and turned to the door, pulling out the keys.

She was calling Stupid off him! No, dammit, kid, shut up! He tried to shout at her but there was no breath to do it with. Stupid still had the presence of mind to lock him in. The kid kept up her insults as he unlocked her cage door. He heard her taunt something about "balls like raisins," and then the chain clanked and the door creaked open. All he could do was gasp for air and watch in horrified anticipation.

He would remember the next forty seconds the rest of his life.

When Stupid stepped inside, his face like a thundercloud, the kid stopped shouting. She shrank against the back of the cage, terror on her face. But when Stupid stepped closer with a nasty grin on his puffy face, her expression changed suddenly. She raised her head, took a quick step to meet him, eyes glaring, and hissed viciously from deep in her throat, showing her teeth, just like that goddam cat of hers, and kicked him solidly in the nuts. In the half second it took for that to register on Stupid's face, she turned sideways and kicked him square in the belly, not a toe kick but a full stomp, with her heel and all her coiled weight behind it. It sounded like a baseball bat hitting a watermelon. Slobber shot out of his mouth. Then she set her leg and kicked him again, higher, in the solar plexus.

Stupid was making garbled sounds like a drowning animal coughing up a hairball, bent over but still standing. The kid stepped to Stupid's left and delivered a third stomp to the side of his knee. Fergus heard the ligaments crunch as they gave way. The guy collapsed heavily on his left side and lay there, rocking in agony, scrabbling his fingers into the wire cage and pulling himself halfway up, still gurgling and blowing spit. It was ugly.

The kid thought so too, judging by the horrified look on her face. She watched him another ten seconds, glanced at Fergus, and then stomped him sharply in the head just over his ear. It was the knockout blow. He fell back against the fence, out cold. Why the hell did she do that?

The kid watched him another fifteen seconds. He wasn't moving. She rolled him with one foot until he was lying flat on the cement. Then she sat on the cement next to him. Huh?

She scooted backwards, up against the guy's waist. Her shoulders moved a bit, moved some more, and finally she stood up. She had his knife from the scabbard on his waist. Of course: that's why she knocked him out. She had to get him where she could reach that knife without him resisting.

She got to her feet and came to the wire between them. Turning her back, she stuck the handle of the knife into one of the openings in the chain link. It sagged down loosely, but she carefully felt for the blade and tried to press the nylon tie that held her wrists together down onto it. The knife fell out. She replaced the knife and tried again, and again it fell out. Fergus wanted to hold it for her but he couldn't budge. He felt like a bus had run over him.

The fourth time the knife stayed in place and she sliced the tie through. With her hands free she dug the keys out of Stupid's pocket—he still hadn't done any more than twitch and gag—and let herself out, locking him in. Then she went to Fergus.

"Ahhh, that's better," he gasped once the nylon strap was gone, carefully flexing his shoulders. He looked up at her and cleared his throat twice. His voice was raspy.

"Balls like raisins? Good one, kid."

"Fergus," she said, laying her hands on his neck, "Be still."

"Can do…ahhh…no problem."

After a bit she moved her hands under his shirt, to his shoulders, collar bones, and upper chest.

"Oh, Fergus," she said, "You're hurt, bad."

"No damn lie," he wheezed. "Hey, not to break up your fun…but…but someone needs to see…if there's anyone in that trailer…and especially if there might be…a usable vehicle out front. I nominate you."

"OK. What about him?"

"The reporter? I dunno. Leave him for the moment. We can decide later."

"What about you?"

"Gimme some minutes to let the adrenalin level out. I ought to be able to get up before long. I won't be winning any races, though. Tomorrow's when I'm gonna be laid low. If we make it to tomorrow. Get going, girl. And be careful. If someone's in there, don't let 'em grab you. You're all we got, now."

The reporter, still slumped against his dog house, was looking at the two of them as if they had suddenly materialized from another dimension. Clio stared at him until he noticed her in return.

"You'll be OK," she said to him. "I'll cut that strap in a minute."

Fergus watched her head off in the direction of the trailer. How great to be breathing again. What we take for granted, he thought.

They had to get the hell out of here. If there were a vehicle they could hot-wire, problem solved. If not, the next option was a distant second. Hide in the woods? Not good. Hobble down the highway and hope to hitchhike before Beard and his pal returned? They'd taken his watch, but if they expected to return by midnight that must be an hour and a half, two hours, away, max. He couldn't hobble far in that time.

He rubbed his face with both hands, reveling in the sensation of being alive. Stupid hadn't busted up his face. As dumb and doped up as Stupid was, maybe Beard's warning not to mess up the prisoners sank in somehow. However it happened he was grateful.

Next door, Stupid was on the road to recovery. He could groan now, and add to the puddle of drool under his mouth. Fergus flashed back to the kid putting him down in seconds. He had seen a lot of combat and more than his share of martial arts movies, but he'd never seen anything like that. A hundred pound girl…. Coombs had told him stories of Ana Darcy's abilities as a fighter. The kid was her daughter, for damn sure. What a great tale to share with Robboman... if he survived that long.

He decided to try to get to his feet. The chain link fencing provided handy finger holds, but even so it took several minutes to pull his bruised and cramping body to the vertical. He carefully rotated his neck, forcing the dizziness to subside. The gutless reporter watched him the whole time. Ah, here comes the kid.

"What'd you find?"

"Just this pack of water bottles. A lot of beer and liquor, but I left those. There's a motorcycle out front under a tarp, but it's all in pieces. There's no one in the trailer. It's filthy. It smells terrible."

"Well, crap."

"Fergus, how far do you think we came from Tasajillo?"

"Ten to fifteen miles, give or take."

"OK, look: I can run back there and get my car and be back here before midnight."

"What? Are you nuts?"

"No. I've run ten miles many times. My mom ran over 30 miles once. This'll be easy. It's downhill."

"Well...."

"And while I'm gone, if you can walk, you can get as far as you can from this place."

She had a point. Even if the hoods caught him, she'd still be relatively safe.

"OK, then. You're on. Let's think about this a minute first, though."

Her shoes looked decent: suede or something like suede, flat heels, Velcro straps. She was wearing dark clothing, but she'd have to turn that windbreaker inside out to hide the reflective strips. When he asked, she said her brother hid an emergency key on the outside of all the family cars in case keys got lost or locked inside.

He had some final thoughts before she departed.

"Those guys left going the opposite direction you'll be running, so they'll probably come back from that direction too. But they might not. You need to get off the road and hide for any and all vehicles. They had a black Suburban, but they could be in something different now. Don't risk contact with any vehicle unless it's a cop car.

"I'll do the best I can to put as much distance as possible between me and this place. See if you can find me two t-shirts or light colored towels or something in the trailer. Let's assume I'll make it as far as the first turn toward town.

I'll drop one of the towels on the oncoming side of the road and keep going. That's your stopping point. If something happens to me and I don't get any further, turn around when you get to it and get the hell back to the Tasajillo police department, got that? Don't risk letting these mugs see you if they're at the trailer here, OK?

"Now, I hope I get farther, and when I see headlights coming from town, I'll drop that towel on your side of the road and hunker down. When you see something like that in the road, pull off and wait. Look in your rear-view mirror. If a crippled, busted-ass former Seal appears in it, that could be me. It could even be me and this fool reporter. If you don't see a towel, then keep on going to the one on the opposite side. Turn back there. Don't go beyond it and don't worry about me. I'll head for the woods where I'll be all right for days. You got that?"

"Yes," she nodded, "that makes sense."

She accepted two of the water bottles, and snugged them into her windbreaker so they wouldn't bounce.

"I'll see you soon, Fergus. Good luck and please be careful."

"You too. You're a trouper, girl."

She started down the dirt road to the highway at a brisk walking pace. About the time she disappeared into the gloom she broke into a trot. The last he saw of her was her hair, tied back in a pony tail, bouncing left, right, left, right.

Well, Fergus thought, ain't this a pisser. Time to get your broken butt in motion, man. He looked at the ring of keys in his hand. Might as well start with freedom of the press.

# Chapter 32

Tucker slowed and turned in past the "Sportsmen's Gun & Pawn" sign and pulled up to the gallery. He cut the engine and turned off the headlights.

"Stay in the truck. I'll be back in a minute," he said.

"No problemo," he said, mocking a gringo accent.

"I mean it. Don't get out and wander around. Schultz has cameras everywhere. He'll see you and get pissed. Smoke all you want but don't get out."

"Yeah, ok."

He mounted the gallery and pressed the buzzer. The latch clicked and he pushed the door open and walked inside. The showroom was deserted, barely lit enough to allow him to find the door to the back. Schultz was at his desk.

"Talk," he said.

"I brought back what we didn't deliver. Six cases."

"A'right. What else?"

"We got that government man. He's in the cooler. Had a high school girl with him, says she's his niece. We had to get her too—couldn't leave her behind to raise a ruckus. And one other...."

"*Another?* What the fuck?"

"There was another guy spying on that government man. We nabbed him too. Couldn't risk him seein' us grab the others. Says he's a reporter."

"You shittin' me? A fucking reporter?"

"I guess. Had a press card and a British passport. Also some kind of fancy phone surveillance gear. He wouldn't tell us what he was after, so we roughed him up a little—only a little, didn't hurt him, much—to make him talk. He said the government man was one of several people that's connected to some celebrity and he was checking them all out. That's all he'd say. He's in storage too. I figured you'd want to handle it yourself."

"Shit, shit, shit. Goddamit, this is gettin' too fuckin' messy!"

Schultz glowered at his desk like he was considering pounding it, but why? What was done was done. And he did want to handle it himself.

"Bring the truck around to the freight door. I'll open it. Back in, all the way in, so I can close it while you unload. Fuckin' government drones are probably looking down on us. Then drive me up there. I'll sort this out one way or the other."

Schultz watched Tucker all the way back to his truck on the security monitors. Then he headed to the blockhouse to let them in, thinking as he walked. He had already selected a good spot for a lonely grave up in the national forest above the shack. Wouldn't require much more effort to make it a triple.

At home, Clio often ran at dusk. Like most people, her mind controlled her body during her waking hours, but on a long run it was the other way around: her body took over while her mind rested, with the result that both body and mind were replenished by the exertion. It was doubly relaxing if it came at the end of a busy day.

Under more favorable conditions, a late evening run down a forested country highway might have been similarly pleasant. The weather—chilly and damp—was ideal for exercise. The ponderosa pine, aspen, spruce, and fir trees around her would have been beautiful, had it not been dark. At least their smell was crisp and clean. The run this night, however, was anything but pleasant.

For one thing, she was having another delayed reaction to violence. She had acted quickly and decisively as she had the week before, but afterwards, her jangled emotions exacted a cost in shattered nerves and regret at what she had done to that dumb, brutal man. But never mind that. There were much more immediate things to worry about now: the imminent danger to herself and Fergus, and, more to the moment, running strategy.

She stumbled once and nearly fell stepping in a pothole, a reminder that she had to devote some of her attention to where her feet were going, not a simple matter in the faint moonlight. She also had to keep alert for headlights from ahead and behind. There had already been two vehicles: a compact sedan with gotch-eyed headlights headed toward Tasajillo, and some kind of truck that looked like a half-size 18-wheeler with a flashing yellow blinker on the top of the cab, headed away from town. She left the pavement for both, standing behind trees until they had passed out of sight.

Still another part of her mind had to be concerned with pacing and endurance. She'd had no food for over twelve hours. Would that affect her performance? She didn't know, but she was too scared to feel hungry. Her normal running pace was seven to eight minutes per mile. Her mother, years ago, had won the Olympic marathon covering twenty-six miles at a little over five minutes a mile. Fergus had estimated the distance at no more than fifteen miles, so she would assume that. She would also assume she had no more than an hour and a half to make the run and then drive back. The drive was about twenty minutes. Unfortunately, since her watch had been taken, all the timing had to be guesswork.

She tried to concentrate on the potholes, the traffic, and the math. Seventy minutes. Fifteen miles. Drat! That was less than five minutes a mile. She didn't think she could run that fast for that long. Even her mother hadn't, and her mother had trained for it. She would have to do the best she could. What to aim for?

She thought she might reasonably be able to run seven minute miles for fifteen miles, but that would take over an hour and a half. She needed to run even faster than that. Five minute miles were impossible—she'd "bonk" before she arrived, slow down and go a little crazy. Six minute miles? That would mean an hour and a half. Maybe she could run that fast. She would try for six and pray it was less than fifteen miles to Tasajillo.

Fergus decided to take a quick look at the trailer before limping off. Maybe he could find a decent kitchen knife, at least. Stupid's knife was a cheapie, worse than nothing. No wonder the kid had trouble cutting that nylon. He shook his head as he yanked the screen door open over the concrete step. That fool reporter would not have made it to lunch on the first day of Seal training, if they had had lunch (which they had not). This guy just had no spine at all.

The kid was right: the trailer was, to use the Navy phrase, a shithole. He'd be very careful about fingerprints. If the local cops rousted this place they would do a cursory check for prints, but if weapons and drugs were involved, as it looked like, that would bring the FBI, among others. Their techs missed little, including DNA in big cases. Best not to touch anything much or sneeze or spit.

The place smelled of stopped-up toilet. All the furnishings were dirty and ragged and crap was strewn everywhere. He did find a usable kitchen knife, not too sharp but at least pointed enough to ruin someone's day. He wrapped one of the towels around it and stuck it in a back pocket. Using the other towel as a pot holder, he flipped open cabinet doors and lifted furniture for a quick look.

There was only one bedroom and only one bed, with a huge sag in it. Maybe this was Stupid's crash pad. The closet had two jackets on hangers and piles of clothes on the floor, and on the shelf…on the shelf…what was that? A green ripstop bag? It looked familiar. Gingerly, so as not to strain his abused muscles, he pulled it down and unzipped it. Hot damn! It contained the stuff they'd taken from him and Clio when they were seized! He dumped it out on the bed. God damn! There was his pistol! The clip was still in it. His Seal combat knife and scabbard. His Swiss Army knife. Their watches. Wallets. Cell phones (with the SIM cards bent in half, the bastards). Everything, even the kid's lip balm. Yee-hah!

Why the hell did they set it all aside like that? He ejected the clip, checked the chamber and restored the pistol to his ankle and knife and scabbard to his prosthesis and slung the bag over his shoulder. Dude! Screw the kitchen knife!

He walked outside loving the feel of the pistol against his ankle. He still felt like shit, but that was fifty percent better than when he went in. A battered broom was leaned against the jam. With great pleasure he opened the saw blade on his Swiss Army knife and sawed the sad-looking head off. It would make a usable hiking staff now. He was looking forward to some serious hobbling.

The reporter was sitting on a garbage can, waiting for God knew what.

"Hey, Mr. Reporter," he said, "got a present for you."

He handed him his wallet and passport. The guy took them with no comment.

"You could thank me, man. Wouldn't kill you. If they took anything else of yours, it might be in the bedroom closet in the trailer. I'll give you two minutes to check."

The guy just sat there.

"Two minutes, man. Then I'm heading down the road to join my niece. She'll be coming back with her car and we're outta here. Come with me and get a free ride the rest of the way."

The reporter looked at him as if they had just met on the street.

"That girl," he said, "your 'niece?' That's Ana Darcy's daughter, isn't it? I finally figured it out. She's Ana Darcy's daughter. That's why you called Ana Darcy."

Fergus's body was trashed but his mind was combat-ready.

"Pal," he said, "you really got some kind of strange bug up your nose about Ana Darcy. This is my sister's kid, and I will admit, some say my sister looks a little like Ana Darcy, but I promise you, she ain't Ana Darcy. She's a sensei. You know, a martial arts teacher? And her daughter is her best student. But that doesn't matter now. Come on, let's boogie on down the road. We gotta put some distance between us and this place, all right? Follow me, man. Let's go."

Fergus turned and began shuffling down the driveway to the highway. He looked back after a minute. The reporter was still sitting on the garbage can.

"I advise you to change your mind, and soon, pal. Go out to the highway and turn left. Walk your ass off, and you might catch up with me, OK? Good luck to you, bub."

And with that, Fergus headed off slowly and painfully into the darkness, his heart lighter than it had been all day.

## Chapter 33

Among her many fears on this horrible night, Clio worried that it was impossible to accurately gauge her speed or the time she'd been running. She had quickly warmed up at her eight minutes per mile pace, moving to seven as her body loosened up and her circulation rose to the challenge. Once she realized she needed to go even faster, she increased her pace gradually until her legs and lungs felt on fire. Then she backed off a little to a speed she hoped she could maintain, whatever it was.

The cloud cover had thinned enough for moonlight to produce shadows of the trees on the pavement. Except for her breathing and light steps, her progress was silent. Once, rounding a bend, she surprised a coyote at the edge of the pavement. Two hand claps sent the beast streaking into the woods.

She hid from another vehicle, a speeding pickup truck full of teenagers singing to a blasting radio. She used that brief halt to take a drink of water and shake her legs out for half a minute while she gasped for air and wiped her face.

She had never run downhill for an extended distance before. It wasn't as easy as she thought it would be. Different muscles, ones she seemingly seldom used, were being called upon. The muscles down the front of her thighs and calves were searingly painful and so tight she feared they would cramp. They felt like they were quivering. She shook them out a few more seconds, dropped the now empty water bottle, and resumed running.

She had enough experience as a runner to know that this wasn't going to be as easy as she had claimed to Fergus. She remembered something her mother had told her that helped when she ran the Olympic marathon: to repeat a mantra, in her mother's case a nonsense children's verse with a catchy rhythm in Luvit, her native language from Thomo. She had sung the tune to her children countless times. Clio began repeating it over and over until it created a stable place for her mind to settle down in.

The next few miles were not as steeply downhill, the curves more gradual, and the straight-aways longer. Surely that meant Tasajillo could not be that far ahead. More than likely there would be houses close to the highway, perhaps with dogs. She did not fear dogs—she had known since childhood how to handle them—but if they started barking that could attract attention. If so, she would deal with it somehow.

The image of the beat-up, badly injured Fergus, making jokes and struggling down the highway far behind her, was never out of her mind. Bodyguard or chaperone, whatever her mother was paying him could never be worth what had happened to him. It was worse because his drawing that terrible man away from her almost cost Fergus his life. The pain she was feeling on this run was little enough for what she owed him.

Her lungs would probably not explode, even if it felt like they were about to. She picked up the pace a little more.

I'm livin' the dream now, thought Fergus, if only those VA docs could see this. The sumbitchin' surgeons at the hospital practically made the patients walk back to their rooms off the operating table. Keep active, they said, exercise, don't lie around. OK, bastards, I got your activity. And man, does it hurt. Haven't felt pain like this since…well, too many times actually. For once, though, the stump was the least of it.

Even if he made it to one of the docs at the elementary school, he'd still end up doped to the gills and pissing blood for weeks. Busted kidneys tend to do that.

Traffic turned out to be a problem. He could see and hear vehicles plenty early, but getting off the road quickly and under cover was difficult. Nimble he was not.

The first vehicle was an old car, not moving too fast, which was fortunate: he stumbled over a limb getting to cover and nearly passed out from the pain of falling on his side. Took three damn minutes to get vertical again.

If the driver had seen him, he'd have thought he was an old broken-down codger who couldn't cross a street without help. Shit, he even had a cane, or the broomstick equivalent. Useless piece of crap—any weight he put on it only pained his battered ab muscles. Screw the broomstick. He slung it into the trees.

The second vehicle to come by was a freakin' Bud Light beer truck. Dammit, but wouldn't a beer be wonderful right now? Three would be even better. And what about that fifth of tequila on the kitchen counter of that trailer? Was it stupid to walk off and leave that, or what?

No, it wasn't stupid. Don't kid yourself, man: you're a cripple, a marginal goddam mercenary for hire, and an escort for a high school girl. But it's still a mission and you accepted it.

Shit, the same thing applied on active duty. Those simple civilian souls who said you were "defending our freedom" were full of horse shit. It had nothing to do with defending freedom. You were a cog in a political machine, following orders. Keeping the oil flowing was about the best reason you were there. But no matter: you and your squad signed up for it and you did it right.

You can do it right now, too. If you don't you're plumb pitiful and a total loser and why bother to live?

Better to concentrate on what you have to be thankful for. March to it, count it off, butthead. Make your doctor proud.

One: still alive.

Two: got no bullet holes.

Three: got no knife wounds.

Four: got no IEDs and no dain bramage.

Five: got no broken bones. Well, might should modify that one. A couple ribs on the left side are doubtful. So let's make that:

Five: got no compound fractures.

Six....

Six....

Go ahead, admit it, man: number six is that damn kid. You're thankful for that hundred pound Tinkerbelle. How crazy is that? In fact, as long as we're doing this, let's add....

Seven: Go, kid, go.

# Chapter 34

Once they were on the road Schultz spent five minutes grilling Tucker on the tactical situation. He must have been satisfied since he merely huffed but issued no torrents of profanity. After that, there was no small talk. Tucker didn't expect any. Schultz never said much anyway, and he was obviously pissed tonight. The tension in the vehicle was high. Tucker drove carefully. Schultz, in the front passenger seat, kept leaning forward to check the passenger side rear view mirror. A few vehicles were going their way, all obviously local, and none stayed with them long in any case.

Schultz had never seen the trailer as far as Tucker knew, so when he slowed and turned in at the gate, Schultz sat up and paid attention. As Fdez got out to open the gate Tucker noted the outside lights were on in back. Not a good sign—he hoped Bagger was not wasted or coked out of his mind.

Schultz noticed it too.

"What're those lights on for?" he growled. "Oughta be dark."

Tucker agreed but said nothing. He pulled around the trailer to shine the headlights on the cages.

Two were empty, the doors hanging open. The one on the right contained one person, lying in a heap. Tucker knew instantly: it was Bagger.

"What the fuck is that?" Schultz shouted.

Tucker put the truck in park and got out.

"Fdez, check the trailer," he said.

Schultz, pulling a pistol from under his jacket, stalked to the dog cages. *It's no great loss if he shoots Bagger,* Tucker thought. *Except we'll have to bury him. Goddam Bagger. How in the hell did three caged people get the better of that dumbass?*

Schultz rattled the door to Bagger's cage. It was locked.

"Hey, jackass!" he bellowed. "You! Get up, you fuckin' melt-down!"

The disheveled mound that was Bagger twitched enough to demonstrate life but seemed incapable of any higher function.

Fdez came out of the trailer. He shook his head.

"Get the flashlight outta the truck," Tucker told him. "Let's look for sign."

He knew better than to try to placate Schultz. He backed the truck in a circle and shined the headlights down the dirt driveway to the gate. He and Fdez began searching the damp dirt down the path to the highway for whatever they could see. The only vehicle tracks were several sets from the Suburban.

"Hey," said Fdez, pointing to the edge of the driveway, "Tracks."

He was right.

"Boss!" Tucker said, "check this out."

Schultz, a life-long hunter, needed only a few moments to read them.

"Three people," he said. "The girl, there. That one, a man in running shoes, and that one, a man in street shoes. He brought up the rear—stepped on the tracks of the other two. All walking. Toward the highway. Gimme that flashlight."

Tucker and Fdez followed as Schultz quickly traced the prints to the pavement.

"They turned south," he said. "Figures. That's toward town. How far is it?"

"The town? Twelve miles or so."

"And how long you been gone?"

Tucker checked his watch.

"About an hour and a half."

"Alright. You guys carrying?"

They nodded.

"Get in the truck. Drive."


By the time Clio ran under the now-extinguished La Placita restaurant sign, she was so near total exhaustion she could barely think rationally. She had no trouble thinking irrationally, however. Contemplating the stretch of highway running through the center of Tasajillo she found herself remembering her annoying friend Shack and his stupid video games. If this were a video game there would be assassins, monsters, trolls, zombies, werewolves, and space aliens waiting to jump out at her from behind each building, not to mention hiding in the trees—and she with no ray gun to vaporize them.

But there were no monsters, no assassins, not even any stray dogs. There were only two traffic lights, blocks away, blinking red. One beat-up pickup truck was leaving the Stop 'N' Shop, and a number of trucks were clustered around a honky-tonk on the other side of the street, with distorted music from an overloud juke box pulsing for half a block.

She jogged at a moderate pace down the pavement, avoiding the sidewalk. Her hair was a problem: it made her an identifiable girl from quite a distance. If only she had a ball cap, she could be a man, or at least a boy, out for a late-night run. Should anyone call to her she planned to merely wave and keep running. But no one else was out.

El Faro was two blocks past the middle of town, where city hall sat. Two pickups were parked in front. There would be a patrol car out and about somewhere, and probably a dispatcher somewhere staying in touch, but no lights were visible in the building.

A light was on in the lobby of the motel. The clerk was probably watching television or sleeping in an adjoining room. She allowed herself the luxury of walking to her car, her lovely, so very precious little car. There were twelve other vehicles parked before rooms, and lights on in two or three.

Her throat and lungs were on fire, her steps wobbly. She nearly cried when she touched the cool metal. Julio had clipped a short Philips screwdriver under the edge of the hood where the wipers nested. Her hands were shaking—for heaven's sake, don't drop the screwdriver into the engine compartment! She felt as if she were under water. Concentrating on each motion, she pulled the screwdriver loose from the spring clip that held it in place and clutched it to her breast. Yes!

A quick look around: no one in sight. She went to the rear of the vehicle, kneeled down, and began unscrewing the screw at the top left corner of the license plate. It came out with little trouble. She pulled the plate away from the frame and the spare ignition key trapped behind it fell into her hand. Yes! Quickly, she replaced the screw.

In the next minute she had opened the door, popped the trunk release, found one of the water bottles Julio had stationed there (bless you, J-man), started the car, had a long drink of water, and started back toward the mountains to rescue poor Fergus, if only she could. Her arms were shaking so much she could feel the car waver as the speed picked up. The dashboard clock read 11:43 pm.

The t-shirt! Please let there be a t-shirt on her side of the road!

Ben Bianchi was having the worst day of his life, and that was saying something, since the previous worst day of his life was only the day before. Here he was, man of the world, bon vivant par excellence, admired throughout the civilized world for his acumen and savoir faire and feared by the world's royalty, heads of state, and big league CEOs: here he was, coming to fully appreciate the wisdom of sending others to do the dirty work, others whom he could supervise in safety while staying close to his champagne breakfasts and silk sheets.

It's a fine thing to write lurid tabloid stories about crime and criminals, but quite another to actually fall in with the criminals. If he had only known he'd be risking his life for this damned story, he'd have let his flaming father stew in the soup that he made for himself. These people were animals, drug dealing, gunrunning, bloody animals!

Even the good guys were vicious—that girl, holy God, that girl! Whether she was Ana Darcy's daughter or not, she was the most violent one of the lot, a truly frightening human being. So sweet and innocent one minute, and a consummate fiend from hell the next. It was like a bad movie...a bad *American* movie. And the end wasn't yet written!

How far had he walked down this godforsaken lane? Who the hell knew? It was far enough to be too bleeding far. His normal exercise routine was to walk from the limousine through the lobby to the elevator. He must have trudged miles this night, painful miles, in the dark, in the middle of a wild, American forest, where mountain lions and bears surely lurked, not to mention ticks, snakes, and worst of all, spiders.

There was no sign of that uncle or whoever the hell that was ahead of him somewhere. There's another character from a bad movie. He'd seen him almost beaten to death, only to get to his feet and walk down the road nearly singing for joy. These people were crazy!

Oh, God, please let a policeman drive by. Anybody will do, really. Well, not *anybody*, not *them*. You know what I mean, God.

A few minutes later, headlights appeared around a bend perhaps a half mile away. The vehicle was unfortunately headed away from town, but any port in a storm, hey?

He stood on the shoulder of the highway and watched it as it neared. In fact, it stopped, just after it rounded the curve. The engine raced several times and then it accelerated suddenly, with a pronounced screeching of tires. The tires screeched again as it stopped suddenly. Then it repeated the previous maneuver. Very strange; this might not be quite the salvation he sought. He stepped off the pavement and selected a tree to hide behind.

The truck sped past, straddling the center line. He heard a radio and young voices shouting and laughing. Teenagers, drunken teenagers. For the love of God, this was like that *Deliverance* movie. There's a thought: deliver me, O Lord! Cautiously, he resumed his interminable progress downhill.

The next vehicle, a few minutes later, was much better behaved and going in the right direction. He stood as it approached, ready to wave it to a halt, when his blood ran cold: it was that cursed black truck! And it was slowing and coming at him! Oh, Christ!

He turned and started to run…where? Into the woods—there was nowhere else. Car doors opened. A voice shouted: "Stop, or I shoot!"

It was two of the same ruffians, but with a big, mean-looking bald one in the front seat who seemed to be the gang leader. He gave the orders.

"Put him in the backseat. Fdez, keep a gun on him. Mr. Reporter, listen to me. Sit there and be quiet and we won't shoot you. We won't even tie you up. But try to run off again, and Fdez will shoot you five times at a minimum. Do you understand? *Do you understand?*"

That was abundantly clear. Yes, he understood. He nodded.

"All right," the big bad bald one growled. "Two to go. Drive. Step on it."

Clio was sure there was no way Fergus could be running. If he could achieve a normal walking speed, say four miles an hour, the farthest he might get would be about five miles. But he was hurt, seriously hurt. He'd not likely get five miles.

That meant she couldn't reasonably hope to see a towel in the road for at least five miles. Since the highway from Tasajillo into the mountains didn't become steep and curvy for at least that long, she was able to drive that part as fast as she dared. After five miles she slowed to the speed limit and paid close attention to the right shoulder.

Her whole body was wound tight as a spring. With trembling fingers she set the vents on outside air in the hope that the chilly breeze would keep her mind alert as she sped along: inside curve, outside curve, inside curve: where was he?

To her horror she almost missed it. She was negotiating an outside curve as the invisible hand of centrifugal force pushed her car toward the oncoming lane and the steep dropoff beyond. The headlights swept across the darkness, over some bushes, back to the highway. The cloth, she realized a fraction of a second later, lay in the darkness close to the car. She stomped on the brakes and squealed to a stop four car-lengths past the towel. She was hyperventilating once again.

Where was he? The hoped-for vision of his form glowing red in the taillights did not come to pass. She was on the point of getting out to search for him when a rapping on the passenger side window nearly made her jump out of her skin. Oh, thank heavens! She mashed the button that unlocked all the doors. She could only see his waist, which moved to the rear door, but he didn't open it. He must need help.

She opened her door and started to get out.

"Wait," he said, looking over the roof. "There's a car coming."

Sure enough, headlights could be seen on the trees round the next bend.

"Turn this thing around and go," he said, urgency in his voice. "Quick!"

He pulled open the back door and got in. The vehicle's headlights came into view as it rounded the next curve. She shifted into reverse and goosed the car backwards while turning. Stomp the brakes. Throw it in drive. Hit the gas. The car fishtailed slightly as it began moving. A Corolla is not a dragster. The front tires shot gravel underneath as it picked up speed.

"It's them," Fergus said, "It's that goddam black Suburban."

Clio nearly panicked. She had no experience with high speed driving. The Suburban was gaining fast. She could hear Fergus fumbling around in the dark behind her.

"Drive as fast as you safely can," he said. "Where's the goddam window button? Ah."

The wind noise increased markedly right behind her head. What was he doing? The Suburban was closing fast. They were going to ram the Corolla! Without realizing it, she began moaning.

"Steady, girl," Fergus said over the roaring wind noise. "I'm going to encourage them to be careful. Don't be surprised."

The Suburban wasn't more than a car length behind them when she heard two quick mechanical crunches from the backseat and then…good heavens! A loud, flat pop—a gunshot! Another! Three more! Fergus had a gun! One of the headlights on the Suburban went out.

Whoever was driving must have hit the brakes: the truck receded quickly, slowing to stay a hundred feet back or more.

"Take that, bastards!" he shouted to no one in particular. "Got more if you want 'em!" Then, to Clio: "Hunker down in the seat, girl. Keep your head as low as you can. They probably have guns too and we might get some return fire."

A wavering, high-pitched "Oooooh" through her nose was all she could manage. The next curve was approaching and she was going way too fast....

"That's their car!" Tucker shouted, as the Suburban's headlights swept over it during the turn. "There's that government guy!"

As they watched, the government man in question dived into the car, which backed up and headed downhill, swerving wildly.

"Smash 'em!" Schultz growled. "This thing is a tank. Give 'em a good smack and send them over the edge. I'll get you another fuckin' truck."

Tucker floored it. The little silver car was not up to forty yet and the Suburban was approaching sixty. It looked like a simple matter to bump the hell out of that tin can.

But wait—a hand with a pistol appeared out the driver's side window! Fuck! The muzzle flashed and flashed some more. One of the Suburban's headlights went out. A spider hole crunched the windshield between him and Schultz.

"¡Ay, chinga!" said Fdez in back, as Tucker hit the brakes and ducked.

Schultz had his pistol out. He pressed the button to roll down the passenger side window.

The Corolla had rounded the curve ahead. Tucker wrestled the Suburban through the turn after it, keeping some distance between them.

"Close in again," Schultz ordered, "and stay low. I'm gonna give that fucker a taste of his own medicine."

A red light was flashing on the instrument panel: *Service engine immediately*," it said

"Boss! Lookit this! The engine temp's redlining! Guy must've hit the radiator. We gotta stop or we're toast."

He was right: the engine was clearly laboring, with a pronounced hiss and streams of vapor issuing from under the hood.

"Stay with him as long as you can," growled Schultz, pulling a cell phone out of his pocket. "I got that fucker's number." He scrolled down his contact list to "B1" and pressed "Call."

Fdez was giddy with excitement. He slapped the reporter on the shoulder.

"It's a bomb! Check this out, dude. Is gonna be cool, man!"

To Fdez's great surprise, the reporter exploded in anger.

"It's a *what*? NO! You can't do that! You bloody sod! Don't you see? It's not him, you silly shite! It's that girl! *That girl is A*...."

## Chapter 35

"What was *that*?" Clio screeched.

There had been a sharp, low whump over the wind noise, as if someone outside the car had hit a bass drum, hard.

Wincing with the effort, Fergus turned around in the backseat and looked out the rear window. The Suburban, on its side and trailing sparks and a rippling plume of flame, was sliding off the edge of the road into the canyon.

"That was car trouble," he said, smiling grimly in the darkness. As ye sow, so shall ye reap, bastards.

"It sounded like something blew up!"

"Yeah, it did, didn't it? Maybe I hit something important in the engine. It was a big target, true."

Clio slowed well below the speed limit and pressed the button to raise the back window. She was shaking and sniffling, trying not to cry, fighting to get her breathing under control.

"That truck? Wha...what happened to it? What about the p...pa...the passengers?"

"It was on its side, slowing down. I didn't see it hit a tree or anything."

"Oh, my gosh...oh, oh...if I'd been...been a minute later," she gasped, "...but, but you had a gun. Wh...where did you find a gun?"

"Checked the trailer before I headed out. Found the bag they stashed all our stuff in. Got it right here. You need your ChapStick?"

"Are you serious? Everything? That's wonderful!"

She slowed the car even more and took a long drink from her water bottle. Her teeth were chattering.

"N...n...need some water?" she asked.

"Yeah, thanks."

She passed it back, her hand trembling when the weight left it. She heard water gurgling out of the bottle.

It was over. They were alive, both of them. Fergus had saved them from being crushed by that big truck. She felt like crying and laughing at the same time.

She forced herself to focus on the road.

The water bottle flopped into the passenger seat.

"You're very un-annoying right now, Fergus."

In the faint moonlight that made it into the car on the driver side he could barely make out the back of her head. She had some kind of tie for her hair, but less than half was tucked into it. It was all over the place.

"You think so? Well since you brought it up, you're pretty un-annoying right now yourself, kid. Good job fetching your car. It was just what we needed."

She took her time getting back to the intersection by the restaurant.

"Go straight through," he said. "Take a right at the next street and go past the motel and come back around from the far side."

"OK," she said. "Why?"

"In case anyone in town noticed you rushing up there and then noticed you coming right back. They might remember that later."

"Oh. OK."

She crossed the intersection and turned right at the next. No other vehicles were out. A related thought occurred to her.

"Do you have another pair of shoes in your room?"

"Yeah, a couple."

"I do too. Maybe we should change them and hide these for a while."

He thought a moment. He figured it out.

"Ah. The tracks we left, right?"

She stopped at a stop sign, started again.

"Uh-huh. The police might remember your run-in with those guys and come by again."

"Good thought."

"Should we call in that...that accident?"

"No. One of them might be able to phone for help. For sure, there'll be debris and skid marks all over the road up there. The next vehicle either way will notice it. Bound to."

She reached the block behind the motel and turned right into the abandoned gas station. The Infiniti was still parked by the service garage.

"That's a rental," Fergus said. "The reporter rented it."

"How do you know?"

"His stuff was in the bag, too, including car keys with an Avis key fob."

She braked at the highway.

"Look," she said, pointing to her right. Five or six blocks away, a police car with lights flashing was turning by the restaurant. "You were right. Someone must have called that in."

"Yeah. Their little party has entered the clean-up phase."

"What was that all about, Fergus?"

"It looked like they were dealing dope for guns—that's what was in those crates they were loading before they left. Lotta money in that stuff. Highly illegal. Didn't want any people making connections. They probably saw that reporter nosing around and got spooked about him too."

She pulled into the space in front of their rooms and shut off the engine and sat there, still shuddering.

"I wonder if either of us can move," she said, opening her door. Her voice was hoarse, her throat raw.

It took determined effort and rubbing the muscles of her thighs, but she got out and stood, legs trembly. Fergus pushed open the rear door.

"Do you see the room key in that bag?" she asked.

"Yeah. Here. You can open up while I get vertical."

They managed to stagger into his room, grateful there were no witnesses. Fergus did a careful slow-motion collapse onto the bed.

"Oh, damn, oh hell, this feels good," he muttered. "I'm cleaning up my language for you, kid."

"Thanks for that. I'll be right back."

She emptied the bag containing their possessions on the bed and claimed those that were hers. She frowned at the bent SIM card but tucked it in a pocket. She took her key and went out to open her own room door. Then she opened their adjoining doors. Fergus hadn't moved.

"How do you feel?" she asked.

"I've been better," he mumbled, "quite recently."

She sat on the bed and took his hand. It took him a half minute to pull it away.

"What are you doing?"

She said nothing. She was nearly exhausted herself.

"Just let me lie here. None of that damned Catholic crapola, all right?"

She could hardly keep her eyes open. A wise retort was beyond her.

"OK. No crapola. I promise. I'll get you some ibuprofen. Then I'm going to take a hot bath. You're on your own, Fergus."

His eyes were closed. She went to fetch the pills, worrying about what she had just felt from his hand. She had experience with many seriously sick people, but could remember none who had had so much terrible pain. She had to do something about that, if she possibly could. But not now. It had to be later.

The bedside clock said 4:26 am. What an odd time to wake up. She slept less than four hours? The rattling hum of the heat pump under the window was a comforting sound. She was so stiff she could hardly budge, but a few minutes of gradual moving and flexing enabled her to return to her bathroom and take a second hot shower. That helped.

The reflection in the mirror over the sink suggested she was ten years older than she really was, and badly in need of a good meal. Yet she wasn't hungry. She ran her fingers through her damp hair again and again, getting it off her neck and shoulders and chilling her skin when it fell back. Fergus was right: she was a kid, an unremarkable, insignificant kid. There wasn't much to her, and not much to look at, all skin and bones and not much of either. Well, her mother wasn't that different, but she had managed all right. But there was no point in worrying about that now.

She looked in on Fergus. He was asleep in much the same position. She went closer. In the faint illumination from his bathroom light, she could see an empty pint whisky bottle on the carpet. She went back to her room to get her little penlight, the nurses' model used to check eye dilation, ears and throats. With its help, she found a partially open drawer in the bedside cabinet where there were two more pint bottles, unopened. She slid them under the bed.

His injuries needed to be inventoried. He hardly changed his breathing rate while she concentrated on feeling carefully along his neck, shoulders, and arms. The darkness didn't matter: she didn't need to see to feel the pain and bruising through her fingertips.

There were several large bruised areas on both arms. His chest and trunk were covered with massive injuries—the long, flat rectus muscles in his abdomen were severely bruised and possibly herniated, but she couldn't be certain about that. The hips and legs had several bad spots, but none likely to cause major, long-lasting pain.

The thug had pounded as hard as he could on Fergus's back, over his kidneys. That would be terribly painful, and the kidneys could be seriously damaged. Checking them could be a problem too, since they did not lie close to the skin. That was worrisome. However her hands sensed what they did, distance from the point of origin was a factor. The skin and blood vessels under the skin were easiest. The kidneys were not far under the skin—not like the spleen or pancreas, which were normally near the center of the trunk—but far enough from the skin to be difficult to sense.

She pulled up his t-shirt and slid her hand under his back to his right kidney. It turned out to be easy to locate because it was in terrible shape. It was like feeling the heat from an open oven at a distance. She wasn't sure she could treat it. The left kidney was almost as damaged. However had he managed to walk five miles with those injuries?

She sat on the bed and regarded his motionless form. He was a grouchy, cynical man, but also good-hearted and honest, smart, courageous, and very, very tough. There was no telling what violence he had lived through, but the concussions he had suffered could easily have changed his personality entirely. He was a lot to work on, more by far than anyone else she'd ever dealt with... Mr. Bianchi excepted. It was too late for him; not so for Fergus.

There were advantages with Fergus: she had a day, perhaps two days, to work on him multiple times. It was also fortunate that the healing he most needed was the kind she felt the most confident providing, involving muscles, tendons, joints, and the circulatory system. The kidneys would be a challenge, but there was no real emergency there. If something was beyond her and he needed a hospital, there would be time for that. In the meantime, she could "practice" on him, in both senses. If she could help restore him to at least the condition he arrived in, she would try her very best to do so.

## Chapter 36

She was just too tired to start on Fergus. The exertion earlier in the evening left her jittery, and her mind would not focus as she needed. A nap was not a choice either. There were too many things that needed doing.

The bent SIM card on the dresser caught her eye. It wasn't bent that much, really. She carefully straightened the tiny chip, laid it on the dresser to see if it was flat, bent it a bit more, checked it again, and installed it in her phone and turned it on. It worked! There was a message! Julio wanted to know where she was and why she wasn't answering her phone. She sent him a text message telling him the phone had gotten wet and that she would call him later in the morning.

That fib was a reminder that she had been in yet another terrible scrape and was going to have to decide how much she should tell her parents about what had happened. That would need to be coordinated with Fergus, one more thing to be done later.

She'd go get some food they could eat in their rooms. Fergus was still sleeping, with his shoes on. She untied them and pulled them off. She'd forgotten about his prosthesis. He had a support stocking on over the stump. She rolled that off. The stub of his leg was inflamed and hot and rubbed raw in several places, but the little tube of antibiotic ointment in her bathroom bag provided temporary first aid for that.

She put his shoes and hers in the green bag that had held their pocket items and hid it behind the ice machine in the alcove outside their rooms. Her own feet were tender but felt better in the little seven dollar blue tennies that were her backup shoes. She reinstalled the emergency key on her car, locked the room doors, and drove to the Stop 'N' Shop, where she bought two pints of milk, two of orange juice, and a small Styrofoam ice chest evidently designed for a six pack of beer.

It wasn't yet 6:00 am but the little coffee shop in the center of town was open. The proprietor, a cheery woman with fat cheeks happily prepared her four taquitos which she packed into her new ice chest.

She felt much better back in her room after a decent breakfast. She was ready to get to work on Fergus.

Fergus, however, was not ready to be worked on.

He was lying about as he had been, with one arm thrown over his eyes.

"Fergus," she said softly, "are you awake?"

The reply was a low groan.

"Fergus…."

"Sore as hell," he said. "Can barely move. And you took off my damned foot. Put it back on. I gotta pee."

"The leg is inflamed and abraded, Fergus. You'll damage it even more. Look, here's the ice bucket. Lie on your side and pee in this. I'll come back and dump it for you. Then I'll look at your leg."

"Screw that! Put it back on, kid. I'll pee like a man, goddammit."

"Please, Fergus. You'd do it if a doctor told you to. You can do it for a kid too."

"Damned if I will, goddammit. I'll…ohhhh."

He tried to raise up a little but failed.

"You see?" she said. "Even with the prosthesis on, you couldn't walk. Your abdominal muscles are too sore. Here's the bucket. Please try. I'll be back."

She returned to her room, unhappy with herself. Her bedside manner needed polish. After five minutes she returned. He had barely used the bucket. The urine in it was a pronounced red. She flushed it and washed out the bucket, thinking. She needed a plan to outsmart Fergus. She returned to the bedroom.

"I need to be in a hospital," Fergus grumbled. "I need to be zonked for a week on painkillers. I need a goddam doctor."

"OK, Fergus," she said, in a tone of capitulation. "I'll take you. Let me put on your prosthesis and we'll figure a way to get you up."

He grumbled while she squeezed more antibiotic ointment on her fingers but didn't resist when she began spreading it over the angry red skin where the prosthesis had fit. She rubbed it in gently, slowing her hands to a stop. Fergus's pain was like a solid wall, not personally painful to her but almost corporeal in its comprehensiveness. Where to start? She closed her eyes and confronted it gradually, directing her fingers to meet it, engage it, to sort it out. Fergus's voice broke through.

"What're you doing, dammit?"

"It's all right, Fergus."

"Goddammit, you promised. No crapola."

"This is not mumbo-jumbo, Fergus. I'm going to make you better."

"Like hell," he managed, between gritted teeth.

"Shhhh," she whispered. "Let me concentrate."

He tried to move his leg away but his abdominal muscles were so locked up he couldn't. She redoubled her concentration, made more difficult because Fergus kept swearing and moaning, but she persisted. She shifted the position of her hands several times to better understand what was what. Mainly, there wasn't enough muscle and skin tissue over the bone. It might grow in, but it would take a long time. Her eyes closed. She stopped listening to Fergus's curses.

Wave after wave of pain, aching, piercing pain met her fingers. Her vision faded, her fingers faded, until finally her mind met the pain directly, embraced it, explored it: the epidermal pain, the pain in the muscles, the painful inflammation of the osseous tissue, the abused nerve endings, all of it. It was not her enemy. It didn't want to be there. She would use it, work with it to help it go away.

Time slipped by. Her mind was on Fergus's body but she never forgot what she was doing. She had lessened the pain from his leg. She was sure of that, and that would have to do for now.

She opened her eyes. Fergus had gone to sleep like others she had treated. The plan was working. She went to the bathroom, washed the ointment off her hands, and returned to Fergus. His blood pressure was high, probably because of the damage to his kidneys. Those needed attention immediately. It would be her first attempt to treat an organ well beneath the skin. She suppressed her anxiety and forced herself to concentrate.

She started with the left kidney, closest to her, sliding her hand under the t-shirt just above the crest of the ilium of his pelvis. The location of the kidney was obvious: it throbbed with pain. Slowly sliding her fingers back and forth with pressure provided by Fergus's weight over them, she concentrated on the sensations. The blood coursing through the body's circulatory system was one of the first signals she had learned to identify. This particular task was especially daunting because of the scale of the damage. The kidneys purified the blood, which she knew she could work with, but she had never worked on such a badly damaged internal organ before. There was no hurry, fortunately. She focused her mind and tried to be open to her senses.

The aura around the kidney was hot, or heavy, or hard…there was no vocabulary to describe the impression. Despite that, she knew that moving her fingers back and forth and repeatedly stroking the area would cool it, or soften it, or thin it out. There was no way to explain it. She remembered combing her own hair with her fingers only minutes earlier: pass after pass, until it flowed smooth and free. Some day, perhaps Dr. Peebles' medical researcher friends could discover if she was clearing up the capillaries in the kidney, or flushing damaged corpuscles through to his bladder, or something else entirely. For now, somehow, with her mind, she was gradually combing the pain out of Fergus's left kidney. This power used to frighten her. Now she didn't worry about it as much. She used it.

She opened her eyes. The kidney was not yet well but she felt sure it was better. Fergus remained asleep, on the near side of the bed. She went to the other side, knelt on the bed next to him, and repeated the process on the right kidney until her back was hurting and the sore muscles in her legs were threatening to cramp up. When she finally stopped, this kidney was better too. The organs were not fully healed, but the fact that she had improved them gave her a little confidence.

It was nearly 8:30. She had never spent so much time concentrating on healing. It wasn't physically arduous but a she needed a change of mental focus. She went to her room, washed her face, and texted her brother that she was busy but could handle a text now and have a chat in a few hours. She drank some orange juice.

Fergus was still sleeping, his face haggard. Time to check the rectus muscles. Those worried her. It was fortunate that they were flat and near the surface: she was normally good with muscles and tendons. A serious injury, however, could require surgery. That was beyond her.

She got a bath towel from his bathroom, folded it several times, and set it on the carpet by the bed to kneel on. Several minutes of gentle exploration under the t-shirt were sobering. He had massive bruising all across his abdomen. It was a wonder no organs underneath had ruptured. Those were difficult to assess definitively, but the malfunction of a major organ would have been detectable. The area of bruising was bigger than both her hands.

Since he was sleeping soundly, she got up, slipped off her shoes, and straddled him carefully so that she could slide both hands under the t-shirt. It was a reasonably comfortable position. Moving both hands together revealed exactly where the toe of that awful man's boot had hit him. As far as she could tell there was no herniation, but there didn't have to be much to still be a problem. Those muscles were thin sheets, basically, and rather delicate. Even a slight gap could allow a partial intestinal protrusion. She'd do the best she could and see what happened.

Once again she focused her mind on Fergus's body, moving her hands in tandem in a sweeping pattern, ribs to pelvis, dozens of times, a hundred times, not daring to press too hard, focusing her mind on combing out the problems: freeing up circulation, reducing swelling, and soothing the tendons and connective tissues.

After uncounted minutes she paused and opened her eyes, straightening her back. Outside the room, someone was loading a car. A man's voice. Doors slammed. An engine started.

She made another survey of Fergus's abdomen and began repeating the slow sweeping motion, but in reverse, from pelvis to ribs, time after time until her mind began to float away. The bruising was lessening.

Fergus mumbled something and turned his head to one side. It was 9:40. She got off the bed and put her shoes back on. She studied him closely. His face was still drawn, but more relaxed. There was a light sheen of sweat on his face, a good sign. His temperature was high but not fevered. That meant his body was working to heal itself too. She needed to check his pupillary response.

"Fergus," she whispered, close to him. "Can you hear me?"

"Mm," he mumbled a few seconds later.

"Fergus. Wake up, Fergus."

"Umm," he said.

His eyes fluttered open, unfocused. Then they focused on her face, inches from his own.

"Umm," he said again. He took a deep breath, then another. "Umm. What day is it?"

"It's Thursday, Fergus. You've been asleep about four hours."

He took several more serious breaths.

"What'd you give me?"

"What?"

"What meds did you give me to knock me out? You must have been to a pharmacy and boosted some wonder drugs or something."

"Nothing. I gave you nothing. You took a couple ibuprofen after midnight. That's all."

"I can breathe now. How come?"

"I worked on you a little, Fergus. That's all."

"You? Just you?"

"Just me."

He stretched his body gingerly.

"Hard to believe."

"You want some orange juice?"

"Uh, yeah. But I gotta pee again, big time."

"Good. This time let's see if you can 'pee like a man.' I'll help you up."

Once she had installed his prosthesis and tugged his legs over the side of the bed, she coached his effort to rise.

"Push up with your arms so you don't need your abdominal muscles much. Just sit there for a bit, if you can."

It took a minute but he managed it.

"That's great, Fergus. Now draw your legs under you and push your weight out over them. Lift with your legs, not your middle."

She stood next to him in case he needed steadying, but he stood on his own, puffing a bit from the effort.

"You did it, Fergus. I'll walk you to your bathroom and then you're on your own. Call me if you need any help."

"I'm like a goddam geezer," he said, as he shuffled toward the bathroom.

"It's pretty good for a man who wanted to be 'zonked for a week.' Go do your business and then I've got some breakfast for you. I'm not through with you yet, shipmate."

Fergus halted his shuffling.

"'Shipmate?' Where the hell did you come up with that?"

"Mr. Coombs said that's what he and Mom were: shipmates. A team, I guess he meant. That's a Navy word, isn't it?"

"Yeah, it is. Shipmates. Hmm. I kicked ass. You kicked ass. We kicked ass. I guess we are a team. What a concept. Stick around, kid. I'll be right back."

And he shut the bathroom door.

## Chapter 37

"Tister! How're you doing?"

"Good, J-Man. How are you?"

"We're good too. What happened to your phone?"

"I got caught in a rainstorm. It got wet. I had to dry it out. It took two days."

"Well, I'm glad you're back. Working hard? Learning stuff?"

"I think so, yes."

"You always say that. I mean really. That health team sounded like the perfect place for you. Are you seriously figuring things out?"

"Well, yes and no. I can't explain what's going on any better, but I'm getting better at using it. But never mind that. It'll take too long to explain now. I'll tell you all of it when I get home. What about you? How did your car do?"

"Oh, man! That was so cool! We set a speed record! Two hundred and eleven miles an hour!"

"That Corolla? Two hundred miles an hour? Are you kidding me?"

"It actually got to 216 mph, but that was after the timing trap. We beat the old record by 36 mph!"

"Gosh, I wish I'd seen that. Congratulations!"

"Not only that, Toyota people were there. They're gonna study the whole system: batteries, drive motors, control circuits. They might wanna use it!"

"Wow! I guess that'll mean another bunch of money, you think?"

"Well, who knows? They bought the rights to look at it for two years. That'll be enough to buy me a fellowship year or two at Rocky Mountain Tech, if I wanna."

"That's wonderful. I'm so happy for you, brother. I hope someone made a video."

"Yeah, they did. The Toyota guys brought a video crew. They're gonna email the video to me. I should have it to show you next week."

"So, how's Mom?"

"Oh, boy. Did you see what she did in Switzerland?"

"Yeah, I did."

"Well, she was kinda bummed for a couple days. We had a little cruise down the Texas coast and then we sorta camped out at the Plan C ranch, and then we checked out San Antonio and an old friend of Mom's in Uvalde. Now we're at the house above the Williams Ranch in Alpine."

"What old friend of Mom's?"

"From when Mom first arrived. A college student hid her out and taught her stage makeup. You remember that story."

"Yeah, I do. So…."

"So Mom found out where she teaches and had lunch with her. She's a high school teacher, theater arts, I think. Dad and I didn't see her. Mom said she was so thrilled that she'd come to see her. Her name's Luisa something or other. She's married and has three kids now."

"Neat. How're the Williams?"

"Mr. Williams was in Houston at some hospital. Mrs. Williams was with him. I forget what's wrong with him but she told Dad he's gonna be OK. So it's just us at Scott and Aunt Ianthe's house in the mountains. They're still in Switzerland. It's real peaceful here, actually."

"When are you coming home?"

"Late tomorrow, maybe, or on Saturday. Dad and Mom wanna see Doro's gallery exhibition. They're thinking about coming up Saturday, if you're gonna be there."

"Uh, yeah, we, uh, finish and pack up Saturday morning, but I could meet you in Santa Fe, easy."

"Have you already been to the exhibition?"

"Yeah."

"You don't sound too enthusiastic."

"Well…Doro did a painting of me. It even looks like me. People were studying it. It's so embarrassing."

"Excellent. Gotta see it!"

"Don't say that, J-Man."

"I'm just kidding—you know that. Did you hear about the visitors?"

"The visitors?"

"You know, the ones Uncle Rothan announced."

"Yeah, I did. What do you think?"

"I think it's gonna mess up our lives. What do you think?"

"I think so too. I don't wanna talk about it."

"I don't either."

"I need to get back to work. Let me know when you all get home, please."

"I will. Hey, Dad bought a new truck. It's great on the road."

"Dad? A new truck? Did he hit his head?"

"He said the three of us wouldn't be comfortable in the old one. I think he was just tired of it."

"Well, I'll see it Saturday. Don't forget to call when you get home, please."

"OK, Tister. Take care. Miss you."

"Miss you too, Gomer. See you soon."

She stowed the phone in a pocket and checked on Fergus. He was coming out of his bathroom, looking jubilant.

"Pee at last! Pee at last!" he proclaimed, "Great God almighty, I can pee at last!"

"You stole that from Martin Luther King. That's not nice," she frowned.

"My apologies. But it's true."

"What was the color?"

"Pink, dark pink."

"OK. That's good."

"It is?"

"It's cleaning up. It's better now. That's good, but it needs to not be pink. It'll take a little longer, I guess."

He was moving stiffly. She watched to see whether he'd sit in a chair or lie down again. He appeared to be considering the chair.

"There's breakfast if you want it," she said.

"Good. I'm ready."

He chose the chair but sat gingerly, without leaning back. She set out the orange juice and milk and got the ice chest from her room. The taquitos were still warm, barely. He didn't care. He drank most of the orange juice and half the milk while consuming a taquito with relish. She forgot to buy coffee, but they made do with the little in-room percolator and coffee packets. He declined a second taquito and lay back down, slowly and carefully, uttering several grunts of pain. She removed his prosthesis. He didn't even complain, for a change.

"Do you have another stocking? This one's got ointment on it."

"Huh? Oh, yeah, in my travel bag. On the left."

"I'll wash it."

He folded the pillow in two and slid it behind his head.

"You did this, huh?" he said, patting his abdomen gently.

"Yes."

"So…you learned to do it, or what?"

"I'm still learning, I guess. That's why I wanted to work with this medical team. I discovered I could do it by working on cats and dogs when I was about eight, but I figured out more from helping my great grandmother. She had blood pressure problems and I found I could tell her blood pressure with my hands and eventually help her control it. That's how I started. I still don't know how I do it."

"I gotta admit, all along I thought that business with you and Coombs was bogus. But now that I've had a turn, I'm rethinking that."

"That was so scary. Dad said a barrel blew up and hit him. He was having a cerebral edema. I could feel his brain swelling fast. I'd never had an emergency like that before. I was afraid he would die in my hands. I had no idea if I could slow it down. It was terrifying."

"I remember that," he said, nodding. "The weirdest night of my life. Me and my team were at the ass-end of the world in the middle of armed hostiles, and who should drop out of the sky in the wee hours but the elusive woman from outer space in her sexy little spaceship, with Rob Coombs, half dead, and a crew that turned out to be her husband and children. And she gives us the scumbag the whole world had been trying to find for ten years."

He shook his head.

"Sheesh, what a night. The corpsman said Coombs should have died in minutes. He figured the guy was just lucky. Come to think of it, I guess he really was. So was I. Bravo Zulu…shipmate. If you don't mind my asking, how did you learn those martial arts moves?"

"I don't mind. Because of Mom. She already knew a lot, but she kept taking classes and I went along. She did a little of everything she could find."

"What's that kicking routine?"

"Oh, I don't know. Savate, and a couple other styles. Mom likes it too. We're both small. Our legs are our strongest muscles."

"True," he agreed. "Hand me that remote, please. I think I'll see what's on the sports channel."

It was on the dresser. She passed it to him. He had another request.

"How about digging out one of those little bottles, too?"

She'd been dreading this.

"Not a good idea, not yet," she said. "Your kidneys and liver are pretty busy trying to get well right now. Don't make it harder on them. Later? Please?"

"If you say so. Makes sense," he said, turning on the TV. "OK. Later."

## Chapter 38

Clio spent twenty minutes washing out Fergus's stocking and straightening the SIM card for his phone until she made it work again. His took a little more effort than hers but to her surprise the little film of circuits on it had not cracked. She put it in his travel bag next to his pistol and knife, grateful he hadn't asked for those particular items to be put under his pillow. She turned in the chair and studied him from ten feet away.

He had gone to sleep watching a basketball game but he wasn't sleeping peacefully. His hands trembled and from time to time he would throw a forearm to one side and slap the bed. Worry lines flitted in his brow and his lips twitched.

She turned down the volume on the TV and checked the time. He'd had a late breakfast and probably wouldn't be ready for another meal until the middle of the afternoon. This was a good time for another round of treatment. Up to now, her experience at repeated sessions with the same person had been limited to her great grandmother, whose need had not been critical. These concentrated, repeated sessions with Fergus were her first with anyone.

She contemplated his sleeping form. Fergus was not a big man, more rangy rather than solid as Mr. Coombs, though Coombs was not that big, either. Both had short, military style hair. Fergus's hair was a shade lighter than Coombs', almost sandy. He would be thought good-looking by most women, with regular features and an earnest cast to his jaw. She had noted one singular thing about him at the airport, though: his eyes, which were keen and suggested alertness and intelligence, an observation which was confirmed over the following days. He and Mr. Coombs had the same self-confidence, probably for similar reasons. Both had undergone the same daunting training and then lived through many potentially deadly wartime experiences. They had nothing to prove to anyone and no need to brag about their experiences. But those experiences had clearly shaped them. Yet Mr. Coombs was relaxed and friendly. Fergus seemed a little wild, and, oddly, a little deadened at the same time.

She rubbed her palms together slowly and kneeled at the end of the bed. Very gently so as not to awaken him, she laid her hands on his foreshortened left calf. She knew instantly his blood pressure had come down and the tissues were less painful. If the silly man had allowed her to treat him ten days ago he could have saved himself a good deal of pain. She couldn't completely heal it, and there would be some pain until the muscles and tendons grew into the new configuration, but it should not be disabling. As she had seen, Fergus could handle a little pain. She spent fifteen minutes on the left calf, using increasing pressure, not stopping until she was sure it was in better condition than it had been. When she finished, Fergus was relaxed in a deep sleep. Now for his kidneys.

She used the same procedure as before, sliding her hand under him and using a slow back and forth motion. The "combing out" process seemed easier this time: not faster, but more sure. She knew from the previous session that she could do it, even though the kidneys were deeper under the skin than the blood vessels and joints she usually dealt with. She was more confident, and could tell his left kidney was situated slightly higher in his trunk. She spent some forty-five minutes on each one.

Over that hour and a half, while part of her mind concentrated on the kidneys, another part drifted unpredictably. A word her father had used several years earlier came back to her. Her mother had been at a low point in her life and no one in the family knew how to help her. Her father, prompted by a passage in a Tony Hillerman Navajo mystery novel, consulted Dr. Melvin Bisti, a professor of Indian studies at New Mexico State University, to see if the Navajo healing ceremony might offer some ideas to help his wife. The problem as Dr. Bisti saw it was that her mother had lost her harmony. The purpose of the elaborate healing ceremony, called the Blessing Way, was to restore the ailing person's harmony. Now, working on problem areas over half of Fergus's body, the concept took on new meaning: it fit her notion of the way she dealt with a vast, complex human soup of tiny pieces of life. It was what she was doing. She was giving Fergus's body its harmony back. Or some of it, at least.

When she was satisfied she had improved his kidney function well beyond what she had done earlier in the morning, she took a break and ate half of one of the two remaining taquitos. It was room temperature but still flavorful and filling.

Then she went back to Fergus, spending an hour on his abdominal muscles. They were fragile and some pain would remain but she judged that he would be able to walk, sit, and lie almost normally. Restoring strength and flexion would take longer.

Since she was in position, straddling his body again, she devoted twenty minutes to two bruised areas over his ribs.

He was still sleeping soundly. She stood and studied him a minute. It was a perfect opportunity to experiment. What could she tell about the organs of his trunk?

She kneeled by the bed and slid her left hand under his back, palm up, and laid her right hand on his abdomen, palm down, and like a doctor with a stethoscope, slowly moved her hands to one area after another, concentrating on the impressions. The kidneys were easy now, like old friends. The small intestine was obvious. She thought she could sense the liver, but everything was jumbled together. The pancreas and spleen were almost impossible to detect, lying as they did with the trachea, lungs, esophagus, and stomach.

It reminded her of sitting at a table in a noisy restaurant. On one hand, it was chaos, but on the other, by focusing selectively, you could overhear something of what was going on at different tables. But it was very difficult. Lots of practice, with different subjects, might help…but who would she get to submit to something so weird? Her brother?

No, definitely not her brother.

This session had taken over four hours. She was tired. She stretched out for a moment on the empty side of Fergus's bed. It wouldn't be good to go to sleep here, but her mind was still registering the profusion of impressions she had received from his midriff.

And then what about…what about his brain?

She had studied anatomy, maybe not in quite as orderly fashion as medical students, but she had read a lot, and remembered much. The brain was a mystery to much smarter people than she was. It was also the most complicated organ in the body, with many lobes and areas, nerves, and blood vessels, all with incalculable, interrelated, multiple functions.

Even before the medical team doctor's guesswork diagnosis of concussion trauma, she had suspected Fergus's brain was damaged to some degree. His extreme jitteriness behind the wheel of her car was abnormal, as were the flashes of temper and other behavioral glitches she had observed. Could she sense that damage? Would it be proper to try? Or would it be prying?

Well, no, it wouldn't be prying. She could not read his mind like some movie mentalist or telepath. Most likely what she would encounter with the brain would resemble other generalized scans she had made of many people: another noisy restaurant, only bigger and louder. But how would she know unless she tried?

She turned her head and checked: he was still sleeping. This was the perfect time.

Turning on her side and extending her left arm, she gently laid her fingertips on Fergus's forehead. He didn't move. She began to concentrate.

What should she look for? It was probably foolish to be looking for anything at this point. Complex impressions took time to build, and even more time to be considered.

But still. Biomarkers. Those would be wonderful to find. She knew researchers were hoping to find biomarkers in the blood, perhaps, or in the cerebrospinal fluid, that would be signs of mental diseases. They were looking especially at the hippocampi, two small areas deep in the cerebral cortex, sources of electrical activity which showed up on EEGs. How would she ever manage to recognize these?

Biomarkers did exist for other conditions. The biomarker for heart disease had been a surprising and welcome discovery that made detection of heart attacks a simple matter. Cholesterol also was detectible through a biomarker. She had learned to identify those herself, but also realized that might have been possible because she knew they were there in the first place. If only biomarkers for concussion trauma could be found....

She was beginning to tune in to the impressions she was receiving from Fergus's brain. The brain, even a sleeping brain, was a hive of activity. At first barely a whisper, after moments of concentration it became a tidal wave of signals, far more than she could process at the moment. Her concentration wavered. Tired as she was, it was too much to focus on at the moment.

Eventually, pondering the possibilities of cortisol and norepinephrin as candidates for biomarkers, she drifted off to sleep.

Forty-five minutes later, Fergus woke up. It took him a few seconds to realize he was looking at a motel room ceiling, and a few more to rejoice in taking deep breaths. Even the ribs he thought might be broken didn't hurt. Maybe they weren't broken after all. Maybe the kid fixed them.

Holy shit! He wasn't alone! He was in bed with his employer's daughter!

There she was, eighteen inches away, sleeping like a bunny, hugging a pillow and breathing softly. Oh, hell!

Her face was peaceful, her relatively sharp features softened in sleep. A thin lock of wheat-colored hair over a corner of her mouth was undulating with her breath. She *should* be tired. She'd been through a hell of a long, physically and emotionally draining experience and then spent the next day working him over on very little sleep. If he waked her, she might be as embarrassed as he was. What should he do?

Before he could devise a plan, her eyes fluttered awake.

"Mmm," she said with a sleepy smile, apparently unembarrassed. That was a relief.

She slid off the bed and stretched.

"I didn't mean to do that," she said, "but I feel so much better. I hope you don't mind."

He glanced at her. Mind? She didn't seem to mean that as a joke. He'd better take it seriously.

"No."

"How are you feeling now?"

"Three and a half or four by five."

"What?"

"Sorry. Navy talk. It means borderline outstanding."

"That's good," she replied. She rolled the stocking over his stump and installed the prosthesis.

"Now, let's see you stand up."

Cautiously, he complied. It didn't hurt as much as he expected it would.

"That's great!" she said. "You're my best patient ever. I mean, no one else has ever needed that much attention. I didn't really know what would happen over time."

"Me neither. I was expecting some kind of massage treatment, like from an athletic trainer, but this was totally different. What exactly were you doing?"

"I don't know exactly, Fergus. There's a professor at the medical school who doesn't know, either. He's the one who suggested I work with this medical team. It was a great idea…but you were even better. I mean, I feel terrible you were hurt so bad, but I'm learning a lot from working on you. I'm grateful to you for that. That's all I mean.

"In fact," she continued, "I'd like to know what you were feeling while I was working on you, if you remember. I've never asked anyone about that before."

He was doing careful stretches, loosening selected joints, moving about the room while massaging and lightly tensing muscle groups. He stopped to think.

"Hard to describe." He paused to think. "I remember when you began. It was like your fingers were charged, like with some weird sort of current. Not electric, not low frequency sound, but something like that. It was subtle, soothing, and it took a while to build up. I thought for a while it was cold, but it wasn't, exactly. Whatever it was soaked in and spread out. It would've felt good even if it hadn't erased the pain. That must have been in the first few minutes before I faded out. I can still sort of feel it now. Were you controlling it, or what?"

"Well, I guess I was. I must have been. But it's not like a switch I turn on or something. I just think about it. I've been trying to understand it but I'm starting to think I never will. Maybe it doesn't matter. Maybe just making it work is what matters."

"Maybe so. It's what matters to me; I know that."

His face was unreadable. She changed the subject.

"So…what should we do now? Are you hungry?"

"Not terribly. I think I feel good enough to take a shower. Let's decide about food later."

She readily agreed and headed to her room to do the same. His shower was refreshing, not quite magical, but one of the best he could remember. Most showers are not memorable. This one was. He was grateful for every minute of it.

Dressed in clean clothes, he considered searching for one of the pints she'd hidden but decided to stretch out on the bed again and simply relax. He didn't take it for granted this time. It was a luxury.

There'd been a lot of rough knocks in his life, including two helicopter crashes and two vehicles destroyed by IEDs. He was all too familiar with the long, painful routine of struggling back into fighting shape afterwards. Several incidents had taken a month or more to recover from, and had involved damn near a whole drug store of medicines, some of which had been hard on him too. This time, after a severe beating less than twenty-four hours ago, he almost felt ready to get back into action. On active duty he *would* be back in action. It was astounding.

The only explanation was the kid and her spooky, gentle ministrations. His initial impression of her as a schoolgirl barely old enough to drive, small, shy, skinny, with pipe stem arms, skinny legs, and shoulders as square as if the coat hanger were still in her shirt—that impression was wrong. She had proven uncommonly self-possessed and utterly competent in surprising ways—and not only by completely stomping two major-league criminals in seconds, and later a third, without using her hands. After that, even more inexplicably, she turned into some bizarre kind of healer, something completely unique as far as he knew, totally without precedent. And very timely.

So her mother came from another planet? Coincidence? Who knew?

He'd love to see what kind of woman the kid would grow into some day.

He picked up the TV remote and started to point it at the television, but a sudden realization froze his arm in mid-air.

That painting.

The painting by that Doro guy. The woman in it...her serene expression, the feeling of peace...the gentle light in her face....

It was beginning to make sense to him.

## Chapter 39

An hour later Clio knocked softly on the connecting door and stuck her head in. Fergus was at the table, putting his pistol back together. A can of oil, a cleaning brush, and some scraps of oily cloth lay on a gaudy color pamphlet of area tourist attractions.

"How are you feeling?"

"Four and a half by five, plus an RCH."

"A what?"

"Oops. Another Navy phrase. 'Just a tiny bit.'"

"OK. Good. What about food?"

"What about it?"

"I'll go get some, if you're ready. You know the restaurants here better than I do. What would you like?"

"That pizza we had last week was pretty good. Could you stand another?"

"Sure."

"It came from that little café the other side of the city hall. Order whatever kind you like and I promise to eat at least half of it."

"I'll be back."

It was a good thing she hadn't said she'd be *right* back. It took her the better part of an hour. He had cleared the table and put his pistol away. She set down two bags as the aroma of hot pizza caressed them both.

"How are your kidneys by now?"

"Better. Not nearly as painful."

"Color?"

"Pinkish."

"OK. That's good. They're flushing out. That's why I got you this."

She reached in the second bag and pulled out a six pack of Budweiser.

"Are you *kidding* me?" he asked, thunderstruck.

"No. Beer will help flush out your kidneys."

He picked one up with a joyful smile, popped the tab, and raised it in her direction.

"Bravo Zulu, shipmate! Cheers!"

He took a generous sip and swallowed.

"Oh, God, that's good. How the hell did you manage this? Do you cast spells too?"

"I ran into Kathy Springer in the restaurant. You know, one of the nurse aides? She said she thought we had left but then saw my car. I told her you caught that stomach bug that some of the others had, and after you'd spent two days in bed you were finally up to eating again, and you really wanted beer with your pizza, but I couldn't buy it for you. So she went with me to the Stop 'N' Shop and got you some."

"So you do cast spells, in a manner of speaking. Very well done, shipmate. You want one?"

She wrinkled her nose.

"No thank you. I hate beer."

"More for me," he said, taking another swig.

They began demolishing the pizza. She slowed down after the second slice, but Fergus kept up the pace. He was on his third and had opened a second beer when she spoke again.

"I think one of the same policemen who talked to you last week was in the café tonight."

"Yeah?" he said, looking sidelong at her as he lowered a string of mozzarella into his mouth.

"People at other tables were asking him about that wreck."

"I bet. What'd you find out?"

"He said they thought it was part of a war between drug dealers. There were four people in the truck. One was killed in the wreck, two others sent to the hospital, and one disappeared."

"Hmm. Any mention of who was who?"

"He thought one of the two they arrested was the big dealer. The other was a reporter, he said."

"Let's buy us a newspaper tomorrow. I bet it'll have more details."

"OK." Her face fell. "And Fergus, the policeman said the truck blew up because of a bomb."

"Hmm."

He thought fast. There was no way he was going to tell her he had repurposed a bomb meant for the two of them. Fortunately, she didn't know much about IEDs. Fortunately or unfortunately, he knew way too much.

"I wondered about that," he improvised. "I fired what, four or five shots? And I was aiming, firing out the left back window with my right hand. I didn't shoot randomly. I aimed at the engine. I thought the gas tank blew up, but who knows? There might've been a bomb there somewhere."

"But a bomb? That's so scary!"

"If the cops are correct, yes, scary. I have experience with improvised bombs. They blow up the guys that put them together more often than you'd think. I wouldn't grieve too much about them. We were no threat at all, and they were trying their best to kill us. They got no better than they deserved."

She stopped with her third slice of pizza. As she watched almost admiringly, Fergus finished the pizza and a third beer. He wiped his mouth and added the crumpled napkin to the pile of crumpled napkins on the table. He discretely stifled a burp.

"Man, that was good," he said. "You get a medal for that, shipmate."

"I'm glad you enjoyed it," she said with a hint of a smile.

She began putting all the trash into the bag it had come in.

"Let's plan a bit for tomorrow, OK? I expect you'll be stiff in the morning, so I'd like to work on you a little more then. In the afternoon if you're up to it, I'd like to visit Mr. Bianchi one more time. I'll call Mr. Baldwin tonight and ask if that's all right. Would that work?"

He wadded up the napkins and dropped them in the bag, adding three empty beer cans.

"Yeah, sure, I think so. Eating his upscale food isn't exactly arduous duty."

"If you don't feel like it, we won't go. What time is your flight Saturday?"

"Two something in the afternoon. Two ten or fifteen."

"OK. Let's take a break. I need to call my family and see if they have a schedule for their visit up here yet."

"You do that," he said, slowly pushing himself erect. "I'll start my break with a happy visit to the little room where the king goes alone."

She watched him shuffle to the bathroom, guessing that he was feeling more pain than he let on. Probably all SEALs were stoic like that: manly men. She swept the remaining pizza fragments into the bag and headed to her room.

Her phone buzzed as she emerged from her own "little room."

"Hello?"

"This is Thornton Peebles, Ms. Méndez. Am I calling at a bad time?"

"No sir, not at all. This is a good time."

"Good. Have you had a useful experience with the medical team over the last two weeks, I wonder?"

"Uh, yes, sir, I have."

"I'm glad to hear it, but I'm not calling to get into that now. I'm sure that conversation would be too long and involved for the telephone. If I remember correctly, your medical team's last day is tomorrow, is that not right?"

"Yes, sir."

"Very good. Well, as it happens, I have spent the day attending a conference on alternative medicine. That's not an area that appeals to many of my colleagues, since its practitioners often shirk the scientific method, but I have found some things here to be of interest. In particular, I have met a gentleman with wide experience in alternative healing, a credentialed academic scholar of the field, who has studied a wide variety of alternative methods of healing and, most importantly, who is acquainted with many of those who use them.

"You will recall the difficulty we had trying to understand your own situation, which conforms to no known standard medical regimen. I think it is possible that this man may be able to shed some light on the matter, or at least provide us both with needed perspective. He is also, I should add, a most approachable and low key gentleman.

"I have mentioned your case to him, anonymously and only in general terms, and he is intrigued, I think it would be fair to say. He might be able to provide helpful context for your abilities, and given his wide background, perhaps even help you to illuminate those abilities in your own mind. Since you are understandably reluctant to being a test subject, I'm afraid my own contributions are at a standstill.

"And so I am calling to ask if it would be at all possible for you to drop by my office at a time of your choice on Saturday and meet with the two of us, however briefly—that is, if it won't interfere with your returning home. I think there's a very real possibility that what you may learn will be of use to you."

"Oh. Uh...well, uh, yes sir, I guess that's possible. Uh...would three o'clock be all right?"

"Yes, it will. I look forward to seeing you at three o'clock, and hearing of your experiences. Thank you very much, young lady. Until then!"

She sat on her bed a minute holding the phone and staring at the ugly tan carpet. Dr. Peebles was such a sweet man. She knew he was genuinely interested in her. So why did she have a bad feeling about this?

Peebles slipped his phone back in his pocket and emerged from the quiet corner of the lobby into the hallway where the hotel's conference rooms were. Everyone in the hall was wearing a convention tag but he didn't see his man. Several small groups were gathered around a food cart and a drink cart, chatting animatedly. They certainly were a varied bunch—made even graduate students look preppy.

Aha, the fellow was still in the last conference room, alone at the rostrum, evidently making notes on some of the handouts that had been given out. He too would have stood out at medical convention but for different reasons. He was obviously Native American: stocky, long black hair in a braid tied back, worn but shiny cowboy boots with a walking heel, jeans, turquoise belt buckle, purple shirt and bolo tie sporting more turquoise, complexion the color of an old penny. He looked up.

"Did you reach her?" he asked.

"I did," he replied, sliding into a front row seat. "She said three p.m. would suit her. I hope that suits you."

"It does. I'd almost come at three a.m. to meet her." He set his pen down and straightened the sheaf of papers. "Almost everything you've told me about her is atypical of the healers I've known or heard of—most unusual."

"You hinted at that earlier. How so, specifically?"

"You mentioned she never worked for pay. That's about the only item she has in common with traditional curanderos and healers, except she doesn't even accept chickens or other offerings. But more important, healers and curanderos are always in and of their communities. She, you say, keeps a low profile and is largely unknown in her community. Also, most healers acquire their skills in middle age. Some are quite elderly. A young girl, almost a child, is highly atypical.

"And then there are her methodologies. She's half Hispanic, you said, living in a Hispanic society. Most curanderos in those communities commonly deal with *susto*, *empacho*, and *mal de ojo*, to name some of the most frequent concerns. *Susto* is caused by fright or sudden trauma, in which the soul leaves the body. The curandero must put it back. *Empacho* is thought to be impacted food in the digestive tract, which the curandero dissolves and removes. *Mal de ojo*, the evil eye, is acquired in several ways, both intended and unintended, and is the product of envy, of either a person or of a person's possessions, particularly when one fails to touch the envied individual. Your young woman does none of that. She is not Catholic."

He paused and looked at his papers.

"I'm sorry if I sound like a lecturer, but I *am* a lecturer.

"Protestant communities, on the other hand, have always mistrusted the inclusion of saints and Catholic dogma curanderos employ, yet they too have historically had healers, especially in rural and isolated areas where access to doctors is difficult or impossible. Healing by faith is sometimes accomplished by the laying on of hands, or a variety of other similar techniques, often during a service with the assistance of the entire congregation. Native American communities with their many healing ceremonies also frequently use communal action for their ceremonies. Your young woman does none of that.

"Instead, as you have mentioned, this girl, or woman, is to a considerable degree a student of scientific medicine, who seeks to intervene directly in the body's biological processes. That, as far as I know, is unique. And, I might add, seemingly impossible. Yet you have personal experience of this."

He scooted his chair back from the rostrum.

"I repeat," he said, "I would come in the middle of the night to learn more about this young woman and her abilities to heal. This," he said, pushing himself to his feet, "is going to be very interesting."

## Chapter 40

The kid had been talking on her phone for at least twenty minutes but then went quiet. Was she asleep? Their adjoining doors were open. He got up to check. She was sitting on the edge of the bed, hands and phone in her lap, shoulders slumped, looking miserable.

"Hey," he said softly, "You all right?"

She nodded. Normally her posture was erect and taut. Now she looked tired, even whipped.

"Bad news?"

She shook her head.

"I don't know, Fergus," she sighed. "I'm afraid I just don't know what I'm doing."

"What do you mean?"

"About healing. I've spent two weeks—two years, really—trying to figure it out, if it's controllable and helpful, or if it's weird and I should forget about it, and I can't decide."

She looked at the phone in her hands.

"I couldn't practice on the patients at the clinic. You're the only person I've tried really hard to help. I think I did help a little…but I'll never find another person to work with. Who would want to? I'm not even sure it would be right to try to work on anyone…because I don't know what I'm doing! I might hurt them instead!"

Surprised, he said nothing for a minute. She went on.

"Like your kidneys. I'd never worked on kidneys before, or any organs except the skin. I didn't know if I could do anything for your kidneys, but I went ahead anyway. What if I made them worse? I'd feel terrible about that. There'd be no excuse for it."

She sniffled. He almost spoke, but she continued.

"I mean, humans are not machines. They're so complex even doctors don't know the half of it. There's no end to the complications. It's human life, after all! Who am I to think I can play with it?"

He shuffled into the room and sat, slowly and carefully, on a corner of the bed.

"I know what you mean, OK?" he said. "I know a little about risk, about how most things are beyond our control. The thing is, you just prepare the best you can and then you do the best you can. SEALs do that. Doctors do that. Why should you be any different?

"Remember," he went on, "I'm the one you worked on, right? I know what it's like to be on the receiving side. That guy hammered on me only yesterday! If it weren't for you I'd be in a hospital bed right now, half dead, high on Oxycontin with tubes coming out of me, pissed off at doctors and nurses, and waiting for a week to pass and hoping I hadn't got hooked on the meds. So I'm not afraid of what you might do to me. Just the opposite."

His face was slightly flushed, maybe from the beer.

"So what if you're still learning this stuff? I'm cool with that. We all have to start somewhere. It's working. I say keep it up; do your best. I'm not worried you're going to hurt me. You wouldn't do that. In fact, if you find something else about me to tune up, have at it. Seriously: anything. Hell, I'm proud to be your first patient."

She smiled, barely, and wiped away the moisture under her eyes with two fingertips.

"OK," she said, "thanks," adding after a second, "I'd like to work some more on those kidneys and abs. In half an hour? Or whenever you want?"

"A half hour. You got it."

He eased back to his own room, grabbed the remote, and carefully stretched out on the bed to search the channels for something to watch, wondering as he did so, Am I getting soft?

Maybe not. A crying woman was not necessarily a special case, but this one was, somehow. Despite her proven combat abilities, she seemed particularly vulnerable, given her mother-from-another-planet situation and this crazy healing business. That wrangle in Afghanistan two years ago, with her supposedly saving

Coombs' life after the big shootout, had seemed way too unlikely to be true at the time. Now he believed it.

Two weeks ago he had expected just another rich brat to keep an eye on. Coombs' employees had any number of outrageous stories about spoiled kids they'd been paid to nursemaid. Miami had plenty, and they usually meant easy money for whoever got the call. But this gig was turning out different. The kid was different. He was starting to respect her. Even like her. Phew.

Yeah, he was probably getting soft.


Forty feet away, Clio had flopped on her own bed and pulled a pillow over her face. Everyone went through spells of depression. She knew that. Maybe she was having one now.

Why didn't Dr. Peebles mention the name of that man who wanted to meet her? Who is he? Maybe that didn't matter, but there was something she didn't like about that meeting. Being put on the spot: that was it. Having to perform. For a stranger. And not even knowing what she was doing. Medical people were sure to realize that. At home, sooner or later word would get out that the girl on Highway 28 could cure you and crowds of people would climb over the wall around their house to find her. That would be horrible: she was neither a doctor nor any kind of professional.

Fergus was sweet to try to cheer her up. As cynical and tough as he was, it really touched her that he would come out of his shell to give her a vote of confidence.

It was getting hot under the pillow. She pulled it off. The bedside lamp didn't make much light. The room was still appropriately dim. She stared at the ceiling.

She'd probably never get a better subject than Fergus. He even gave her permission to look for "other things" to fix up. She had worked on Coombs' brain, but never really examined a brain before Fergus. That had been exciting, strange but exciting. She didn't think she would do him any harm, but really, how could she be certain? It would be smart to ask him once more just to be sure he really meant it. One way or another, she suspected that his brain was where she might find some of those "other things" that he said she could "tune up."

And so, to the muted sounds of some televised sports event in the next room, and with many uncomfortable thoughts—of what she was going to tell her mother, her hazy post-graduation plans, and the sure-to-be unpleasant strains on her family when the new group of Thomans arrived—she drifted into a light sleep.

She roused at the sound of a marching band and crowd noise. Fergus must be watching a football game. She'd slept forty-five minutes. It was time to get to work.

She looked in on him. He was propped up in bed looking comfy. A can of beer was on the bedside table.

"Ten minutes?" she said.

"Good," was the reply.

She pulled fresh clothes out of her travel case and went into the bathroom to put on a t-shirt and cargo shorts and tie her hair back. No street clothes this time. This was going to be a serious session. She had to concentrate and she had to be comfortable.

She started out of the bathroom but stopped in the doorway a minute, thinking. She knew from the previous session that she could receive impressions from his brain, dense, chaotic impressions that bore no relation she could discern to cranial anatomy. They were different only in quantity from the impressions she'd gotten from patients at the medical clinic, and even from Dr. Peebles and Mr. Bianchi. Her brother might call it background noise, but that was just at first. Eventually, with a little practice, concentration, and reflection, she had started to learn to isolate selected parts of the body's input, like Fergus's kidneys, muscle groups, and joints. She could try that with the brain. This past Tuesday one of the doctors had told her concussion damage could be seen by the newest scanners. If that was so, if there was something there detectible by a scanner, then there might be a chance she could detect it herself.

Her only strategy was to focus her mind, be open to what she found, and try to analyze it. She would have to be extra careful about actually affecting anything. That was a pathetically vague strategy, but that was all she could do, like Fergus said. It had produced results before. Well then, better get started.

She stepped to Fergus's doorway. He turned off the TV. She would start with his leg, get him relaxed, and move on from there. She ran through the sequence yet again, preparing her mind. She might never get another opportunity like this.

After the kid's ten minute warning he visited the bathroom again. He moved there and back pretty well, though he couldn't have carried combat gear and certainly wouldn't be fully operational yet. He lay back down and turned off the TV when she appeared in the doorway.

She stood there several minutes. She'd changed into a snug gray t-shirt, shorts, flip-flops. Not a bad looking kid at all: skinny but not bony. Had a nice little hourglass shape, with arms curved in at the waist to match. She came to the foot of the bed. She was looking in his direction but not at him, more like *through* him, her face soft, as if her mind was somewhere else. Her sharp features could be scary when she was angered—he'd seen her look that way twice. Normally she looked like your basic kid, an alert kid. He'd seen her with this particular expression before, but he couldn't place it. Finally her eyes focused and she came to herself. She kneeled, removed the prosthesis, and began with his stump.

Her hands were warm. She massaged the muscles vigorously, squeezing up and down the length of the calf for a good while, then stroking firmly from the knee to the end. The strange warm coolness began about the time she started that odd humming. It made him drowsy.

"Try to stay awake if you can, please," she said. "I need you to roll over in a minute."

He tried. She continued putting the chill on his leg for many minutes but he just couldn't stay alert for it.

At some point he became aware the mattress was rocking. She'd climbed up on the bed and straddled his hips. Oh, lordy, now there was a sensation. She pulled his t-shirt out of his pants, slid her hands under it, and began stroking his sore abs. Soon the ache was receding under wave upon wave of cool tingling. It was warm, too—a totally bizarre feeling. She looked to be somewhere else, eyes unfocused, peaceful.

That was it! That's what it reminded him of—the angelic face of the woman in the painting: the same, sweet serenity, as if everything was going to be all right, as if whatever the future might bring, good or bad, their present little world was golden, and the rest didn't matter. Oh man, how had that Doro guy been able…been…he must have…that's how.…

"Fergus, wake up please. Can you hear me?"

"Erg."

"C'mon, Fergus. Say something, please."

"Mmm. Yeah.…"

"Are you awake?"

"Sorta."

"Fergus, did you hurt your neck sometime? You seem to have problems with the vertebrae there and your shoulder and elbow. Am I right about that?"

"Umm…uh, yeah. Heh…hel…chopper crash. An' a IED. Laid up a bit over those."

"OK. You told me I could work on whatever I found, right? Can I do that?"

"Wh…sh…sorry. Can't make m' mouth work. Sure. You fin' anything that c'n be improved, give it a sh…shot."

"All right. I'll try. I'm going to roll you over. Help me, if you can."

It must not have been pretty, but he soon found himself on his stomach with his head hanging off the edge of the bed. She seemed to want it there. She was standing over him, exploring his neck, gently moving his head side to side or raising it fractionally, and pressing on the vertebrae with her fingers. All he could see was kid feet: small, narrow, and springy, smooth young skin like on the rest of her except for angry pink bands across the top of each foot and some redness around the little toes—not bad for running twelve miles in street shoes. The toes splayed slightly as she moved over him to work on his spine and shoulder.

His neck was tingling, the warm coolness spreading into his shoulders. He was so relaxed he missed whatever followed. But whatever it was, it was good.

Clio had no awareness of causing those she treated to feel tingling, heat, cold, or anything beyond simple contact. Simple contact was all she felt herself. If anything, the process worked in reverse: she received impressions, sensations, or input, or whatever the accurate term was, from those she worked on. Fergus was able to describe being on the receiving side in more detail than anyone heretofore. His descriptions, unfortunately, were of little help in improving her knowledge.

From age seven she had worked several years with Epifania Guajardo (whom she called Tía Fani), whose specialty was animals. That elderly, crotchety-sweet woman had worked miracles seemingly from instinct and insisted that Clio do the same. Clio had powerful golden eyes, she said, ojos poderosos, and she was certain Clio was destined to be a great healer. At first she cooperated just to placate the ancient woman, but she eventually gained a small measure of competence when treating dogs, cats, Tía Fani's goats, and even quarter horses at Stallman's Stables.

Tía Fani never worked on people, though, perhaps because she didn't like most people. It was only by happy accident Clio learned that what worked with animals also worked with her beloved great grandmother. Later, after several traumatic experiences at age 15 when she intervened successfully with concussion-induced brain swelling (Rob Coombs) and a cerebral stroke (her grandmother), she decided to temporarily suspend her pursuit of pharmacology and study medicine itself in an attempt to understand her perplexing abilities to diagnose and heal.

However, after several years of study she was coming to believe that traditional medicine, both books and doctors, had nothing to say about her kind of healing. Likewise, her efforts with the medical team had offered minimal enlightenment—but her extended sessions with Fergus were a revelation. Fergus had eventually understood what she was trying to do to him, and even collaborated with her. She might never understand where her ability came from or how it worked, but partially thanks to Fergus, she knew it did work.

So as long as Fergus was available and willing, she would do her best for him…and for herself.

Finding several of Fergus's old injuries was particularly gratifying. The injuries hadn't been serious enough to be noticeable from watching Fergus move, and as far as she could tell from her examination they weren't excessively painful. She took that to mean her ability to detect older, mostly healed injuries was accurate, at least in this case. The cervical vertebrae in his neck seemed to be calcified to some degree, and she concentrated hard on that area without knowing if she had helped. She also did what she could to soothe the nerves and improve the circulation of the blood in that general location. She treated his shoulder in a similar fashion, but the affected area was larger and would probably still bother him on occasion. She could work on them more tomorrow, though.

Now for his kidneys. Since he was on his stomach, access was easier and the treatment went quickly. They felt reasonably healthy, well on the way to full recovery. She could not have explained how she knew.

There he was, spread out on the bed, breathing comfortably. He had had a lot of pain and violence in his life, most recently because of her. She had little confidence in whatever her healing abilities amounted to, but perhaps, in some small way, she might be repaying him for what his service had cost his body.

Slowly and carefully, she managed to pull him fully back on the bed and turn him over, straightening his rumpled clothes so he wouldn't look like someone had thrown him there. Now came the moment she'd been looking forward to and dreading at the same time.

He was lying diagonally on the bed, his head near the pillow. She kneeled on the carpet, laid a hand softly on his forehead, and closed her eyes. Over the minutes which followed she moved her hand to both sides of his forehead, temple, and jaw.

More minutes passed. Her position was wrong for using both hands. She got up and lay with her head on the pillow, body down the edge of the bed. That worked nicely. Fergus's head was against her chest and she could place her hands on both temples, over his ears, under his jaw and throat, behind the ears. She took her time, trying dozens of placements, returning to previous ones again and again. The only sound in the room was the thrumming of the ancient heat pump under the window. She didn't hear it.

After two hours she had had enough. It was late. Fergus would probably sleep the rest of the night. The room was a comfortable temperature but she straightened him on the bed and pulled the bedspread and blanket over him.

She returned to her room and got ready for bed and lay down, reviewing what little she knew about the brain and its many components: the cerebellum, the cerebral cortex, prefrontal cortex, temporal lobe, Broca's area, neurons, dendrites, synapses, myelin sheathing, the corpus callosum connecting the two hemispheres, and so on—it was incredibly complicated. A human was basically a bag of electro-chemical protoplasm tied together by electrical impulses—nervous signals—whether sight, sound, touch, smell, or cerebral, which somehow she seemed able to detect. She was a fool to think she might ever understand it.

And yet she had received copious impressions which would take days to absorb. They had been chaotic, yes, but there were patterns there, a system of some kind. She felt it in her soul. She recalled Dr. Peebles' musical analogy of a symphony orchestra. What she had found was like a thousand symphony orchestras each with a hundred musicians, all warming up at the same time—not making music, but not making random noise either. Despite the cacophony, there were patterns. For one thing, if you could analyze the noise of all those musicians, you would find that the sounds would be grouped around the notes on the musical scale. The scale might even be reconstructed. For another thing, the qualities of the sounds they produced would also form groups and patterns: brass sounds, strings, woodwinds, high pitched, low, overtones, harmonics. If one were expecting music, it would not be there. But if one were open to looking for any kind of pattern, there would be some. Deriving their significance was another matter altogether.

It might be the same with the brain: discrete thoughts, for example, might not be recognizable, but other things might…if only one knew what, and how to interpret them.

She would sleep on it. Experience had shown that time helped her progress in understanding her impressions.

Maybe she would dream some kind of answer. The purpose of dreams was a mystery to scientists and doctors. Her brother Julio theorized that the brain had to "reboot" regularly, just like a computer or erasing a blackboard, to get rid of old data and clean the circuitry so it would continue to operate at maximum efficiency.

Was Fergus truly asleep when she examined his brain? Could he have been dreaming? Would his fully awake brain be different? Maybe he would allow her to have a trial when he was awake.

Clio loved irony. It did not escape her that she was wondering about dreaming as she drifted off to sleep.

# Chapter 41

The red digits of the cheap motel room clock said 5:23. Floating midway between wakefulness and sleep, Fergus let his thoughts wander. It was easy. He didn't hurt anywhere.

For the first time in a long time Celine was in his reverie. Celine: so lovely, such a sweet-tempered woman. Back in college he had majored in international studies in order to have classes and subject matter that would enable him to be closer to her in her own major in Sinology. Looking back now, it seemed improbable that an active, bumptious young man should be drawn to her shy warmth and gentle ways, but they had had three blissful years together, and then three increasingly unhappy years, before he'd driven her away. She could never understand, could never accept, why he wanted to join the Special Forces and go to war. He had been obsessed about it at the time—he had to be, to survive three years in the Special Forces—but now, he couldn't understand why he had done it either. Their separations were terribly difficult, but coming home was even harder. The smallest things made him angry. It was painful to recall how much he had changed. How had she stood him as long as she had?

He could only hope she was finally happy with her second husband, the professor or whatever he was. She had never lost her temper; she even had the heart to forgive him, fool that he was. In the darkness, his eyes stung. Funny how things turn out. Who would have predicted that she would be the tough one? And who would have predicted he would someday be able to admit that?

A car engine being started outside roused him to check the clock again: 6:08. He had to pee, big time. Using his arms for leverage, he sat up without too much difficulty. As long as he didn't rush it, his muscles worked fairly well. Hallelujah. Good work, kid.

A clean support stocking and his prosthesis lay at the end of the bed. In the process of putting the damned rig on, he noticed the drawer in the night stand was not shut completely. He pulled it open. She had returned his two remaining pints of Johnny Walker Red. It hit him like a verdict from a judge: she knew he'd been sneaking drinks, but she felt he was well enough to drink again if he desired. He hadn't fooled her, but she trusted him anyway. Was that wise?

He closed the drawer, put on the prosthesis, and made it to the bathroom without a problem. Somehow it no longer felt right to keep thinking of her as "the kid." Except for being young she was a lot more than a "kid." She was whip-smart, quick-thinking, a martial arts whiz, could outrun a greyhound, and was one hell of a healer of the afflicted. Plus her mother came from another planet. No indeed, not your average kid.

He stretched a bit to test his residual stiffness and walked to the window and pulled the curtain open a bit. Her car was gone. That must have been the engine that woke him up. He tried walking the length of the room. Twice was enough to convince him that he could indeed move around well enough to not attract attention in public. He changed to a fresh t-shirt and washed his face.

As he came out of the bathroom the curtains suddenly glowed a dull yellow, fading quickly to black. A car door slammed. She was back. A few seconds later he heard her lock click and door open. A light went on in her room. He stuck his head in.

"Hey," he said.

"Good morning," she said. "I see you're up."

"Yeah, moving pretty good, thanks."

"That's great. I'll give you a tune-up later. How about some breakfast?"

She set two bags on the table.

"Excellent," he said. He realized he had a newfound desperate need for taquitos in the morning. He pulled out a chair and sat down.

"Oh, and I got a newspaper," she added, looking into the bag. She pulled out a copy of the Santa Fe *New Mexican* and handed it to him, continuing to unpack cartons of orange juice, milk, two cinnamon buns in cellophane, and two apples. He found the story on the second page: "One Dead, Three Injured in Suspected Gun-running Incident."

She glanced at the headline as she passed him a taquito and poured some orange juice.

"That policeman said two were injured," she said.

"Yeah," he replied, folding back the page and spreading it out on the table. "This says that one fled the scene but was captured later."

There were four photos with the story. Two were probably old police booking shots: a middle-aged man with a scraggly beard and lined face and a younger Hispanic man with a thin ring of beard around his chin, hooded eyes, and a tattoo on his neck. The other two were more conventional photos: a middle-aged man with a pudgy face, bald head, and crazy eyes, and a photo which Fergus tapped with his finger.

"Holy crap! Look at this! This guy! His name is Bianchi! It says he's a reporter!"

"What?" she gasped, hopping to her feet "Let me see that!"

She stood against Fergus's shoulder as they read through the article. She smelled of talc.

"This is the missing link!" he said.

"The what?"

"Old man Bianchi told me the jerk who tried to kiss your mother in public was his son, and that he would almost certainly want to get even with her for putting him in his place. Who better to do that than his own son? This fellow here must be the grandson of the old fellow we've met."

"Oh, wow. But…." She furrowed her brow.

"What?"

"How did they find me? How did they connect me with her?"

"Good question. I wondered about that too. All along I thought that reporter was after me, not you. It wasn't until you unlocked his cage and took off running down the road that he said he figured out the reason I called Ana Darcy was because you were her daughter. I thought he was nuts. I never called your mother. What?"

Her face had gone pale.

"No, you didn't," she said. "I did. I borrowed your phone and sent her a text. Remember? My phone battery had died!"

"Aaah," he said, looking down at his taquito. "That means someone was monitoring your mother's phone. Not my phone: *hers*. They traced the call back to the closest cell tower to Tasajillo. That's not hard to do, really, but usually it's governments—CIA types and other spooks—that do stuff like that. Newspaper reporters have done it, though. Hey, this thing is getting cold. Let's think and talk as we eat, OK?"

He dosed his taquito with salsa from the little plastic container and dived in. She didn't appear to be enjoying hers.

"What is it?" he asked, after several bites.

"This was all my fault. All this trouble, people getting killed and injured."

"How do you figure?"

"My phone is secure. It can't be traced. I thought one little text message would be OK. I was stupid!"

He swallowed and took a slug of orange juice. Her eyes were shiny. She looked about to cry. He set down the bottle.

"All right, here's the opinion of a security expert, OK? If I were your CO and you were in my command, yes, I'd be pissed…excuse me…I'd be ticked off that you committed a possible security breach. That kind of thing happens. But in this case it didn't result in any deaths. Remember, we stopped those bozos from hassling that young mother, right? We put some serious hurt on them, made them look bad. That's plenty reason for them to shadow us afterwards. I mean, we weren't hiding. They knew exactly where we were.

"But it turns out there's another guy on my trail—mine and yours—the reporter. I bet these mugs spotted him and picked him up. That's why they were together."

They thought about that while he finished his taquito. He unwrapped a cinnamon bun and took a bite.

"Not too fresh," he muttered, "but I'll eat it. Here's another thing. Those gumballs never asked us a single question, did they? They just hauled us off and locked us up and then what? They went to fetch that fat guy with the beady eyes. Why? Why did they do that? This article suggests he's the one behind the gun-running. He owns a gun store. They've gotta be working for him. They must have thought we—no, they must have thought that *I* was a threat to their operation. Why? I ask you: why?"

He looked evenly at her while he drank more orange juice. Her face was blank.

"I bet I know why," he went on. "They saw this tattoo." He raised his forearm. "Those cops sure looked at it. It's the SEAL seal, you might say, famous among military people and even the general public. I bet they suspected that I wasn't just a medical orderly, but a plant, a secret agent, embedded with the visiting medical team, sneaking around after lawbreakers like them. That's why they went to get the big boss, and why they wanted to kill me. You had nothing to do with that, Clio, nothing at all."

He paused and looked at the cinnamon bun. They both realized that was the first time he'd ever called her by her name. After a few seconds, he took another bite of the bun.

"That makes sense," she said quietly.

She poured herself some milk. They resumed their breakfast. She pulled the paper to her and read the article.

"This says Bianchi had some broken bones, but would be released in a few days."

"Yeah," he said, adding after a pause, "You're wondering what he's going to do then."

"If he writes about me, there's no way I can prevent it."

"I guess not."

"Except to decide what to tell Mom."

"Big problem."

"Really."

"Well, you're seeing Bianchi senior this afternoon, aren't you? He said he would do what he could."

"Oh, I know. That poor man has his own problems. He can't be worrying about mine. Let's not think about that now. What would you like to do this morning?"

"I don't care...."

She shot him a glance. Uh-oh. They'd been through this before, and he'd been kind of flippant about merely following her around. She hated that.

"...but I think I could stand a little sight-seeing. That brochure I ruined with gun oil listed some interesting stuff around here. We could go look at some of it."

Her face lightened. She smiled.

"OK," she said, "That'll be fun."

They finished their breakfast and she "tuned up" his abs and kidneys. They dressed for the occasion and headed out.

Fergus suggested that they first drive to where they had been imprisoned and count the miles. The gate had yellow police tape across the opening and Clio didn't slow down, but the distance turned out to be slightly over thirteen miles. Their calculations had to be approximate because of uncertainty about the timing. Fergus had retrieved his watch shortly after she left and could only estimate how long she had been gone. Clio remembered the time on the dashboard clock when she began to drive back but had to guess how long it taken her to get the hidden key and start driving. She was astonished to calculate that, even allowing several extra minutes, she had averaged just under six minutes a mile. She hadn't known she could run that fast that long, even downhill. Fergus was impressed too, and said so.

They spent the rest of the morning driving a wide circle three quarters of the way around Santa Fe. Fergus discovered that northern New Mexico was a totally different region from anything he had seen in the United States. It was unique: almost solid Indian reservations and national forests. There were more places of interest than they had time to examine, but they did visit a few, including several pueblos, the renowned sanctuary at Chimayo, famous among Catholics for its healing properties, and Kasha-Ketuwe Tent Rocks National Monument, with its bizarre, conical sedimentary formations, evidently a result of eons of erosion. He wasn't up to hiking the trails, but there were observation points from which he could get the idea of the place. He loved the open sky, the adobe buildings and flat roofs with vigas (pole beams) sticking through, the chili and garlic ristras hanging by doorways and in arches, and even the battered old trucks and cowboy hats on the men.

For lunch they stopped at what looked to Fergus like an ordinary burger joint, but he soon learned differently. They did have burgers, but he decided to try the chicharrón burrito, basically a taquito with added pork crackling cubes. It was fatty but delicious. The kid, his shipmate, had a cardboard tray of three crispy tacos, sloppy concoctions of beans and meat, spicy chilies, and enough lettuce, cheese, and chopped tomatoes to deserve salad dressing. They were delicious too. He knew that because she gave him one before eating the other two.

She laughed to see him pull extra napkins out of the dispenser to clean the grease off his hands and face.

"You should have also tried the cheeseburger with green chili strips," she said.

"Roger that," he said. "Let's return this way and stop here again and I'll do that."

The morning was way more fun than Clio expected, largely because, for a change, Fergus seemed to be enjoying himself too. He talked more, was more interested in his surroundings, and seemed less nervous in the car. The heavier traffic they encountered as they headed to Mr. Bianchi's condo in Santa Fe didn't seem to bother him.

Might her examination of his brain last night be a factor in that change?

Not necessarily. There were other possible explanations. They had shared a frighteningly close call with violent deaths, for one thing, which was a perverse sort of bonding event. For another, they had been physically close for hours and hours as she worked over much of his body with her hands. She had also discussed medical matters with him, a fairly intimate business.

Also, he was in much less pain than he had been. Surely that would make for a less cranky sightseer. As far as his brain went, she hadn't attempted to heal anything. She had merely collected an enormous flurry of sensations, which she was still pondering.

On the other hand, though, her "healing," with Fergus as with others, was not consciously done. She had almost never been aware of trying to heal, or correct, or fix anything. She simply concentrated on the impressions, as if trying to understand them. "Healing" was what her patients reported afterwards. With Dr. Mitchell at the hospital, for example: she detected his shoulder joint problem quickly, and then focused on it until the level of pain she detected was alleviated. The actual means by which the alleviation was achieved remained a mystery. So perhaps she really had helped Fergus's mental problems, merely by examining them.

But that made no sense, none at all. It was so frustrating! No wonder she had so little confidence in her abilities. She still didn't know what they were.

The same housekeeper, Alice, met them at the door. She showed them to a sitting room at the front of the condo, with filmy drapes over big windows looking out on the sculpted landscape of the entrance. She told Fergus the cook would be in shortly to offer him some refreshment and led Clio down the hall to the door to the sunroom. She paused with her hand on the doorknob.

"He's been very low the past few days," she said. "I think he's asleep now. I'll tell him you're here."

"That's all right," Clio said. "I'll tell him, if I may."

Alice thought a second.

"Of course," she said with a nod, opening the door for her.

He was in his recliner under a lap robe, apparently asleep. The room was dim, the curtains open enough to leave the room in the reduced light of a cloudy afternoon. Music, some opera or other, was playing. She turned down the volume, moved a stool next to him, and sat.

He had lost weight since her last visit, and he hadn't had that much weight to spare. His face was gaunt, the skull underneath the papery skin quite evident. His appearance reminded her of a photo she had seen of the mummified King Tut, which she had found creepily sobering. With careful observation she could see his chest slowly rising and falling. On the end table at his left was a framed reproduction of Doro's painting.

She watched him for several minutes. As a younger girl she would have been frightened by such a solemn sight, but she was not frightened. With the soft light, quiet music, the stillness of the room, and the knowledge that the stars and the Milky Way galaxy were wheeling eternally overhead, somehow it felt holy.

After several more minutes she gently laid her hand on his. She was ready for what she would feel and it did not shock her. She clasped the thin hand between both of hers and let the sensations wash over her. The seconds passed. He took a deeper breath. His eyelids fluttered.

"Good afternoon, sir," she said.

His eyes opened a little. His lips twitched.

"Ms. Móntez," he whispered. "So lovely to see you again. Thank you for coming."

"It's an honor, sir," she replied, quietly.

"I'm…sleepy. I…. Please, Ms. Montez…see Axel…. Baldwin."

"I will, sir."

His eyelids closed. The hand between hers briefly gripped her fingers. She laid a hand on his shoulder, bent forward, and kissed his temple softly. Moving the hand to his neck, she closed her own eyes and leaned her head against his. She stayed like that a long time.

Fergus ignored the magazines and television in the sitting room. He sat in a fine, leather wing chair and thought about his life while a man outside expertly edged the lawn along the curb. He was still thinking twenty minutes later when a sleek Acura sedan pulled up and that Baldwin fellow got out.

"Ah, Mr. Fergus," Baldwin said as soon as he entered. The perfect assistant: immaculate dresser, good with names. "Ms. Móntez must be with Mr. Bianchi?"

"She is, yes."

"I'm afraid the doctors are not encouraging. Mr. Bianchi is now on what they call hospice care."

"Sorry to hear that," Fergus said. "It's a sad situation."

"It is, truly. Yet Mr. Bianchi has faced the end with his usual fortitude and foresight. Only yesterday, he gave me instructions which pertain to your niece, and which I have since carried out. He directed me to inform you both of the details."

Fergus waited. He nodded.

"In case you have not already learned, the reporter pursuing your niece is his grandson."

Fergus nodded again.

"Mr. Bianchi has taken steps to prevent his grandson from ever writing about your niece or getting anyone else to write about your niece. Not to be too specific, he has made him president of one of the corporation's non-news divisions, with the stipulation that if anything about your niece should ever appear in one of SANECOR's publications, he will be removed from his position and his severance package will be cancelled. We feel certain that he will comply with this, and that you and your niece may be confident that this episode is over.

"I regret that I must attend an online board meeting in ten minutes, so I must ask you to convey this information to your niece, if you will, please."

"Gladly."

"In case you might need to contact me in the future, here is my card. May I say that Mr. Bianchi and I have been most impressed with your niece. She is an extraordinary young woman."

"Thank you. I agree."

He was still at the window ten minutes after Baldwin drove off when the kid returned, looking serious, very serious. She walked straight to him. Without missing a beat he opened his arms and hugged her.

She hugged him back.

## Chapter 42

On the drive back to Tasajillo, Fergus told Clio what Baldwin had said about young Bianchi's conditional promotion. Clio did not react, saying nothing at all until they were five miles from town.

"We'll need some dinner pretty soon. I'm sorry, but eating out tonight doesn't sound good—I'm not quite ready for noise and cheerful people. Plus, I'm tired of eating in the rooms. Would you be willing to take some food to the park at the end of town and eat outside?"

"Sure," he said. "It's a nice evening for it."

"What would you like?"

"Hmm," he said.

She glanced at him. He had a twinkle in his eye. For two weeks he'd been stubbornly deferential about choosing restaurants but now could make a joke about it. He was messing with her, a little, but she wasn't in a mood to reciprocate.

"How about this?" she said. "The Tuli café makes a good burger. Get one with cheese and green chili rajas and see how you like that."

"Great idea. I think I'm gonna miss these green chilies."

While she waited for their food he crossed the street to the Stop 'N' Shop and bought a can of Bohemia beer.

They ate at a picnic table overlooking the creek that flowed by the town to the east. Six or seven young teens were playing an informal game of soccer on the grassy area beyond some well-worn swings and a slide. The sun was close to dropping behind the mountains. At the moment the evening was clear and crisp.

They ate without talking. His food was good. The green chili strips made the cheeseburger into an exotic, memorable meal, and the beer was perfect with it. She was eating her burrito automatically, her face blank.

"You OK?" he asked.

She looked up as if she'd forgotten he was there.

"Uh-huh," she replied.

He tilted his head as if to say "Really?"

"Oh," she sighed, "It's just...I've never been around a dying person before. It kind of got to me."

"I didn't see him," he said. "Was it sad, or scary, or what?"

"No, not that. It was...quiet, peaceful. It was strange. I mean, it's a life, ending, but I actually felt close to him." She shook her head. "I guess you've seen a lot of that, huh?"

He looked at the soccer players. They were straggling off the field, kicking the ball from one to another.

"Some. In war, death is violent, and it's...unnatural, you might say, highly unnatural. It gets to us, even if we pretend it doesn't. But a rich old man, fading away in his fancy house, with cooks and doctors and caretakers everywhere? I mean, we all gotta go sometime. Doing it the way he's doing it doesn't seem so bad."

"It's not bad," she replied. "It's mysterious...majestic, somehow. See, my mother's people think of everything as part of a cycle. They say that our bodies are composed of elements made in the stars, and that they'll return to the stars to be made into something else eventually."

"Pretty far out."

"No, it's true. Even our astronomers say that. The big bang produced the lighter elements, like hydrogen and helium, which compressed together to form stars, and the stars made all the other elements, including the ones in us. But a complete cycle would take billions of years."

"Is that their religion?"

"Well, kind of. I don't understand it myself. They think that being born and living and dying is the universe working like it's supposed to. Everything does it, the planets and stars too. Today, I saw it myself, I guess, up close. I couldn't help thinking about it. I still am."

"Man," he said, "that's pretty heavy. I'd never have thought of it like that."

She watched him studying the remaining french fry fragments, eating selected slivers. His spirits also seemed down, but surely for some other reason. She tried a question.

"You've been quiet too. Not about Mr. Bianchi, though, right?"

"Uh...no. I've been thinking about the potholes in the road of my life. I've screwed up a lot. It's been on my mind lately. I don't know why."

"You?"

"That surprises you?"

"Well, yeah. I mean, you're a war hero, and a SEAL, the best of the best. You and your team took out the world's worst terrorist. And so here you are, minus a foot, but still young. Your life isn't even half over."

"Well, thanks for that," he said with a rueful smile. "But among other things, there's also my personal life." He folded up the paper his fries had been on. "I might've told you I'm divorced. It was my fault. Completely. I was a jerk. She's a wonderful woman and I loved her totally. I still do. She remarried, happily, I hope. I miss the intimate part of it too but I don't wanna go into it."

"Oh, I'm so sorry. Was the divorce after you were out of the service?"

"Yeah."

He held the paper bag up to her. She dropped in the debris from her hamburger and on a whim laid her hand on his.

"Your pain is back," she said.

"Yeah, gettin' stiff, a little."

"I can fix that, later."

He tossed his wadded-up paper into the bag and looked skyward. "The sun's down. It's getting chilly out here. Why don't we head back?"

"OK. I need to go by the Stop 'N' Shop on the way back. I'm out of shampoo."

Once again, their car trip was silent. She was considering the impressions she had just gathered from Fergus's hand. His revelations about his sad marriage caused her to rethink what she had felt with his brain the night before. Previously, she had wondered if some of the strange patterns she had found might be related to the concussion-induced trauma she was almost sure he had suffered. Now that she knew his marital problems had come after his military service she wondered if the trauma might have been a factor in the marital discord. Her visit to the Stop 'N' Shop was an impulse, but so what? Most of what she did with healing was from impulse.

With the medical team departed, the parking lot at El Faro Motel had only three cars in it. They were unlocking their respective doors when she spoke.

"I'm going to shower and then pack. Can I tune up your abs in about an hour?"

"You bet. I'll shower and pack too. I think you could make a living being on call for busted up goons, if you wanted."

"I might. I'm starting to like it," she replied as she opened her door and went in.

He finished his shower before she did—no surprise there. As he emerged from his bathroom dry and clean-shaven he heard her hair dryer whining and things clanking on the counter. It didn't take him long to pack. He left the case open on the counter next to the television, sat down, and poured himself one finger of Johnny Walker while she walked back and forth across the doorway folding clothes and, it looked like, putting them in a suitcase on the bed. For several minutes, she was on her cell phone.

The hot shower had eased his sore muscles somewhat and the booze relaxed him a little more, but he could still stand some attention from his semi-extraterrestrial therapist. He was starting to like it too.

He was on the point of pouring another shot of Johnny when Clio peeked in.

"Remember this?" she said, holding up the green rip-stop bag. "Surely it's safe to claim our shoes now. Would you like the bag?"

"No, thanks" he said. "I don't need a souvenir of that night."

"I'll give it to my brother," she said. "He loves gear bags." She set his shoes on the counter next to his bag and took her little gray flats out. "My family is home," she added. "We'll meet them at the art gallery tomorrow and go to lunch and then I'll take you to the airport."

She rolled up the bag, and disappeared into her room. In another minute she was back. She stood behind his chair and laid her hand on the back of his neck. Oddly, he was pleased she hadn't asked to get started.

"You're nice and relaxed," she said, "but I feel the stiffness. Let me zero in on it."

She had him stand and move his neck and arm around to suit her while she placed her hands here and there. He didn't have a full range of movement in that shoulder and she explored it until the joint protested and she was satisfied. Then she had him assume the position: on the bed, head over the edge.

It was much like before: eighteen inches below his face, two cute little rows of kid toes, and above, unseen fingers probing and moving his head back and forth, up and down. The cooling effect and the tingling sensations began together. He found it easier to stay awake this time. Maybe it was because he was getting more familiar with the process, or maybe she wasn't giving him the full whammy.

Then she had him turn over so she could work on the shoulder: more pinching, rubbing, massaging. Those little fingers were stronger than they looked. She must have spent ten minutes on his shoulder.

"Now for the recent stuff," she murmured, moving to his kidneys. He was getting seriously drowsy but he didn't fight it. From experience, he knew it would be fine. When she finished with those, she straddled his hips again and began stroking his abdomen under the t-shirt. Good God, how could that not help? Gradually, amid pleasant (and unmentionable) thoughts, he drifted out of consciousness.

Clio was so thankful to have a subject for extended treatment. She was feeling more in control of what she was doing. The fact that she still didn't quite know *how* she was doing it didn't bother her as much as it had. She'd had feedback, and she knew she really was doing some good.

After all, the second day she had worked on Fergus, she had discovered the old injuries to his neck and shoulder, and had been able to improve them. She could not completely correct those problems, but by concentrating on the general area of the injury she thought the various tissues would function more smoothly. She was more confident of what she was doing with his kidneys and abdominal muscles. She already had worked on them successfully. By the time she had finished the present session, over an hour later, he was soundly asleep.

Now there was plenty of time to return to an area she was much less sure about: his brain, the most complex organ in the body. She had more patient history this time: not only her deduction that Fergus had some degree of concussion trauma, but also that one of the major "potholes on the road of his life," an unhappy post-trauma marital conflict and divorce, might have resulted from it. The two might even be reinforcing each other in a vicious circle of tension.

Last time, the storm of input she had received had been daunting, and confusing. Even so, she suspected there had been an order to it all, somehow. Would her ability to discern patterns have improved? And if it had improved, would she be able to concentrate on them and perhaps affect them? The possibility was exciting…but also a little scary.

As before, she lay where she could hold the back of Fergus's head against her chest. She checked to make sure her hands could conveniently access most of his scalp. Then she took three long, slow breaths, closed her eyes, and focused her mind on the impressions flowing into her.

In just a few minutes she understood something that had confused her before: it took the accumulated input of multiple hand placements to form an overall impression of the brain. As far as she could tell, there was no identifiable center of activity. Images from PET scans she had seen suggested there might be, but she found the entire organ was humming with activity and she needed many minutes to form a comprehensive impression. It was like walking around a house peeking in the windows. Only with patient effort could one form any coherent impression of the interior, however tentative that impression might be.

Her former analogy with orchestras tuning up simultaneously seemed less accurate than ever. She recalled a movie she had seen which had a bead curtain in a doorway in several scenes. She enlarged that concept: a big room with a high ceiling, with rows and rows of bead curtains hanging close upon one another, millions of beads altogether, filling the room completely. But the strings of beads were free-floating, and could separate and recombine with other strings of beads constantly, in an ever-changing swirl of patterns...with her free to float among them, to observe their constant shifting, to hold out her hands, as it were, and run them through her fingers so the strings would part and reform constantly.

That was more satisfying, closer to what she was feeling. But these weren't beads, exactly. Instead, she sensed them as having textures, for lack of a better term: some smooth, some round, some jagged, some clumped together, varying endlessly. They were not identifiable as "thoughts" per se, but nonetheless seemed connected somehow, discrete entities, perhaps electro-neurological patterns, of a real human mind. They might be emotions—she sensed loneliness, anger, longing, and more...but it was impossible to pursue them. She didn't really want to.

Being inside another human brain was incredibly intimate, almost a union, like nothing else she had ever experienced. She was swimming underwater, in effect, through the living center of Fergus's actual being.

The room and the outside world faded away as she concentrated as never before, holding Fergus's head tight against her, unaware of her hands moving from forehead to temples to crown, front to back, side to side, swimming ceaselessly through the mysterious beads, moving them aside, combing them out, finding their edges and boundaries and connections, feeling the consistencies change, reform, and combine with others in endless sequences, on and on and on, until she was no longer sure which were his and which were hers.

## Chapter 43

Chico Bustamante, a long-haul truck driver finally home after three weeks driving a big rig coast to coast four times, had been gently eased out of Chope's Bar by the sypmathetic bartender at three in the morning. His road skills were so befuddled that on the way home he was unable to prevent his truck from driving into an electric pole in the very center of Tasajillo, causing the airbag to knock him unconscious and a transformer to short out and explode with a sound not unlike a mortar shell landing too close for comfort, prompting dogs to start barking frantically and lights to come on in nearby houses.

Two blocks away, the attenuated blast caused a shift in the REM sleep pattern of former Navy Lieutenant Ian Fergus. He had been dreaming that he and his ex-wife Celine were making passionate love in a canvas-covered tree house in the Seattle Arboretum during a midnight rainstorm. That this was illogical, given that Celine hated camping, did not occur to him. The concussion from the exploding transformer caused the aerial love nest to morph into his former canvas hooch in Camp TARFU, Afghanistan, which was on the ground, not in a tree, and which happened to be in the process of receiving a visit from a tiny space ship floating down from another planet. Out of it stepped "the kid."

She had lovely, long, straight dark blonde hair and a sweet, knowing smile. Trailing the scent of honeysuckle, she walked straight into his hooch, which had a big, red cross on the entrance flap. He followed as if he had been ordered to. Since this was a dream, he was unsurprised to find a double bed there, with the kid standing at the end of it, waiting for him. Somehow he had been seriously wounded (though he was leaking no blood and had no holes in him). He lay down in order for the kid to restore him to health.

Still with that sweet face, the kid climbed onto the bed and sat on his hips, at which point he knew he would be healed of his injuries, whatever they were. As if in slow motion, she crossed her hands at her waist, clasped the hem of her t-shirt, and pulled it over her head inside out, her hair cascading over her shoulders and perky little breasts. Then she leaned forward with an angelic smile and glowing golden eyes and kissed him softly on the cheek.

Around that moment, Tasajillo's lone police officer on the night shift was racing past the El Faro motel to the accident scene with his siren wooping. It wasn't absolutely necessary at that hour of the morning but regulations allowed it, it wasn't a bad idea in the interest of public safety, and it would be a not-too-subtle reminder to the community that their tax money was being spent in protecting them. It was loud enough even through the heavy drapes and the humming air pump to rouse Lieutenant Fergus to a state of near-wakefulness. He found himself sweating and puffing in the darkness as if he had run a hundred yards.

He had been dreaming, right?

Dreaming?

*Right?*

Yes, it was a dream, surely it was a dream. But it was so vivid, so completely real. Half in a panic, he sat up. In the dim light leaking out of the barely open bathroom door, he found his prosthesis at the end of the bed and slipped it on without the support stocking and made his way to the bathroom. He relieved himself, washed his hands and face, and stared at his reflection.

The face in the mirror showed surprise at the precise moment he realized that he didn't hurt anywhere, and it hadn't hurt to urinate. He moved his left arm in a complete circle. It was easy, and it didn't pain him. Astonishing as that was, it was the dream that was still electric in his mind: the kid!

Could she have…?

No. No, of course not.

Could he have…?

Well…no. No, certainly not. And especially not if she had not. It had been a dream, only a dream.

So why could he still recall the thrilling warmth of her skin against his?

Hey! He was in his briefs! Where were his goddam pants?

Holy hell, what had happened to him? What the damn hell had happened to him?

A little shakily, he returned to the bedroom and sat on the edge of the bed. In the dim light, there were his pants neatly folded on the far corner of the bed.

The adjoining door was ajar. It was dark in the kid's room. The bedside clock showed 04:26 am. Odd—the same last four numbers as his Navy ID number. He slipped off the prosthesis and lay back and stared at the ceiling.

The pillow smelled of honeysuckle.

When the kid's alarm beeped he was sitting in one of the two chairs in his room fully dressed. The bed was made and the television was on with the sound muted. He'd watched a little of some rodeo but found that didn't suit his mood as well as the college girls' volleyball game he had on at the moment. The girls were superb athletes, all tall, slim, and quick, with excellent killer instincts and teamwork, sort of like the kid, writ tall.

His thoughts wandered. From time to time he regarded the three strands of cobweb-thin, sixteen inch-long hair draped over the arm of the vacant chair. He had found them in the sheets.

A light came on in her room. He heard her bathroom door close and the plumbing perform its various functions. He still hadn't formed a strategy. What could he ask her and not look like a total fool?

Several minutes passed. She knocked gently on his door and stuck her head in.

"Good morning!" she said cheerily.

"Good morning," he replied, his voice a little rusty. He turned off the TV.

She pushed the door partway open. She was wearing new gray jeans and a long sleeve crewneck turquoise t-shirt.

"How are you feeling?"

"Great. Excellent."

"Nothing needs tuning up?"

"No…."

His voice left something unsaid.

"What?" she asked.

"Uh, I seem to have lost my pants last night."

"Oh, right. Sorry about that. You still had that bruised area on your right thigh. I couldn't work through the jeans. While I was treating that I found another area in the knee on that side. Did you injure that at some point?"

"Um, yeah. High school football."

"Well, I think I improved that too. It was probably a sprained tendon. It must have healed funny. It would take surgery to fix it, but I reduced the inflammation some."

"Ah. Well, thanks."

"I couldn't put the jeans back on, so I just left them off and covered you up."

"Right."

"Why don't we load the car and check out? We can get breakfast on the way to Santa Fe and try someplace new."

"Good. I'm ready to go."

Ten miles down the road he tried again.

"Three days," he said, shaking his head.

"Huh?"

"Really, two and a half days after getting pounded good, and I'm over it. I feel as good as I did before. No: I lied. I feel better, a lot better."

"That's wonderful!"

"You're telling me. You're an ace, shipmate."

"Thanks!"

"How long did that session last night take?"

"How long? I don't know. I was kind of zoned out, I guess you'd say. I usually concentrate so hard I lose track of the time. It must've been about two hours total."

"Hmm. I had no idea."

Crap. He wasn't going to get an answer that way. Well, all right then. Try the direct way.

"Last night I had a weird dream." He watched her. Her expression didn't change. Her eyes were on the road. "I dreamed my ex-wife and I were making love. And then blammo: she became you. You and I were making love. Would you know anything about that?"

He watched her closely. Her eyes widened in what looked like surprise.

"Me? I have no idea what you might have dreamed. Like you said, dreams are weird. I've never asked anyone I treated if they had strange dreams afterward, but that might be a good idea. Maybe I upset your biorhythms. I'll have to ask other people that question." She glanced at him with a twinkle in her eye. "I hope it wasn't a scary dream," she added.

"Not hardly," he said, giving up. "Just, like I said, weird."

# Chapter 44

Doroteo Mendoza, Doro, was having yet another good day. His father's son, his Mexican rancher father's misfit son, was not doing too badly on his own after all. The oldest son, an upcoming rancher, and the second child, an eminently eligible daughter, were his father's pride and joy, but he seemed relieved when the third child, the gay one, headed off to art school and then the United States.

On the other hand, his grandfather would be very proud of him. His success would be a partial return for that enlightened gentleman's investment in his grandson's Bellas Artes education. After only three years on his own, the grandson was soon going to be making a living from his art—highly unusual for a young artist.

He politely excused himself from conversation with the gallery owner and several gallery visitors when his very favorite cousin Clio arrived. Something important had happened since seeing her nine days earlier, and he could hardly wait to tell her.

The first time she visited the gallery he had been surprised to see she had a chaperone. It was not unknown in Mexico for a young girl to have a companion away from home, though chaperones were generally older women. Clio had told him he was an uncle and maybe he was, but Doro was a keen observer of people, especially men, and he suspected this man was more than just an uncle. He was only about ten years older than Doro himself, trim, confident, and alert though being subtle about it. Doro judged he would know how to not suffer fools, especially around his niece. It seemed likely that her parents had arranged for this particular man to accompany their daughter because they wished a higher, more physical level of security for her. It was a little odd, given that this was the United States, but she was completely worth it in his opinion.

As for Clio, the first time he'd seen her she had taken his breath away. The way the planes of her face brought her sharp features into harmony, and her keen hazel eyes changed with her mood gave her a presence like no one he had ever seen or imagined. Her quick mind made a perfect match with her appearance. In less than twenty seconds he knew he had to paint her. Later, she astonished him again when she vanquished the bullies who had attacked him—and astonished him even more when she repaired the beating they had given him. After doing that, of all things, she kissed him. Like he told his friend Mark, it was as if he had been understood and blessed at the same time. From that moment to this he had harbored an extraordinary spiritual love for this young woman, his distant cousin.

He shook hands with the chaperone—the man gave off serious male vibes—and embraced cousin Clio tenderly. The companion wandered off to study the art while Doro, in typical courtly Mexican fashion, politely drew her out on her happenings, mostly routine, before she asked him for his own news.

"Ay, prima! Tengo que decirte: your painting was sold!"

"It was?" she said, concern in her face.

"¡Sí! That rich man, Bianchi, bought it. For $100,000! ¡Imagínate! What's the matter?" he asked.

"That's wonderful, Doro. But he's terribly sick. He won't have long to enjoy it."

"I know. Es una lástima, de veras. I didn't see him. His assistant, Señor Baldwin, talked to me. He gave me two envelopes. One is for me. This one is for you." He pulled a small envelope, the size of a thank-you note, from his shirt pocket and handed it to her. The paper was parchment-like, and heavy. "He said we would know when to open them."

"Oh, my goodness. He must have meant, after, after...." She hesitated.

"Sí, I think so too: después de que fallezca...." He took her hands, still holding the envelope, between his. "I had to sell it, prima. Señor Baldwin said they wanted me to use the money to stay in Santa Fe and start a studio."

"Oh, Doro, that's so sweet." She started weeping. "That poor man."

"I know," he said, hugging her again. "But it means I'll be here for good. We can visit from time to time!" Over her shoulder he saw her parents approaching. He patted her and stood back. "Ajá. Aquí vienen tus padres."

She slid the envelope in a back pocket and composed herself quickly.

"Don't tell my parents who bought the painting, please. I'll explain later."

At the far end of the room, Fergus was admiring one of Doro's watercolors, a running stallion, seen from the front. He knew from sad experience that watercolor was one of the most difficult of media, but this stallion, sparely limned in broad, vigorous hues, looked full of life and completely and expertly rendered. Clearly, Doro was not a duffer as an artist.

He was planning how he might chat up the elegant gallery owner when Ana Darcy and husband and son arrived. This was only the second time he'd seen her, and much less dramatic than the first time, though considerably more elegant. Then, she'd been half undressed, covered in soot, and smelling of cordite. Now, she looked right for an art gallery, in sharp black pants, white blouse, and a crisp, lightweight burgundy parka. Her hair was different, curly and short, and she wore black framed glasses. He'd not have recognized her had he not known.

He was going to give the family time to greet each other and chat a bit, but before he could saunter over Ana Darcy herself came to greet him. To his surprise, she gave him a quick hug and two air kisses.

Two years earlier he'd shaken hands with the President of the United States and hadn't been half as thrilled.

"It's great to see you again, Fergus," she said, retaining his right hand in hers. "I hope you've had an uneventful two weeks."

"It went by in a flash." That was a lie. "I'd do it again any time." That was true, with qualifications.

"We so appreciate your service, sir," she said, "now and before. You must meet my husband and son again. We'd like to look at Doro's art briefly, but we'd be honored if you would join us for lunch, please!"

"It would be a pleasure, ma'am."

And so it turned out, to his surprise—not that the family was not fun, because they were, but because his normal tenseness in non-military groups was not a problem. He relaxed. He enjoyed himself.

Which is not to say his mind didn't wander throughout the meal. For one thing, he was happy that he'd not put his foot in his mouth before a remark from Clio made it clear that Doro did not know her mother was "Ana Darcy." Nor did anyone say a word about Ana's newsworthy photo-event at the Davos Conference. OK, fair enough. He and the kid would say nothing about their close call with death at the hands of the crime underworld, either.

Over another outstanding meal of New Mexican-style cuisine, probably the last he'd enjoy for a good while, the six of them had an agreeable time together. It was evident that Doro had not seen the family for some time himself, yet the parents smoothly included both newcomers into their conversation. Matt Méndez and his son Julio were about like he remembered them from that crazy night in Afghanistan: reserved and self-controlled, just like men should be. It was incredible to think that this normal-seeming family was the only one like it on Earth, with the wife from another planet, and twins half from it. They were perfectly ordinary on the one hand, and on the other they were unique in all the world—two worlds, really.

Fergus remembered that his mother used to say that people were basically the same everywhere. She probably said it after Ana's big splash at the Olympics and her interview afterward. He'd been a freshman in high school then, and Ana had made an unforgettable impression on him. If anyone had predicted at the time that he would eventually meet her and work with her and for her, he'd have thought they were crazy.

And now he was having lunch with her and her family. It would be fun to tell the story of these two weeks to the only person to whom he could mention it, Rob Coombs. He'd leave out the erotic dream starring Ana Darcy's daughter, of course. That memory, still vivid and embarrassing, he would keep to himself.

Clio had been watching the time. They had to make their farewells before dessert to make it to the airport on time. The drive would be less than an hour.

Once they had left Santa Fe behind, Clio spoke up.

"I'm sorry about all the trouble we had these two weeks, Fergus," she said. "It should have been easy, but instead it was terrible. I'm so glad you were there for me when I made that goof at the motel."

He thought about that a second before laughing out loud. It was the first time she had ever heard him laugh.

"Don't mention it," he replied. "That was trivial. I'm really glad *you* were there to put down that ox at the trailer and set us free. Then you ran thirteen miles chop chop to fetch the rescue vehicle and set us free again. That was outstanding. Not even a SEAL could have done that."

"Well, those men would have crushed this little car with us in it if you hadn't shot up their truck," she said.

"That was basic markmanship. The thing is, I should have been hospitalized for a couple weeks after that. You repaired the damage in two and a half days. I still can't believe that. I'm in your debt more than you are in mine, way more. You're an ace, shipmate. I mean that: big league."

A shiny blue pickup in the left lane suddenly cut in front to let an even faster sports car zoom by. Clio braked to maintain a safe distance. Fergus didn't freak out.

"Oh," she said. "Well, thanks."

"Seriously," he went on, "Coombs made your mom an honorary SEAL. I think you ought to be another."

"That's crazy. Please don't. I'd have to explain it to my mom."

"You have a point. You could be one hell of a combat medic, though. You could save lives, girl."

"Oh," she replied. She thought a minute. "Maybe. I don't know. I hate to see suffering, and pain."

"Yeah, everybody does. Soldiers say they get used to it, but they really don't. It corrodes the soul eventually."

They were nearing the airport. Traffic was heavy. Neither said much more until Clio pulled up at the departure terminal. Fergus's bag was on the backseat, not in the trunk, but Clio set the brake and got out anyway. They stood there.

Her face was forlorn.

His was unreadable.

"Thank you, Fergus," she said, "for everything."

"Don't mention it. Thank *you* for everything," he replied.

She hugged him impulsively. Her eyes were glistening.

"You take care, now, shipmate," he said, patting her back and releasing her.

He hoisted his bag, smiled quickly, and headed into the terminal. She watched him move into the crowd until a traffic cop's whistle and rumbling passenger shuttles called her back to her car.

It took fifteen minutes to drive to her appointment with Dr. Peebles at The University of New Mexico while her mind churned with conflicted thoughts.

It was Saturday afternoon and the campus was deserted but the old building was open. Dreading the mysterious visitor, she started up the stairs. Dr. Peebles would never trick her, but this just felt wrong. She resolved she would not be trapped into "performing" for a stranger.

Despite his life-long immersion in the science of medicine, Thornton Peebles was enjoying his acquaintance with a genuine scholar of alternative medicine. The man, to his credit, tempered his enthusiasm for healing and healers and his own childhood experiences with a rigorous researcher's careful dispassion.

Over the half hour they'd been chatting, his guest had jotted down a number of accounts of healers for the possible interest of his new acquaintance: Don Pedrito Jaramillo of south Texas, *Border Healing Woman*, a biography of Jewel Babb of west Texas, and *The Hummingbird's Daughter*, the story of Teresita Urrea, the "saint of Cabora," from northern Mexico and later El Paso and Arizona, all well documented (if not scientifically examined) cases of healers in the area. He was adding the "Indian doctor" of Liverpool, Texas when Peebles raised a finger.

"Ah!" he said. "I think she's here. That was the door to the stairwell."

A few seconds later there was a soft knock on the door.

"Come in!" he said.

The door opened and Clio Méndez appeared. She started in surprise.

"Dr. Bisti!" she said.

"Clio!" he responded, getting to his feet.

"You know each other?" Peebles said.

"I've known her family for years," Bisti replied, embracing her quickly. "I had no idea you had skills as a healer, my dear."

"How do you do, sir," she said, shakily.

"Very well, thank you. And you?"

"I'm…ok."

"And how is your lovely family?"

"They're fine. I just left them. We were at an art gallery in Santa Fe which is showing works by a cousin of ours."

"But this is astonishing!" Peebles said, showing Clio to a chair. "To think that you already know each other!"

"The Méndezes and I are on the board of the Juárez Academy School in Mesilla," Bisti replied. "I've known Clio and her brother since they were in primary school. Her parents are great supporters of local education and cultures in all their manifestations." He turned to Clio. "I remember you worked a while with a local curandera, didn't you? I thought that was research for a school project. Oh, my, this is wonderful."

"She has just completed two weeks helping with a rural medical clinic," Peebles said. "She and I had hoped that working in such a busy, less formal medical environment would provide her an opportunity to test her skills in a variety of medical situations. Is that what you found, Ms. Méndez?"

"Uh…well, maybe. I'm not sure. I saw lots of people of all ages, and I made tons of impressions. But I haven't sorted them out very well yet. It takes time. I can't explain any of it yet. I'm sorry. I'm nearly exhausted, really."

Both men were instantly sympathetic, and Clio managed to politely maneuver herself away from them after another twenty minutes of pleasantries and a copy of Dr. Bisti's list of healers. The only cost was a promise to meet with both gentlemen at some point in the near future.

She stopped in a first floor restroom and washed her face and back of her neck with cold water and was headed back home ten minutes later, still puzzling out her situation.

Traffic was light.

The atmosphere of Dr. Peebles' office always impressed her. Books and journals were stacked everywhere. Medical charts, degrees, and plaques covered the walls. One ancient bookcase contained a worn doctor's bag and dusty old-fashioned scientific equipment from a druggist's lab. The office had always appealed to her as a good place to puzzle out her strange abilities.

It was common knowledge that the human body was a complex, swirling electrical-chemical-neurological network, some of which could be measured by modern instruments. Perhaps that is what she was detecting, using only the instrument of her body. Peebles' offer of a controlled experiment to investigate was tempting but too public for her taste, though nothing else seemed to offer hope of an explanation. Maybe she could enlist Julio in the effort.

She leaned to the passenger side and pushed the sun visor out to block the late afternoon sun.

Julio could figure a way to measure anything, surely. Still, that was only half the problem: she seemed to not only detect cellular electricity but also affect it, an even bigger mystery. However did she control it, if that was what she was doing? It was so very weird. *She* was so very weird. But then why wouldn't she be? Half of her came from another planet.

Even if she didn't completely understand how she did it, it was wonderful to be able to help people. But the long range consequences to her of doing so were looking decidedly unattractive.

A black Suburban coming up fast behind her on the Interstate nearly gave her heart failure, even though she had seen the previous one blow up in her rear view mirror. As it pulled into the passing lane and went by her she saw it carried a mother and father and a crowd of children in back. She let out a shuddering breath.

Really, she had a lot to be thankful for, not least her dear little car, as clean and neat as it had been two weeks ago…when it very easily could have been a crumpled wreck at the bottom of a canyon with two bloody bodies in it. Taking another deep breath, she set the cruise control to a safe 65. Three hours and a little more to home: plenty time to worry about the days and weeks just past… and ahead.

# Chapter 45

Coomb's bright red pickup truck was easy to pick out among the cars and trucks jockeying along the curb of the arrival terminal. Fergus waved and jumped in as Coombs barely stopped. They shook hands quickly.

"RobboMan! How's the new dad?" he said, buckling his seat belt.

"Welcome back, Fergus! Doing pretty good, thanks, better than Michelle. She's up at all hours. At least her mother's here to share the load. Full time job, taking care of a teeny one. She's cute though. Sweet-natured. Just like me."

"Outstanding. I wanna see her one of these days soon."

"You bet. We'll do it. I got a picture…hold on. Later."

He cut off his comment as he checked the mirrors and zoomed into merging traffic. Fergus held on but managed not to panic. Once they were comfortably up to speed, he spoke again.

"Thanks for picking me up, man. You didn't have to do that."

"I wouldn't for anyone else, but you're a special case. I had to hear how the job went with our favorite customers. Everything smooth?"

He changed lanes quickly and passed two trucks and a car. Coombs drove like a fighter pilot.

"Smooth? Well, let's just say that all's well that ends well. It makes quite a tale. We'll be at my condo in ten minutes. Come on in for a spell. We can't do it justice unless we're drinking a beer. Might need two. Like they say, you ain't gonna believe this shit."

Thirty-five minutes later, with two beers down, Fergus had reached the point in his narrative when he and Clio had arrived back at the motel, beat up, run down, shaken, and in major pain.

Coombs had stopped him five minutes into the story to confirm that neither he nor Clio had been permanently injured and that there would be no long-term consequences for the two of them or for World Security Services. Once reassured, Coombs allowed him to resume his narration with only a few clarifying interruptions.

"You mean those guys blew themselves up with their own bomb?"

"Yeah, they did, the dumb fucks. Evil to him who thinks evil, right? Didn't some French guy say that?"

"Probably."

"Doesn't matter. Mind you, I didn't tell Clio I found a bomb on her car or that I returned it to sender."

"Course not. No need to know. Bravo zulu, shipmate, way to go. And are you telling me she actually stomped a three hundred pound oaf with her hands tied behind her back?"

"Totally. Thoroughly. Took her about thirty seconds. Damnedest thing I ever saw, I swear. And one of the most welcome."

"And then she ran twelve six-minute miles to go get her car?"

"Closer to thirteen."

Coombs shook his head.

"Jesus."

"Yeah, man."

"Mother and daughter. Un-freakin'-believable."

"But wait. There's more. You need another beer?"

"I better not.... Aww, hell, let's split one. This is too good. I'll text Michelle that I'll be home in a half hour."

Fergus returned from the kitchen with a beer and a glass. He poured half into the glass and handed the bottle to Coombs. Coombs wrinkled his brow.

"I'm sorry about this, Fergus," he said. "If I'd known things would get this hairy, I'd not have got you into it."

"Well, like I said in the truck, all's well that ends well."

"Hey, wait," Coombs said. "What day did all that happen?"

"Wednesday night. Three days ago."

Coombs thought a moment.

"You said that big guy beat the hell out of you, right?"

"Half killed me, or a little more. Don't spread it around."

"But you're not busted up. In fact, when you got in the truck I was going to point out you're not even limping. You look great. How can that be, only three days later?"

"You wanna guess?"

Coombs shot him a sharp glance.

"Clio?"

"You got it. You remember she was with that medical outfit to practice her healing. I thought it was bullshit, frankly. I know she supposedly kept your brain from exploding, but I figured that was hooey." He tilted his glass and watched the beer and foam swirl. "Now I know it wasn't."

"I'll be God damned. What'd she do?"

"I made it to the bed and lay there a couple hours, feeling worse and worse, cramping, severely bruised, probably bleeding internally. I was ready for an ambulance, man, or a corpsman with the needles of oblivion. She started working on me in the wee hours while I bitched at her to knock it off, and the next thing I knew I woke up and felt better."

"How'd she do it?"

"Beats the shit out of me, but she did it with her hands. Massage, light massage and manipulation. It was not your typical massage. It felt great, but it was cool and electric at the same time. I tell you, I was sold after the first session, but she did four more or so over the next two days. Cleared up my busted kidneys, my abs and lats, and my goddam stump, which the VA hospital couldn't do shit with. She even found an old high school football injury and fixed that too. Seriously, man, I haven't felt this good in years."

Coombs scraped a strip off the label on the bottle with a thumbnail and shook his head again.

"Holy crap," he said.

"You said it," Fergus replied.

"And we can't tell a freakin' soul."

"Not even her parents. But *we* know."

Coombs drained his bottle. Fergus finished his glass.

"Well then, I might have a deal for you, if you want it."

"What?"

"Got a great job coming up. Diplomats. Economic summit. South American finance ministers. Easy, pays great, might go a week. Takes six bodies but we only had five. I was gonna send Hayes, but he was going to have to cancel a vacation. Since you're in such good condition…. Only hitch is it starts tomorrow. Are you up to that?"

"Damn straight. Ready for duty."

"Outstanding," he said, getting to his feet. "Thanks for the beer and the briefing. You and I could write a book about those two women, but no one would believe it. What is it about that family?"

"Except for being from another planet, I have no idea. But I enjoyed briefing you, since I can't tell anyone else," Fergus said, setting the glass down. "Let's do this again sometime. You haven't told me all your Ana stories. I'm in the club now. I'm cleared for it."

The reunited Méndez family had assembled for a festive first dinner back home: Clio and Julio, Ana and Matt, Matt's parents Bert and Julia, and Bert's mother Abuelita. There was much catching up to be done. Clio's strategy was to let Julio to do most of the talking for the two of them. He was the one who had had the real adventure, after all: setting a world speed record for an electric Corolla. He even showed off a t-shirt and trophy to prove it. For her part, she said her experience with the medical team was routine, almost boring. Fergus's name came up only briefly in response to a question from her mother. Clio answered almost dismissively, as if Fergus had been merely part of the background, and leaving the impression that she was a little annoyed to have had him along. Her mother did not press the matter.

No one mentioned her mother's trip to the Davos conference and the famous ear-pulling incident (though Clio definitely planned to ask her about that when they had some private time). The omission was no surprise, since Julia, their grandmother, though as sweet as ever, still suffered the effects of strokes she had years before. Only a month ago she tried to order egg rolls in a Mexican restaurant and on another occasion worried that Chinese gangsters from the detective novel she had just finished were lurking outside the family compound. She couldn't be trusted to keep the biggest secret in the family, that her daughter in law was from another planet.

On the other hand, Clio noticed that Abuelita, her 95 year old great-grandmother, had not missed the juicy news from Davos. A few minutes after Grandma Julia had gone up to bed she leveled a knowing look at Ana and in a low voice uttered one of her many dichos, the proverbial wisdom of New Mexico:

"Aunque el mono se vista de seda, mono se queda."

Clio shot a glance at Julio, who returned it with a gleam of amusement. Abuelita, as usual, had hit the nail on the head: a monkey dressed in silk is still a monkey.

It was only much later that night, when her parents had retired to their bedroom in the front of the house and she and Julio had moved to theirs in the back, that Clio could press Julio for the rest of his story: it was time for some twin talk. She sat cross-legged on her bed with her big cat Raisin, folded up like a sphinx and purring contentedly. Julio sat in her desk chair.

"I wanna know more about this girl at the hunting lodge," she said. "Dad barely mentioned her, so that means he's covering something up. Let's have it, Bubba."

"Aww, she was with her father, some big oil guy from Houston. She was supposed to meet her boyfriend to go see the Texas Mile, only he never showed. She was bored. We took her to the track, that was all."

"So what was she like?"

"Fancy clothes like a rhinestone cowboy's dream. Rich. Spoiled. Not that s-m-a-r-t. Real pretty, though, like a model." He laughed. "The first time she saw me she thought I worked there. She ordered me to get her a Coke."

"You're kidding!"

"No. I went and got her one."

"You didn't!"

"It was funny! She never realized I did it for a joke."

"Dad said you took her to the race."

"*I* didn't. *We* took her to the race. Since she'd been abandoned."

"So…did she find out you weren't just a waiter?"

"Yeah. She got talking to the racing team. They must've made it sound like I was a genius. Her attitude did a 180."

"I bet. So then what?"

"'Then what' nothing! We took her back to the lodge!"

"Oh, no, gomer! You can't fool your tister. C'mon, J-man. Tell me about that 180! I know there's more!"

"Well, just a little."

He was blushing. She was right. There was more.

"She wanted to have a party, to celebrate the speed record. Except we were the only two young people there."

He paused.

"Yeah?" she prompted. "So…?"

"She wanted to sneak some beers and have a slumber party out in the brush. She was going to bring a pillow."

Clio slapped her thighs.

"Are you kidding me? Bubba! That was your big chance! What did you do?"

"My big chance? You can't be serious! I mean, maybe it was, actually. But…I couldn't. I just couldn't. I played a dirty trick on her. I told her Dad and me had somewhere to go that evening. I said the next night would be OK, and she agreed to that. But Dad and I left the next morning."

"You ran out on her!"

"Yeah." His face clouded. "You think I was an idiot."

"No! No, I don't, not at all. Just the opposite. It didn't feel right, did it?"

"No. It felt wrong, actually."

"Good for you. It's gotta feel right. When it does, you'll know it. Don't you think?"

He looked at her strangely.

"You think? Well, yeah, I hope so. I didn't realize that until I had to choose." He put down the pencil he had been twiddling. "Y'know, twin stuff works two ways. I'm thinking you're hiding something yourself—maybe your own big chance? With some handsome intern? You weren't saying much at dinner. I told you mine. Now you gotta tell me yours. It's only fair."

She hopped up, went to the doorway, and peered down the hall toward the front of the house. Reassured, she pushed the door almost closed and retook her seat on the bed.

She regarded him a second.

"You're right. There was something."

"And you didn't tell Mom and Dad. I knew it!"

"No, I didn't tell them. I'm not going to, either. Fergus and I nearly got in serious trouble."

"*What?*"

"Shhh! Not so loud!"

"How?"

"Well, it was last week. We'd had a long day. We were resting in our rooms before going to eat when I heard a woman screaming outside…."

Very carefully, Clio proceeded to relate a "based on a true event" story, revising a few details to suit her purpose: she had rushed to the defense of a woman and infant being hassled by a strung-out ruffian. She was dealing satisfactorily with that individual when a second and third appeared. She ended up smashed against the hood of the woman's minivan, leaving Fergus to deal with the other two, which he did, though at the cost of many bruises.

Fergus advised the woman to go elsewhere, carried her—Clio—to her room, and dealt with the police when they arrived.

He was cramped up and sore and not ready for work the next morning, so she spent several hours working on his injuries. After another session that evening, he was up and around and soon recovered the rest of the way. That was the end of the matter as she related it.

To her surprise, Julio wasn't shocked to hear that his sister and her body guard had beaten up three thugs. He had only one question.

"I don't see why you can't tell Mom. You both did good…."

"Well, partly it's because I thought from the beginning that having a body guard was ridiculous. I just couldn't stand it if Mom said she told me so. But also, it's because of what I did with Fergus. He went to sleep like my patients tend to do…so I took a chance and checked out his brain too."

"You what? Why?"

Those were excellent questions, and as she hoped, they kept Julio from grilling her further about the fight and possibly discovering the even worse business of the deadly scrape she and Fergus had barely lived through. Instead, she rattled on about the details of her experiment to try to help Fergus with his concussion-related problems. The more she went on, the more it seemed to confuse Julio. That was fair enough. She was confused by it too. Finally, Julio admitted it.

"I don't get it. What's the problem?"

Her face fell.

"For one thing, I always ask for permission before I work on someone. I didn't ask Fergus because he was in too much pain, but the second time, when he was feeling better, I did ask him if he wanted me to do some more, and he said yes. But I didn't specifically ask if I could work on his brain."

"So?"

"See, when first I picked him up at the airport, he was jumpy. And nervous, and grouchy. And then he went crazy fighting those two guys. I had to stop him. I was afraid he was going to kill them. Later, one of the doctors at the clinic figured he had concussion trauma. He said scanners could detect it, but there was no treatment for it. So…when I was treating his bruises and he went to sleep, I decided to see what I could tell about his brain. He didn't give me permission, but I did it anyway. I shouldn't have done that."

"Oh. I see now. Well, what happened when you did?"

"That's the other thing, the one that worries me most. It scares me, really. I…I connected, I guess, with his brain, somehow. It was so weird I can't describe what it was like…sort of like wandering around in the dark, bumping into things but not knowing what…way confusing. I still don't know what it was. Maybe electrical signals? I mean, I was inside a human mind! I just don't know, Bubba!"

"Whoa. Tister, that's wild."

"I know! But the funny thing is that after that, his personality changed. You saw him at lunch: he was relaxed. He talked like, well, like Mr. Coombs would have, like a regular person. But he hadn't been like that at all before. It must be because of something I did. Only I don't know what I did! I didn't think I did anything!"

"Oh, jeez. That's cool." He thought a second. "But it's not very scientific."

"No, it isn't. It's scary."

They looked at the Raisin, eyes closed, apparently at peace with the world. Julio rolled the pencil between his thumb and index finger.

"OK, so it's not scientific," he said. "But you seem to make it work somehow. Maybe you do understand it, on some other level. Maybe you just need to give it time."

A moment passed.

"I'm tired of all this," she said.

"All this what?"

"Healing. I thought I could experiment, practice, maybe figure it out. Learn to control it. Use it. But it's not happening. I feel like stopping, just quitting. Before I hurt someone…."

He considered that.

"That'd be too bad," he said, finally. "You've done a lot of good—saved two lives, in fact. You'd never hurt anybody."

"Of course not. Not on purpose. But I don't understand it, Bubba! I was inside a person's mind! Who am I to fool around with someone else's mind?"

Her original purpose had been to distract Julio from the desperate trouble she and Fergus had survived, and she had done that. But she had done it too well. She had distracted herself too.

Julio only had one thing to say.

"Wow."

## Chapter 46

Most of the public schools in the Las Cruces area let out at 3:00 pm or 3:30 pm. Juárez Academy, however, was a private school. Known for its high academic standards, every school day had an extra hour devoted to tutoring, by teachers, parents, and student volunteers. It was optional, but generally well attended. The students, and the families of students, were serious about education.

When the bell rang at 4:00 pm this particular Friday afternoon several dozen students and tutors began packing up their materials and heading out to the street, among them the Méndez twins, Julio and Clio, who had been tutoring middle school students. The supervisor, Dr. Alice Chamot, wished them a good weekend, adding "We're going to miss you guys next year."

They left thinking about next year and the future generally without needing to say a word to the other. Julio was digging his car keys out of his jeans when Clio stopped short.

"Hey, isn't that Delia?" she said, tilting her head toward a slight girl walking away from them, halfway down the block. A chilly wind was whipping her hair behind her.

"Delia Iriarte? Yeah, I think so," Julio replied. "What about her?"

"Her grandmother usually picks her up, but it looks like she's walking home."

"You know where she lives?"

"I think it's about a mile away. Let's see if she needs a ride. Here, take my books to the car."

She trotted after the girl. Julio unlocked the RAV-4, stashed their book bags in the back, and started the engine to get a little heat going. The school had only about 300 students K-12, and he knew a little about most of them. Delia was a sixth grader. He didn't know if she was an orphan or her parents lived somewhere else, but her grandmother was the only adult he had ever seen her with. She had to be one of the many at the school on 90% scholarships. Some of those were underwritten, anonymously, by his parents.

Clio returned with the girl in tow. They settled into their seats.

"Delia's grandmother has a headache today," she said. "We'll take her home." She turned in her seat. The girl was fussing in the back with a book bag half as big as she was. "Is her headache unusual?" she asked her.

"No. She has them often. Sometimes for days."

"Hmm," Clio mused.

Julio knew what Clio was thinking. A week ago she had said she was tired of healing. Now we'll see about that, he thought. She turned back to him.

"Let's stop at that botánica behind the church. They have something that might help her."

"OK, sure," Julio replied.

"Do you know who Doña Dolores is?" she asked the girl.

The girl, wide-eyed, shook her head.

"She's a curandera. She lives about five miles from here. I was her assistant for two years. I learned a great remedio for headaches from her. We'll see if it'll help your abuelita."

Clio only needed five minutes to emerge from the store with a small brown paper bag.

"Got it. Let's go," she said.

Delia directed them to an old neighborhood on the edge of Las Cruces. Built in the traditional style, each block was a long, single story adobe building divided into six residences, some with brightly painted doors and window frames, a few others faded and peeling. With pine beams protruding from the walls all the way down the block, some doorways arched, and strings of chiles and great clumps of cactuses and ornamental plants along the curb, it was an attractive neighborhood, if obviously low income.

Delia's grandmother's house was the second from one end. The living room was tiny and dark, the air still. Julio could see a small kitchen at the back. It wasn't until Delia spoke that he realized the grandmother was lying on the couch.

"I'm home, Grandma," she said, "¿Cómo está?"

The woman removed a cloth from her eyes and tried to focus on the visitors. She wasn't as old as Julio had expected, maybe between 40 and 50.

Clio stepped forward.

"I'm Clio Méndez, ma'am. This is my brother Julio. We're students at Juárez too...."

Julio had never watched his sister work as a curandera, though he had seen her treat their great-grandmother, and watched her in a panic, treating the injured Rob Coombs. She was very smooth with the woman. He was not surprised.

In Spanish, she explained that she had been an assistant to Doña Dolores. The woman had heard of her. Doña Dolores, Clio said, had a tea which was a good remedy for headaches, and if the lady was willing, Clio would give her some. She agreed.

She gave the packet of tea to Delia and explained how to make it and suggested she save the package so they could get more if they needed it. The girl went to the kitchen. While she was gone, Clio freshened the damp cloth the woman had had over her eyes and worked in a couple of drops from a tiny bottle she took out of the paper sack from the botánica. Telling her she would try to cool her head while the tea was making, she gently laid her hand on the woman's forehead and covered it with the cloth.

After several minutes Julio detected the pungent, soothing odor of peppermint. Delia returned a few minutes after that with a steaming cup of tea.

"She's sleeping," Clio whispered. "When she wakes up, you can give her the tea. It works just as good cold." She got to her feet. "She might sleep a couple of hours, but that's OK. She'll feel much better."

The girl thanked them shyly as they left. Julio said nothing until they were back on Highway 28.

"Well, you did it again."

"Did what again?"

"Worked on a brain. You put her to sleep, didn't you?"

"Yeah. I did."

"So maybe you're not that tired of healing."

"Well, what could I do? Doctors can't do much for migraines, and it's expensive when they try. I've treated migraines successfully several times. I know how to do that. The woman was really in pain and that made problems for Delia. So I helped two people."

"You don't sound that happy about it."

"I'm not. Well, not exactly. I mean, think about it. She'll tell her friends, and when they get headaches or something else they'll try to find me. Curanderas would love the extra business, but I don't. That's why I said the tea and peppermint was one of Doña Dolores' remedies. They're not. The tea is regular tea. The peppermint is a remedy used by curanderas and therapists, but not usually for headaches. I just hoped the scent would take their minds off me."

She sighed.

"I'm still tired of it, Bubba."

Julio steered around a beer can.

"Maybe. But whatever...I think you're awesome, sis."

Twenty minutes later they found their mother in the kitchen, humming to herself and cooking furiously.

"Whatcha fixing, Mom?" asked Julio.

"Tomatillos! From the garden," she said. "We had lots. They won't keep long, so I'm seeing what I can make with them. I really missed New Mexican food."

"What's that?" Clio asked, pointing to a steaming pot.

"Oh, that's the posole," she said. "There are tomatillos in that, and this is tomatillo guacamole, to go under the chiles rellenos, in the oven. And those," she said, indicating bowls of cheese, onions, cabbage, radishes, cilantro, and tortilla chips, "are the garnishes."

"Wow. It smells great," Julio said.

Clio popped a radish slice into her mouth. Out the window, their new pickup, with a half dozen square hay bales in the bed, was turning in the driveway. It rolled past the house, probably to the barn.

"Mijo, would you go tell your father to clean up and come to the table, please? Tell him we'll eat at Abuelita's house."

"Sure, Mom."

"Mija, would you carry these dishes over there, please? I'll bring the rest in a minute."

"Sure, Mom."

After the festive Friday night meal, the extended Méndez family accepted Grandpa Bert's invitation to watch one of his favorite movies from the Golden Age of Mexican cinema, the 1951 comedy *A.T.M. A toda máquina,* starring Pedro Infante and Luis Aguilar.

Once Julio realized the dialog was 1940-style snappy Spanish, it was filmed in black and white, and the stars often broke into corny romantic songs, he sneaked out to his family's house to spend some quality time with the living room computer.

Clio found her mind wandering too, but her cell phone saved her by beeping plaintively, giving her an excuse to her to retreat to Abuelita's kitchen.

She had a text message from Doro: "Prima--puedes abrir la carta."

"Opening the letter" could only mean the letter from Mr. Bianchi, and that had to mean the poor man had passed away. The news hit her harder than she expected. She retraced her brother's path to their house, passing by him in the living room (as he mumbled "You too, huh?" without looking up from the screen) to her bedroom. Already near tears and afraid she would cry when she read the note, she slipped out the back patio gate to seek the privacy of her shop in the barn. Raisin followed, sensing her upset condition and hissing uneasily.

She snapped on the lights and heater and laid the envelope on the counter. The shop was a narrow, long room with work surfaces and equipment on one side and several chairs and cabinets against the opposite wall. Raisin hopped into one of the chairs, the better to keep track of whatever was happening. On the counter before her were three jars of macerated herbs infusing. She pulled down a paper coffee filter from the shelf, spread it in the filter cone, and set it over a clean quart jar. Carefully, she poured the thick liquid into the cone and watched it begin to drip through. Then she opened the envelope.

It was a full sheet of parchment-like paper, folded twice. The lines, handwritten with a fine-point fountain pen, were more even and well-formed than she expected, despite a couple of blots:

*My dear Miss Montez,*

*I cannot tell you how much it has mattered to me to have known you these past two weeks. Your simple kindness to a complete stranger has renewed my faith in humanity when I no longer thought it possible. I am so grateful to have met you, and especially at this late time in my life.*

*Do not mourn me, and do not give up on the rest of us .You must not stop caring for people. You are needed.*

*The painting is yours. Mr. Baldwin and your cousin will handle the details.*

*My best wishes to you and your family.*
*G. Bianchi*

She flashed on the memory of that frail old man, wracked by disease and dying, still protecting her from the intrigues of his son and grandson and even thanking her for her feeble attempts to help him. But the emotional peak had passed and the tears were not coming....

Raisin swiveled her ears toward the door and chirped. Most likely a family member was approaching or the cat would have hissed. She slid the letter under a brochure on the counter. There was a soft knock and her mother peeked in.

"I saw the light," she said, pausing just inside. "Daughter? Is something the matter? That phone call?"

"It was a text message. One of the elderly people I tried to help died today."

She flopped down in one of the chairs. Her mother sat next to her, with Raisin on the third chair.

"I'm so sorry. That's too bad."

"I worked on him several times, but it was no use. He was just too sick. He was a nice man."

There was no way she was going to tell her mother the man was the father of the man whose ear she had pulled.

"You can't help everyone, daughter."

"Oh, I know. I'm just tired. Tired and confused." Her voice shrank to a whisper. "There's so much I don't know about healing."

"Surely that's normal. No one knows everything. We just do the best we can."

Fergus had made the same point. But what if people still died?

"I guess so," she whispered.

The first filtration had finished. She stood and put a new paper filter into the cone and set it over a second jar while her mother rubbed Raisin's shoulder. A moment passed.

"I came to you for another reason, daughter. I owe you an apology."

"You do? For what?"

"For insisting that Fergus be with you those two weeks. I was probably being overprotective, but I just couldn't go to Switzerland while I was worrying about you being by yourself all that time. I know you didn't like it, and it turned out to be unnecessary. I'm sorry, daughter. In your place I would have been unhappy about it too. Please forgive me."

Clio picked up the second jar of macerated herbs and began pouring it slowly into the filter paper.

"That's all right, Mom," she said over her shoulder. She smiled a secret smile at the dripping slurry. "Fergus worked out pretty well."

Former Army Ranger J. T. "Justin Time" Butts turned onto Fergus's street.

"It's the next to last on the right," Fergus said. "Blue reflector, down low."

"Roger," Butts replied, adding, "It was a good week but I'm glad it's over. You didn't have to pick up the check for all of us just now."

"Well, hell, seems like I've stiffed you guys the past few months. I probably owed you."

"You probably did. Didn't expect you to come back from New Mexico like you'd had two weeks leave in the Bahamas. That must have been a good job."

"Body-guarding a kid. Easy. Parents paid nearly double. You'd be in a good mood too."

"And you're not limping. You didn't piss and moan all week like you used to. How come?"

"Ah. Well, the kid I was watching was volunteering with a traveling medical clinic. They had docs and therapists out the yin-yang. One of 'em turned out to be excellent."

"Yeah? A doc?"

"Hell no."

"Therapist, then?"

"Yeah. A young one. Cute. Really had the touch."

"Man! We could use someone like that!"

"No lie, geezer. If you ever save up enough to pay her to come here, I'll see if she's willing to work you over. Here we are. Thanks, J. T. See you Monday."

Coombs' diplomat-watching job truly had gone well, Fergus reflected as he unlocked his door. It was just like Coombs promised: clean, straightforward, good food and reasonable hours. He surprised himself at the wrap-up party: he hadn't pissed off anyone on the team and had even enjoyed a hamburger and two beers with them at their favorite watering hole. He really did feel like he had had a restful vacation earlier, despite getting nearly beaten to a pulp, shot, and blown to hell.

He took a hot shower and changed into more comfortable clothes. What to do next? He'd been in the habit of drinking steadily in the evenings, but that didn't appeal now. In fact, tomorrow, Saturday, he might put on his blade prosthesis and try a little running. Might get some of his edge back. It was still there if he'd just work some of the dullness off.

There was his carry-on bag in the corner where it had been all week after he had grabbed the clothes out of it. He should put it back in the closet, after double checking to make sure he hadn't left anything in it.

The damned thing had a dozen little zippered compartments, mesh pouches, lanyards, and other crapola all through it. One of the little baggy pouches on the right side had a wad of paper under it. He pulled it loose and flattened it out. It was a receipt from Chico's Liquor Barn. He thought a second. He had kept the carry-on bag at the end of the low dresser in the motel room. He'd probably flipped the paper wad at the trash can and missed; caught the bag instead.

He started to zip up the bag when a flash of light on the bottom caught his eye. A fragment of a mirror? He slid it out from under the rightmost pouch. Not glass: it was a piece of shiny Mylar, with tiny lettering across it. It was a little envelope with one side torn off. He held it closer to his eyes. The left edge was missing, but the rest said "…-ctronically tested for reliability." He turned it over. In bold white letters, that side said "TROJ…."

What? *What?* Thoughts hit him one after another like bullets from a machine gun. He hadn't tossed this out. The kid had to have done it, and she missed the trash can too. Probably in the dark. Where had she got this? He'd been with her the whole time…the shampoo! She'd gone into the Stop 'N' Shop for shampoo, but returned without any. Said they didn't have her brand. That's when she had bought it.

Oh, Jesus, the dream, the dream he couldn't forget. *It wasn't a dream!*

He collapsed slowly into a chair as images flooded back. He'd been two-thirds asleep with her sitting over him, reveling in the soothing electricity of her smooth, cool hands on his wrecked abs…after that…after that, what? Drowsiness. Hair cascading down. Warm breath. Scent of honeysuckle. Young, firm skin. Total, all-encompassing peace….

He realized he was staring at the carry-on bag.

Holy hell, holy sweet hell. His client's daughter. And not just any client. And not just any daughter. When he asked her about his dream she lied like a pro. And then her last words at the airport were to thank him for "everything." He had thanked her back, and meant it. She'd saved his butt and then made him better than new…and now, to his amazement, even better than that.

Another image was floating somewhere in his mind. It took several seconds to coalesce: that painting again, by the artist/cousin she had also healed. He'd never forget that picture. How could he? He had lived it: the woman's glowing golden eyes and tender compassion for the damaged creatures under her hands, seeming to say, "All is well, all is well. No matter what, you are loved."

He caught his image in the mirror over the dresser. The face there was smiling at him.

## About the Author

Al Past is a retired English and linguistics professor, husband, father, grandfather, musician, house builder, and photographer. He lives on a ranch in South Texas.

## About the Distant Cousin series

Ana Darcy Méndez is still the only extraterrestrial with her own blog:

http://www.anadarcy.blogspot.com,

which is a companion for the novels, containing background about Ana's native language, Luvit, an extended interview with Ana on the history and culture of her home planet, Thomo, and photographs, maps, and so forth to accompany the stories.

Just for fun there is also a collection of Ana's mostly successful poly-national cooking experiments, exhibits of the arts and crafts of Earth that have fascinated her, selections of our poetry and music that she loves, Mexican-American proverbs and language games from her family's life, puzzles, astronomical news, ideas on early childhood education, and more, including many photos of cats.

Made in the USA
Charleston, SC
01 May 2014